Bohemia in London

Also by Peter Brooker

BERTOLT BRECHT: Dialectics, Poetry, Politics

NEW YORK FICTIONS: Modernity, Postmodernism, the New Modern

MODERNITY AND METROPOLIS: Literature, Film and Urban Formations

A GLOSSARY OF CULTURAL THEORY

MODERNISM/POSTMODERNISM: a Critical Reader

Bohemia in London
The Social Scene of Early Modernism

Peter Brooker

© Peter Brooker, 2007

All rights reserved. No reproduction, copy or transmission of this publication may be made without written permission.

No paragraph of this publication may be reproduced, copied or transmitted save with written permission or in accordance with the provisions of the Copyright, Designs and Patents Act 1988, or under the terms of any licence permitting limited copying issued by the Copyright Licensing Agency, 90 Tottenham Court Road, London W1T 4LP.

Any person who does any unauthorised act in relation to this publication may be liable to criminal prosecution and civil claims for damages.

The author has asserted his right to be identified as the author of this work in accordance with the Copyright, Designs and Patents Act 1988.

First published in hardback 2004
Paperback edition published 2007 by
PALGRAVE MACMILLAN
Houndmills, Basingstoke, Hampshire RG21 6XS and
175 Fifth Avenue, New York, N.Y. 10010
Companies and representatives throughout the world

PALGRAVE MACMILLAN is the global academic imprint of the Palgrave Macmillan division of St. Martin's Press, LLC and of Palgrave Macmillan Ltd. Macmillan® is a registered trademark in the United States, United Kingdom and other countries. Palgrave is a registered trademark in the European Union and other countries.

ISBN-13: 978–0–333–98395–9 hardback
ISBN-10: 0–333–98395–5 hardback
ISBN-13: 978–0–230–54692–9 paperback
ISBN-10: 0–230–54692–7 paperback

This book is printed on paper suitable for recycling and made from fully managed and sustained forest sources. Logging, pulping and manufacturing processes are expected to conform to the environmental regulations of the country of origin.

A catalogue record for this book is available from the British Library.

A catalog record for this book is available from the Library of Congress.

10 9 8 7 6 5 4 3 2 1
16 15 14 13 12 11 10 09 08 07

Printed and bound in Great Britain by
Antony Rowe Ltd, Chippenham and Eastbourne

Contents

List of Illustrations	vii
Preface	viii
Acknowledgements	x
Maps: Soho, Fitzrovia, Bloomsbury; Kensington	xii

1 **Bourgeois-Bohemians** — 1
   Bohemian personae — 1
   Bourgeois-bohemians — 10
   Bohemia in Babel — 23

2 **'The Nineties Tried Your Game'** — 27
   French connections — 27
   Bohemian empire — 29
   On or around 1908 — 41

3 **'Our London, My London, Your London'** — 52
   Enter Ezra, transatlantic bohemian — 52
   Very English, violently American — 60

4 **Nights at the Cave of the Golden Calf** — 72
   A shadow play — 72
   The dancer and the dance — 79

5 **1914: 'Our Little Gang'** — 93
   Rebels, allies, enemies — 93
   Bohemian girls and new freewomen — 102

6 **Café Society** — 113
   Two for Dieudonné's — 113
   Paint the legend: the Restaurant de la Tour Eiffel — 123

7 **The Nerves in Patterns** — 132
   'An ex-dancer, I believe' — 132
   'Some of the actor in Tom' — 139
   Pierrot, un peu banquier, on Margate Sands — 148

8 Bloomsbury's Bohemia	**158**
Temps perdu, temps retrouvé	158
About 1910	168
Notes	178
Bibliography	186
Index	195

List of Illustrations

1. The Empire, Leicester Square, 1905 (postcard)
2. Sir William Orpen, *The Café Royal*, 1912
3. Pagani's Restaurant, Great Portland Street, 1910
4. ABC Tearoom, 1901
5. Ezra Pound, c.1913. Photo by E.O. Hoppé
6. Wyndham Lewis. National Portrait Gallery, London
7. Henri Gaudier-Brzeska, c.1913
8. T.S. Eliot outside Faber and Gwyer, 1926
9. Church Walk, Kensington, 1957
10. South Lodge, Kensington, in the 1910s. Photo by Wallace Heaton
11. Lloyds Bank, Cornhill, 1920s
12. 46 Gordon Square, Bloomsbury
13. Frida Strindberg, 1915. Photo by Arnold Genthe
14. Iris Barry
15. Vivien Eliot in the Eliot's flat in Crawford Mansions, WI
16. Lady Ottoline Morrell, c.1910
17. Anonymous sketch in the *Daily Mirror*, 4 July 1912
18. Wyndham Lewis, *Study for a Wall Decoration in the Cave of the Golden Calf*, 1912 (lost)
19. Wyndham Lewis, 'Cabaret Theatre Club Poster', 1912
20. A visit to Wilfred Scawen Blunt, 18 January 1914
21. In the garden at Charleston, 1928. Photo by Vanessa Bell

Preface

Everyone can tell a bohemian: he's an artist or artist type, a poseur, a degenerate, a hanger-on; dressed the part but not exactly the real thing. And anyway, the real thing – or was it the real bohemian – went out with the nineteenth century.

In this book I see the bohemian as a conspicuous example of the modern artist; committed in gesture, polemic, poem and painting to the subversive force of an aestheticising temperament in the face of a resilient conformism and bare-faced commodity culture. As Charles Baudelaire had understood, on two counts, identifying this type and the continuing tensions structuring the role of the artist under modernity: the '*flâneur*' goes to the market seemingly to observe but in reality to find a buyer, while the 'dandy's' disdain for the female struggles with the knowledge of a shared regimen of self-fashioning.

Baudelaire's modernity produces the dandy, the decadent or aesthete, hybrid types moving between isolation and the crowd, commodification and autonomous culture, an idea of the masculine and the feminine. I'm interested in how the bohemian who is also a modernist responded to these tensions in the seismic shift of the new century when the magnetism of the urban metropolis of London was at its strongest. This 'bohemian modernist', I suggest, emerges as the very expression of this transition in the cultural sphere; the hybrid male persona who has learnt that 'art', the 'artist', and the 'bohemian' type are themselves commodities. One result was that 'he' became 'she' or 'they' with a new product, the fugitive 'little magazine' which counters while it mirrors the ephemeral novelties of commercial modernity.

This leads me to consider not simply individual artists, though many, canonic and otherwise, are immensely interesting, but to situate these figures in modernism's non-conformist groups, coteries and loose associations, themselves united to the point of fierce division over art's form and function and an idea of the experimental life. The creative outcome was various – a magazine or masterpiece, perhaps; or no more and no less than the length of a man or woman's hair, the cut of a jacket, the shape of a hat, the fall of a dress, an earring, a cane, the choice of one café rather than another. For the bohemian is the figure in whom aesthetic and cultural style, artistic strategy and personal bearing, male and female, come together.

But singularity is defined against type. The bohemian belongs to Bohemia and as modernist he or she similarly finds a new role in the dissenting enclave which is there and not there, a real and symbolic place in the shadows of the bustling imperial metropolis. My interest in the coteries of early modernism is an interest in the places they met – the 'at homes', garden parties, teashops, studios, salons, cafés that mapped an alternative city in Edwardian and Georgian London. We know this side of modernism through the legendary anecdotes by which the individual biographies are often told: the meetings between Pound and Lewis at the Vienna Café or Eliot and Woolf in a taxi in Richmond; parties at South Lodge and Garsington; the double dinner of Imagists and Vorticists at Dieudonné's; gatherings at the Restaurant de la Tour Eiffel. Many of these totemic incidents are remembered and mis-remembered, embroidered, fictionalised, conjured out of next to nothing. I want – certainly not to correct these stories – but to embed them in the culture of the period and in an account which knows it too is a re-telling.

Virginia Woolf said how she thought of the past in terms of 'scenes' and wondered how similar this was to novel writing and if other people accessed the past in the same way. I believe they did and do and that it is indeed like novel writing. I want to investigate these scenes to see how they are composed and what they mean. At points I attempt different kinds of writing and reconstruction to do this. This I see as consistent with my overriding interests: in the coordinated relations between self-fashioning personae and symbolic places, in modernism as an emerging aesthetic and art of life, and in the accompanying, inescapable fictions of the cultural record.

Acknowledgements

I would like to thank the following for permission to quote from manuscript sources: for quotations from Iris Barry, The Edmund Schiddel Collection, Special Collections at Boston University; from Vivien(ne) Eliot, Yale Collection of American Literature, Beinecke Rare Book and Manuscript Library; the Bodleian Library, Oxford and the Estate of T.S. Eliot; from F.S. Flint, the Harry Ransom Humanities Research Center, the University of Texas at Austin; from Ford Madox Ford, David Higham Associates; from Patricia Hutchins, the British Library; from Wyndham Lewis, the Division of Rare and Manuscript Collections, Cornell University Library.

Illustrations

I would like to thank the following for permission to include images:

Front cover: Tate, London 2003; Back cover: Biddy Peppin; Bridgeman Art Library (Sir William Orpen, *The Café Royal*, 1912); Division of Rare and Manuscript Collections, Cornell University Library (Wyndham Lewis, *Study for a Wall Decoration in the Cave of the Golden Calf*, 1912); English Department, University of Reading (Ezra Pound, c.1913); National Portrait Gallery, London (Wyndham Lewis, c.1914); Harry Ransom Humanities Research Center, University of Texas at Austin (Church Walk, Kensington, 1957; a visit to Wilfred Scawen Blunt, 18 January 1914); Houghton Library, Harvard University (T.S. Eliot outside Faber and Gwyer, 1926; Vivien Eliot at Crawford Mansions); Lloyds TSB Group Archives (Lloyds Bank, Cornhill, 1920s); Mary Evans Picture Library (The Empire, Leicester Square; ABC Tearoom, 1901); New Directions Publishing Corporation (Henri Gaudier-Brzeska, c.1913); Tate, London 2003 (In the garden at Charleston, 1928); The British Library (Anonymous sketch in the *Daily Mirror*, 4 July 1912); The Edmund Schiddel Collection, Special Collections at Boston University (Iris Barry); The Museum of the City of New York (Frida Strindberg, 1915); Wyndham Lewis and the estate of the late Mrs G.A. Wyndham Lewis by kind permission of the Wyndham Lewis Memorial Trust (a registered charity) (Wyndham Lewis, 'Cabaret Theatre Club Poster', 1912).

Acknowledgements xi

I am pleased to thank the British Academy for the award of two small grants for research visits to the USA. Special thanks, for a long time now, to Peter Nicholls, for unfailing encouragement and suave criticism; thanks to Paul O'Keefe and Biddy Peppin for their generosity. Thanks for ever to Liz, 'going round and round still, dancing, still dancing'.

Every effort has been made by the Author and Publishers to secure permissions for all relevant works, and if any have been missed we will be happy to rectify the situation at the earliest opportunity.

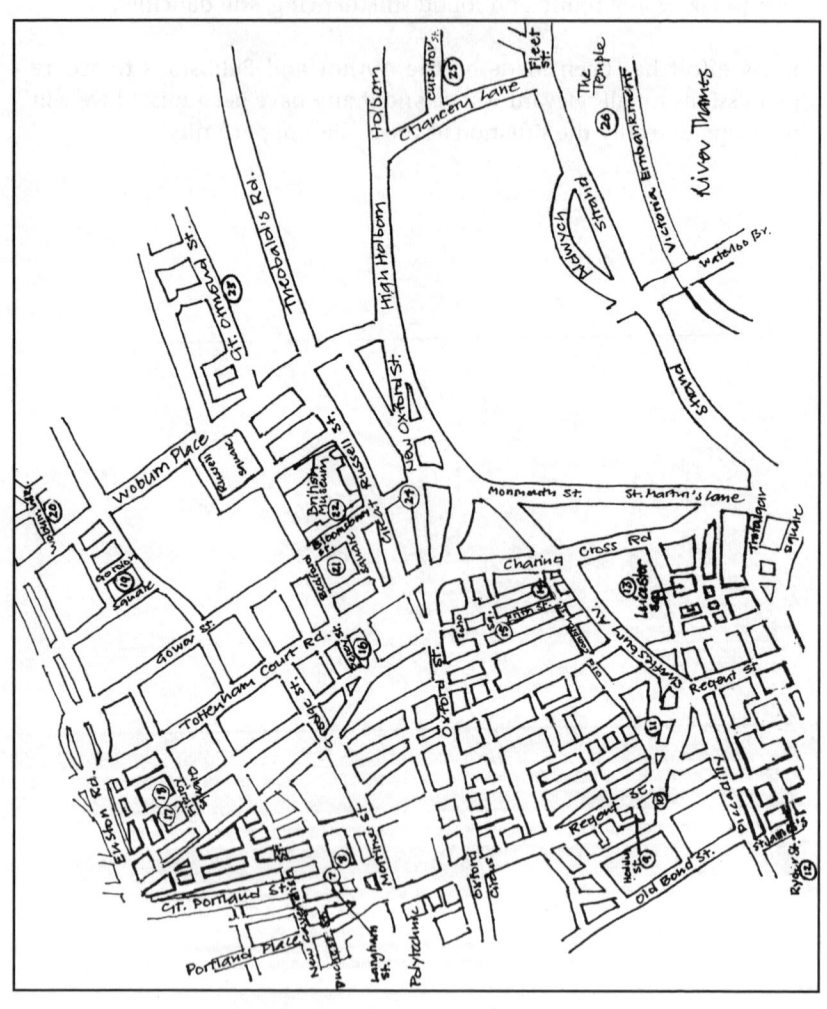

Kensington

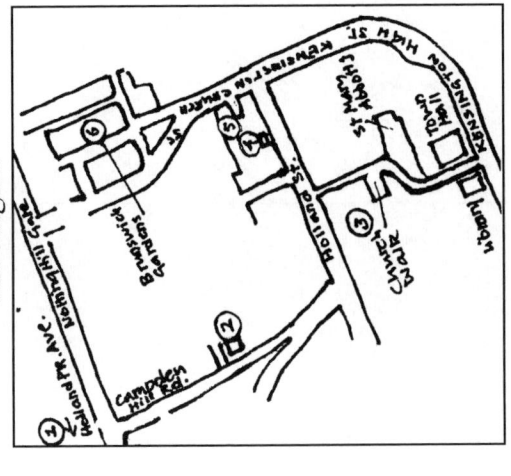

Key sites

1. *The English Review* offices, 84 Holland Park Avenue
2. South Lodge
3. 10 Church Walk, Pound's lodgings, 1909–14
4. Miss Ella Abbott's teashop
5. 5 Holland Place Chambers, the Pounds' home, 1914–19
6. 12 Brunswick Gardens, home of Olivia Shakespear
7. 48 Langham Street, Pound's lodgings, 1908–9
8. Pagani's Restaurant, 42 Great Portland Street
9. The Cabaret Club, Heddon Street
10. John Lane and Elkin Matthews' bookshops, Vigo Street
11. The Café Royal, 68 Regent Street
12. Dieudonné's, 11 Ryder Street
13. The Empire Theatre, Leicester Square
14. Belotti's Ristorante Italiano, 12 Old Compton Street
15. 67 Frith Street, scene of Hulme's 'at homes'
16. Restaurant de la Tour Eiffel, 1 Percy Street
17. 29 Fitzroy Square, home of Virginia and Adrian Stephen 1906–11
18. Omega Workshops, 33 Fitzroy Square
19. 46 Gordon Square, home in 1904–6 of the Stephen brothers and sisters and subsequently of Vanessa and Clive Bell
20. Woburn Walk (then 'Buildings') where both Yeats and Dorothy Richardson had lodgings
21. 44 Bedford Square, home of Lady Ottoline Morrell
22. The *Egoist* offices, Oakley House, Bloomsbury Street
23. The Rebel Arts Centre, 38 Great Ormond Street
24. The Vienna Café, New Oxford Street
25. The *New Age* offices, Rolls Passage, off Cursitor Street
26. Fountain Court, The Temple, home of Arthur Symons

1
Bourgeois-Bohemians

Bohemian personae

Act One
In the Garret

A broad window from which an expanse of roofs, covered with snow is seen. At right, a stove. A table, a bed, a wardrobe, four chairs, a painter's easel with a sketched canvas and a stool: scattered books, many bundles of papers, two candlesticks. A door in the centre and another at left. Rodolfo [a poet] is looking pensively out of the window. Marcello is working at his picture, 'The Crossing of the Red Sea', with his hands benumbed by the cold.

Act Two
In the Latin Quarter

A crossroads. Where the streets meet a kind of square is formed: shops, vendors of every kind. To one side, the Café Momus ... The crowd is large and varied: bourgeois, soldiers, maidservants, boys, girls, students, seamstresses, gendarmes, etc ... The café is very crowded so that some bourgeois are forced to sit at a table out in the open.

(Puccini, 1983: 73, 96)

Giacomo Puccini's opera *La Bohème* opened in Manchester in April 1897 and transferred to Covent Garden in October. The trial of Oscar Wilde had taken place in May 1895, the same year as the publication of George Du Maurier's *Trilby*. The opera and novel helped put one idea of the artist into popular circulation while the trial sent another to prison and into exile. In the wake of Wilde's 'dismal' trial, said Ford Madox Ford, a brow-beaten and resentful public 'simply steam-rollered out' the remains of nineties' aestheticism, inviting the 'Typical English Writer' and 'Typical English critic' to step into the void (Ford, 1921: 199, 39). 'Poetry was finished', declared Ford, and what followed, in the best of 'those dark days' was a devotion to the art of fiction and the social novel (200, 39). This was the era of late Henry James, Galsworthy, Bennett and Wells. And of Ford himself, though his family connections with the Pre-Raphaelites, and with James, Joseph Conrad, and subsequently with Ezra Pound and other younger artists, meant that he, quite uniquely, bridged the overlapping generations up to the First World War. Not until 'Les Jeunes', as Ford termed them, arrived upon the scene was there anything new, he said – only then to discover that this new, when it appeared in the person of Wyndham Lewis, saw fit to dump a couple of embarrassing old has-beens like Ford and Conrad. They were *'Foûtou*! Finished! Exploded! Done for!' (Ford, 1932: 400). So Impressionism was blasted off the face of the literary planet by modernism, though of course nobody at the time called the new movement this. Nor was it, nor could it be, entirely new. 'Les Jeunes' did not instantly step clear of the shadow of aestheticism, as we shall see, nor of its associated idea of the artist. Wilde was a type of the bohemian-dandy whose 'private artistic morality' (David, 1988: 7) came to pose a particular threat to the norms of bourgeois heterosexuality. Wilde's trial and its consequences meant few would follow him in this respect. Not, at least, the 'Men of 1914', as Lewis labelled Joyce, Eliot, Pound and himself, though sexuality remained an issue in their lives and work. Meanwhile, the success of *La Bohème* and greater commercial triumph of *Trilby*, whose spin-offs ran into Trilby shoes, sweets, kitchenware, and the soft Trilby hat (David, 1988: 23) meant that a less troubling idea of the youthful heterosexual bohemian artist could take hold.

'Bohemianism', in these texts and the popular imagination, embraced both the figure of the artist and an idea of the artistic life. All this had a beginning, if there ever was such a time, in the short narrative sketches of Henri Mürger's *Scènes de la Vie Bohème* (1845–49).[1] Mürger distinguished, in a way soon forgotten, between the three classes of 'unknowns', 'amateur' and committed bohemians whose dedication to their art steered them through poverty and doubt. Bohemia was, he announced, 'a stage in artistic life; it is the preface to the Academy, the Hôtel Dieu, or the Morgue' (Graña and Graña, 1990: 45). The setting of these stories in the 1830s and in Paris – 'Bohemia only exists and is only possible in Paris', wrote Mürger (ibid.) – suggests a synchrony between the emergence of the down-at-heel artist as urban rebel and the new technologies and commercial impetus characterising European cities in the period of modernity. Both tendencies do begin earlier of course and the bohemian inherits much from the figure of the Romantic artist in English and European traditions, as well as from Edgar Allan Poe, and perhaps especially from the French proto-symbolists, Théophile Gautier, Gérard de Nerval and Charles Baudelaire, in pitting a personal style and aesthetic against the codes and priorities of industrialising societies. This opposition could take different aesthetic, social and sartorial forms and express different alliances – with students and the *demi-monde*, peasants and proletarians, gypsies, tramps, insurgents and conspirators. For Marx, as Walter Benjamin reports, the 'Bohème' was associated with the figure of the 'professional conspirator', a plebeian type recruited from displaced, itinerant soldiers whose irregular tavern life was devoted to terroristic fantasies of immediate government overthrow (Benjamin, 1973: 11–34, 72). Benjamin likens the poet Baudelaire directly to this indeterminate class: 'What Baudelaire expresses' he writes, 'could be called the metaphysics of the *provocateur*' (14). The much discussed type of the *flâneur* is another such symptomatic figure, associated with the apache of the left bank, the prostitute and ragpicker, and at once an habitué of the city but distanced from its middle-class crowds in manner and occupation (53–61, 96–8).[2] The artist adopted an attitude towards society of indifference, mockery or spleen – 'I want to raise the whole human race against me', wrote Baudelaire (14). In this mode the male artist was pointedly idle and elusive, having rejected the claims of routine work and a settled abode. He was instinctively given to the spirit of revolt: promiscuous, immoral, and immodest; in one inflection a careless womaniser, in another an effeminate dandy, all in the name of art and an alternative to established canons of taste, bourgeois respectability and the marketplace.

The bohemian alternative could be expressed, then, in a painting or poem or the habits of the creative life and generally found too an associated location in sections of the new metropolis and in the studios, cafés, tearooms, bookshops, libraries and editorial offices which mapped out an artistic subculture. Here was the large and motley crowd of the Café Momus, whether in Puccini, Mürger, or real life Paris. 'Everyone went there', confirms Hugh David: 'foreigners, prostitutes, the aristocracy, the *nouveau riche* and the young denizens of Bohemia' (1988: 27). But, still, to take effect the bohemian challenge could not be confined to a café ghetto or discrete subculture. If the bohemian was also a 'serious artist' and chose fame and influence rather than dissipation and self-destruction (and the possible legend of an early death) he, since it was invariably a he, must gain recognition in the public sphere. Hence the exhibitionist protests, the proclamations and manifestos and the public appearance of the artist as 'Artist'. The first public entry of the bohemian as self-proclaimed Romantic and sworn enemy of the bourgeoisie, occurred, argues Mary Gluck, at the opening performance of Victor Hugo's *Hernani* at the Théâtre Française in February 1830. Hugo's supporters appeared in a wild array of costumes – 'in pea green jackets, Spanish cloaks, waist-coats à la Robespierre, in Henri III bonnets, carrying on their heads and backs articles of clothing from every century and clime' (Hugo in Gluck, 2000: 356). Costume was therefore employed as a weapon against bourgeois convention. Rallying the bohemian side was Théophile Gautier, poet, journalist and proponent of art for art's sake. His spectacular appearance 'in a scarlet satin waistcoat and thick long hair cascading down his back' was a 'particular insult', Hugo felt, to bourgeois eyes (ibid.). Gautier was the bohemian as ostentatious dandy, his unforgettable red waistcoat an unrepeatable example of fashion as anti-fashion (Gautier in Graña and Graña, 1990: 359–64). More often the life of artistic dedication and poverty was to find a more seemingly natural outward expression. Being an artist meant wearing rough, open-necked shirts, silk neckties, corduroy jackets and trousers, an Inverness cape, slouch hat, long hair and optional full beard or wispy facial hair. It meant life in a garret, the bonhomie of fellow male artists and a sweetheart who was a dancer or working-class *'grisette'*. This is the figure the public met in Du Maurier's *Trilby* and Puccini's *La Bohème* and in Augustus John who played the part of womanising Romany artist with serious gusto. Thanks to such examples, the bohemian rebel of the nineteenth century became the clichéd 'artist' of the twentieth. Ford, for one, deeply resented the 'sartorial tyranny' which resulted (1921: 200).

Cliché, therefore, somewhere along the road to the academy, hospital or morgue, was the more immediate fate awaiting the bohemian and the oppositional modern artist the figure represents. If the bohemian was too much of an outsider he was of little account, but if, on the other hand, being an artist meant little more than wearing the standard uniform then he was a tame, even comical type. The bohemian was a nonconformist, that is to say, whose non-conformity was at risk at all points, from indifference, parody, convention and compromise, since simply to survive, however close to the bread-line, required some means of livelihood, support or patronage. To do more and succeed as an artist required openings, in galleries and magazines and journals. It was precisely at this point, therefore, in the artist's relations to an artistic establishment and the workings of commodity culture that the battle lines were most sharply drawn and crossed. The man of letters, as Baudelaire had said, 'goes to the market place, as a *flâneur*, supposedly to take a look at it, but in reality to find a buyer' (Benjamin, 1973: 34). But if this was the case, if art was indeed part of the very operation it opposed, what price a revolt against bourgeois values?

There were three significant confrontations between the artist and the public in London literary life before the end of the century which tested this relationship. Swinburne's *Atlanta in Calydon* (1865) had made him a popular hit and he responded by cultivating the role of 'ultra-sensitive, highly strung and carelessly Bohemian poet' (David, 1988: 10). His *Poems and Ballads* in the following year gave him a different reputation, however. The periodical press was disgusted at its veiled sexual reference and 'unspeakable foulnesses' and Swinburne was branded a prime agent of the 'Fleshly School of Poetry' attacked in 1871 by Robert Buchanan. In a second incident, later in the decade, James Abbott McNeill Whistler's impressionistic *Nocturnes* earned the contempt of John Ruskin. Whistler, so Ruskin famously charged, had 'flung a pot of paint into the public's face'. Whistler defended his technique and integrity but was as much as anything defending his flamboyant personality. He was awarded a farthing in damages which seemed only to confirm how this affair of art and artists was a rum piece of theatre put on for public consumption. Both incidents were a mere prelude, however, to the trial of Oscar Wilde. In this most sensational showcase of bohemian artist versus public, Wilde risked himself, we might think – since he could have avoided arrest – and lost. In the courtroom his famed wit and irony fell on deaf ears and left the judge bewildered by a life of expensive corruption – 'of the most hideous kind among men'. To do such things Wilde 'must be dead to all sense of shame' and a sentence of two years hard labour was 'totally inadequate' (Hyde, 1948: 339). Outside the Old Bailey, in the early evening of 25 May 1895 a prostitute among the crowds shouted she was sure he'd 'ave 'is' air cut reg'lar now!' (330). This unlooked-for alliance of his lordship and a street whore in the name of the regular life was symptomatic. Both ends of society joined in an expression of public disdain for the subversive figure of the artist, making sure he was the outsider he claimed to be.

If middle-class society was affronted by its nineteenth-century bohemian artists, therefore – and the affairs of Swinburne, Whistler and Wilde showed it was – it was also very ready to demonstrate how it could exercise the apparatuses of the law and public opinion, most crucially in the new mass medium of the popular press, to ridicule and revenge itself upon the bohemian challenge. Interestingly, however, the assorted ranks of law and order had other strategies to hand than vilification and expulsion. George Du Maurier, for instance, had been a *Punch* cartoonist and pseudonymous author of two parodic novels on the life of the aesthete before the appearance of *Trilby*. And Oscar Wilde himself, in happier times, had been pleased to recognise his reflection in the figure of Reginald Bunthorne at the opening of Gilbert and Sullivan's comic opera *Patience* in 1881 (David, 1988: 14–17). A pot of mockery, so to speak, had already been flung in the face of the artist, who, flushed with such fame, could only smile back. Subsequently, *La Bohème* and *Trilby* offered to redraw the figure of the artist along less degenerate lines than earlier, setting a more regular, hot-blooded romantic type against a melancholy but really quite jolly background.

Cleaned up, in one way or another, the bohemian image could therefore be made to serve society's own purposes. Judging from the account in Arthur Ransome's *Bohemia in London* (1907), the seedier aspects of recent history had been speedily erased. On a day in Spring 1904, Ransome, who was to gain lasting fame as a children's author, threw up the life of a publisher's errand boy in south London for the first-hand experience of bohemian life in Chelsea and Soho. His sojourn took him to the Embankment, artists' studios and French cafés but not to the Café Royal where both Wilde and Whistler had held sway. He makes no mention of them or other named contemporary artists. His bohemians are unknowns like himself – one, an abandoned 'poet' in 'huge felt hat' with 'a wealth of thick black hair' and enormous beard, confesses he is a bank clerk in evening disguise (126–9) – or they are the ghosts of 'bohemians' past: Carlyle, Hazlitt, De Quincy and the denizens of eighteenth-century coffee houses. Ransome frequents foreign restaurants, smokes a clay pipe, has a merry time and engages in deep conversation about art and philosophy. Drink flows but no one gets drunk, no one drinks absinthe, and no man or woman has sex. Somehow, though, there is romance. Ransome's bohemian ends married, a successful 'civil servant, or a respectable man of business' and worldly-wise. Bohemia is something a young man enters 'like a tavern' and leaves by 'the door into the registrar's office' (276, 281). Oats were sown as they must be to make a steady married bourgeois life the life it is.

Hugh David suggests Ransome's Bohemia is a sentimental picture of 'a second-hand lifestyle' which is out of touch with 'the real artistic life of London' (1988: 54–5). It's difficult to disagree. All the same, it's clear that the entire record slides across the surface of first-hand authenticity and second-hand contrivance. Mürger's stories, for example, for all their interest in the 'official Bohemia' edit and refashion scenes from his own youth, making him, as David says, simultaneously, 'chronicler' and 'creator' of his own life and legend (26). Truth and reality, as always, but here perhaps more self-consciously, are inevitably constructed and the props and iconography of Bohemia were evidently vital to its conspicuous display of anti-bourgeois values and taste. If the bohemian persona came, in one way, to appear conventional and false, therefore, it could not, in another, have been more real or material. For the art of the period belongs to a burgeoning commodity culture whose money values and commercial display Bohemia loved to hate and was determined to out-stare, though it could only do so in the same discursive universe with a counter image of its own.

Mary Gluck believes the bohemian gesture had become anachronistic by the mid-nineteenth century (Gluck, 2000: 373–4). It is more accurate, with David, to see the French example and the aesthetes of the English nineties as 'the Bohemians of the moment' (David, 1988: 8) – on the understanding that if aesthetes were to some degree bohemian not every bohemian was an aesthete. The bohemian was the product of and reaction to changing forms of modernity, and the persona correspondingly altered. Benjamin accordingly sketched 'the various generations of the *bohème*, from the *bohème dorée* of Gautier and Nerval; the *bohème* of the generation of Baudelaire, Asselineau, Delvau; and, finally, the latest proletarianised *bohème* whose spokesman was Jules Vallès' (Benjamin, 1973: 11).[3] In London, the Edwardian and Georgian years saw a further modulation in this figure as this period moved away from the aestheticist example and as relations between artist, public and artistic establishment entered a new phase. A first sign of this, within two years of the diluted, licensed holiday of Ransome's *Bohemia in London*, was the beginnings of Imagism at the Poets' Club led by T.E. Hulme. Hulme and his associates prized a hard, clear impersonality over the soft, 'feminine' and intuitive modes of Romanticism and Impressionism. The resulting bohemian persona was a curious hybrid, newly defined if not always newly attired; in part in thrall still to a past Romantic image and the lure of Paris, in part a tough-minded opponent to its sentimental residues and the bullish philistinism which commanded the imperial metropolis of London. In much the same way, modernist abstraction was receptive to the new technologies of mass production shaping this society while it looked to compete with its influence. One further complicating factor, as we have seen, was that this society had scored a double hit in defeating the degenerate aesthete and producing a bohemian to its own liking. The modernist artist emerged, therefore, not only in the context of a mixed indebtedness to and rejection of Romantic and Victorian modes, but in company with this popular stereotype. The result, I suggest in this book, was not a single new type of 'the modernist bohemian' but the strategic adoption of different bohemian personae.

This occurred, what is more, at a time when the artistic life broadened its social composition. Given contemporary social changes this is not surprising. The arts recruited men and women from the new lower-middle class and from the provinces as well as from wealthy landed families with a long-standing interest in the arts. They were joined, of course, in the commonly remarked upon feature of modernism, by émigrés from Europe and the USA. Another change was the role of women. The nineteenth-century bohemian was invariably male. Women were 'girls', seamstresses, dancers, 'grisettes', courtesans and prostitutes. This pattern continued, but in the wake of the turn of the century 'new woman' and contemporary suffrage campaigns, women came much more to the fore as independent figures in political and cultural life. They wrote and painted and edited magazines. Also, changing attitudes to sexuality and marriage, in particular – and this one might think was in its way an inflection of the Wilde case – meant that an overtly political struggle was accompanied by a transformation in social-sexual relations and identities. The 'men of 1914' are unquestionably important players in the modernist coteries and café society of London in these years but many others participated in linking formal artistic innovation with an experimental social aesthetic which vied with bourgeois norms. Ezra Pound remembered the café society of the London years as creating 'a sort of society or social order or dis-order' (Paige, 1971: 306). It is an important insight. For if modernist Bohemia posed an alternative to established codes it did so in two ways. Firstly in creating a unity, however temporary, of ideas, practices and settings and a consequent social solidarity across differences of generation, gender and social class; and, secondly, in reverse but complementary fashion, by posing an open, dialogic and 'irregular' model to the compulsively unifying dominant order. The internal differences, rifts, rivalries and animosities within and across the social-artistic groupings of modernism were themselves, that is to say, a part of the experiment.

The delicate dynamics of these external and internal relations came to a crisis in the war years: a time both of heady solidarity and internal friction and of growing disenchantment and hostility between artists, press, and public. As Ford Madox Ford remembered it, 'Les Jeunes' had found, indeed created, an enthusiastic public for themselves by 1914 (Ford, 1921: 136–7). If this was no longer true in the post-war years it was partly because this public had been unsettled by the trauma of historical events, partly because of internal changes, some all too obvious, in personnel and circumstances. By the end of the decade many of modernism's leading innovators were dead, traduced, in self-exile, or separated from the unifying base of a literary or artistic grouping. Pound's *Hugh Selwyn Mauberley* (1920) offers a retrospect over these problematic distinctions of poet and public in its portrait of the now anachronistic aesthete Mauberley. Mauberley recedes from the world of letters, his hedonism supplanted by the hardness of the final poem 'Medallion' – indebted to Gautier's 'sculpture of rhyme' rather than to his red waistcoat or endorsement of *l'art pour l'art*. Pound's poem lambasts the signs of modernity ('The age demanded... A prose kinema... we have the press for wafer / Franchise for circumcision'; Pound, 1968: 206, 207). But principally, as is well understood, it is a farewell to London, an indictment of England's careless ignorance of its own traditions and failure to support the modern artist. The 'Doctrine of the Image' replaces Impressionism and the poem enacts this, but the image of the newer type of artist remains unclear. At least in the poem it does, for in Pound's own person it is clear enough. Infuriated by a variously pusillanimous, censorious and pedantic literary establishment and deprived, as he saw it, of a livelihood in literary journalism, Pound decamped predictably to Paris where an idea of the liberated bohemian existence was still alive.

In London the immediate post-war years witnessed an end to the collective life of modernist experiment. This brief moment of little more than a decade therefore, between the approximate dates of 1908 and 1920, provides the historical markers of this book. Book and history end therefore before the appearance of the major works of modernism from Eliot and Joyce. In my view these works belong to another phase, a modernism of the text, we might say, which emerges in a separated way from the embryonic cosmopolitan modernism of the earlier years. What survives in our time is a cultural memory of this modernism in the making. It will be obvious that I believe this is of more than nostalgic interest. The texts of the modernist canon lift off into a long and full life. Something was lost, however, and certainly lost to London. For in detaching itself from the adventurous, volatile, artistic and social life of its apprentice years, modernism parted from an informing culture – one which in its very incoherence and heterogeneity, presented a fullness the ensuing era lacks.

I mean to suggest, therefore, that we will gain from a broader understanding of the social character of modernism in the years in which it came into being. I want to reflect on what this involves in the following chapters but firstly to consider the changing figure of the bohemian in relation to a singular individual, Wyndham Lewis, and a single text, Lewis's novel *Tarr*.

Bourgeois-bohemians

Lewis recalls how in early 1909 he visited Ford Madox Ford's *English Review* offices at 84 Holland Park Avenue, Kensington. He 'silently left a bundle of manuscript' with his name but no address and returned some weeks later to be presented, much to his surprise, with the proofs of his story 'The "Pole"' and subsequently his first publication in England (Lewis, 1984: 130). Douglas Goldring recalls this first encounter differently. Ford, he says, told him on the evening of Lewis's visit how Lewis – 'tall, swarthy... with romantically disordered hair, wearing a long black coat buttoned up to his chin' – had made his way up the stairs to find Ford in the bath, 'a large sponge in one hand and a cake of soap in the other':

> After announcing in the most matter-of-fact way that he was a man of genius and that he had a manuscript for publication, he asked if he might read it. 'Go ahead', Ford murmured, continuing to use his sponge. Lewis then unbuttoned his coat, produced 'The Pole' and read it through. At the end, Ford observed 'well, that's all right. If you'll leave it behind, we'll certainly print it'. (Goldring, 1943: 40)

In *Return to Yesterday* (1932) Ford remembered things differently again:

> He was extraordinary in appearance ... he seemed to be Russian. He was very dark in the shadows of the staircase. He wore an immense steeple-crowned hat. Long black locks fell from it. His coat was one of those Russian looking coats that have no revers. He had also an ample black cape of the type that villains in transpontine melodrama throw over their shoulders when they say 'Ha-ha!' He said not a word.
> I exclaimed:
> 'I don't want any Tzar's diaries. I don't want any Russian revelations. I don't want to see, hear or smell any Slavs.' All the while I was pushing him down the stairs. He said nothing. His dark eyes rolled. He established himself immovably against the banisters and began fumbling in the pockets of his cape. He produced crumpled papers in rolls. He fumbled in the pockets of his strange coat. He produced crumpled papers in rolls. He produced them from all over his person – from inside his waistcoat, from against his skin beneath his brown

jersey ... All the time he said no word ... At last he went slowly down those stairs. I had the impression that he was not any more Russian. He must be Guy Fawkes. (1932: 390)[4]

Jeffrey Meyers, Lewis's major early biographer, believes Ford's story as told to Goldring was 'apocryphal' (Meyers, 1980: 27). True, Goldring admits Ford's anecdotes were often untrustworthy, but adds that if this event 'didn't happen, it ought to have done' (1943: 40). Meyers does not consider that this account may have been as much Goldring's story as Ford's and that Goldring was himself helping the record fit the way things should have been. Indeed, we might view both tales as boosting the mythology of Ford's *English Review*, and redounding to these authors' own prescience and key role in the story of literary life which came to revolve around Ford and Violent Hunt's *South Lodge*. But Lewis was himself also evidently at work on the enigmatic persona of 'Wyndham Lewis, artist'. Goldring comments knowingly that he had 'never seen anyone so obviously a "genius"'. It suited Lewis too to be thought 'a mystery man without a past', as Meyers puts it (1980: 30). Ford thought that he was Russian or a Pole, or Spanish – as did others – until he discovered 'his costume was the usual uniform of the Paris student of those days' (1932: 390) or, as he writes of the Lewis character in the novel *The Marsden Case* (1923: 4) 'all these things were the products of a sojourn in Bohemia, not of foreign birth'.

But if not actually 'foreign', Lewis was not obviously 'English' either. The crew of an English cargo ship on which he once travelled needed to assure themselves that he was 'an English gentleman' beneath all his 'wildness' and 'strangeness' (Lewis, 1984: 251). His years in Paris, Spain, Germany and Holland between 1902–1908 rubbed away the worst effects, he said, of an English education: 'I became a European', he wrote (121). And Ezra Pound agreed: Lewis was 'the rarest of phenomena, an Englishman who has achieved the triumph of being also a European' (Pound, 1960: 424). Thus Lewis returned from Bohemia 'almost as a foreigner' (Lewis, 1984: 251), with a perspective not unlike that of the 'foreign auxiliary' F.T. Marinetti, who visited England from early 1910, and with whom for a time Lewis brewed up a double plot against the complacent aestheticism of the English establishment. The hair, the coat, the heavy silences of the bohemian Lewis were the outward signs, therefore, of the dedicated 'artist' intent on estranging a moribund national culture. At the same time this self-created image was also a 'front', an embodied public programme deliberately separated from Lewis's private life. His sexual liaisons and marriage he notoriously secreted in this second compartment and, as if to compound the enigma, shifted his London base across addresses in Ealing, Chelsea, Soho, Bloomsbury and Kensington (Farrington, 1980: 12). That these private and public realms were not so separate, however, is evident from his attempt to theorise this very division in his writings. Here too he developed the argument for multiple personalities or personae which was ironically of a piece with his private inaccessibility.

In all this, Lewis joined, with Goldring, Ford and many others not only in contriving a personal legend but, at the same time, in administering to the remembered hues of a pre-war idyll. This cultural myth is at work in Ford's reflections in 1932 on a day in late June 1914 when 'I stood on the edge of the kerb in Piccadilly Circus and looked at London' (1932: 399). He felt 'free and as it were without weight. It was a delicious day...the flower girls had brought with them a perfect mountain of colour...The Season...was at its height'. But still Ford is ready to leave, to bid farewell to literature, and stood there 'taking my last look at the city' and up at the sky when 'on that night all London was blacker than the grave' (414). In not dissimilar vein, Lewis, writing to Sturge Moore in 1941, remembered 'how calm those days were before the epoch of wars and social revolution', a time of companionable talk 'in the last days of the Victorian world of artificial peacefulness' (Meyers, 1980: 27).

'The years immediately preceding the war,' John Rothenstein avers, 'were cosmopolitan and revolutionary' (Farrington, 1980: 8). Vorticism he sees as the artistic culmination of this complex history. After the war, writes Richard Cork, 'the whole heady context of pre-war London, which provided such an ideal environment for the fermentation of experimental ideas, had vanished for ever... Vorticism was virtually forgotten' (Farrington, 1980: 29). These views sum up the attraction of the period, of course: a time remembered in anecdote and incident as a moment of new beginnings and lost promise, of what once was and might have been. Such thoughts plainly belong to a retrospective postwar mythology of the earlier period. But it is true too that the period was being composed, written and rewritten, as it occurred. Lewis in particular, both by instinct and design, made and remade himself in the figure of the mysterious rebarbative artist while simultaneously revising his work and writings in these London years and beyond. This was true of the story 'The "Pole"' (a generic term, Lewis points out, for a stranger and artist) and the other related short stories later collected in revised form as *The Complete Wild Body* (1982). And it was true of the material of the novel *Tarr*, which was begun in 1907, re-written and first serialised in 1916, and further revised for a new edition in 1928.

Most biographical accounts see Lewis as a bohemian in Europe, a Vorticist and then 'Tyro' and 'Enemy' in the London of the war years and 1920s. Paul Edwards, for example, identifies the figure of the bohemian with the Romantic myth of an 'authentic lifestyle' associated with ' "primitive" people uncontaminated by industrial and bourgeois values' (Edwards, 1996: 30). In this account Lewis is a bohemian in the period of his visit to Brittany from which the early stories derive and of his admiring association with the 'gypsy' Augustus John. Freeing himself from this model and the naive assumption of a life outside the entailments of bourgeois modernity, Lewis, says Edwards, 'became free to role-play instead' (33). But the figure of the bohemian was in fact never free of urban life or bourgeois commercial values. Rather, he (sic) was a particular product of and reaction to this emerging modern society. Role-play was not an alternative to a bohemian life style, therefore, so much as its very essence. Edwards concludes that Lewis was pitched between the Romantic and postmodern artist, the one locked in an impossible quest for authenticity, the other destined to recycle the 'always already' available materials of an abundant but finite contemporary culture. To put this differently, Lewis was positioned precisely as a 'modernist' artist, committed alike to experiment, innovation and the social and political role of the artist, but able to maintain a critical position in advance of a failed and invasive society only by continual change and re-invention. The different 'Wyndham Lewises' we see in Paris and in London are the result – all of them, in my view, versions of the Bohemian artist as outsider and scourge of bourgeois society and the artistic establishment. *Tarr* presents some of the variations on this bohemian type, a set of portraits of the artist as it were, at the same time as, in Lewis's reworking and rewritings of the text, it enacts this very process of self-revision in his own artistic life.

The novel had its beginnings in a story written in 1907 or 1908 and grew out of Lewis's six itinerant years in Holland, Madrid, Munich, and especially Paris where he went after school and student life at Rugby and the Slade School of Art. At the Slade and subsequently in Paris and Brittany, Lewis fell under the spell of the older and already celebrated Augustus John. 'Near John', he wrote to his mother, 'I can never paint, since his artistic personality is too great' (Rose, 1963: 9). Whatever weight we attach to this, Lewis's own personality, as both painter and writer, did not assert itself until his arrival in London in late 1908. In Paris, after divesting himself of the effects of the British public school system, he began his education, 'in many directions', one of which was to create a Wyndham Lewis who an old school fellow would have found unrecognisable: 'I still went to a tailor in Brook Street for my clothes, but persuaded him to cut them in to the oddest shapes. My hair was abundant and was now worn extremely long' (1984: 250, and see 121).

Carefully tailored but short of funds, the floppy-haired, foreign-looking, brooding genius made the legendary climb to Ford's office and entered English cultural life, a somewhat late developer at twenty-seven. Exhibitions with the Camden Town Group, the Allied Artists Group and at the Second 'Post-Impressionist' exhibition led to a short-lived association in 1913 with Roger Fry's Omega Workshops and a permanent animosity towards the aesthetics and social style of Bloomsbury. At the end of the same year he met and entertained Marinetti and the following year began the Rebel Arts Centre and, in consort with Pound and others, launched the Vorticist movement and its journal *Blast*. He settled at this time in Percy Street, next door to the Tour Eiffel Restaurant, earlier the home of the one-time Poets' Club led by T.E. Hulme, who Lewis had also met in 1913. The Eiffel Tower became the base for Vorticist gatherings and Lewis decorated an upstairs Vorticist room; the whole enterprise a direct rival to Bloomsbury and the Omega workshop five minutes walk away in Fitzroy Square. If Lewis launched Vorticism, it launched him too. Much like the artist figure Arghol in his drama 'Enemy of the Stars' who in his encounter with mankind (the character Hanp) 'is destined to become "Arghol" – a mass produced persona, a false self, a crowd creation' (Chapman, 1973: 22) so Lewis became the artist-propagandist-showman, 'Mr. Wyndham Lewis', the newest sensation on the 'A' list at society drawing rooms and salons (see Lewis, 1982: 46–55). But if lionised on one side, Lewis was loathed on the other. As prowling 'verbal pugilist', in Richard Cork's description (Farrington, 1980: 23), he goaded opponents into the ring, even such a one as Lytton Strachey, who reacted on Bloomsbury's behalf to an early Lewis story with an 'Ugh!'. 'The total effect was *affreux*', he exclaimed, and 'the deleterious influence' of Lewis's company a certainty (Chapman, 1973: 83).

At Percy Street, meanwhile, Lewis determined to enlist, but also, since septicaemia from an earlier uncured bout of gonorrhoea delayed his departure, to leave some more robust artistic legacy of his 'work' rather than his 'name', to adopt a distinction drawn by Pound (Pound, 1960: 423). Thus he returned in the summer of 1914 to the materials of his earlier life in Paris, pasting new sections of what was to be the novel *Tarr* to the core story of a German art student, Otto Kreisler, which he had said was 'just finished' in 1909 and again, 'finished' or nearing completion in 1910 and 1911 (Lewis, 1990: 361–2). The revised and expanded novel was completed in November 1915 and left in Pound's hands while Lewis was at the front. It was published in the *Egoist* magazine from April 1916 and then as an *Egoist* edition in July 1918 (1990: 365–70).

In *Rude Assignment* Lewis remembers Paris as a heavenly period of indolent curiosity. The city 'was the great humanist creation of the French', it was 'the perfect place to live in ... expansive and civilised ... its multitude of café-terraces swarmed with people from every corner of the earth' including 'an immense student population' who relished its 'divinely disputatious' liberal and bookish culture (1984: 120–1); 'that Paris', he adds, 'will always remain for me the geographical source of all life and light and true happiness' (250).

In *Tarr* (1918) Paris was less this bohemian idyll of later memory than the more tawdry world of 'bourgeois-bohemians' busy being artists. The Knackfus Quarter is 'given up to Art' and occupied by artists in 'corduroy trousers' on 'the operatic italian model' (1990: 21). Americans and Germans rent the apartments and Italian models festoon the square. Lewis's satirical sweep across this world performed, said Pound, 'a huge act of scavenging; cleaning up a great lot of rubbish, cultural Bohemian, romantico-Tennysonish, arty, societish, gutterish' (Pound, 1960: 429). For Lewis, as for Pound, these were pretty much the same sort of rubbish. Certainly in one early gust in the novel they attach themselves to one figure, the character Hobson, who serves to set off Lewis's chief protagonist, Tarr. Hobson is customarily identified with Roger Fry and thus with Bloomsbury; he is an indolent pseudo-artist who has 'no right' to the artist's standard long hair, old hat and shabby tweeds (34). Hobson is the artist type, 'uniformly *out of uniform*', 'a crowd ... a set' not an individual; he represents 'the *dregs* of Anglo-Saxon civilization! ... a mixture of the lees of Liberalism, the poor froth blown off the decadent nineties, the wardrobe-leavings of a vulgar Bohemianism with its headquarters in Chelsea!' (29, 34). The background to his activities are, Pound confirms, 'more or less Bloomsbury. There are probably such Bloomsburys in Paris and in every large city' (1960: 428). The contretemps between the two men takes place in a Paris café but might just as well have been in Fitzroy Square or Percy Street where Lewis sat writing, throwing punchy insults in a new round of the row begun in 1913.

Thus English Bloomsbury is transported to this Parisian stage and shown back to the English readers of the *Egoist*, a flaccid imitation of a feeble French original, whose hat Tarr knocks off on Lewis's behalf. Paul Peppis sees a radical contrast between Tarr and James Joyce's contemporary portrait of the artist. Whereas Joyce's artist embodied an individualistic idea of the ego favoured by the *Egoist*'s editor, Dora

Marsden, Lewis, Peppis argues, presents a corrosive critique of the magazine's ruling assumption of an autonomous, self-determining 'single subjectivity' (Peppis, 2000: 136). Peppis connects this difference with the impact on Lewis of the experience of war. Certainly these years were a period of revision and repositioning, and the direct experience of war was to significantly alter Lewis's thinking. However, if anything, the war persuaded him that the geometric forms developed in Vorticism 'were bleak and empty. They wanted *filling*' (Lewis, 1984: 139). He increasingly adopted 'a humanist naturalism in art' (Sheppard, 1989: 524) which, after 1917, became associated with an emerging auto-critique of Vorticist abstraction and vitalism thought now to be complicit with the violence of war.

Tarr is difficult to place in this period of concentrated rethinking, but while it rejects the concept of the 'indivisible ego' targeted in *Blast* 1 in favour of the externalised and emptied self of Vorticism, it also ridicules the extremes of a Vorticist subjectivity. It does not dispose of the ego, therefore, so much as de-compose it into the 'new egos' announced in *Blast* 1, only then to expose these new types of the artist to the satirical chemicals of the social-sexual world of the novel. The end product is less the 'anti-individualist' novel Peppis describes than the double-voiced '(anti-) Vorticist' hybrid described by Richard Sheppard.

Lewis employs Tarr in the novel as one of his 'showmen' (1990: 15) for this 'new sort of person; the creative man' (29). This new type is above the philistine populace and above sexual appetite, for in him the normal person's sexual energies are re-channelled into the creation of 'the Artist himself' (29). 'Surrender to a woman was a sort of suicide for the artist' (214). 'Life' too, accordingly, 'is art's rival and vice versa' ... '*deadness* is the first condition of art' (298, 299). A statue has no soul other than its 'lines and masses'. 'No restless, quick, flame-like ego is imagined for the *inside* of it. It has no inside' (299, 300). These ideas certainly accord with Lewis's emphasis elsewhere. His 'new egos' are porous: 'individual demarcations are confused and interests dispersed' (Lewis, 1997: 141). Characters in the novel experience this instability – though, like Tarr who feels a part of himself 'purloined' or 'captured' and held hostage by Bertha (Lewis, 1990: 72), they for the most part sense this as a threat to an assumed coherent self. From the outset, however, Tarr's sexual appetites, as dismissive as he is of them – and of the woman Bertha who is their initial object – compromise his claims to be the artist of his own self-image. Nor, apart from some passing references to cubism, is there anything to suggest that his own work or that of the other would-be artists comes close to realising these ideas.

Hastings, Mary Borden Turner, and Nancy Cunard, were casually entered into by Lewis but often left the women distraught. This cavalier abuse of women went with a disgust of childbirth and a callous indifference towards children. Lewis is said once to have told Kate Lechmere that he dropped and killed his baby by Ida (Meyers, 1980: 22).[6] Another story tells how when Iris Barry returned from hospital with their new baby, she had to wait outside Lewis's studio until he had finished having sex with Nancy Cunard (Meyers, 1980: 91–2, but see O'Keefe, 2001: 226). We find this offensive. But that, after all, seems to have been the point. For here was another face of the legend: 'Wyndham Lewis, heartless Lothario' to complement the Vorticist firebrand.

The record sometimes tells another story, however, as in the case of Iris Barry. The Barry–Nancy Cunard story is not one that Barry's papers corroborate. Also, though Lewis's final letter to her in April 1930 (six months prior to his marriage to Gladys Anne Hoskins) rejecting all association between them is shockingly cruel, their correspondence earlier in the 1920s after their affair had ended shows him to have been a measured but supportive friend who gave her money and advice and showed some concern for the daughter Masie (Schiddel).[7] Their son, Robin, if such he was, Lewis never recognised. Also, as we have seen, Lewis came to revise and indeed reject the anti-humanism of the Vorticist aesthetic. *Tarr* is part of that process, most strikingly in the figure of Anastasya. She is an independent cosmopolitan woman ('My parents are Russian. = I was born in Berlin and brought up in America. = We live in Dresden'; Lewis, 1990: 213) who moves unchaperoned about Paris streets. She is more than Tarr's equal in debate; a drinking companion, gourmet and erotic temptress who is moved more by sexual desire (which she awakens in the 'schoolboy' Tarr, 295) than possessiveness ('You won't hear marriage talked about by me', 307).

The new conditions which outdated 'the old form of egotism' meant, wrote Lewis in *Blast* 1, that the 'THE ACTUAL HUMAN BODY ... now, literally, EXISTS much less' (Lewis, 1997: 141). He preferred to keep both art and life free of the messiness of the body – of the crowd, the sexualised woman, babies and children – until the violent physicality of combat and death at the front persuaded him otherwise. Thus his painting and portraits turned to a semi-naturalistic depiction of the human figure. Anastasya's figure is full; she is a provocative and larger-than-life physical presence, not in this respect unlike the series of Tyros Lewis was to paint in the early 1920s. 'She exuded personality with an alarming and disgusting intensity' (Lewis, 1990: 100). Her appearance is exotic and non-conformist and moves in an inventive vocabulary across classes and culture: thus she wears 'a heavy black burnous, very voluminous and severe' with an 'immense and sinuous' hat (99). Her 'large ornamental bag' suggests 'the herbs and trinkets, paraphernalia of the witch' (98) and she feels 'herself a travelling circus of tricks and wonders, beauty shows and monstrosities' (100). Later she combines a coat 'all in florid redundancies of heavy cloth, like a Tintoretto dress' with the 'plain dark blouse and skirt... and open-work stockings' of a working girl (294). To the 'ridiculous amateur' Tarr, whose de-humanising obsession with her size only reveals his amplified desire, she is a 'big brute', a 'hulk', a 'mass', an 'ox' (214, 294, 297). He cannot, all the same, resist her perfection: 'The upper part of her head was massive and intelligent. The middle of her body was massive and exciting... the weight was in the head and hips. = But was not this a complete thing in itself?' (300–1). In Anastasya, in short, to our surprise and perhaps to his own, the misogynistic Lewis presents the combination of sexualised body and intelligence that Tarr and Kreisler deny or fail to achieve. In her the novel truly discovers its main character, a 'new sort of person' who implies 'an egoistic code of advanced order, full of insolent strategies' (99) well beyond the explicit model she has served to critique.

Anastasya does not simply resolve the novel's masculinised polarities, however, certainly not so as to proffer a newly constituted version of the unified indivisible ego. For one thing, her 'personality' is a consciously gendered construction and not a 'universal' model. 'Quite used to being looked at, she had become resigned to inability to avoid performing' (100). Her – in the context, remarkable – combination of 'the geniality of public character and the genius of sex' (100) derives from this controlled self-awareness of herself as a woman. Secondly, while Kreisler, Tarr and Bertha move in and out of a repertoire of standard roles, Anastasya confidently embraces the mobile, decentred role-play which in them is a sign of self-alienation. 'I don't like being anything out and out,' she declares, 'life is so varied. I like wearing a dress with which I can enter into any milieu or circumstances. That is the only real self worth the name' (133).

This is an unexpected subversion of Lewis's thinking in 'The Code of a Herdsman'. There the artist is warned only to come down from the mountain and consort with the vulgar crowd wearing 'masks and thick clothing' (Symons, 1989: 30). The Herdsman enjoins him to 'Cherish and develop, side by side, your six most constant indications of different personalities... Leave your front door one day as B.: the next march down the street as E. A variety of clothes, hats especially, are of help in this wider dramatisation of yourself' (26). Thus Lewis stepped out in the several guises, including the necessary hat, of the bohemian artist – boulevardier, Spanish gigolo, Vorticist provocateur, war artist and post-war Tyro – to engage in a suspicious, critical but inevitable commerce with the bourgeois herd. Here, in Anastasya, the strategy of multiple identities is redeemed of its fear and contempt of the social mass to produce a gendered, manifestly embodied example of the theatrical, perfomative self that Lewis's theory otherwise reserves for the elitist male artist.

But does Lewis contemplate a male equivalent to Anastasya? First of all, in her active sexuality, independence and unchaperoned movement across Paris, she is herself 'male' as these activities were customarily gendered – she guesses Tarr views her as 'not properly a woman' because of her intelligence and good sense (Lewis, 1990: 296). Her equivalent would be consequently 'feminised', though in the manner of her own female identity not that of its stereotypes. In the 1928 version of *Tarr* Lewis made changes to the syntax and presentation of character to produce the more 'straightforward novel' he spoke of in the 1910s (Lewis, 1984: 139). He did not, however, develop the character of Anastasya. She departs both versions of the novel in a matter-of-fact sentence, 'Tarr and Anastasya did not marry. = They had no children' (Lewis, 1990: 320), leaving the stage to Tarr. Lewis did not choose therefore to explore the innovative, 'metahumanist' type she represents (Sheppard, 1989: 530). He did, however, make a small relevant change elsewhere. *Blasting and Bombardiering* contains an amplified version of the section 'Morpeth Olympiad Record Crowd' from 'The Crowd Master' in *Blast 2*. Here Lewis describes Cantleman as a 'rough bohemian' and 'suffragette' (1982: 66); he was, he says, 'my character, my fictional diarist' and adds, on the description 'suffragette', 'I've just put this in. The editor of *Blast* would never have admitted that he was a suffragette' (66n).

In the mid-1910s Lewis shared the pages of the *Egoist* with Dora Marsden's 'Individualist' editorials and the feminist and suffrage arguments that the paper had continued to run since its earlier life as the *Freewoman* and *New Freewoman*. *Blast* 1 contained a story by Rebecca West and an address 'To Suffragettes'. The first presents a politically active, sexually alive woman locked in marriage to a murderously jealous husband. The second, for all its patronising tone, suggests an affinity between suffrage militancy and Vorticist tactics. The 'rough bohemian' (the post-Romantic manly bohemian) and male 'suffragette' (the militant, womanly bohemian) etch in a transgressive coupling to match the confident and open performativity represented by Anastasya. In both her character and this small change, suggestive and curtailed as they are, we sense both the possibilities brought to the surface by the cultural and political agitation of the period, and note how these were minimised and set back by war and its aftermath.

The old order, Lewis announced in his post-war review *The Tyro* in 1921 was 'suffering from every conceivable malady' (Lewis, 1970: 3). The underlying malady in the life of the resilient bohemian Lewis in this later phase especially was that, like Tarr, he has no 'social machinery' (Lewis, 1990: 23) – or rather had been robbed of it. For here too, there was a decisive difference between Lewis and his characters. Tarr was not, we should remember, the leader of an artistic movement, nor are the novel's characters placed in anything faintly resembling the network of productive and disputatious associations between men and women artists in the London of the 1910s. The idea of an artistic community – 'Co-operation, group-genius' – Tarr writes off as 'a slavish pretence and absurdity' (313). Lewis, on the other hand, wrote to his mother from France that his only loyalty was to his artistic contemporaries: 'I dont [sic] want to get killed for Mr. Lloyd George, or Mr. Asquith, or for any community except that elusive but excellent one to which I belong' (Rose, 1963: 81). Lewis retained his faith in a 'New Epoch' beyond the war and *The Tyro* was one of its vehicles. In 1920 'starting all over again' he founded Group X, ten artists of whom five had been associated with *Blast*. Their one exhibition took place at the end of March at the Mansard Gallery. His own solo exhibition 'Tyros and Portraits' was staged in April 1921. The two issues of *The Tyro* were largely single authored but its arguments were plainly more than individualistic (Chapman, 1973: 27–30).

Thereafter, in the middle 1920s, Lewis went 'underground' into a period of intense study to emerge in his last bohemian persona as the crowned 'Enemy', the lone black knight used as the insignia of his third short-lived review published under that title between 1927 and 1929. The social maladies were such that they required the combined medicines of sociology, philosophy and politics to cure them and the result, published between 1926 and 1930 – years which also included the revised text of *Tarr* and the *Complete Wild Body*, was the four major volumes, *The Art of Being Ruled* (1926), *Time and Western Man* (1927), *The Childermass* (1928) and *The Apes of God* (1930). Like other modernists, and especially Ezra Pound, Lewis drew a heavy line between the artist in the expanded role as social and political sage and prevailing tendencies in Western modernity. In this battle he comes to represent the modernist extreme; an estranged, reviled and neglected but fiercely independent critical voice: the 'solitary outlaw' he proudly announced in *The Enemy*. For all the considerable interest of his later work and career, something had been distorted and lost – the possibilities of a fluid, experimental, theatrical self sketched above and what had supported and inspired this: the cosmopolitan and revolutionary pre-war environment referred to by Rothenstein and Cork. In that earlier time there had been some working 'social machinery' and sure signs of the diverse, dissenting products of a collective bohemian life.

Bohemia in Babel

A second retrospective account of this pre-war ethos tells us more of what this bohemian London meant before it was ploughed under by events. John Cournos's novel *Babel* appeared in 1922; a relatively unnoticed addition to the *annus mirabilis* of modernism as it entered its 'canonic' phase – with all this development entailed for the isolated epic modernist.[8] Cournos depicts the Vorticists as 'Dynamists' and associates their machine aesthetic with the overwhelming temptation to join in the mood of national unity at the outbreak of war. The war solves all manner of contradictions as the differences housed in Babel fall into oneness. Lewis had seen how the anti-humanist abstractions of Vorticism were complicit with the dehumanised violence of war, and Cournos, if he to some extent confuses Vorticism with Futurism, is right to see how *Blast*'s nationalistic *brio* could easily turn into a patriotic chant.[9] What is particularly significant, however, is the way in which the novel acknowledges the force of difference and contesting values – in spite of the protagonist Gombarov's theoretical commitment to artistic unity and yearning for personal stability. This is given wide artistic, economic and political dimensions in the novel. However, it is the story of Gombarov's relation to women and his depiction of the tense, dialogic culture of London, which is most striking. London is the Babel of the title but its vibrant, compelling and confusing life represents the general critical state of the contemporary world, and is also internalised as a Babel of the mind. Modern society is heterogeneous and international all at once (Gombarov loses his virginity to a Parisian courtesan in Florence in a bed made in Massachusetts by Puritan hands) and his brain rings out a 'medley of discordant tunes' (Cournos, 1922: 37). He is Jewish, Russian, American, a 'monk and roué' (62) at war with himself, pulled one way towards home, wife, children and the other towards romance, adventure and art. He faces, in other words, the choice of bourgeois or bohemian. The first is represented by his respectable middle-class American fiancée, Winifred, who promises to help discover 'the especial thread that is my true self' (62). Gombarov has however chosen art and like Hudson in *Tarr* – and like Lewis – chosen to look the part. He abandons a job in journalism in America for the artist's life in Paris and arrives in 1912 at his cherished destination, London, dressed in a 'wide-brimmed felt hat, his artist's black wing tie' and 'longish hair' (90). He is enthralled by the sights, shapes and sounds of London but notices too how unnoticed he is, unlike in America or Paris. The city sweeps up outsiders and newcomers in an impersonal variety. Later, as he visits Speakers' Corner in Hyde Park, he realises that this acceptance of difference and disputation is central to the character of the city:

> the significance of Marble Arch was that it represented the modern world and its contending ideas in microcosm. There was no unity, the world was here visible in all its fragmentary nature, restless in all its fractious contradiction. (124)

This 'tolerance, the by-product of a complex, many-tongued civilisation' he realises was what 'kept men from jumping at each other's throats... Only some great intolerance... might weld together the fragments of this island into one single expressioned face' (124). It followed that tolerance did not 'unite a world' but 'broke it up'; 'it implied that a community with a million persons might have a million different opinions... a million discordant voices' (124–5).

As Gombarov struggles to maintain his own creative life, he comes slowly, as if out of the fog afflicting the city, to reject Winifred and the life she represents. The tolerance he has observed confirms instead his bohemian rather than bourgeois self and informs his relations with a Jewish prostitute, Judith, and a suffragette, Lucy. Both women are placed on the social margins, and are, while independent in their cultural and sexual attitudes, deeply conscious of disadvantage and oppression. Cournos suggests an affinity between these women and the struggling artist as outsider. Their circumstances and independence bring them together but also rule out a long-term relationship. There is no tacking between bourgeois and bohemian options of the kind Lewis indulges in, therefore. The male artist does not seek nor find compliant women. Rather there is passion, pain and a recognition of difference to the point of incompatibility and respectful separation as the women and Gombarov go their own ways.

As he strives in London to support his creative work, Gombarov becomes involved in various artistic movements of the day, as did Cournos. He meets Tobias Bagg (Ezra Pound), Hugh Rodd (T.E. Hulme), the 'Primitives' (Imagists) and contributors to 'The Self' (the *Egoist*).

The satirical edge Cournos gives these portraits did not produce a novel of Lewis's type, nor a form to match the perception of internal and cultural struggle. However, Cournos does, in his account of a Gaudier-Brzeska character, named Jan Maczishek, describe an art which embraces opposites: 'the primitive, savage spirit incarnated in mechanics, cruelty with nuance...a Maori spear and the French machine gun' (346). And there are other correspondences. Gaudier-Brzeska was the bohemian type to Cournos's steady journalist. Nevertheless, there is a way in which Gaudier-Brzeska's rounded Vorticist sculptures find an echo in the rounded shapes of the London Gombarov so delights in and the domed capacious structure of the British Museum, 'the greatest yet of all repositories' (93). This too in its 'preservation of fragments, and fragments of fragments' of extinct civilisations (93) brings the Babel of the past into the Babel of 'multiple faced' modern London (328). Thus Cournos finds in the physical city and in sexual and social relations a double analogy in cosmopolitan Vortex London for a Vorticist aesthetic equal to the internally fraught Babel of modern society. The tower is tottering and so too is modern man ('I am Babel, a full-thoughted, tottering modern man'; 328) before the false unity of war. The world is suspended nonetheless at a prior, fleeting, moment: the 'new person' is after all a kind of machine, 'a kind of gramophone disk...capable of gathering onto itself and recording the voices of its proximity, voices harmonious or querulous, vulgar or full of refined nuance, as the case may be, now warring among themselves' (63). Elsewhere, this idea of a modern personality finds its appropriate urban medium in jazz improvisation, 'a many-tuned medley...an ultra modern music shaped out of discords' (89), something you danced to in company with others with the full 'social machinery' of the body.

Cournos does not produce a modernist form to accompany his modernist notion of a riven, mobile subjectivity. No more did Lewis explore the joint potential of a confidently performative female sexuality and modernist form. Few if any did. Jessica Dismorr's work provides a final striking sense of a possibility along these lines however. Dismorr joined the Rebel Arts Centre and exhibited as a Vorticist in 1915, in 1917 in New York, and as a member of Group X in 1920. She signed the Vorticist manifesto and contributed illustrations to *Blast 2* as well as a set of prose poems. The third of these, 'June Night', reports on the precarious and jagged excitement of the metropolis from the top of a bus – reminiscent of Cournos's first sight of the city also from a bus on a June evening. She separates from her boring, romantic male escort and feels herself a 'strayed Bohemian' (Lewis, 1981: 68).

Jane Beckett and Deborah Cherry argue that Dismorr's perception of the 'throbbing' crowded bus, the 'mews and by-ways', 'unplumbable depths' and 'widening circles of alarm' that she escapes to is gendered feminine (Beckett and Cherry, 2000: 67, 68). The sense in this text of places out of reach or out of bounds and, in Dismorr's 'London Notes', of the city's inner, hidden places is consistent with the dark 'scrypts' (script and crypt combined) and cave-like spaces in her own paintings and the work of her Vorticist colleague Helen Saunders (Beckett and Cherry, 2000: 68–72). The representation of figures in their painting is machine-like and by that token does evade the binary registration of sexual difference (70–1). Thus, what had been gendered and embodied, as in the written text of Dismorr's 'Monologue' in *Blast* 2 becomes now anonymised according to the dictates of modernist impersonality. In so far as an expression of sexual difference only bolstered the subordination of women, therefore, we might view the de-sexualised figures in Vorticist drawings and paintings by women artists as a radical gesture. Still, this is not the radical representation of woman, in mind and body, we find in Anastasya ('I – am – a *woman*; not a man', she assures Tarr; Lewis, 1990: 296), or approach in Saunders and Dismorr's prose pieces.

One is left with a stray thought. Helen Saunders helped paint the 'Vorticist Room' in the Tour Eiffel Restaurant in 1915. This is generally unrecognised and as such symptomatic of the commonplace discrimination of the 1910s and its continuation in our own times. We might wonder if Saunders or Dismorr contributed in any way to the murals at the Cave of the Golden Calf, the subterranean nightclub off Heddon Street for which Lewis and others were commissioned. Here, after all, was an urban dark space, a bohemian dive humming with sexuality and invention. Did Vorticist women artists go there? Did they dance? Did Lewis dance?

2
'The Nineties Tried Your Game'

French connections

In August 1875, Stéphane Mallarmé paid a short and frustrating visit to London (Mackworth, 1974: 40–1). He had lived for a year in London in 1862–63 when he'd stayed in rooms in Panton Street at the heart of the French quarter in Soho, and returned again to the city in 1872. Panton Street was at that time a street of quiet working families, seemingly transplanted from some modest provincial town 'that was neither quite France nor quite England' (7), and wedged between the hard men of the Black Bull tavern, the prostitutes of Windmill Street and the equally squalid Rupert Street, abutting the mayhem of Leicester Square. At six o'clock an army of street harlots, beggars, con-men and assorted villains rubbed shoulders with dapper gentlemen on their way past illegal boxing matches to expensive brothels. Mallarmé was young, poor and devoted to poetry. With his companion, Marie, who passed as but was not yet his wife, he had come to learn English so as to gain proficiency as a teacher and improve his reading of Edgar Allan Poe. They went for walks or watched from their top window – an ordinary but telling image, for the visit was to produce the poem 'Les Fenêtres', one of the founding documents of French symbolism. On one of their walks too, to Hyde Park, the couple encountered the London fog which was to swirl its way through Impressionist and early modernist art of the city. The sensation of a surrounding impalpable reality and distant 'morbid outline' in the half-invisible city confirmed Mallarmé in his poetic ideal: to reach for a profound evanescent truth beyond the real – the magnificent view beyond the window of the 'dreary hospital' of 'Les Fenêtres' (Mallarmé, 1977: 71).

In London in 1875 he planned to meet connoisseurs and active enthusiasts of France and French letters, such as John Payne, Arthur

O'Shaughnessy and Edmund Gosse. Above all, he hoped to meet Algernon Charles Swinburne who had expressed his admiration for Mallarmé's translation of Poe's 'The Raven'. In the event Swinburne proved elusive and Gosse and O'Shaughnessy were out of town. Payne later remembered Mallarmé as a diminutive 'Parisian type' trotting about Bloomsbury trying to locate Swinburne – as if, Gosse added, 'by the light of pure instinct' (Mackworth, 1974: 41).

Mallarmé's experience pointed up an intriguing difference between Parisian and London literary culture. The long-established French quarter of Soho had attracted skilled craftsmen and women as well as low-life types, and from the 1870s, bands of exiled Communards, to the centre of London. But French literary culture had not yet affected English customs. Perhaps, comments Mackworth, Mallarmé 'never quite understood that...one could not simply drop into a certain café or restaurant and be sure of finding a few poets who would tell one where the others were to be found' (40). 'In London', she adds, 'there were few meeting places of this sort' (40–1). Instead, Mallarmé made his way to the British Museum Reading Room, armed with letters of introduction from Gosse and O'Shaughnessy. There Richard Garnett would facilitate his research on the long-awaited edition of William Beckford's *Vathek*. Gosse, O'Shaughnessy and Garnett were members of a generation of English men of letters employed by the British Museum. Later examples, who were in their own small ways to usher in the grander figures of modernism, included Laurence Binyon, R.A. Streatfeild and their associate Sturge Moore. The Museum tearoom and the nearby Vienna Café would also play their part in this story. In fact, therefore, Mallarmé had been introduced to precisely one of those places in London where you could drop in and find a few poets who would put you in touch with a few others.

In 1875, the Café Royal was not yet a fashionable meeting place and the Cheshire Cheese in Fleet Street was little known beyond a small literary coterie. Both emerged as significant symbolic sites for artistic life and this was itself an expression of a further change in the relations of English and French art and literature. A number of English and French writers experienced and contributed to this change, among them Swinburne, W.E. Henley, and George Moore, Mallarmé and Paul Valéry, and most notably perhaps Paul Verlaine and Arthur Rimbaud, who lived together as lovers in London between 1872–73, before Verlaine's return in different circumstances to lecture in London and Oxford in 1893. The Café Royal was established by the Frenchman Daniel Nichols (Daniel Nicolas Thévenon) in 1865. By the 1880s, it was the special haunt, along with a changing entourage, of Whistler and, subsequently, Wilde. These two, and others of less renown, shared the ground-floor Domino Room with 'a whole tribe of the *fin de siècle demi-monde*', among whom Hugh David numbers 'down at heel aristocrats, cells of foreign anarchists, check-suited bookmakers, unsuccessful artists, criminals, pimps, prostitutes, and lookers-on' (David, 1988: 106). In 1884, Daniel Nichols acquired the Empire and in 1887 converted it to a variety theatre. If the Café Royal was French in origin, in décor, in its menus, regimen and social tone, its clientele were English, British or American. And if the Empire was French owned and in some ways cultivated a lavish French atmosphere, it belonged firmly in the tradition of English popular entertainment.

But these were only the most opulent and sensational examples of a new more cosmopolitan London social scene and nightlife. Music halls – or 'theatres of variety' – invaded the West End, finer and larger in their baroque, well-lit splendour than most West End theatres or opera houses. By the 1890s many even included short films on the bill. Hotels, meanwhile, began to offer restaurant dinners and Soho was dotted with French and Italian cafés, offering seven-course meals for around two shillings. By the light of day the city consolidated its role as an imperial capital, commanding European admiration for its business supremacy and prowess on the world stage. And by the turn of the century there were sure signs of the other changes that would declare London a 'modern' city: an increased population, the growth of the suburbs, new forms of office work, a generation of commuting clerks and secretaries, department stores and restaurant chains, advertising, a cheap popular press, the underground and motorised transport. Cultural sensibilities matched and parried these developments in a transformation that was in its own way 'modern': eclectic, fragmented, impersonal. To become modern, said Arthur Symons as early as 1892, poetry must respond to the experience of the city (Holdsworth, 1974: 11). He had London in mind and sought consistently to catch at this new reality in his own prose and verse. The first and enduring model, however, for Symons as for others, was not London, but Paris.

Bohemian empire

The Welsh-born Symons emerged as the leading ambassador for French poetry in London, the go-between Mallarmé had wished to be. He attended Mallarmé's Tuesdays in the early 1890s, he invited Verlaine to lecture in London, edited the *Savoy* ('the most ambitious', the 'most satisfying achievement of *fin de siècle* journalism', said Holbrook Jackson, 1976: 48) and, above all, drew on his personal acquaintance with the French poets for his influential *Symbolist Movement in Literature* (1899). This was an expanded and revised version after discussions with Yeats of the earlier essay, 'The Decadent Movement in Literature' (1893). The term 'Symbolism' was to be preferred, said Symons, since it heralded poetry's return to 'the main road of literature ... to the one pathway, leading through beautiful things to the eternal beauty' (Symons, 1958: 4). Decadence had been a by-way, an 'interlude, half a mock interlude' which referred at best to a matter of style, such as the 'ingenious deformation of the language, in Mallarmé, for instance' (ibid.). Decadence had named much more than this in the earlier essay, however; it bore 'all the qualities that mark the end of great periods: an intense self-consciousness, a restless curiosity in research, an over-subtilizing refinement upon refinement, a spiritual and moral perversity'. If the 'classic' was a model of literary and cultural health then decadence was a disease, 'its very disease of form' reflecting 'all the moods, all the manners, of a sophisticated society; its very artificiality ... a way of being true to nature' (Holdsworth, 1974: 72, 73). Arguably, the essay was describing the French writers Symons most admired: the Goncourts, Verlaine and Huysman. In the event he tempered these sentiments but the air of decadence hovered and was to return in a later retrospective account of his bohemian days in London.

Yeats was concerned to distance himself from the more sordid aspects of the nineties and his doctrine of symbolism was part of this attempt. To Symons's notion of the artist as a cosmopolitan wanderer, Yeats, as Max Beerbohm reported, sombrely replied that 'an artist worked best among his own folk and in the land of his fathers' (Lhombreaud, 1963: 127). Yeats's influence persuaded Symons to dispense with that part of his argument which described the 'impressionist' attempt to capture a fleeting moment, along with the associations with self-conscious artifice, indolence and perverse curiosity. Decadence now named more the 'attitude' he identified as Wilde's special contribution to the decade (Jackson, 1976: 85). These are significant, but perhaps in the end minor adjustments. In the broader sweep of things, as examples or moments in the aestheticist movement, decadence and symbolism combined to suggest experimental verse technique and idiom, new subject matter, and the idea of the 'abnormal' poet, in Symons's description, who was as much at odds with society's manners and morals as with literature's established conventions. In the 'Decadent Movement in Literature' Symons had talked of the character Des Esseintes in Huysmans' *A Rebours* as representing 'the effeminate, over-civilised, deliberately abnormal creature who is the last product of our society' (Holdsworth, 1974: 78). In *The Symbolist Movement in Literature*, it is Verlaine who exemplifies the type of the artist who is above society's rules, since these 'are made by normal people for normal people, and the man of genius is fundamentally abnormal. It is the poet against society, society against the poet, a direct antagonism' (Symons, 1958: 44).

Behind this argument lay Walter Pater's injunction to the poet in the 'Conclusion' to *Studies in the History of the Renaissance* (1873) to experience the sensations of the moment with all their intensity, 'to burn with a hard gem-like flame'. For to live for the instant was to make an art of life. Symons's essays, following after the trials of Whistler and then Wilde, helped embody the implications, in personal and social bearing, of the literary aesthetic Pater had introduced, encouraging an open 'affected' connection between personal, sartorial and literary styles. At one point, already known as a leading translator and populariser of French verse, Symons confirmed his literary sympathies by having a suit made in Paris – an apparently superficial but no less serious and more public gesture than writing a poem titled 'Décor de Théâtre' or 'Clair de Lune'. Holbrook Jackson who drew on a lengthy passage from Symons's conclusion to his *Studies in Prose and Verse* to sum up 'the attitude of the Eighteen Nineties', confirmed the connection in this 'new epoch of artifice' of a fascination for the urban and 'the new Dandyism'. The artificiality of the period 'needed an urban background' and expressed itself in 'the art of posing' – a dandyism of clothing and 'temperament' combined (Jackson, 1976: 15, 108, 110, 112).

'Where is your Montmartre, where is your Quartier Latin?' Symons's friends asked when they arrived in London. 'We have none', he answered, 'because there is no instinct in the Englishman to be companionable in public. Occasions are lacking ... for the café is responsible for a good part of the Bohemianism of Paris and we have no cafés ... nothing in Cafés Royaux and Monicos and the like can have the sort of meaning for young men in London that the cafés have long had and still have, in Paris' (Symons, 1918: 164). This from *London: a Book of Aspects*, first published in 1908. Others thought differently. Arthur Ransome felt he had found Bohemia in Soho in the previous year. Max Beerbohm, on first entering the Café Royal, had exclaimed 'This indeed is life!' (David, 1988: 102); Verlaine, reports Symons, 'adored' the Café (Symons, 1923: 3). Shaw sometimes dined there but avoided bohemian society. D.H. Lawrence detested and satirised it viciously (Deghy and Waterhouse, 1955: 98, 152–5).

Evidently there were contrasting perceptions of the Café Royal. So too were there of London and London locations, prepared, in effect, by poets' words and painters' images. Symons himself – like many of his contemporaries – saw the city through the canvases of Whistler and the texts of Pater and Baudelaire. Thus, in words which echo all three: 'The especial beauty of London is the Thames, and the Thames is so wonderful because the mist is always changing its shapes and colours, always making its lights mysterious' showing 'reflections of golden fire, multiplying arch beyond arch' (1918: 138–9). So he muses, 'and I found myself gradually trying to paint, or to set to music, to paint in music, perhaps, those sensations which London awaked in me...above all those which seemed to lead one into "artificial paradises"' (166).

In one way, though, Symons was of course right in what he said to his French visitors. London was not Paris. The 'foreign quarter' of Soho was not the 'Quartier Latin', but an 'impression' of Paris and more distantly, Italy. What Symons realised too, however, was that if it lacked the 'uniform brightness' of Paris, the 'real London' was 'a picture continually changing, a continual sequence of pictures' (138). It was more changing, syncretic and cosmopolitan than Paris and in its variety combined the imprint of European cities and customs with something more indigenously English. Hence Ransome found his way to Bohemia in Soho through its associations with an English eighteenth and nineteenth-century literary past. He wasn't looking for Paris or French symbolists so much as for Hazlitt, De Quincy and Carlyle. His logical destination, given such a quest, was 'The Cheshire Cheese', an ancient chop house frequented, so it was said, by Johnson, Boswell and Goldsmith. But then, Fleet Street was on the fringes of Ransome's map, and had more to do with the world of work he'd left behind than the holiday world he wanted to join. The Rhymers' Club was over and didn't conjure up his idea of bohemianism.

Symons had belonged to that other earlier world, and brings it to mind once more in an essay of 1923 on the Café Royal. Here, though he repeats the remarks quoted above of 1908 ('we have no cafés' like Paris), he concedes that 'Our only equivalent is the Café Royal' (1923: 2). As the 'hot nights and heated rooms' of the Café come back to him, he relishes the thought of 'rare and radiant conversations' with Augustus John 'on the soul in art, on the flesh and the spirit, on the beauty of absinthe and of the exotic beauty of Iris; on serpents, gypsies, the Russian ballet, Giorgione' (4). Oppressive but companionable enough, we might think. The truth of Symons's 1890s, however, was that if his steps took him to the Café Royal he was drawn back, by way of the unshakable image of

Paris, first to his rooms at Fountain Court in the Temple, and thence to the Strand and the magnet of Leicester Square. 'Only Soho is Bohemia' he declares in this essay – though still not in the 'literal sense' (4). Unlike Mallarmé thirty years earlier Symons was ready, though, to enter the fray, Baudelaire's 'bath of multitude': a jumbled society in Soho of the debonair and degraded, of upper-class gentlemen and high-class prostitutes who mingled in the Empire Theatre's wide 'promenade'. The doors of the Empire and Alhambra opened upon a world where middle-class ladies and their daughters, actresses, dancers and prostitutes appeared in confused proximity, where the soul of art and the brooding poet consorted with sinuous female artistes and a boozy populace. The music hall was indeed a 'theatre of varieties', where English vaudeville and French exoticism combined in an idiom of 'double entendres'. The ballet at the Empire was the 'ballet divertissement', the Maitresse de Ballet was a Madame Katti Lanner; girls in skin-tight costumes performed 'tableaux vivants'. But the theatre was after all 'the Empire', its Britishness unmistakably emblazoned on its programmes in flags, banners, crests and the figure of Boudicca (Weightman, 1992: 78–9).

During 1895–96, Symons shared rooms at the Temple with Yeats. Yeats had 'never liked London' but the quiet and solitude of the 'real' fountain at Fountain Court made it more agreeable and 'as if in the country' (Yeats, 1955: 322). Both men were then aged thirty and fellow members of the now fading Rhymers' Club. They had met Verlaine in Paris in 1894 and must in this year have discussed the ideas in Symons's 'Decadent Movement in Literature' (1893) and the French poets he knew and read to Yeats. Symons took hashish, in imitation no doubt of Baudelaire, and though neither he nor Yeats much liked alcohol, they at one time tried taking two whiskies a night, thinking they needed to be more dissolute if they were to be great poets. The experiment lasted a month before they returned to their preferred late night drink of hot water (Hone, 1971: 122). Their ideas were as connected and distinct as their rooms, which were joined by a narrow passage. As Symons liked to remember, Yeats recalled how 'if anyone rang the bell at either door, one or the other would look through a window in the connecting passage, and report. We would then decide whether one or both should receive the visitor' (Yeats, 1955: 322; Symons, 1923: 5). One caller who was for Yeats alone was Mrs Olivia Shakespear – the 'Diana Vernon' of a group of love poems – who rescued him from 'unctuous celibacy', either at this time or later when he moved to the greater privacy of Woburn Walk (Ellman, 1973: 107). For his part Symons entertained 'a woman called Kate who was married and had two children', most likely her sister too, and a stream of young girls from the Empire and Alhambra for 'ballet tea parties', amongst them 'Lydia' with whom he had an affair until 1896 (Beckson, 1977: 70–1; Beckson and Munro, 1989: 101, 59, 212). Here too Leonard Smithers, bookseller and publisher of erotica ('a scandalous person' thought Yeats; 1955: 328) called to inaugurate the *Savoy* magazine with Symons as literary editor and Aubrey Beardsley as art editor.

From the Temple, Symons 'used to wander at night with Yeats and with Image and others' usually in the direction of the Café Royal and Leicester Square (1923: 4). Yeats was not a regular at the Café Royal (though he was remembered on one occasion, 'all long hair, sloppy tie and velveteens'; Deghy and Waterhouse, 1955: 82) and may have veered off for another assignation. For the others, Bohemia in Soho beckoned not from a café terrace but from the twin palaces of the English music hall and the Crown tavern sandwiched between their stage doors: 'for a year or two before, [before 1894] to the end of 1896', said Symons, 'I never haunted the Café Royal so much as I haunted the historic "Crown"'. Here 'poets and painters and others' discussed 'aesthetics and metaphysics...to the accompaniment of the cheerful clatter of the Alhambra and the Empire ladies' (1923: 3). In the environs of Leicester Square, Symons found fellow artists, much of the subject matter of his verse, and his professional métier as the 'scholar of the musical hall', as Yeats had christened him, filing his research reports in the next day's papers and writing a regular column for the *Star*. At the Crown they met the fellow Rhymer, Ernest Dowson, who at one time conducted Symons on his own bohemian itinerary to supper at a cabman's shelter. Dowson, said Yeats was 'gentle, affectionate, drifting'; full of personal charm, religious, but given to dissipation. 'Sober he looked at no woman; drunk he picked the cheapest whore.' The last time Yeats saw him he was pouring out of glass of whisky in an empty corner of Yeats's room, 'The first today', he murmured over and over (Yeats, 1955: 311–12, 399).

The Crown had vanished by the early 1920s, not long before the Empire itself was closed and converted into the Empire Cinema (Weightman, 1992: 43). 'Selwyn Image and myself only have vivid recollections of those midnights', Symons muses (1923: 3). And already in 1908, the memory of his nightly walks, alone, or with Yeats, Image and others, from the Temple to Leicester Square is obscured by the disappearance of twisting lanes, especially the treasured Holywell Street, caused by the widening of the Strand, and by the invasive noise and disruption of the 'machine' (the gramophone, the telephone, the underground, the motor bus). 'It is the machines ... that have done it' he laments (1918: 146). A world had been lost. The French poets he had lauded had died: Verlaine in 1896, Mallarmé in 1898. Pater had died in 1894, Beardsley in 1898, Wilde in 1900. And so too soon had the Rhymers: Dowson in 1900, Johnson in 1902, and Davidson in 1909. In 1908 Symons himself suffered a mental breakdown. Yeats who had been his closest associate (Symons was 'the best critic of his generation ... the most sympathetic, and understanding of friends') visited him two or three times and then according to Rhoda Symons in 1917, 'now studiously avoids meeting him' (Beckson and Munro, 1989: 198).

Symons recalls the earlier time between 1893–96 in essays fifteen years apart, recycling passages in a mechanical but defiant affirmation of a retreating past. The effect is that if Soho is never truly Paris, it is also in a sense never truly here and now in these accounts but serves, like the earlier London, as a counter-memory against personal loss and the destructive time of modernity and 'progress'. This is nostalgic, of course, but it also has a stronger force. In a sentence from 1908, repeated, in an insistent present tense, in 1923, Symons writes how, 'In Leicester Square you are never in the really normal London: it is an escape, a sort of shamefaced and sordid and yet irresistible reminder of Paris and Italy' (1918: 153; 1923: 4). The abnormality of Soho's foreign quarter, itself a prelude to the cultivated artifice of the musical hall ballet, served as the physical analogue of the perverse curiosity of the 'deliberately abnormal' artist figure (Holdsworth, 1974: 78). Symons's conception of 'The World as Ballet' set its fairy-tale spectacle, make-up and lithesome dancing girls against the 'natural' world which it surpassed. 'The dance, then, is art because it is doubly nature: and if nature ... is sinful it is doubly sinful'. The dancer, was 'all pure symbol' (Holdsworth, 1974: 81, 82). Such thoughts lead him to think of 'the world as a puppet-show', a spectacle of automatic, phantasmic gesture. Like the memory of Paris in Soho, the symbolist poet and symbolical ballet presented a world of 'irresistible' and sordid, somewhat sinister, illusion. This was what decadence and Bohemia meant – the place of the artificial, the more and less than human world across the footlights of marionettes and fairy tale; the scene of intense sensations, of perverse refinement, of excess and distortion concentrated in the ecstatic moment it was the task of the artist to capture. In short, Bohemia was a self-conscious affront to the received norms and values of aesthetic and moral taste – something false, soiled, sordid, ostentatious; words Symons uses of the 'foreign people' of Soho (1918: 15) – which lurked inside English ways and ideas; the 'other' which walked the twilight streets of the English metropolis.

But if Symons was drawn in and drawn downwards by this irresistible 'undesirable' foreignness, he invariably pulls back to a bland plateau where all is in truth innocence and charm. Thus, if Verlaine was one day the beggarly prince of the dissolute life, he yearned on another for bourgeois respectability with the young wife he'd deserted, and was in all things child-like, a genius blessed with an incorruptible naivety, a 'real, almost blithe, childishness' which set him beyond the ordinary dualisms of good and evil (Symons, 1958: 43–6). An equivalent jockeying between spontaneous intimacy and blithe impersonality shows itself in Symons's own relations with the crowd and with women. Thus it was that he one evening announced, to Yeats's astonishment, that he 'was never in love with a serpent-charmer before' (Yeats, 1955: 335). 'I fell casually in love with woman after woman', as he was to put it; soon they 'ceased to exist for me; they were non-existent. I had taken up with others' (Beckson, 1977: 70). The result, before this later directness, was a rhetoric of implication which, in a change of register, he shared with the popular musical hall and variety acts which traded in innuendo. Were the trysts and friendships – with Minnie Cunningham, Ada and Lizzie Vincent, Minnie and Ada Kelly, Louie Bryant, Cassy, Violet, Lydia – innocent or sexual, fantasised or real? (Beckson and Munro, 1989: 95, 99, 101). Lionel Johnson saw only the flat enumeration of impressions and the pursuit of 'commonplace pleasures' in Symons's verse: ' "a London fog, the blurred tawny lamplight, the red omnibus, the dreary rain, the depressing mud, the glaring gin-shop, the slatternly shivering women... that and nothing more" ' (Yeats, 1955: 307).

Literary London took more offence than Johnson and was scandalised by Symons's tale of passion with a 'Juliet of a night' in 'Stella Maris' in the first issue of *The Yellow Book*. The poem was, as Symons said to Verlaine, 'un peu osé' for an English review (Beckson, 1977: 105). The English press and public opinion, fired up by Wilde's trial, took against Beardsley's illustrations to Wilde's *Salome* and he was dismissed from *The Yellow Book* (Yeats, 1955: 323). Here was the avenging power of the 'normal'. The profound divisions in *fin de siècle* society surfaced at such a moment, but were everywhere present; in literary culture as elsewhere – as the names Kipling and Henley, Yeats and Dowson, Gissing and Shaw, Beardsley and Wilde, plainly show. The imperialist poet and dissolute artist criss-crossed the same city, the social realist sat down with the aesthete. So too, even in the safe bohemian haven of the Empire Theatre, did the decadent and the moral campaigner. In 1894, Mrs Sheldon Ames, of the National Vigilance Association, and Mrs Ormiston Chant, came purposely to scrutinise the activities of the promenade and the dancers on stage. The *ballet divertissement* began:

> Company after company of girls, in costumes of delicately contrasted tints, march, troop, or gallop down the boards, their burnished armour gleaming and their rich dresses scintillating in the limelight ...

The *première danseuse* enters:

> To see her advance on the points of her toes, her arms curved symmetrically above her head, a smile of innocent child-like delight on her face ... is an experience indeed. Then her high-stepping prance around the stage, her little impulsive runs and bashful retreats ... her final teetotum whirl, are all evidently charged with a deep but mysterious significance. (Weightman, 1992: 79-80)

Thus an entranced reporter for *Harpers New Monthly Magazine*. Mrs Chant saw something else:

> To begin with, there was one dancer in flesh coloured tights and I used no opera glasses at first, but at last had to use them to see whether she even had tights on or not, so nearly was the colour of the flesh imitated. She had nothing on but a very short skirt – which when she danced and pirouetted flew right up to her head, and left the rest of the body with waist exposed except for a very slight white gauze between the limbs. (Weightman, 1992: 81-2)

Mrs Ames presented her outraged findings to the London County Council Music Hall and Theatres Committee: 'The Empire was the worst place she knew in civilised countries'. The Licensing Committee determined that the Empire should erect a screen between the promenade and the dress and upper circle and banned the sale of alcohol in the auditorium. The theatre was as a result threatened with closure until one evening in November the matter was decided by a crew of young men who kicked at the woodwork supports and tore down the canvas. Symons replied to the campaign in a letter to the *Pall Mall Gazette*. The Empire was 'a place of entertainment, the most genuinely artistic and the most absolutely unobjectionable that I know in any country' (Beckson and Munro, 1989: 107). If Mrs Ames and Mrs Ormiston were puritanical – arguably they showed a keener sense of what was transgressive in an age when women's legs were not publicly displayed – Symons was disingenuous, though his tone was that of the practical liberal ('Vice, unfortunately, cannot be suppressed' and matters at the Empire were at least 'managed with ... discretion'; ibid.).[1]

That there was more to tell is suggested by his late 'Confessions'. Essays under this title appeared in 1926 and were assembled as Symons's *Memoirs* (Beckson, 1977). One such was 'Bohemian Years in London' (70–4). Like other essays in the collection, it is a patchwork of repeated passages and meandering anecdote, though in this instance Symons's reminiscences acquire a remarkable change of tone. Thus, where he had earlier yearned for London's 'supreme sensation', he says now that he desired, 'the city's corruption' (71). What was formerly 'irresistible' is here 'revolting', a 'fearful attraction' (71). He sees himself drifting from virtue, relishing 'the vicious, morbid, fantastic, abnormal' to become, without qualification, 'a vagabond, a Wanderer, a Bohemian' (72). Such thoughts echo and confess to the earliest descriptions of decadence. But what we sense too is a fear of failure and lost reputation. Hence the picture of himself as a callous Casanova, quoted above. Hence, too, a self-aggrandising comparison throughout the essay with earlier literary masters. Thus Symons gives himself 'an evil reputation' like Paul Verlaine (72). Like Byron, Swinburne and Rossetti, he has been reviled and misunderstood by the press. Like Shakespeare and a host of others, from Marlowe to Meredith, he shares the 'abnormal' perversity of genius. Above all, he insinuates a comparison with Baudelaire – aloof, malicious, contemptuous, and in his God-like divinity and diabolism, 'inexplicable' (71, 74).

At one moment the essay refers, revealingly, to a lesser figure: 'I had then', Symons writes, 'and have had since, much of the fever and turmoil – but none of the unattained dreams – of a life like Dowson's' (73). The parenthesis is crucial. Dowson's life corresponds point by point to the figure of the bohemian of limited talent whose destiny in Henri Mürger's *Scènes de la Vie de Bohème*, lay in 'the Academy, the hospital, or the morgue'. Symons wrote an 'Introduction' to an edition of Mürger's stories, titled *The Latin Quarter*, in 1901, and opened with these same words. This volume was reprinted in 1908 and shadows his recycled account of Dowson, published first in 1896, as an obituary in 1900, and again, in whole or in part, in different volumes between 1902 and 1907. The words above on Dowson, without the comparison to himself, occur in the original essay. But chiefly one feels how the two essays, on Mürger and Dowson, could be transposed one with the other. Dowson was young, charming, poor, half-starved and in miserable lodgings, in love with a restaurant owner's daughter, a poet but 'not a great poet' (Symons, 1905: v). Thus one half of the bohemian type. For all his delicacy, however, Dowson became, says Symons, 'quite another sort of person... almost literally insane' under the influence of drink (xiv, xv). He drifted through bouts of sordid dissipation towards the morgue. The point of the comparison in Symons's 'confession' is clear. He means, in his own disordered state, to save himself from the taint of a failure like Dowson's. Hence the qualification – 'but none of the unattained dreams' – and hence the elevation of himself to the level of literary greatness.

'Bohemian Years in London' therefore accentuates the 'double life' of the bohemian Symons sees in Dowson and in himself. The Empire and music halls of Soho had been the particular scene of this tension. But while this late essay releases his decadent other, Symons does not explore the ambiguities of his sexual attitudes, nor the dual and confused sexual identities bestowed upon women, nor the proximity of art, literature and pornography which shadowed the dualism of the flesh and the spirit in the period. What he sees only is that the collocation of purity and sin is 'inexplicable'. The explanation is not far to seek, however. Symons wrote in his introduction to Mürger how the child-like bohemian remained unaware of the governing force of 'the intangible, inexplicable monster than we call Society' and nickname 'the Bourgeois, the Philistines, the Jews' (Symons, 1908: viii). Both sides of his Jekyll and Hyde artist were determined by art's unavoidable relations with 'normal' society in the moral arena as in the marketplace. Symons chose to 'escape' society, rather than negotiate the still socially situated role of the bohemian artist. To maintain the 'abnormality' of genius, the 'foreign' other to received opinion in the press and moral crusaders alike, could neither ignore, mollify, compromise with, nor convert society to itself. To live along the line of this double life required an ironic cunning Symons did not possess. No more did an 'evil reputation' avert the underlying plight of the modern artist set in and 'against society'. For, before the final destination of Academy, hospital or morgue, lay another danger – the trap of the stereotype; the pose of artist as 'Bohemian', 'Decadent', 'Rhymer': precisely the figure society could dismiss all too easily as 'an artist'.

The *fin de siècle* was shaped – one might say, distorted – by this double life. The high minded was joined to a cheap, low-life sensuality, the artist tied to the despised bourgeoisie, art to the marketplace. We can see these ambiguities, contradictions and compromises everywhere: in the schizophrenic, vagabond dreamer, Paul Verlaine – at one moment excluded from the salon of Ford Madox Brown as a sexual deviant, and, at another, would-be respectable bourgeois husband; in the temptations of the rituals of the Catholic Church to erstwhile aloof and rebellious free-thinkers and hedonists; in the production of the *Savoy*, a magazine devoted to artistic virtue published by a purveyor of clandestine literature. In Soho, too, the 'variety' of the musical hall extended to the double spectacle of the demi-monde and the earnestness of moral crusaders. And in the Café Royal, where Wilde held court in one corner, his ne'er-do-well brother, Willy Wilde, and the tipster and racing fraternity occupied another, the loud suits of one set vying with the others' bohemian corduroy (Deghy and Waterhouse, 1955: 73–4). The Rhymers were a symptom of this ambiguity. Yeats, their co-founder contributed to – while he undercut – the mythology of its members as disorderly romantics. They were a 'revolt against Victorianism' (Yeats, 1955: ix), their sad fates a warning against the tragic logic of Pater's doctrines, but were, at the same time, personally gentle and studious, and, in company, modest and polite to the point of boredom. In an interesting interpretation, Hugh David sees in this rather grey sobriety a version of the bohemian come into its own as distinctively English (David, 1988: 47). The upper room of the Cheshire Cheese, Bernard Bergonzi agrees, witnessed an attempt 'to combine French literary café life with Johnsonian conviviality' (Bergonzi, 1973: 27; and see Jackson, 1976: 115).

For Yeats, though, it was in the end either all or nothing, and in *The Oxford Book of Verse* of 1936 he had decided, in an act of considerable nonchalance, that it was the second. 'Then in 1900', he famously declares, 'everybody got down off his stilts; henceforth nobody drank absinthe with his black coffee; nobody went mad; nobody committed suicide; nobody joined the Catholic Church; or if they did I have forgotten' (Yeats, 1964: 217). Yeats forgets not only Johnson and Dowson (whose death, it might be said, provided him with the marker of 1900), but Davidson's suicide and Symons's madness. Arguably, by this time, in the mid-1930s, Yeats had not only tired of the old story, but needed another history to confirm himself as the modern poet he had become in the 1910s. Drawing a line under the Rhymers released him from his late-Romantic past into his post-Romantic present. To backdate this change by a few years brought him conveniently and more decisively into the modern world.

The truth is less tidy than this of course. There was no day or month when the 'modern' arrived. The late Romantic and the post-Romantic overlapped through the late 1890s and into the new century. There were other survivors than Yeats, after all – among them, Ernest Rhys, Victor Plarr, Selwyn Image and Elkin Matthews – who belonged more to the age before 1900. Yeats had distanced himself from the externality and rhetoric of the Victorians, but came then to find the 'slight, sentimental sensuality' of his own generation 'disagreeable' (1955: 326). There was a way, however, that these now passé forms and tones had combined with signs of the new, as T.S. Eliot was to discern in Dowson's 'Cynara': a mixture of Swinburne and 'a new and irregular' spoken rhythm (Eliot, 1996: 396). Bernard Bergonzi amplifies this on behalf of the nineties' poets. Dowson, in particular, he suggests, strained a borrowed diction 'to breaking-point in his attempt to convey' – successfully Bergonzi thinks – 'a novelistic complexity of the erotic life' (1973: 29). The idea of 'novelistic complexity' suggests the example of Henry James, and, in turn, of Flaubert, and thus the standard of poetry as well written as prose which Ford impressed upon Pound who put it to Yeats, and which both men shared with the distinctly modern Eliot. We find this earlier, too, however, in Symons who, writing in 1904, had looked to Browning and to the Elizabethan and Caroline lyric for a model of direct spoken language in poetry (Holdsworth, 1974: 15). The modern was dispersed in these ways through the 1890s and the 1900s. Time, so to speak, was itself schizophrenic. And not surprisingly this gave rise to some conspicuous anachronisms, to some thoughts and figures who seemed out of key with the march of events – now startlingly in advance, now behind the pace of their times.

On or around 1908

One way to consider this in-folding of the modern and pre-modern is to reflect on the course of events passing through a particular date. Let's first of all imagine. It's 30 October 1908 and Ezra Pound is dining at Pagani's Restaurant at 42 Great Portland Street, just north of Oxford Circus. Baedeker's guide of 1908 noted the display of drawings and autographs of artists, opera singers, and actors in its upstairs 'artists' room' and recommended its coffee. Pound was to use the restaurant regularly, though whether he was to any extent directed by Baedeker we don't know. He had arrived in London from Venice in August 1908. It was fitting therefore to eat at an Italian restaurant where he could enjoy a 'few words of Italian' with the waiters (Carpenter, 1988: 101). But it was also quite simply close to his lodgings. He had stayed briefly in 1906 at a boarding house at 8 Duchess Street and had now returned to the same address. And Duchess Street, just up from Langham Place, was five minutes from Pagani's.

October 30th, was Pound's twenty-third birthday. No doubt he sketched a letter home in which he reflected on the past and planned for the future. He had in the space of less than a year gone from an abortive spell teaching at Wabash College, Indiana, which ended in February, 1908, to Venice, where he stayed from March to August, and come then to London. He needed, he reckoned to his father, 'a good six weeks to get realy (sic) underway ...' (Carpenter, 1988: 98). Money was a problem. He arrived with £3 and three weeks later was down to a shilling (5p). For a short time in September he shifted to Islington. A draft arrived from his father who would henceforth send £4 a month and Pound moved back to Marylebone, next to the Yorkshire Grey pub off Great Portland Street. He could have eaten at the Yorkshire Grey. Like Yeats, though, he seemed not to drink alcohol, and preferred teashops and restaurants to pubs.[2] For company at Pagani's he had (shall we say) three or four copies of his *A Quinzaine for this Yule*. This was his second volume of verse, drawn from his Venice notebook and whose London publication he had told his father to announce back home in Philadelphia as imminent. In the event he paid for the printing of this as for his first volume, *A Lume Spento*. A hundred copies were printed in late October by Pollock & Co. in Mortimer Street, within walking distance of his lodgings. This time he would be luckier, though. There was more calculation in the title – which said 'Christmas' rather than 'Dante' to its readers. Would a waiter, the restaurant owner, perhaps, appreciate a copy? They sold well enough, anyway, for the renowned literary publisher Elkin Matthews to order the production of a further 100 copies under his own imprint. Matthews had earlier offered to take some copies of *A Lume Spento*, so Pound had two books displayed in Matthews' shop window in Vigo Street before Christmas. This wouldn't, on 30 October, have seemed such a bad prospect.

Pound was already a curious combination. A 'Latin Quarter type' as the affair at Wabash College (where he put a chorus girl up for the night) had suggested to students and college authorities, and a go-getting careerist American who thought big. Symons would have approved of his escapade in Indiana, but Wabash would have sounded like the very faintest echo of the real thing. Latin Quarter types belonged to the European metropolis. In London, Pound was an ambitious outsider, determined to make a hit 'in this bloomin village' as he termed the city (Carpenter, 1988: 98). On first meeting him, Dorothy Pound was put in mind of James's *Roderick Hudson* (Pound/Shakespear, 1984: 4). Ezra, she remembered, was always 'the most American thing going' (Kenner, 1973: 486). To Mary Moore in the USA he wrote how he was in hopes of meeting 'several people of the kind one reads about' (Carpenter, 1988: 98). He needed 'contacts' – a word he was to use for the retrospective

Hugh Selwyn Mauberley (Life and Contacts) (1920), and one with a particularly American ring. But Pound's comment to Mary Moore reveals something else too. He came to London, as he made clear, to learn from Yeats (Hall, 1977a: 47), someone he had read and read about. He didn't come to view London. And in this respect he thought small.[3]

Outside Pagani's there was probably the scent of late autumn fog, the clatter of horse-drawn cabs and the drum of the first motorised cars and omnibuses back and forth from Oxford Circus. The first department stores stood on Oxford Street. In late June, in Hyde Park, there had been the second of two mass demonstrations on behalf of women's suffrage. Pound had tried the Regent's Street Polytechnic (the 'Polytechnique' as he styled it) for a teaching post in the first month of his stay (Carpenter, 1988: 98), but 'life and contacts' didn't much seem to take in the signs of modern London. Nor at first the by-ways of Bohemia. The Café Royal, Soho and Leicester Square were a short walk away. A bus ride took you to the Strand and the Cheshire Cheese. There's no record of Pound having paid its upper room a visit in homage, however. He had included a poem, 'In Tempore Senectutis'. *An anti-stave for Dowson'*, in *A Lume Spento*, and in 1915 remembered that 'In America ten or twelve years ago ... One was drunk with "Celticism", and with Dowson's "Cynara", and with one or two poems of Symons' "Wanderers"' (Pound, 1960: 367). But what, in 1908 did he know of, or, rather, in what *way* did he know, Yeats and the Rhymers? Did he know how fascinated Symons and Davidson – to say nothing of French poets and painters – had been by London, or know at this time of Ford's popular *The Soul of London* (1905)? Did he know – one year after the riots at the first performance of Synge's *Playboy of the Western World* – of Yeats's involvement in the Abbey Theatre, and that Yeats, who he'd come to London to meet, spent half his time in Ireland?

The answer lay in his poetry. As Hugh Kenner has shown, the first and next two volumes, *Personae* and *Exultations* (1909), also from Elkin Matthews, were flooded with the hypnotic cadences and verbal tricks of the Yeats of *Poems* (1895) and *The Wind among the Reeds* (1899) – mixed in with borrowings from Rossetti, Swinburne, Villon, echoes of Dante, and imitations of the Provençal troubadours (Kenner, 1988: 79–81). 'London, deah old Lundon', as Pound put it to William Carlos Williams in February 1909, was 'the place for poesy' (Paige, 1971: 7). For the young Pound this meant a place of words (even words like 'poesy', thrown in with a bit of mock cockney); an echoing room of the European Romance tradition, starting from and returning to the 1890s. London was the point where all this seemed to be concentrated on the page. Dorothy Shakespear responded to this in Pound. So too, did

Harriet Monroe – one of those who purchased his early verse at Matthews's shop in 1910 and was beguiled by 'the strange and beautiful rhythms of this new poet, my self-exiled compatriot' (Wilhelm, 1990: 100). It was on the strength of this that she agreed in late August 1912, four years after Pound's arrival, to his becoming 'foreign correspondent' for *Poetry* magazine. Dorothy Shakespear had asked the important question, however. 'Are you a genius? Or are you only an artist in Life?' she wrote in the opening entry in her 'Notebook' after first meeting Pound in February 1909 (Pound/Shakespear, 1984: 3). Her anxiety echoed the distinction in Henri Mürger's *Vie de Bohème* between the poseur and the real bohemian. Reviewers were preoccupied by it too. Was Pound or was he not the genuine article: was he essentially 'a poet'? 'Mr Pound is an American', wrote F.S. Flint, as if in answer, 'and a hotchpotch of picturesqueness made up of diverse elements – in literature, words from divers tongues – is the American idea of beauty. Thank heaven that Mr Pound is a poet also' (Homberger, 1972: 65).

Pound's was therefore a bookish, literary London; more a *musée imaginaire* than a physical city. In this respect, the two places that did count for him at the start made perfect sense. The first was the British Museum Reading Room where Mallarmé had found English men of letters at home. Pound received permanent admission there in October 1908 to research the Latin lyricists of the Renaissance and so began a daily routine of study. In the Reading Room he wrote the lectures which became *The Spirit of Romance* and which he gave in 1909 at the Regent Street Polytechnic. And there too in April 1909 he wrote 'Ballad of the Goodly Fere', which he hawked unsuccessfully around Fleet Street, and checked up on the verse form for the poem 'Sestina Altaforte', based on a war song by the twelfth-century troubadour baron, Bertran de Born. The second poem proved an important breakthrough. It appeared in Ford's *English Review* (June 1909), and was, as such, the first poem Pound published in an English magazine. On 22 April 1909 at the Eiffel Tower Restaurant he loudly performed the sestina's elaborate rhyming pattern in a war-like voice worthy of de Born and had to be screened off. The restaurant stood on the corner of Percy Street and was used for meetings of the Poets' Club headed by T.E. Hulme. Later Wyndham Lewis was to live next door and the restaurant entered upon its long life as a symbolic bohemian venue. Pound could have walked down Percy Street on his way to and from the British Museum. As far as the records tell, however, before Spring 1909, it was a blank. By then Pound had his public persona ready. He braved the London traffic, Ford remembered 'waving his cane as if he'd been Bertran de Born about to horse-whip Henry II of

England' (Norman, 1969: 46). Bellowing in a Philadelphian accent which Ford found 'disconcerting' (Goldring, 1943: 47), Pound strides into view like a transplanted Don Quixote. But, unlike Quixote, he was not so much dreaming as posing (*vide* Dorothy's question above). He had defended the 'gloomy', 'disagreeable' tone of *A Lume Spento* to William Carlos Williams in October 1908 by arguing that the poems were 'dramatic lyrics' written in character (Paige, 1971: 4). As the poem 'Histrion' had put it, 'Thus am I Dante for a space and am / One Francois Villon, ballad lord and thief' (Pound, 1977: 71). Pound was drawn to de Born in particular because he was a strategist who moved in and out of role: a minstrel who could turn his hand equally to war songs or love poems. He offered a template, so to speak, and for now at least, for an eclectic Yankee troubadour looking for an angle in modern London.

As it turned out, therefore, the 'picturesque' and the 'poet' in Pound were not quite as separate as Flint had thought. But to pull this off required the right look. Photographs of Pound in 1909 show him in winged collar, wearing a tie and buttoned woollen cardigan beneath a nondescript jacket. He is clean shaven – and his hair is piled to one side. In a group photograph taken in 1914 (Figure 20), Victor Plarr, to Pound's right, wears the same type of collar and tie and what looks like a frock-coat. F.S. Flint, to Pound's left, wears what would still pass as a conventional lounge suit with turn-down collar and tie. Yeats, known in the nineties for his bohemian velvet, cravat and cape – but soon to be offered and to refuse a knighthood – on this occasion wears a wide double-breasted suit, his left hand grandly raised to his lapel. Pound's shirt collar is outside his velvet jacket, his tie hangs loose, he wears spats and has acquired a thin moustache and tuft of beard. He had also acquired a cane, as Ford noted, a turquoise earring, and was careful about his tailor (he went to 'Cotton of Holland Street...Poole for high swank' he told Patricia Hutchins; Hutchins, 1965: 130). Brigit Patmore remembers him ordering a 'a snug-waisted full-skirted overcoat of tweed, the blue of delphiniums, and the buttons were large square pieces of lapis lazuli'. Thus attired he swept up Kensington Church Street, his hat pulled over his eye, a cane swinging from his hand. 'He was at ease in masquerade,' she comments, it kept him 'inviolable' (Patmore, 1968: 61).

This way he could be 'a poet', ' "every inch a poet" ' as Douglas Goldring put it (1943: 40), without uttering a word. Perhaps the early Yeats had again set an example. More likely it was James McNeill Whistler, whose dandified appearance said 'artist', but whose canvases and reputation said irascible, innovatory, anti-establishment 'American artist in Europe'. Pound's 'To Whistler – American' was one of the first two poems he published in *Poetry* in October 1912, but Whistler had served as a kind of proving ground for Pound since 1907 at least, when he drafted two essays on the painter (Beasley, 2002). In Philadelphia, before his departure for Europe, he had made a present of Whistler's 'Ten O'Clock Lecture' to H.D. (H.D. 1979: 17) and signed his poems to her with a gadfly in imitation of Whistler's butterfly. At this same time he began also to copy Whistler's clothes – 'the best model he could think of at present', says Carpenter (1988: 63). A decade on, the same model seemed still to work. In 1916 he wrote to Iris Barry advising her to look out for someone on Wimbledon Station who wore a boutonnière, carried 'a perfectly plain ebony staff' and looked, so he was told, 'more like Khr-r-ist and the late James MacNeil Whistler every year' (Paige, 1971: 85).

After the British Museum Reading Room, the second place of importance for the young Pound was Elkin Matthews' bookshop in Vigo Street, just off Regent Street and round from the Café Royal. Matthews and John Lane had been at the hub of literary production in the 1890s and Pound reckoned them still 'the twin peaks of Parnassus' (Hutchins, 1965: 58). They had long gone their different ways, however, and Matthews, Carpenter comments, was 'no longer a fashionable figure' (1988: 98). He still published the Rossettis, Swinburne and Yeats, had published Synge's *Riders to the Sea* in 1907 and had just brought out Joyce's *Chamber Music* (hardly the modern Joyce) on the recommendation of Arthur Symons whom he also continued to publish. What mattered now, though, was not so much what was on the shelves as who was in the shop. For here, in 1908 and 1909, Pound met the surviving 1890s, in the persons of Ernest Rhys, Selwyn Image and Victor Plarr, along with Laurence Binyon, keeper of prints and drawings at the British Museum, Orientalist, translator of Dante, and poet. Binyon's *London Visions* was published by Matthews alongside Pound's own volumes. From this point of intersection the contacts radiated and a social geography came into view. Pound 'devoted' his Sundays to Plarr and dined in Hampstead with Rhys – when he notoriously played up to the image of poet by eating a tulip. Here he met D.H. Lawrence, whom he entertained at Pagani's and put up in his room in Kensington, and also May Sinclair (they too dined at Pagani's) who in turn introduced him to Ford Madox Hueffer who had taken Lawrence along to Rhys's dinner. Another roundabout set of introductions originating with Matthews led him to the young Australian poet Fredric Manning who introduced him to Olivia and Dorothy Shakespear. Olivia Shakespear, herself a novelist, was Lionel Johnson's first cousin and the 'Diana Vernon' of Yeats's poems. She and Dorothy accordingly managed Pound's long awaited introduction to Yeats: all part of 'being in the gang & being known by the right people' as Pound wrote to his father (Carpenter, 1988: 107).

It was a small world, as Pound had intuited, based, as he had not expected, in the 'village' of Edwardian Kensington – where the Shakespears, May Sinclair, Edgar Jepson, Gilbert Cannan, Ford Madox Hueffer and Violet Hunt all lived. Here too he met not only literary types but members of the English middle class and aristocracy who were friendly to the arts. In some ways Pound looked familiar to this society, a belated, honorary Rhymer who could be invited to lecture and read at middle-class salons. But he was also a strange American whose manners belonged to another world. The strategist Pound wanted at first to join this English society though he had little sense of the nuances of social class and decorum on which it depended. Some 'contacts' also didn't come off, such as with George Prothero editor of the prestigious *Quarterly Review*, as we shall see. But this was later, in 1914, by which time Pound's London had taken quite a different shape.

For his first four years in London Pound was in his own words 'behind the times'; 'out of key' and 'out of date' like the 'E.P.' of the poem *Hugh Selwyn Mauberley* (Pound, 1968: 94, 205). Arnold Bennett, the 'Mr Nixon' of this poem certainly thought so. Pound had met Bennett in 1911; the snobbish aesthete to Bennett's 'commoner' as Pound later saw it (Brooker, 1979: 209). For Bennett, being up to date meant writing popular books and journalism for big money, to the tune, in 1912, of an astonishing £16,000. The bohemian nineties had tried to hold themselves aloof from the market place and failed – 'And give up verse, my boy,/ There's nothing in it' (212). Printing your own poetry, publishing with a minority literary publisher or in small magazines in financial straits, like Hueffer's *English Review*, was not the way to get on. Someone else who agreed with the estimate of the out-of-date Pound and had an astute eye on the literary market place, if not with the same pecuniary ambitions as Bennett, was T.S. Eliot. Pound's early poetry struck him as 'rather fancy old-fashioned romantic stuff' (Hall, 1977b: 95). Pound crossed the Atlantic to join a European tradition. For Eliot, who read their immediate predecessors in England and France more critically than Pound, there was no usable tradition. The question was 'where do we go from Swinburne? and the answer appeared to be, nowhere' (Eliot, 1996: 388). This was not a question Pound would have asked of Swinburne – or of Yeats, who the young Eliot reckoned as no more than 'a minor survivor of the' 90s' (ibid.). Eliot evidently needed to look elsewhere.

In September 1908, the month after Pound's arrival in London, Arthur Symons travelled in the opposite direction to Venice. It was symptomatic that their paths should run this way. In late September, without any warning, Symons suffered a mental breakdown. He was brought back to London in the care of two male nurses, placed in a sanatorium in Crowborough, Sussex, and then, in November, in Brooke House, Clapton where he was declared insane (Beckson and Munro, 1989: 120). He made a remarkable but partial recovery and Pound noted this in a letter home the following September (Wilhelm, 1990: 38). He had met Symons briefly at Olivia Shakespear's, who Symons had known in 1895 of course as Yeats's mistress (Carpenter, 1988: 133). In other circumstances, it might have been Symons who introduced Pound to Yeats as well as to the work of the French symbolist poets. As it was, Pound did not catch onto their importance for some time. Instead he came away from this meeting with an extra item to set off his bohemian attire: the turquoise earring he wore in Kensington given to him by Symons's companion, Alice Tobin.

Pound did not stop to consider the significance of Symons's illness, which was that the nineties – whose best magazine and best critical book Symons had produced – was indeed at an end. On the other side of the Atlantic, Eliot knew there was no living tradition and no poet in England or America 'who could have been of use to a beginner in 1908' (Eliot, 1996: 388). For him, the breakthrough came not through Yeats, nor Symons, directly, but through Symons's criticism which offered the vital entry into the 'poetry of another age and...another language' (ibid.). While a graduate student in philosophy at Harvard, Eliot discovered the 1908 re-issue of Symons's *A Symbolist Movement in Literature*. He found he was able to read past Symons, to 'dissent' from his findings (1996: 401) but on the way to encounter a kindred spirit and inspiration in Jules Laforgue. He purchased three volumes of Laforgue and his enthusiasm took him in 1910 to Paris where he also read Corbière – who Symons had omitted. In these poets, as in their predecessor, Baudelaire, Eliot found less a model or master than at once a revelation and confirmation that you could write about 'unpoetic' contemporary urban subjects in a modern, ironic, conversational tone (1996: 390).

Modern, ironic, unadorned free verse: Eliot's poetry of 1910 and 1911 belonged to the twentieth century while Pound's ('fancy old-fashioned romantic') belonged to the nineteenth by way of the thirteenth century. In these years Eliot composed what would appear 'unchanged' in 1917 as 'The Love Song of J. Alfred Prufrock' (1996: 176). When Pound first read Prufrock in 1914 he proclaimed Eliot had 'modernised himself *on his own*' (Paige, 1971: 40). The fact was he had been modernised outside the orbit of Pound's influence or reckoning of the modern. Perhaps the difference between them was the difference between Paris and Venice. Eliot shared with the French symbolists and with Symons and others of the English nineties, a sense of the modernness of the modern city. His perceptions were mediated, like Pound's, by his reading – of Baudelaire, of Charles Louis Phillippe's *Babu of Montparnasse* which 'stood for Paris' and by the poetry of the elder Rhymer, John Davidson (1996: 405, 398). Whistler's scenes of the Thames embankment hang too like a backdrop to Eliot's daylight version. But these authors and works served once more to confirm an intuition rather than point a new direction. Eliot 'had a good many dingy urban images to reveal', he said, and these images of the 'yellow evening' and 'vacant lots', of window panes, broken bricks and chimney pots seen in New Cambridge, Boston, he overlaid with their echoes elsewhere in a lexicon of lonesome and tawdry city streets (1996: 398, 109–13). 'So it was', he recalled, 'that for nine months of the year my scenery was almost exclusively urban, and a good deal of it seedily, drably urban at that. My urban imagery was that of St. Louis, upon which that of Paris and London have been superimposed' (1996: 107).

Eliot's very early poems of 1910–11 including 'Rhapsody on a Windy Night', the 'Preludes', 'Prufrock', and two poems written in London in 1911, 'Interlude in London' and 'Interlude in a Bar' (1996: 16, 51), are of this type. When he came to Bedford Place, Bloomsbury, and before he met Pound, Eliot was struck by the noise of the city and saw this area as a cosmopolitan, 'foreign' place of many voices: 'English, American, French, Flemish, Russian, Spanish, Japanese' (1988: 55). We're put in mind of John Cournos's *Babel* as well as the voices of *The Waste Land*. The early poems catch at the other, generic side of this diversity. But if Eliot shares this idiom of the city with earlier poets, he also inherited a strain of what Symons called the *maladie fin de siècle*, an intensely self-conscious, nervously fragile apprehension of the world, balanced between the sublime and the degraded. This is the 'art of the nerves' Symons discovered in Laforgue. And 'Here, if ever', he concluded 'is modern verse'; catching at 'all the restlessness of modern life' (Symons, 1958: 56, 60).

Eliot tested out the decadent modern option when, in Paris in 1910–11, he prowled the darkened sidewalks of the city, eyeing less the antics of the avant garde than, says Gordon, 'the prostitutes and maquereaux of the Boulevard Sebastopol...and the men who nosed after pleasure, especially men who had never known it' (Gordon, 1977: 40). This seedy Parisian nocturne is re-evoked, Gordon suggests, in the London poem 'Interlude in a Bar'. The later 'Paysage Triste' (1914) too, is closer than Eliot might have liked to Symons. The poem's speaker stares at a young girl on an omnibus, 'An almost denizen of Leicester Square' who 'would not have known how to sit, or what to wear' at the opera (Eliot, 1996: 52).

The contrast with this London experience was Oxford where Eliot first met Vivien Haigh-Wood. She was working as a governess; she painted and studied ballet. If Eliot's poem seems almost like a Symons's poem, Vivien sounds almost like one of the Symons's dancers. Almost. Neither could find the easy bohemian manner Symons boasted of. Eliot moreover found the nineties' notions of evil puerile (Eliot, 1970: 72) and would have thought the same of Symons's pretensions to an 'evil reputation' alongside Verlaine and Baudelaire. For Eliot, as events were to prove, sex and sin were intensely difficult matters.

There was a lighter side to this serious modernist but even this brought a chill. Symons's chapter on Laforgue described the poet as 'strictly correct, in a top hat, a sober cravat, an English jacket, a clergyman's overcoat, and in case of necessity, an invariable umbrella under his arm' (1958: 56). 'That is the Possum', declares Hugh Kenner (1975: 134). We see in the distance the figure Eliot was to become: the dandified persona of ironic, pedantic modern poet as city banker and, further off, editor and director of Faber and Faber. In a sense, though, he was already this. Laforgue confirmed him in a look and attitude; 'scrupulously correct' but a 'travesty of correctness', as Symons put it (1958: 56). The enigma was set, turning this way and that to show the sentimental face of Pierrot, the stance of the musical hall comedian, and an echo of the suited tramp and modern day clown, Charlie Chaplin, a figure from vaudeville who, from 1914, the year of Eliot's arrival in London, appeared larger than life on flickering cinema screens. Chaplin's 'egregious merit', said Eliot, was that he evaded the apparent realism of the cinema. He 'invented a rhythm' and this he shared with the acting style Eliot admired in the indicative social gestures of Marie Lloyd and the impersonal style he'd seen in the actors, Ion Swinley, and Léonide Massine (Eliot, 1923: 306). Swinley, said Eliot, 'makes himself into a figure, a marionette'; his simplified and abstract performance belonged to a future art of the stage. And this was exemplified, above all, by Massine, the premier dancer in the post-war years of the Ballets Russes, who Eliot saw perform and arranged to meet personally in the early 1920s. Massine's ritualised movement 'symbolised' emotion; he was 'the most completely unhuman, impersonal, abstract' (1923: 305). Eliot was drawn theoretically to this abstract 'mask-like beauty' as a solution to the unreality of conventional realism and saw here too a way to play against the conventional type of the poet and find his own stage rhythm – a bit crude, a bit playful and a bit over-dressed; sly possum and stiff-suited Mr T.S. Eliot.

3
'Our London, My London, Your London'

Enter Ezra, transatlantic bohemian

'Game!' Ezra leaped forward, planting a low return that Hueffer scrambled vainly to return. 'Hard luck!' someone half laughed. Hueffer ignored the call and immediately sent back a soft underhand serve. It fell in the tram-lines, bounced twice but was scooped back by Pound who sprang as if to help the ball over the net, his polychrome shirt flapping in the breeze. Hueffer pushed his belly forward and lunged, missed and missed again. 'My set!' Pound pronounced. Ford took up a position on the base line, threw the ball high into the sun and hit it hard on the first bounce. Pound anticipated from a sitting position as Hueffer's serve arced out of play. 'That's love all', Hueffer called.

The tennis court stood on the opposite side of 'South Lodge' on Campden Hill Road, Kensington and was part of a large garden rented by Violet Hunt for parties. Once Pound knew there was a court he had seized on the idea of playing tennis and the overweight Hueffer (later Ford) had agreed. They played, the way Pound danced and Hueffer talked, without rules or constraint, spinning the game into the irregular form that suited them both, ill-matched though they were. 'It was beyond anyone to umpire or score', said Brigit Patmore (1968: 55). Sometimes there were doubles with Pound and Hugh Walpole, Amber Reeves and Kitty Rome, which could only have added to the irritation of some and the fun of others. 'Ezra! Ezra!', Violet Hunt's parrot squawked as the players returned to the house.

(Hunt, 1926: 114; Goldring, 1943: 47;
Carpenter, 1988: 132)

This was in 1909. It was a year when the character of Pound's London and his own artistic persona began to take shape. It was the year too, most probably, when, in one of modernism's legendary set-pieces, he first met Wyndham Lewis (Lewis guessed it was in 1910) at the Vienna Café close by the British Museum. Both men made a significant early appearance in Ford's *English Review* though whether either registered this or knew anything of each other's work is doubtful. The Vienna Café, Lewis remembered, had a distinctive triangular first-floor room with a glass ceiling 'which reflected all your actions' (1982: 280). The motives and emotions at their meeting were far from transparent, however. The café had been adopted by readers and officials at the British Museum including Laurence Binyon who effected the first introduction ('his bull-dog, me ... Lewis ... Mr T. Sturge Moore's bull-dog' as Pound painted the scene in the *Cantos* (1975b: 507)). Lewis didn't remember himself as anybody's bull-dog. He was an 'idle student', biding his time, who 'looked like a *moujik*' but 'bought his clothes in Savile Row or Brook Street' (1982: 272, 273). Somehow he had slipped easily into this company of mandarin scholars on his return from Europe. For Pound it was an introduction to English class attitudes, cultural snobbery and complacent racism. He was dismissed in advance as 'Jewish' and American, and Lewis, when they met, was surly and indifferent. On a second meeting, perhaps in an attempt to flatter Lewis, perhaps in a show of rakish fellow feeling, Pound suggested in reference to a question about a prostitute, that Lewis looked like someone who was likely to know the answer. Lewis did not deign to reply: It did not appear to be 'a remark addressed to *me*', he said (271).

In time, Lewis came to think of Pound as 'one of the best' and 'one of the best poets' (1982: 271) and his assessment of Pound's situation in London was extremely perceptive. The 'cowboy songster ... in a tengallon hat' of the early meetings proved indeed 'violently American' (274, 275) and could make no headway against the prejudices of this learned and distinctly English elite. Looking back, Lewis reflects he could not 'see him stopping here very long without some such go-between as Ford Madox Ford' (275). Lewis was half right, for Pound had another prime objective in London: to meet and learn from W.B. Yeats, the aesthete to Ford's worldly editor. In most ways Ford and Yeats had little in common – they were 'NEVER at same dinner', Pound insisted (Hutchins, 1965: 94) and were 'in diametric opposition' in their views on poetry (Pound, 1913: 125). Nevertheless, their respective ideas of poetry as 'an exact rendering of things' and like music presented themselves as the two joint possibilities for poetry in Pound's 1913 essay 'Status Rerum'. Yeats was 'the greatest living poet' he said to William Carlos Williams (Paige, 1971: 7), as ever urging Williams to catch up, while Ford became the person 'I would rather talk poetry with [though this did not easily include Yeats's poetry]...than...any man in London' (1913: 125). Pound had some catching up to do to himself, and when Ford fell into a famous fit of laughter at his *Canzoni* in 1911, the shock yanked Pound forward a couple of years out of the hazy world of antiquated imitations of the troubadours ('stale cream puffs' as Pound later judged his early verse) into the harder light of Imagism. Yeats was to learn a similar if gentler lesson from Pound and did therefore learn indirectly from Ford, who himself, we might say, talked a good poem but did not often write one. A harsh critic of the early Pound (someone like T.S. Eliot) might say that this was true of him too and that such 'talk' was precisely what attracted these opposites together. Neither, however, was unself-critical or uncritical of each other. If Ford, in one mood, was happy to think of himself as 'the doyen of living writers of *Vers Libre* in English' (1921: 198), he realised too that his own 'impressionism' was washed out by the imagist technique of 'les jeunes'. His 'On Heaven' Pound praised as 'the best poem yet written in the "twentieth-century fashion"' (1960: 373), but his 'On a Marsh Road' provided Pound, in Ford's phrase 'dim lands of peace', with an example, surviving way beyond the original, of how not to write ('it dulls the image' said Pound; 1960: 5). Pound therefore absorbed, tacked and negotiated between these models, finding his own feet as he went – on the literal journey, appropriately enough, between Ford in Kensington and Yeats's rooms in Woburn Buildings four miles across London in Bloomsbury. 'I made my life in London', he remembered, 'by going to see Ford in the afternoons and Yeats in the evenings' (Hall, 1977a: 36).

His mornings were a different matter. Pound first met Ford as editor of the *English Review* through May Sinclair when he was living in Langham Place and spending much of his time at the British Museum. He moved in August 1909 to a simple first floor bed-sitting room in 10 Church Walk, tucked off a lane running from between the library and Town Hall in Kensington High Street through to Holland Street. Its contents would have served for the stage-set of a latter day *La Bohème* – a mahogany washstand which doubled as a desk, a divan, cane chairs, a shallow bath under the bed, along with the expected books and manuscripts and in time one or two more distinctive decorations such as Gaudier-Brzeska's 'Embracers' and paintings by William Henry Hunt loaned by Violet Hunt. It was close to the Metropolitan railway and buses but near enough to Soho and the British Museum Library for Pound to walk.

Chiefly it was 'nearer to most of my friends' (Carpenter, 1988: 127). Humble as it evidently was, Pound's bed-sit and the environs of Church Walk have acquired symbolic value through the reiterated inventories and associated memories of his many visitors, including F.S. Flint, Brigit Patmore, Ford, Lawrence, Robert Frost and his sometime neighbours, Richard Aldington and H.D., who lived opposite.[1] From this base-room, Pound began to arrange his diary and to re-arrange the world of London letters. He rose late, prepared filtered Dutch coffee, and if we are to believe the portrait in Aldington's *Death of a Hero* (1929), embarked upon his morning toilet, which included scrupulous attention to his nails and the fierce brushing of his hair, for the best part of a further hour.

With the money from the 'Ballad of the Goodly Fere', published in October in Ford's *English Review*, Pound also bought a 'suit' – this was the outfit, awaiting the turquoise earring given him by Arthur Symons's companion, Alice Tobin, on an occasion at South Lodge, by which he became known: a broad, loosely knotted tie worn with an open-necked shirt, a grey velvet 'suit' jacket or the tweed coat with lapis lazuli buttons, Italian trousers and spats. Thus attired he 'sallied forth in his sombrero with all the arrogance of a young, revolutionary poet who had complete confidence in his own genius' (Goldring, 1943: 47). He 'briefly attained' the peak of 'high swank' he said in moments of prosperity – which 'annoyed elderly brit/literatus' (Hutchins, 1965: 130). If not annoyed, others were certainly struck and, like Goldring, sometimes suspicious of Pound's show of 'transatlantic bohemianism' (Goldring, 1943: 47). His long-time model, as we have seen, and as Lewis detected in the combination of delicacy and toughness in Pound's manner, was James McNeill Whistler. Ford, in a change of heart that took three pages, conceded that truly Arthur Symons, not he, ought to be called 'the doyen of living writers of *Vers Libre*' (Ford, 1921: 201). And Symons had likened Whistler to his consummate decadent poet, Paul Verlaine: both were artists of 'the poetry of sensation, of evocation: poetry which paints as well as sings' (Holdsworth, 1974: 75). The line could then run, in something like the route Pound took, from decadence American style to symbolism and so to Symons's sometime flat-mate and the inheritor of the nineties, W.B. Yeats.

Ford himself had a quite considerable literary pedigree connecting him to James and Conrad, and personally to the Rossettis and Pre-Raphaelites, as did Violet Hunt. Ford was born Joseph Leopold Ford Hermann Madox Hueffer, the son of a German-born music critic, Dr Franz Hüffer, and the younger daughter of the Pre-Raphaelite painter, Ford Madox Brown. Mrs Hueffer's sister had married William

Michael Rossetti, elder bother of Dante Gabriel. By the time he met Pound, Hueffer, as he then was (he changed his German sounding surname to 'Ford' during the war) had written two collaborations with Conrad and some twenty-five other books, including studies of Rossetti and the Pre-Raphaelite Brotherhood. Hueffer, however, was anything but bohemian. Being 'cowed' and 'hammered' by the Pre-Raphaelites from an early age probably saved him, he said, 'from absinthe in Soho' (Ford, 1921: 200). An encounter as a young man with Symons and Verlaine at a concert at St James's Hall only scared him off further. And falling victim to the rules and regulations of bohemian costume ('You might or might not wear a red tie; might or might not wear a blue linen, turned-down collar, an inverness, a virgin beard, a slouch hat'; 203) determined him on a double formula of inconspicuous self-effacement and a poetry of direct observation of the common life: since 'just as in our persons we poets must pass in a crowd, so must our verse' (204). This sounded nothing like Yeats or Pound; nor for all its consistency did it exactly tally with the picture of Ford the fluent French-speaking, sometime German baron cum English country gentleman. His identity and allegiance could shift across the parts of his name and background, and as David Garnett remembered him during the period of the *English Review* his eccentricity was in conspicuous full flight: dressed in a 'magnificent fur coat' and 'glassy topper' he 'drove about in hired carriages; and his fresh features, the colour of raw veal, his prominent blue eyes and rabbit teeth smiled benevolently and patronizingly upon all gatherings of literary lions' (Garnett, 1953: 129). Also, for all his wonted ambition 'to pass unnoticed' (Ford, 1921: 202) Hueffer's name appeared in the papers over the scandal of his affair as a still-married man with Violet Hunt. The situation was more trying and corrosive for her (worse, she said, than the embarrassment of handing out suffrage leaflets at Kensington underground station). Henry James, who had been a friend to them both, found her situation 'lamentable, lamentable, oh, lamentable!' (Hunt, 1926: 96) and cancelled her visit to him at Rye.

Though some older acquaintances stayed away from South Lodge as a consequence, the mixed social gatherings and the parties continued up to 1914 and the advent of Vorticism and Ford's departure for the front. The halcyon days were, as ever, short-lived. Pound was 'in and out all day' feverishly attending to odd jobs in the house or garden when not playing tennis 'like a demon or trick pony' or 'inebriated kangaroo' and wearing Violet Hunt's 'Connemara cloak or the editor's old Rossetti coat... – with serenity' (114). 'Wonderful young ambitious poets of his *trompe*, confirmed artists of all kinds, mingled in our courts with the wistful Walter de la Mare and the spanking Amy Lowell, the sinister but delightful Madame Strindberg with her marmosets, painters like Jacob Epstein and Wyndham Lewis and Richard Nevinson and Gaudier Brjeska' (114). Regular guests included Gilbert Cannan, May Sinclair, Edmund Dulac, Brigit Patmore, Phyllis Bottome, H.D. and Aldington, who all lived in Kensington, while others included Skip and Kathleen Cannell, Jessie Chambers and D.H. Lawrence, John Cournos, Kate Lechmere, Rebecca West, and on one occasion Christabel Pankhurst, the 'Queen of our Cause' who stood, at Violet Hunt's insistence, diplomatically grasping a sheaf of pamphlets behind her back while engaged in polite conversation with 'the darling Die-hard of the opposition', Mrs Humphry Ward (113).

The garden parties at South Lodge give a sense of the broad sociality, across different arts, different moral and political opinions and different generations, of this Kensington-based circle. The combination of established and new writers in the *English Review* (Hardy, James, Conrad, Wells, Galsworthy, Bennett, Yeats, Tolstoy, Anatole France, Emile Verhaeren, Rupert Brooke, Lawrence, Flint, Pound and Lewis) reflected this same openness. At the same time, all this was a sign of change, as South Lodge bore witness, in the passage from Victorian to Edwardian to Georgian society. In Goldring's view, the contributors to the *English Review* (which coincided with his role as Ford's secretary) 'fell into two sharply divided categories' – Ford's old friends and confrères and writers of the coming generation (Goldring, 1943: 39). Although social discipline was relaxed in the Edwardian years, 'The middle classes', Goldring comments, 'as Violet found to her cost, clung desperately to Victorian conventions and to appearances of respectability' (71). Her misfortune was that her 'irregular union' with Ford came before what she termed the post-war 'differentiation of the standard of manners' and altered attitudes towards marriage and divorce (73). Hunt and May Sinclair, and Rebecca West, of course, were active in the suffrage and contemporary women's movement. Ford was a supporter and his pamphlet 'The Monstrous Regiment of Women' struck the liberal note in this respect at South Lodge. Pound and Lewis remained distant and patronising, however, and for all Ford's commonly acknowledged editorial 'genius' on the *English Review*, its pages, as reviewed by Goldring, included only three women contributors, one of whom was Violet Hunt (55).

The art of manners evidently changed more slowly than the manner of art. The artist Lewis, especially, rocketed forward, dumping Ford and Conrad into the literary past. Ford and Pound held together across their own generations and the passage from Impressionism to the dictates of

Imagism. Perhaps this was to their credit, as it was to Pound's credit and gain that he found a way between Ford and Yeats. Playing both parts on either sides of the net gave rise to a schizophrenic performance along the way but in the event the dictum 'that verse must be at least as well written as prose' (Ford, 1921: 201) won hands down: game, set and match. In the next phase too, Pound arguably left Ford behind, if on more genial terms than Lewis. Nonetheless, they shared something else across these earlier and later movements. If Pound's bohemian swank disturbed the 'brit/literatus', so did all this endless talk about the technicalities of verse, the idea of the poet as a professional rather than learned amateur, and Pound's free way with the icons of the English tradition – which, in the colonising way of this tradition, included the classics which the upstart Yankee Pound dared to translate. Remembering the scene in the Vienna Café, we can see that what held Ford and Pound, and Pound and Yeats, together was that they were not conventionally or not at all English. Ford welcomed the interplay between America, France and Europe, and believed the 'three nations of the Atlantic seaboard form one civilisation...not of material interests but of the humanities' (Ford, 1921: 105). Pound was to argue similarly, but did not see, at least not with Ford's resignation, the brick wall of 'militant amateurism' standing in its way (ibid.). The war years strengthened this opposition. Pound was accosted by a navvy as a ' "Jurrman...or szum kind ov a furriner"' (Pound, 1975b: 503) but Ford was a more likely suspect and, one way or another, feelings of patriotism decided him to change his surname. At 10 Church Walk, Pound had railed impotently at the bells of St Mary Abbots nearby. John Cournos, who took over the room after Pound, was disturbed by the hymn singing of a nonconformist household opposite and told how holding a copy of *Blast* up against the window miraculously brought it to a halt (1935: 268). Radical art didn't have anything like this kind of success against the louder clamour of war. What's more, in what was the most aggravating discovery for the already irascible Pound, it only hardened English contempt for loud foreign interlopers who ignorantly flouted the rules of the game.

Pound had a way with chairs. He lounged, as in the photograph used as the frontispiece to *Pavannes and Divisions* (1918) and in a painting by Lewis in the late 1930s. In Paris, he was never forgiven for breaking a favourite chair of Gertrude Stein's and turned to making his own unbreakable outsize armchairs out of planed planks, nails and canvas seats (so large, said Ford, 'that once you sat down, there you lay until someone pulled you out'; Ford, 1934: 174). He flung himself into frail chairs in Kensington homes and at South Lodge broke a cane and gilt chair by tipping it back and was henceforth provided with a substitute from the kitchen (Bottome, 1944: 71; Fletcher, 1937: 59). Nonplussed he set about the social furniture. Before his arrival at South Lodge it was the convention, there as elsewhere, for young men 'to wear top hats and "London clothes" and to carry gloves and canes' when calling for tea (Goldring, 1943: 46). Pound put paid to this ritual in his assumed role of 'social master of ceremonies' (47). At Yeats's Monday evenings too, after a patient start while he waited for Yeats to notice him, Pound soon commandeered the entire event.

Woburn Buildings were down a stone-flagged passage (now Woburn Walk) off Upper Woburn Place near the British Museum, in what was then a working-class district of Bloomsbury. Yeats's two rooms at no. 18 were above a cobbler's and a workman's family who soon knew him to be a 'toff' because unlike the other residents he alone received letters (Hone, 1971: 179–80). He had moved there in 1896 after sharing an apartment with Symons at Fountain Court, partly because of the expense, partly to receive his then lover Olivia Shakespear ('Diana Vernon'). The two remained on close terms in later years and it was she who first introduced Pound to Yeats in May 1909 (Wilhelm, 1990: 36). At the Shakespear's home Pound had gone into raptures at the thought of sharing the same hearth-rug as Yeats (Carpenter, 1988: 105; Pound/Shakespear, 1984: 3). Once he was accepted he was more at Yeats's elbow than at his feet, even taking it upon himself to improve the phrasing in a group of Yeats's poems for *Poetry* (Carpenter, 1988: 191). On the first evening Pound took Goldring to Woburn Buildings, he 'dominated the room, distributed Yeats's cigarettes and Chianti, and laid down the law about poetry' (Goldring, 1943: 49). Yeats was asked to sing 'Innisfree' ('over-praised' in Ford's opinion) but was 'unfortunately... completely unmusical, indeed almost tone deaf'. The result was 'a sort of dirgelike incantation' which sent Goldring into barely suppressed giggles (49). At least Goldring was spared the more difficult ordeal of a double act between Yeats and the equally tone deaf Pound whose singing voice sounded, even to Yeats's ears, 'like something on a very bad phonograph' (Homberger, 1972: 39). Truly, Yeats's music was at its best not in reading or chanting but in the combination of metre and 'effective speech' (ibid.). Dorothy Richardson, who at one time lived across the way from his rooms, saw shadowy figures seated and standing, engaged in 'talking, talking... and, chiefly, being talked to, by the tall pervading figure, visible now here, now there, but always in speech' (Richardson, 1939: 65). John Cournos, who Pound also introduced to Yeats felt he was in the 'uncontradictable' presence of genius. 'Here was great talk. Yeats himself is the greatest talker I have ever met. I myself sat for the most part silent, drinking in this talk with an avid eagerness' (Cournos, 1935: 237). Another visitor responded with less reverence. William Carlos Williams had been a fellow student and close friend of both Pound and H.D. at the University of Pennsylvania, and had decided to combine being a poet with being a doctor. He was pursuing medical studies in Leipzig and joined Pound in London in March 1910. He sampled 10 Church Walk and suffered Pound to cram in the sights, which included Turners at the National Gallery, the Elgin Marbles and the Tower of London along with a visit to one of Yeats's evenings. Yeats read Ernest Dowson by candlelight: 'not my dish' said Williams. He felt the 'intense literary atmosphere' was 'thrilling, every minute of it', but 'fatiguing in the extreme... It seemed completely foreign to anything I desired. I was glad to get away' (Williams 1967: 114, 117).

Yeats's main room held a settle and leather armchair, a chest containing his manuscripts, astrological papers and tarot cards, a table with two candlesticks, a bookcase with editions of Blake and William Morris and on the walls works by Blake and Beardsley, a painting by Rossetti, and others by Pre-Raphaelite artists (Hone, 1971: 180). It belonged to a different era than Pound's room, though – tarot cards and Yeats's mysticism to one side – Ford Madox Ford would been very familiar if not altogether comfortable with its décor. Apparently, he never attended Yeats's evenings. Carlos Williams, a purer product than Pound of Ford's proto-Imagist teaching and of his desire for a verse of common things and people, responded, we might say, on behalf of the modern Ford. The difference was that Williams reacted as an American – though not as Pound's, nor H.D.'s, nor Cournos's, nor Eliot's kind of American. Pound simply saw Williams as parochial and off the modern tempo. What Williams wanted, however, though he was only to know this as he reflected on these early years, was something that would be emphatically but not exclusively 'American'. Pound, and Eliot especially, he later saw as betraying this cause, not to Paris or modern European art movements to which Williams was himself open, but to the English. This was the 'foreignness' mingled with a preciosity left over from the nineties that he detected at Yeats's and in Pound's London.

Very English, violently American

The streets and park were busy with ladies in sable stoles, serious couples, children bursting with health, housemaids, gentlemen's gentlemen and errand boys running, cycling, weaving in and out of the carriages. The others waited for Pound in the 'piazza' as he liked to think of the courtyard below his rooms and sallied forth, Aldington suited, at a brisk walk, Pound in his grey velvet coat, with long strides, his head up, discoursing on metrics; the women behind, puzzling over a Greek term, feeding the grateful ducks, the gulls wheeling above them at the Pond on their way to the National Gallery, a bus ride to Hammersmith or Golders Green, or – to satisfy Hilda – to take tea at the Grosvenor Gallery, at the British Museum or to stop first at the 'café des artists' as they termed it, the small teashop run by the expatriate American, seeker after civilisation and proud owner of a signed copy of Pound's Quinzaine for this Yule, Miss Ella Abbott, on Holland Street.

'Here!' Pound set down copies of two magazines. 'For your blue pencil'. He pushed them across the table to his companions. 'Mais ils sont toujours en vogue, des Imagistes', he flung himself back, 'modern stuff / mostly by Americans'.

'To America, the future!' Brigit raised her teacup half to the shop and half towards Pound.

'And just what are you gonna make of this, monsieur l'américain?' drawled Pound.

Eliot smiled his smile and took the letter Pound handed him. He read silently and turned to the signature. 'Is this Flint?'

'More bullshit as I fear I must make clear to him.'

Eliot read aloud, '... And "there is no difference except that which springs from the difference of temperament and talent between the imagist poem of to-day and those written by Edward Storer and T.E. Hulme"'.

'Again!' exclaimed Pound. No difference between the / the Hellenic hardness of our own H.D. and Storer's custard!

'And no mention of Aldington', Brigit and Eliot exchanged glances.

Pound let out a 'Pshwaw! Nor of Fat Fordie, you might say.' He took the letter. 'And now this prod at me' – he found a weasely cockney accent, ' "where you 'ave failed is in your personal relationships"', he eyed his companions, ' "you spoil'd everthin' by some NATIVE incapacity for walking square with your fellows". So, he don' like AMERKANS, don't he? And then this' – in daintier tones – ' "You must not PRESUME because of my diffidence and timidity in conversation that you were illuminating me in the long hours of stuccato discourse (STUCCATO!) with which you have favoured me on divers occasions". Oh, NOT at ALL, I MUST NOT PRESUME to have illuminated the poor benighted blockhead, Mr F.S. "Frenchie" Flint of Lunnun Town'.[2]

Frank Flint was a Londoner who left school at thirteen. He joined the Civil Service as a typist when he was nineteen and learned Latin and French at evening classes and eventually mastered ten languages.

In 1909, the year he met Hulme and Pound, he married his landlady's daughter and privately published the collection *In the Net of Stars*, dedicated to her. One thinks, almost inescapably, of the aspirant to culture, Leonard Bast, in Forster's novel, *Howards End* of 1910 or of Eliot's flowing crowd of downcast commuters moving across London Bridge just before 9.00 am. But Flint was more original than Bast and knew contemporary French poetry as well as, and perhaps before Eliot; certainly before Pound. He wrote a regular and learned 'French Chronicle' from 1912 for *Poetry and Drama* and was one of the first contributors of the new generation to the *New Age* which he joined as poetry critic in 1908 (Martin: 1967, 146–7). He was reserved, a scholarly journalist if an average, and, by instinct, Romantic poet, who sometimes got depressed and into scrapes, probably about money. Pound and Flint often met, most likely in company at the ABC in Chancery Lane or at the Tour Eiffel Restaurant, and at one time when Flint had hit bad times Pound invited him and his wife, along with H.D., to dinner. They had omelette which Mrs Flint, 'a hapless little cockney' to Flint's 'derelict poet', in H.D.'s words, found reason to criticise (Crunden,1993: 211–12).

When Pound dined out with others he showed off. And it worked. We go on telling the story of how he chewed a red tulip at a dinner given by Ernest Rhys in Hampstead, or how, on another occasion, over a roast dinner at South Lodge and for the edification of Lawrence and Jessie Chambers, Pound pierced an apple, sliced it into quarters and gobbled it down, to show 'how an American eats an apple' (Norman, 1969: 57–8, 52). At 10 Church Walk he offered his guests preserved apricots and demonstrated how to eat them: 'between forefinger and thumb with the other fingers outstretched like a star...' before 'with raised chin, [he] opened his mouth and bit cleanly into the fruit with his very white teeth, managing to finish it in two bites', his fingers emerging from a silk handkerchief 'impeccably unsugarcoated' (Patmore, 1968: 67–8).

Flint was an English autodidact and somewhat displaced in English class society. Pound was very American as Lewis and others, including Flint, clearly saw. He was, Dorothy Pound reflected, 'the most American thing going' (Kenner, 1973: 486). Some of the time Pound played up to this, but unlike William Carlos Williams he was by ambition an 'American Europeanist' in Donald Davie's description (1975: 23). This meant he was not at first conscious of the kind of distinction which struck Williams between Europe and England. London, for Pound, represented the cultural and 'intellectual capital of America'; it was 'the place for poesy' as he wrote to Williams, the home of the highest art, and Yeats was simply 'the greatest living poet' (Paige, 1971: 7-8). His way into literary society and his route to Yeats proved, as suggested above, to be narrower than 'London', of which he knew only part. 'Pound's London' indeed turned out to be 'Pound's Kensington' as he insisted to Patricia Hutchins (Hutchins, 1965: 18), an area 'SWARming with artistic types' and something like 'a high class Greenwich village', as Ford remembered, the significant difference being that its inhabitants were typically 'wealthy, refined, delicate and well-born' (Carpenter, 1988: 130). Kensington was in other words a bourgeois enclave, home to a professional and business class with a sprinkling of minor aristocrats given to artistic patronage, and typically, as in the persons of Olivia and Dorothy Shakespear, who were so vital to Pound's early years in the city, it was 'English'.

The Shakespears were 'an advanced household' suggests Hugh Kenner. He probably has in mind Henry Hope Shakespear's 'Sunday painting', said to have influenced Dorothy's early work, Olivia's half dozen novels and her social and literary connections. Though the Shakespears were unrelated to William Shakespeare (Olivia, however, liked to spell the poet's name without the final 'e'), they could more genuinely claim a distant family connection to the novelist Thackeray and to the ancient English family, the Talbots, as recalled by Pound in the *Pisan Cantos* (1975b: 515; and see Davie, 1991: 233; Wilhelm, 1990: 248-9). Olivia was also first cousin to Lionel Johnson who had introduced her to Yeats. In Kensington she was a close friend of Lady Low who made her drawing room at De Vere Gardens available for readings, entertained Pound to dinner and helped organise 'Three Lectures on Medieval Poetry' by him at Queen Anne's Gate 'by kind permission of Lord and Lady Glenconner' (Pound/Shakespear, 1984: 89). Another connection, Mrs Eva Fowler, who shared Yeats's interest in psychic and occult experiments, had Pound to lunch, and sponsored three further lectures in Mayfair in 1913 (179). She was a long time friend of the poet, Frederic Manning, who first introduced Pound to the Shakespears and who, along with Yeats, was billed as chairing one of Pound's lectures at Queen Anne's Gate. Pound knew 'all the Swells' as Lawrence remarked (Stock, 1970: 97) and not only benefited from his entree into this social set but calculated in his own version of the compact between English bourgeois and transatlantic Bohemian that this was the way to get on. In 1913 he wrote home about a 'terribly literary dinner' with Tagore, Maurice Hewlitt, May Sinclair, Evelyn Underhill, and George Prothero. Prothero, soon to be Sir George Prothero, and historian at the Foreign Office, was editor of the *Quarterly Review*. He has a later role as villain of the piece in prompting Pound's departure from London. At this date, however, Pound sought his patronage or rather his pages. In June 1912 he had confessed to Dorothy Shakespear how much he wanted to 'entrench myself behind' the *Quarterly*'s covers and 'shall be horribly mortified if it don't come off' (Pound/Shakespear, 1984: 125). Meantime he pursued a more temporising campaign with Dorothy herself. She had inherited her mother's looks and 'modelled her social life quietly [?] on mine' said Olivia (49). 'She was ' "very *Kensington*" ', said Agnes Bedford (Kenner, 1973: 493), 'very English' and not ' "awakened" ' said H.D. (Wilhelm, 1990: 151). If early 1909 found Pound, partly through Olivia Shakespear, already 'by way of falling into the crowd that does things here' (Paige, 1971: 7), he was subsequently to fall rather awkwardly in his relations with mother and daughter into the tangle of English proprieties.

'What did a young woman like Dorothy Shakespear expect of life in the early years of the century?' asks Kenner. We do not know, he implies, since we have 'no sense of the fine line' those years 'were demarking between matrimony and liberty' (1973: 293). It is a crucial insight, which, if we do not now fully appreciate it, names the all-important distinction felt by Violet Hunt and by Olivia Shakespear on her daughter's behalf. A woman's position in society depended upon treading the right side of this line. There was no alternative for Dorothy therefore. 'She *must* marry', Olivia wrote to Pound, 'but obviously can't marry you' (Pound /Shakespear, 1984: 153). Not only did his income fall well below the required £500 per annum, his manners struck the wrong note. She passed onto Dorothy that he 'really must *not* in London wear that turn down collar, with a black coat' (92). He '*ought* to go away'; Englishmen didn't understand his 'American ways' and Dorothy simply could not go about with him 'American fashion' until she was thirty-five (154).

Pound did not see a world of English or Americans so much as artists and non-artists. And an artist, in an ethereal echo of Lewis's Tarr, should not marry: 'it ought to be illegal' he wrote to his mother, 'if the artist must marry let him find someone more interested in art, or his art, or the artist part of him, than in him. After which let them take tea together three times a week. The ceremony may be undergone to prevent gossip, if necessary' (Carpenter, 1988: 105). As it turned out things pretty well took this course. Dorothy was entranced by the artist. In her 'Notebook' she wrote in one dreamy breath of his face and hair and beautiful soul, 'He has conquered the needs of the flesh', she decided, to devote himself to the ' "highest of arts" – poetry'. He 'is not as other men are', she learned from Fredric Manning, 'He has seen the

Beatific Vision' (Pound/Shakespear, 1984: 5, 9). For his part, Pound regularly took tea with the Shakespears, stalled, travelled to the United States and in Europe and had affairs, or, perhaps more accurately, platonic liaisons, in the courtly manner learned from Romance literature, with Bride Scratton, Brigit Patmore and the younger, unmarried, Phyllis Bottome. In the United States he had been linked with 'Mary Moore of Trenton' and had been practically engaged to H.D. in Philadelphia.

Hilda Doolittle came to London in 1911, enjoyed its freedoms and teashops and accepted the editorial advice from Pound that made her 'H.D. Imagiste', the by-line he suggested under her poems and recommended as '*modern* stuff by an American' to Harriet Monroe at *Poetry: A Magazine of Verse* (Paige, 1971: 11). H.D. realised that Pound and Dorothy had an understanding, and in Paris and Italy with Pound and Richard Aldington, took up with the latter. They agreed on a 'modern marriage' – which seemed to countenance extra-marital involvements on Aldington's part with Dorothy Yorke and then Brigit Patmore, and on hers with D.H. Lawrence and John Cournos and later with Cecil Gray (Wilhelm, 1990: 132–3). H.D. had a still-born child in the war years and a daughter in 1919. Her memoir of Pound makes much of his visit to her at this second date in a nursing home in Ealing, he in operatic guise with black soft hat and ebony cane, and of his anguish, his 'only real criticism' being that it was not his child (H.D., 1979: 30).[3] The marriage of Pound and Dorothy Shakespear followed six months after Aldington and H.D.'s in April 1914. His finances were no better, but Dorothy was now 27 years old and there was probably nothing else for it, if only 'to prevent gossip'. Pound imagined, he told Sophie Brzeska, that they would live in 'mutual tolerance' (Carpenter, 1988: 234). There were very few guests at the wedding and a somewhat faded passion in the marriage. Whether tactlessly, or because he was oblivious to such matters, Pound moved with his new wife into an apartment in 5 Holland Place Chambers, Kensington, on the same floor as H.D. and Aldington.

In marrying Dorothy Shakespear Pound 'had *married* England', suggests Donald Davie (1991: 233). He had the chance therefore, Davie argues, of moving into a unified and in many ways 'attractive' and 'admirable' English establishment (224). Davie is thinking of George Prothero's reaction of October 1914 to Pound's appearance in *Blast*. 'I am afraid', wrote Prothero, 'that I must say frankly that I do not think I can open the columns of the *Q.R.* – at any rate at present – to any one associated with such a publication as *Blast*. It stamps a man too disadvantageously' (Pound, 1960: 357–8). Pound never forgot this rebuff which came to stand as a symbol of the hidebound and pusillanimous attitudes of that same establishment. He over-reacted, says Davie. Prothero was saying things are too hot for now. But perhaps Davie forgets how much life and art in London had changed by late 1914 and how Pound responded to these changes. Pre-war Edwardian society presented a transitional but still in many ways Victorian society. Pound entered stage right and stage left, by turns the scholar and gypsy. If some saw an erudite, kind-hearted companion, teacher and dedicated artist behind the pose, or could accept this pose as a homage to the English nineties, others saw a pretentious clown. His own behaviour, moreover (his table manners, the chairs, the clothes, the over-extended courtship) hardly suggests he was an astute reader of the social codes of Edwardian London. No more at first did he read its literary codes – as well, say, as another kind of English outsider like F.S. Flint, or as well as Ford. If he quarrelled with Flint, he absorbed the shock of Ford's ridicule of the volume *Canzoni*. Ford, said Pound, rolled on the floor at 'my jejune provincial effort to learn, *mehercule*, the stilted language that then passed for "good English" in the arthritic milieu that then held control of the respected British critical circles'. This milieu he glosses as 'Newbolt, the backwash of Lionel Johnson, Fred Manning, the Quarterlies and the rest of 'em' (Cookson, 1973: 432). *Canzoni* had been dedicated to Olivia and Dorothy Shakespear. Had Pound meant this volume to join him more firmly at once to the 'respected critical circles' of a publication such as the *Quarterly* and to the 'England' represented by the Shakespears to whom Johnson and Manning had in different ways offered to connect him? Ford anyway encouraged him to ditch both the verse and the society. His earlier books Pound admits in 'Salutation the Second' were 'twenty years behind the times'. Instead the 'little naked and impudent songs' of *Lustra* from 1913–15 would cock a snook at the literary establishment and 'Ruffle the skirts of prudes' (Pound, 1968: 94, 95). If Pound had indeed married England in 1914 he was effectively divorcing it in the same year, as the parts of the 'translatlantic' American and aspirant English persona began to unravel.

And what of Dorothy Pound, née Shakespear? What she desired, she had written, as if in answer to Hugh Kenner, was that she 'may understand the chivalry and trust and joy of a great love' (Pound/ Shakespear, 1984: 9). She had been prepared to live through the romantic genius Pound, had devotedly worked as his assistant, and waited. She must have wondered at the transformation of her society, her London, and of her troubadour metamorphosised into a trouble-maker. They went for their honeymoon to Stone Cottage, Sussex, where Pound had worked the previous winter with Yeats and where he was to work now on translating the Japanese Noh plays. At some time, quietly in the background, her painting changed from conventional landscapes to the Vorticist designs used for the cover of Pound's *Ripostes* (1915) and included in *Blast* 2. She was not thinking of art at this time, however, she said, so much as 'trying to make out what sort of creature I was going to be living with' (Kenner, 1973: 488).

Pound's career in the following half dozen years seemed to spin forward in a whirling rhythm of mounting fame and frustration. He stepped out in 1913 as an Imagiste, in 1914 as a Vorticist, and began work shortly afterwards on the Fenollosa papers which were to result in *Cathay* (1915). Further translations, with Yeats, of the Japanese Noh plays, and of the Roman poet Sextus Propertius were to follow, as were the first drafts of the *Cantos*. He was 'Poetry Correspondent' of *Poetry*, involved in the *Little Review*, a regular contributor, sometimes under different names, to the *New Age* and the *Egoist*, a tireless promoter of Brzeska, Joyce, Eliot and Lewis with publishers and with the New York lawyer and collector, John Quinn. He assisted other figures such as H.D. and Aldington, Robert Frost and John Cournos. He was at the magnetic centre of things – Vortex Pound – and this was 'The Ezra Pound Period' as Iris Barry termed it (see Brooker, 2002: 38–45). More than anyone in these middle years between 1913 and 1917, Pound laid the fuse that ignited in the explosion of modernism.

His milieu accordingly shifted, from middle-class Kensington to Belotti's Ristorante Italiano, the 'cheapest in London', on Old Compton Street in the polyglot, cosmopolitan environs of Soho (Hutchins papers, August 1953). Here he presided as poet, pedagogue and propagandist. Barry came to London in 1916 after a flurry of letters earlier in the year (Paige, 1971: 76–97). Pound's to her – offering support and encouragement along with the severity of his blue pencil and an impossible guide to a 'Komplete Kultur' – were entirely in character, as was the dandified personage who met her in London and spoke in tongues as they walked across a wind-swept Wimbledon Common. Pound, she reported, deployed an accent in which 'American mingled with a dozen assorted "English society" and Cockney accents inserted in mockery, French, Spanish and Greek exclamations, strange cries and catcalls, the whole very oddly inflected, with dramatic pauses and *diminuendos*' (Barry, 1931: 159). He introduced Barry to the changing London scene and brutally presented her to Lewis – 'P said, I whore', as she later revealed (Schiddel, Barry profile, 1942/3). At least one critic believes Pound too had an affair with Barry (Schiddel, Cassidy letter, 25 February 1976). Edmund Schiddel suggests Barry was bisexual and was known in

London lesbian circles and it seems likely both she and Pound had a relationship with Maud Gonne's daughter Iseult (Schiddel, letter, 21 October 1977). This was, said Pound, the most sexually active period of his life (Wilhelm, 1990: 153). 'Mary Butts was one of the four young girls who were given the works by Ezra that year in London', comments Barry, and Wilhelm names Bride Scratton, Brigit Patmore, and Iseult Gonne as women with whom Pound had affairs in London (153, 101, 196–7; and see Carpenter, 1988: 331–2). Barry's essay on Pound says nothing of any of this but it is clear that the 'differentiation of the standard of manners', in Violet Hunt's decorous words, was rapidly taking effect in the sexual mores and conduct that characterised a now younger, anti-bourgeois bohemian generation.

As it stands, in the public expression she chose to make, Barry's memoir evokes an active and varied artistic community, driven by Pound's energy and purpose. Propelled by the polemical fireworks of Vorticism and the undeviating commitment of Harriet Shaw Weaver's *Egoist* operation, modernism surfaced with an agenda full to bursting. That at least is one picture. At the same time for all the vitality of artistic and social experiment, London was empty. 'There is nothing doing here' Aldington wrote to Amy Lowell seven weeks into the war; 'I think nothing new is done here', said Pound in August 1915. He had declared ' "England" ' was 'dead as mutton' as early as 1913 and in 1915 used the same phrase of English verse (Paige, 1971: 24, Crunden, 1993: 267). Pound became fatigued, easily aggravated and an increasingly offensive irritant to others. He fell out with Fletcher, Lowell and Flint over Imagism; he quit *Poetry* magazine in exasperation at their delay in publishing Eliot and his own Ur-Cantos; he ceased to act as Foreign Editor of the *Little Review* and gradually withdrew from the *Egoist*. Elkin Matthews had fussed over the text of poems in *Lustra*, took exception to *Homage to Sextus Propertius* and was to turn down the collection *Quia Pauper Amavi* in 1919. The publisher, John Lane, had earlier insisted that two lines of his 'Fratres Minores' in *Blast* 1 were blacked out, and Pound's translations became the butt of pedantic scholars. Barry points to the issue of censorship as bonding the Pound coterie under the banner of freedom of expression and their war against 'Mrs Grundy' (1931: 163); but this too indicates a change, confirming how modernism, once launched, fell foul of prevailing morality and conservative aesthetic taste. The bohemian Pound no longer sought patronage so much as autonomy, principally in the form of an independent journal which would publish himself, Eliot, Joyce and Lewis, though this was, of course, in turn, impossible without financial backing. The 'tough guy' came to the fore, shouldering the troubadour to one side, six guns blazing at a row of artistic, economic and political targets. *Blast* had been a possible organ for the new movement but lay wrecked by the combined effects of war and provincialism. After Prothero closed the *Quarterly*'s doors to Pound, so other doors, to *Poetry*, the *Little Review*, the *Atheneum* and *Outlook*, closed too, some by Pound's own doing, by the end of the decade. Other than his journalism for the *New Age* he had little source of income. There were the close relationships with Eliot and Lewis and the discipleship of younger artists, but Flint's outburst in a letter to the *Egoist* in 1917 showed the depth of animosity of sometime friends towards him: 'The truth is we are all tired of Mr Pound', wrote Flint, 'His work has deteriorated from book to book; his manners have become more and more offensive; and we wish he would go back to America.' The elderly and not so elderly 'Brit/literatus' joined in antipathy to his American ways. British literary folk 'are tired of his antics... tired of his "Wild Westisms" ... those of us who were once associated with him and are so no longer for very good reasons, detest him with the heartiest of loathings' (Texas, 21 February 1917).

The role of 'Enemy' suited Pound less than it did Lewis. His manner had been as gregarious, if pushy, as his talk and work were heteroglot. The uncompromising stance he was henceforth driven to adopt determined his destiny as another modernist giant in exile. This was not the immediate or only outcome, however. When Pound commented directly on Prothero's letter in print, he saw it as of a piece with the *Quarterly*'s attack on John Keats in the early nineteenth century and by extension an attack on the artists he, Pound, had championed – Eliot, Lewis and Brzeska. In some ways Prothero's reaction was a small thing. We can all the same understand Pound's frustration, precisely at its combined triviality and power. He stood personally to lose part of his livelihood but also detected a larger issue. This was not the cause of art simply as it might have been for the nineties aesthete, nor of 'modernism' pure and simple, but of 'civilisation'. This was *Blast*'s theme and was the theme in 1918 and 1920 of Pound's related studies of Henry James and Rémy de Gourmont, the second of which closes with Prothero's letter and Pound's reaction to it. Civilisation, these essays argue, 'is individual' but depends on the broad circulation and distribution of ideas in the metropolis and on cultural contact and exchange between nations. The line ran through the cities of Paris and London, Pound wrote, and so in principle to the major cities of America. Henry James stands 'On this side of civilisation', 'the hater of tyranny' who had striven 'to make two continents understand each other' (Pound, 1960: 296). To recruit James and the USA to Pound's project presented some difficulties, however. For once America had failed to respond to James's 'great labour', the master confirmed his own preferred allegiance in June 1915 by adopting British nationality. One of the witnesses at this procedure, so it happened, was his close friend and neighbour from Rye, George Prothero. It is very likely Prothero would have agreed with James on the irregular relation of Violet Hunt and Hueffer and that James would have agreed with Prothero on a man's involvement with *Blast*.

De Gourmont, Pound begins the second essay of this pair, belonged, by contrast, to another age. He was open to new work and ideas, his essays presented 'the best portrait...of the civilised mind from 1885–1915' (344) and Paris was open to civilisation. De Gourmont had warmly supported Pound's proposal for a 'periodical to maintain communications between New York, London and Paris' (356) and Pound includes De Gourmont's letter alongside Prothero's rejection. But what was left of Pound's metropolitan triangle in 1920? America had proved obtuse, London had failed him and was soon to figure as the hell of Cantos XIV and XV. And there were some of course who thought Pound had failed them. Flint, for example, and then to Pound's surprise, William Carlos Williams. In the autumn of 1920, after a trip to Venice and Paris, Pound returned to London to discover Williams's open rejection of Eliot and himself as models for American writing: 'E.P. is the best enemy United States verse has' declared Williams (1969: 24). He learned too that he had been sacked by the *Atheneum*. The transatlantic alliance had come apart. There was nowhere to turn therefore but to its one remaining base, 'The Island of Paris', in the fitting title of a series of letters Pound published in *The Dial*. From here he hoped still to effect a cure; a 'poetic serum to save English letters from postmature and American letters from premature suicide and decomposition' (Pound, 1920: 406). The physician was working long distance, however. By late December 1920 the Pounds had moved to Paris and he was to return only once to London, forty-five years later.

Most of us would regard the works of artistic modernism as surviving, indeed as critiquing, the limitations of post-war London and England's impoverished idea of civilisation. Something other than the texts of modernism, however, also stayed 'in the place of memory' to adopt a phrase Pound was drawn to in Cavalcanti. As Pound wrote to Ronald Duncan in 1938 'After all there *were*, in London dining circles or a *weekly* meeting of us and periphery. There was circulation from room to room in at least going concerns which wrote and published. It was a sort of society or social order or dis-order' (Paige, 1971: 306). Elsewhere, he warns Patricia Hutchins against putting 'all the DIFFERENT Anschauungs of the different writers in any one "period" attitude'. Instead, he suggests we think of an irregular shape, a 'literary rhomboid or whatever non-form or aggregate existed' (Hutchins papers, 11 September 1953; 1 March 1957). The perception of a two-sided 'order/disorder' captures much of what I have wanted to convey about this changing literary community in Pound's changing London. The essays on Henry James and De Gourmont, along with the related 'Provincialism the Enemy', set the metropolitan civilisation of both Paris and London against prejudice, dogma and conformity. For Pound this civilisation entails, in words that have a surprisingly contemporary ring, 'not a levelling' or 'elimination of differences' but 'a recognition of differences, and the right of differences to exist' (Pound, 1960: 298). The problematics of order and disorder Pound sketches in the letter to Duncan governed the rest of his work and thinking. However we view this outcome, their coexistence in Pound's defence of difference in Edwardian and Georgian London give that time, location and literary formation its complex, still compelling quality.

4
Nights at the Cave of the Golden Calf

A shadow play

> *I have caught you dancing round the golden calf. But that's not what I have against you. What I have against you is that you haven't danced round the golden calf quite enough!*
>
> (Cournos, 1922: 230)

> Unaware of the approaching disasters of the First World War a wave of creative activity seemed to be sweeping London... Ezra's driving force was everywhere.
>
> (Patmore, 1968: 75)

> Those marvellous summer days before the crash, were crowded, for young men who danced, with pleasures and excitements of which it is difficult, after an interval of thirty years, to disentangle the details. The season of 1914 was a positive frenzy of gaiety. Long before there was any shadow of war, I remember feeling it couldn't go on, that something *had* to happen... In that amazing twelve months before "the balloon went up" I do not remember seeing a great deal of Ford and Violet. Once or twice I encountered them late at night at The Cave of the Golden Calf.
>
> (Goldring, 1943: 71, 70)

> Two years ago I happened to find in New York my engagement book for 1914... [it] was an amazing, packed affair. From the middle of May to the end of June... – there were only six days on which I did not have at least three dinner and after-dinner dates. There would be a dinner, a theatre or a party,

a dance. Usually a breakfast at four after that. Or Ezra and his gang carried me off to their night club which was kept by Mme. Strindberg, decorated by Epstein and situated underground.

(Ford, 1932: 410)

Tried the cabaret on Tuesday with the FMHs – Konody and Czernikoff on the premises etc. till 3.20 am.

(Pound/Shakespear, 1984: 230)

The Cave of the Golden Calf
9 Heddon Street, Soho, London
Situated in a basement just off Regents Street, Britain's first ultra modern nightclub was founded in 1912 and attracted all the intelligentsia of pre-war London. Dramatic Vorticist decorations by Wyndham Lewis and Jacob Epstein provided the backdrop to legendary scenes of drinking and dancing, where bohemia literally rubbed up against aristocracy, whipped up until dawn by a ragtime band and a famously frenzied gypsy fiddler. Events were regularly punctuated by dramatic outbursts from the club's founder owner, the notoriously beautiful and volatile Frida Strindberg, second wife of the Norwegian playwright, whose rapid departure to America in 1914 marked the club's closure.

(Buck, 2002)

...certain transactions of a disagreeable nature caused me to sever my connection with the Omega, and as there is no purpose in returning to such matters here, I will pass on to my next milestone, namely 'The Cave of the Golden Calf'. I believe I am going backwards, but I have not to hand any record of the actual date.

Strindberg, the Swedish dramatist, had a number of wives, one being a Viennese. This very adventurous woman (whose favourite remark, I recall, was 'je suis au bout de forces!', although, often as I heard her say it, I never saw her in that condition, her 'forces' being at all times triumphantly intact) rented an enormous basement. Hence the term 'Cave'. She had it suitably decorated with murals by myself, and numbers of columns by Jacob Epstein: hired an orchestra – with a frenzied Hungarian gypsy fiddler to lead it – a smart corps of Austrian waiters and an Austrian cook; then with a considerable amount of press-promotion she opened as a night-club.

With the Epstein figures appearing to hold up the threateningly low ceiling, the somewhat abstract hieroglyphics I had painted round the walls, the impassioned orchestra, it must have provided a kick or two for the young man about town of the moment. It was about my first job: and if I had acquired the taste for alcohol (as I had not) I might have got a kick or two myself. As it was I had to try, and as best I could, to cope with a patroness forever *au bout des forces*.

(Lewis, 1984: 134–5)

The Cabaret Club had a rulebook (with 40 rules) and a General Committee headed by the *New Age* critic P.G. Konody which included Frank Harris and the composer, Granville Bantock. Membership was 5 guineas, but reduced to 1 guinea for fifty supporters representing the arts, such as Violet Hunt and Ford. In addition 'out of deference to their personalities' certain artists were given honorary membership and had their bills shifted to wealthier patrons: 'you cd/even get eats fr free if you took 'em at Frida's table', Pound reported (Mullins, 1961: 99). Membership also entitled patrons to the edifying pleasures of the Cabaret Theatre Club which on Sundays from 9.15 pm presented new or neglected works, including in its first season plays by Aristophanes, Dostoievsky and Strindberg. A music programme included pieces by Pergolesi, Mozart and Schoenberg's *Pierrot Lunaire*, performed shortly after its Berlin debut in October 1912 (Strauss, 2001: 180). All this was extra however. The heart of the club was its main arena, the Cave itself. Guests were greeted at the club's entrance by Eric Gill's provocative, playful bas-relief of an evidently male golden calf and led in, past Lewis's huge abstract depiction of carnival, 'Creation' (which later became 'Kermesse') positioned on the stairs, down into the realm of Spencer Gore's and Charles Ginner's hunting and jungle scenes and Epstein's caryatids – plastered iron pillars sculptured in relief and painted in brilliant colours. In the Cave's interior stood the idol of the calf once more, in a larger gilded sculpture by Gill. The associations with the primitive and animalistic in this subterranean haunt were unmistakable and the Cave echoed knowingly with the Old Testament story in which the Israelites 'offered burnt offerings and brought peace offerings; and the people sat down to eat and drink and rose up to play' (Exodus, 32: 6). Diners were placed at small tables set before the slim stage, where the cabaret ran through its own varied menu, and the evening wore on into the early hours. The night before it opened, on 26 June, the arena looked '"like a construction site or a ruin"', all was '"mortar and limestone dust"' (Strauss, 2001: 179). The panic was averted by Bokken Lasson, a friend of Strindberg's, who brought her own know-how and pierrot costume from the Cabaret *Chat Noir* she ran in Norway. Lewis's freshly painted drop curtain stuck to the stage floor and there was no electricity or gas for the planned 'artist's meal', but the show went on: Lasson sang to her own guitar accompaniment, Margaret Morris danced to Grieg, Señor Matthias danced 'dances fraught with the spirit of Spain and the passion of the Latin blood' and an actor read Wilde's *The Happy Prince* (*Sunday Times*, 30 June 1912; in Cork, 1985: 105).

Above all, it was the Cave's décor and associated graphics which gave it its integrated conceptual identity, extending from the massive wall paintings by Gore and Ginner and the contributions by Epstein and Gill, to the details of the membership card, also designed by Gill, and the advance advertising – a poster, preliminary prospectus, brochure, envelopes, a programme and menu designed by Lewis.[1] The brochure announced, manifesto style: 'We want a place given up to gaiety, to a gaiety stimulating thought, rather than crushing it' (Yale). Its patrons responded to the call for a season of after-hours revelry and the Cave drew on the broadest of arts, from music hall to magicians to Marinetti to keep them amused. And they too, its members and their guests, were as bold and as various as the cabaret – attired in evening dress, tweeds, 'or even flannels', one journalist noted, smoking cigarettes, and adding their voice in French, Spanish, Russian, German, Swedish to the 'babel of tongues' (Cork, 1985: 104). The Cabaret Club therefore appeared to pull off a magic trick of its own, mixing a cocktail of the popular and avant-garde, the English and the cosmopolitan. 'We do not want to Continentalise', the brochure continued, 'we only want to do away, to some degree, with the distinction that the word "Continental" implies, and with it the necessity of crossing the Channel to laugh freely, and to sit up after nursery hours' (Yale). Here then, in London, at last, was a cultural scene to equal if not surpass Paris, 'the first English Artists Cabaret', as the 'Preliminary Committee' announced to the press (Yale), set down in an underground corner of the imperial capital which was for now, at least, European. This localised heterogeneity operating below the surface of moral and cultural conformity is what gives the Cave its distinctive identity as a social and artistic space; the whole shaken into being by its shockingly adventurous but unified decorative scheme. Frida Strindberg inspired, and with Spencer Gore, orchestrated this scene. She was, as Ford put it, 'trying to build up a Palace of all the Arts', and doing therefore what modern artists were themselves, in other ways, trying to do (Strauss, 2001: 251). If the palace toppled after eighteen months – though Ford does not draw this comparison – it again shared its short life and poor management with other ventures, the

English Review and Rebel Arts Centre, for example, which he and other modern artists were involved in.

Meanwhile in the cockpit of the Cave, artists and beau monde, journalists, debutantes and guardsmen mingled in the presence of unashamedly modern art. They paced themselves through the Cabaret's nine course 'souper' at 5/- per person – if they were not favoured by the generosity of the Maitresse, and listened, on some evening in 1912 or 1913, to 'a gypsy orchestra or the strident tintabulation of a band of Coppersmiths... followed by a reading of Modernist poetry; a melodramatic declaration from the inexhaustible Frank Harris'; the dancing of Margaret Morris and her Greek Children and the 'less predictable' Betty May before 'Ford Madox Ford presented of all things, a series of shadow plays' (David, 1988: 116)

Of all things, a series of shadow plays. 'I wrote a shadow play for Mme Strindberg' said Ford, 'and had to act it myself in place of the lovely actress who should have done it. A too ardent admirer of Mme. Strindberg had stolen the manuscript because he could not bear to let my play be produced' (1932: 411).[2]

That cellar was gloomy, dim, and so cavernous that sounds seemed to die away in dim distances, though the place was not really so large.[3] *Behind my back the young people were talking in whispers. Madame was wavering towards us, a rather shapeless black shadow, coming deviously, between the little tables, her face gradually swimming up, chalk white /.../. A waiter in his shirt sleeves was at my elbow. He bore on a silver tray four admirable – four wonderful – sandwiches that contained immense prawns, a long-necked green bottle of Moselle and a tall, greenish drinking glass.*

I ate ravenously /.../ This was not of course my milieu, but it was extraordinarily soothing /.../ Above-ground people were disagreeably odd. Here everything was so foreign and so oriental that I asked even myself no questions. /.../ Madame too, drifted right across that dim illumination. She approached an irregular greyish column. Light existed – and a terrific white wooden pillar like a beaked man with a scarlet tongue – a Caryatid I think it is called. Other white caryatids existed all round me, more dimly, as if they supported the roof of that vast cellar. All had scarlet details, the heads of hawks, cats, camels, and the white of their paint gave small shining reflections. Madame, invisible, had I suppose switched on some electric light. A pinprick of light existed behind the sheet and grew to a pale glare, a flat black serpent wavered across, rather dimly. /.../

Madame drifted before me, a waiter carrying a chair behind her. She sat down, leaning half across my table and took the Gargantuan peach that was still beside my left hand. /.../ She said:

Nights at the Cave of the Golden Calf

'*The dinner was it good?*' *without looking at me. /.../ It had been a miraculous dinner. /.../ Madame had loosened her furs; her shoulders showed alabaster white, and her rounded oriental features. /.../ She had in her hair a necklace of enormous pearls. She said:*
'*Charles!* ... *But you are not Charles!*' *quite languidly. She added: 'Then you must be Mr. Jessop!*' *She had no aspect of caring in the least /.../
A waiter was at my elbow with a long, greenish document. It was folded down its length; a triangular corner turning up showing the figures £7 14 6. Madame reached slowly across the table and took languorously the long greenish document. She tore it into innumerable green-grey triangles and showered them over the head of the waiter. /.../
I suppose she took me for a kindred spirit. Alas, I was nothing so fine. For she was a kind, voluptuous, abstracted creature. Heaven knows what she thought about. /.../ I believe she was a millionairess, losing hundreds of pounds every night. For the love of Art? To brighten London? /.../ God knows!*

A high note, like the overtone of a bell, had been vibrating round that little pink cell from outside – for a second or two. And then there were hoots – sudden and very disturbing. It was then two minutes past eleven /.../ My shadow play was on ... The shadow play was imbecile in a silly class of thing – a burlesque of Romance. A man is attacked by a cobra and an assassin at the same moment. The cobra bites his little finger – which of course is irrevocable death; but at the pain he starts aside, and the descending yataghan of the assassin cuts off the little finger. So the hero is saved from his oriental adventures – the assassin was of course a Deceived Husband – and returns to Europe with a heroine from behind the grille of a harem, to open a tobacco shop.

This not very amusing story in my bombastic words Miss Honeywell declaimed. /.../ She reclined on her golden throne, gilded laurels in her hair, her face pallid and stiffened, like an ivory mask in the dim light that fell through the sheet, and black draperies ran from her, half across the stage, whilst the non-representational snakes, assassins, and harem-grilles wriggled across the illuminated sheet. She looked ten feet high!

And then, suddenly...I had not the least idea how she did it: the light did not even go out. She must have had a superb athletic physique; for there she was, crosslegged, in the middle of the stage, in front of the sheet, in scarlet trousers, rolling a cigarette, with a beam of limelight that George Heimann was casting on her. And you know she was just a little midinette, exclaiming with the voice and accent of a London typewriter girl – the half falsetto, piquant, ironic intonation:

'And who is This... this graceful figure, cross-legged and rolling the fragrant weed in the window of the Emporium, No 32 ... ' – and so on.

She looked so little and cockney and brave – who had seemed so immense, so classical, and so despondent. And the scarlet trousers and the tight sapphire blue bodice, the colour and the light!

Intellectually I know that she brought down the house, for the Guardees and stockbrokers and German Jews made her repeat the last seventy words of it three times running /.../

It was then half past one; and the place was dreadful; the thin air tight in the lungs; the lights too bright; the dreadful white pillars leering. /.../

Madame's negroid orchestra set up a crash of sound. Madame had South American mulattos, Barbadoes, quadroons, and Cuban octoroons, not to mention Bowery Buck negroes, in her orchestra already in July, 1914. The mad, bad tune of that day was 'All night long he calls her' – and the dance the tango, though that was really a misnomer for the South American Cielito /.../

I danced a great many dances with Miss Jeaffreson, who was an admirable person to hold, and whose step went exactly with mine, /.../ I danced with Marie Elizabeth; she did not dance well; she was too stiff....

And then there was Miss Hamnett. She arrived with Gaudier. And suddenly there were the others, Cournos, Aldington with Hilda and Ezra and Lewis who I'd imagined as a shadow fellow, a cloaked and steeple hatted replica of my George Heimann. He was gloomy, Byronic and violent, and incomprehensible. I had thought at one time that he was going to punch my head.

'Will you never smile, only grimace at us?' Nina had tried at him. 'Or will you dance?' She pouted the words of 'Popsy Wopsy' and twirled towards and away from Lewis, a small laughing thing in her short hair, her bright stockings and flat shoes like a girl's. They had met in Paris and she had danced there, naked, she said, or with veils, when Lewis was full of the idea of Blast.

Lewis was then with Kate Lechmere but ignored her. Violet had come in with them though she hated the bright lights and the paintings.

'Can you do nothing with him my dear?' she said, looking after Lewis.

'And who is this Brjeska?'

'He is doing a sculpture of Ezra. It is for South Lodge, they say'.

'Gaudier-Brzeska', said Aldington,' is probably the dirtiest human being I have ever known. And in this heat!'

Violet stiffened. 'His shirt is clean. On all occasions'.

'Is he really so poor? And why "Brjeska"?'

'He has taken his sister's name...'

'Though he is French and Brjeska is...'

'Polish'. It was Cournos. 'Sister, mistress – what does it matter? He is the most simple, generous soul. Why, he has given me a drawing and a sculpture I admired. That is why he is poor and will continue poor.'

'Isn't he adorable?' Nina again, laughing. 'In Putney we stole some marble and he will do my torso.'

'Ezra's head on Nina's body!' Aldington guffawed.

Brzeska brushed past them. 'Is that Murry?' he steamed. The young Middleton Murry had decided to run a magazine called 'Rhythm' with Katherine Mansfield. She had once acted as a commère at the Club. Not very well, it was said, though she looked very pretty in Chinese costume with her beautiful dark hair.

'It is Brzeska! not Bizeska!' Gaudier interrupted them,'My name is B r z e s k a!'. He stared at Mansfield, 'I will have nothing to do with your "Rhythm".'

The low room was full now of gesticulating figures, dancing, shouting while the primitive forms of ragtime throbbed through the wide room. Ezra was dancing alone. Was this a Vorticist dance? The Turkey Trot? The Bunny Hug? He moved slowly, rigidly against the beat. As he turned he offered Brigit Patmore his hand.

'Ezra I cannot', she smiled, 'you know I cannot'. He turned again expressionless, his hands spread out and his arms gyrating at angles until he approached Hilda, her head bent to catch the earnest words of Cournos.

'Come, oh my Philadelphians!' he called.

'No Ezra, I never could and you never could.' Pound turned again pointing his chin and was joined by Brzeska, leaping, his arms aloft.[4]

'London was adorable then at four in the morning after a good dance. You walked along the south side of the park in the lovely pearl grey coolness of the dawn'. The sparrows, then the blackbirds, then the thrushes became like the sounds of an orchestra and choir. 'Then as like as not, you turned into the house of someone who had gone before you from the dance to grill sausages and make coffee. Then you breakfasted – usually on the lead roof above a smoking-room, giving onto a deep garden. There would be birds there too. Those who cannot remember London then do not know what life could hold. Alas ... ' (Ford, 1932: 410)

Looking back on the pre war years I realise how lucky we had been. Our world seemed so secure ... I was young, beautiful – so everyone told me, though I always doubted it – and had exciting friends. The world seemed mine. (Patmore, 1968: 76)

The dancer and the dance

'I never much cared for the Golden Calf', remembered Douglas Goldring (1943: 70). He was one of the 'young men who danced' and after dinner and before going dancing, he liked to look in at a theatre or music hall, such as the Tivoli, the Oxford, or the Palace, where 'one could listen to Marie Lloyd, Vesta Tilley, George Formby, Little Tich, R.G. Knowles, George Robey, Victoria Monks – a whole galaxy of stars all of whom were at their brilliant best' (72). This was a taste Goldring shared with A.R. Orage, T.S. Eliot and with Lewis, who included the music hall comedians, actors and actresses, George Robey, Shirley Kellogg, Harry Welden, George Mozart and Gaby Deslys amongst the 'Blessed' in *Blast* (Tickner, 1997: 102). Ford, too, had made regular use of the music hall while editor of the *English Review*, effectively using the Shepherd's Bush Empire as his second office (Goldring, 1943: 32). Goldring had been Ford's secretary at the time and they shared, he says later, an 'enormous admiration' for the dancer Adeline Genée at the Leicester Square Empire. 'Her entries were incomparable. She thrilled the house from the first moment of her emergence from the wings on her miraculous toes' (72).

This was the ballet as Arthur Symons had understood it at the turn of the century. Like others, however, Goldring was electrified by a spectacular transformation in the world of dance in contemporary Europe. Above all, 'the wave of creative activity' Brigit Patmore saw sweeping across pre-war London brought with it the Ballets Russes, who performed in London for the first time at Covent Garden in 1911. Goldring continued to prefer Genée to the Russian performers but for Brigit Patmore, the Russian dancers, Nijinsky, Pavlova and Karsarvina, were unforgettable (1968: 75). Others, too, were full of admiration. During the Ballets' summer season in 1912, Lady Ottoline Morrell welcomed Diaghilev, Nijinsky and the designer Leon Bakst to her salon in Bedford Square – where at different times Henry James, Arnold Bennett, Lewis and members of Bloomsbury were also guests. 'She was entranced with the wild music of Stravinsky, the bizarre oriental sets and costumes of Bakst and, above all, the faunlike genius of Nijinsky.' 'Lady Morrell is so tall, so beautiful, like a giraffe', Nijinsky responded (Darroch, 1975: 125–6). John Gould Fletcher went 'at least a dozen times', three evenings a week, during the Ballets' last London season before the war at Drury Lane in July 1914. Here he saw Léonide Massine, Karsavina and Chaliapin and was thrilled by the 'great acting, great singing, great dancing, great music and great stagecraft', and 'fierce sensuousness of the naïve barbaric rhythm of semi-Asiatic Russia' (1937: 152–3). Massine had replaced Nijinsky in 1914 and returned with the Ballets after the war to become 'maître de ballet' and principal choreographer. Ottoline Morrell entertained the new company to jam and black tea at Garland's Hotel and invited them to Garsington (Darroch, 1975: 225).

In this way the Ballets Russes became an established ingredient in the consciousness of 'high Bohemia'. Tom and Vivien Eliot as sometime guests of this middle-class social set were magnetised. The woman called Edith in Eliot's 'Eeldrop and Appleplex' has elements, says Seymour-Jones, of his young wife Vivien and of 'Scheherazade', the subject of one of the troupe's most famous ballets 'inspired by the sexuality and exoticism of *fin de siècle* decadence'. By association, Vivien was 'sexuality incarnate' (Seymour-Jones, 2001: 194). Vivien had studied ballet technique and Brigit Patmore remembers how one Sunday, coming home from a dance hall in Queensway, Vivien fancied she could do a step like Karsavina and practised it in a chemist's shop with Eliot in studied support (Patmore, 1968: 85). On another occasion, in 1919, the three of them went with St John and Mary Hutchinson to see the Ballets Russes, and in 1922, when the company returned to the Coliseum (otherwise a music hall) Eliot asked Mary to arrange a meeting between himself and Massine – who appeared, he wrote 'more brilliant and beautiful than ever' (Seymour-Jones, 2001: 331). The meeting took place and Eliot was delighted. He praised this second 'golden age' of the Ballets Russes in the *Criterion* in 1923, hailing Massine's 'completely unhuman, impersonal, abstract' acting style, and 'in all probability', says Seymour-Jones, Massine visited Eliot in his private rooms in Burleigh Mansions, which overlooked the Coliseum where the Ballets Russes had performed (Eliot, 1923: 305; Seymour-Jones, 2001: 349).

The Ballets Russes was wild, bizarre, naive, barbaric, entrancing, beautiful. Alongside the dangerous appeal of this exotic other, the Eliots' ballroom dancing at Queensway on Sundays seems somewhat provincial. At least, recalled Patmore, Eliot didn't count *sotto voce* '*one*-two-three, *one*-two-three' (Patmore, 1968: 85). And at least, from the point of view of their dance partners anyway, unlike Pound, Eliot did take lessons. In this respect the Eliots were very ordinary and much like other young couples who paid to learn the new steps at the many new dance studios which sprung up across London. Eliot remembered this ordinariness in *The Waste Land*, not least in his 'O O O O that Shakespeherian Rag – / It's so elegant / So intelligent' borrowed from the music-hall song 'That Shakespearean Rag' of 1912. The typists and clerks of Eliot's London may not have gone to the Golden Calf, but they danced the same dances, including 'the grizzly bear' (which is mentioned in the music-hall song) and the 'bunny hug' and 'turkey trot' that Edgar Jepson saw Pound trying out at the Cave. Young working-class women, reports Evans, 'flocked to dance halls where young men would treat them to drinks and join in the faddish "tough dancing". The raw sexuality of dances like the slow rag, turkey trot, bunny hug, grizzly bear, and "shaking the shimmy" horrified the middle classes' (Evans, 1989: 161; and see Hargrove, 1998).

Both ends worked against the middle, as it were. The lower and upper orders in their equivalent cultural garb of the 'popular' and 'artistic' rubbed shoulders in the intermediary realm of suggestive dances, fads and fashion where all that was new mingled. 'Within days of the premiere of *Schéhérezade*', writes John Drummond, 'the combinations of blue and orange, turquoise and violet found their way to the dressmakers of Paris. Poiret and Paquin created "le style Bakst" and within a few weeks it was all the rage' (1985: 22). As ever, London followed Paris which on this occasion transported Russian goods. Thus it was that Brigit Patmore could see, on the same 'wave of creative activity', Pound and others 'launching a new movement in poetry' and Paul Poiret, the celebrated Paris couturier, 'launch[ing] a new style with colours and patterns inspired by the Russian Ballet' (Patmore, 1968: 75). And thus her thoughts on Nijinsky, Karsavina and Bakst glide within the space of a sentence to a memory of the 'evening dresses made in rich brocade and decorated with Russian–style crowns' she wore for nights at the opera or ballet (76). Other women, Violet Hunt and Kate Lechmere, amongst them, were similarly influenced. Violet Hunt adopted a 'Futurist' or 'Vorticist' costume – the terms were flexible (1926: 123) and Beckett and Cherry wonder if the fashionable 'oriental' gown of a kind 'popularised by Paul Poiret and the Ballets Russes' worn by Lechmere for press photographs at the Rebel Arts Centre was her own design or purchased in Paris (2000: 66, 130n.83). Nancy Cunard wore a design by Poiret at a ball when she persuaded Eliot into a rendezvous with her rather than dinner with the Hutchinsons (Seymour-Jones, 2001: 333).

The impact of the Ballets Russes on fashionable society was connected more broadly, therefore, with changes in manners and taste and thus, indirectly, with the innovative work in interior decoration and textiles at the Omega Workshops and the Rebel Arts Centre. This extended sense of creative activity was linked also to women's finding more confident forms of self-expression. By their very nature, dance and clothing are a medium for the display in public places of body shape and movement and therefore of a changing semiotics of sexuality. This took more modest and more explicit forms, of course, and the 'artistic', erotic or blatantly sexual meanings of dance and costume were frequently an issue. The avant-garde and popular and the polite and vulgar therefore moved in an uneasy consort together on the dance floor of society and in the mixed clientele of the Golden Calf. Here, as Osbert Sitwell remembered,

Figure 1 The Empire, Leicester Square, 1905

Figure 2 Sir William Orpen, *The Café Royal*, 1912

Figure 4 ABC Tearoom, 1901

Figure 3 Pagani's Restaurant, Great Portland Street, 1910

Figure 5 Ezra Pound, *c.*1913

Figure 6 Wyndham Lewis, *c.*1914

Figure 7 Henri Gaudier-Brzeska, *c.*1913

Figure 8 T.S. Eliot outside Faber and Gwyer, 1926

Figure 10 South Lodge, Kensington, in the 1910s

Figure 9 Church Walk, Kensington, 1957

Figure 11 Lloyds Bank, Cornhill, 1920s

Figure 12 46 Gordon Square, Bloomsbury

Figure 13 Frida Strindberg, 1915

Figure 14 Iris Barry

Figure 15 Vivien Eliot in the Eliot's flat in Crawford Mansions, WI

Figure 16 Lady Ottoline Morrell, *c.*1910

Figure 17 Anonymous sketch in the *Daily Mirror*, 4 July 1912

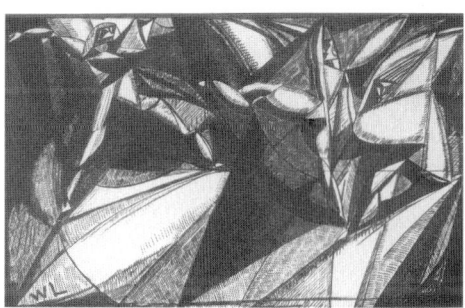

Figure 18 Wyndham Lewis, *Study for a Wall Decoration in the Cave of the Golden Calf*, 1912 (lost)

Figure 19 Wyndham Lewis, 'Cabaret Theatre Club Poster', 1912

Figure 20 A visit to Wilfred Scawen Blunt, 18 January 1914
From the left: Victor Plarr, Sturge Moore, W. B. Yeats, Blunt, Ezra Pound, Richard Aldington, F. S. Flint

Figure 21 In the garden at Charleston, 1928
Back row: Frances (Marshall) Partridge, Quentin Bell, Julian Bell, Duncan Grant, Clive Bell, Beatrice Mayor. Middle row: Roger Fry. Front: Raymond Mortimer

'the lesser artistes of the theatre, as well as the greater, mixed with painters, writers and their opposite, officers in the Brigade of Guards'. Past midnight it became 'a super-heated Vorticist garden of gesticulating figures, dancing and talking, while the rhythm of the primitive forms of ragtime throbbed through the wide room' (Sitwell, 1948: 208). In this mêlée, whether in clean or unwashed shirt, moved Gaudier-Brzeska, 'the archetypal Bohemian artist of the day' (Gregory, 1958; 108). In Ford's eyes, before he noticed Gaudier-Brzeska's 'personal beauty', he was indistinguishable from the 'crowd of dirty-ish, bearded, slouch hatted individuals, like conspirators'; he looked like 'one of those dock rats of the Marseilles quays' (Ford, 1921: 176, 180). But then, on another night, when this hot-house, high-life, low-life dive was raided by the police they found the place 'full of the wives and aged mothers of Cabinet Ministers' (141).

The popularity of dance prompted the rapid invention and adoption of new styles – chiefly from France and the USA and especially in the 1910s 'when America went dance mad' (Stearns and Stearns, 1968: 95). Among these styles, along with the tango and waltz, there were the Apache dance, associated, almost indistinguishably, with the stage and the street theatre of the gangs of Paris's Montparnasse; the work of the experimental solo performers, Isadora Duncan and Loïe Fuller, both Americans, both famous for the sensuality of their performances and sexual frankness of their personal lives; and the 'primitive' ragtime bands and dances from America's jazz capitals. All these were in some way in play at the Cave of the Golden Calf. As Lisa Tickner demonstrates, the figures in Lewis's *Lovers* echo the positions adopted in the 'Danse des Apaches' performed at the Empire Theatre and illustrated in a dance manual of the time (Tickner, 1997: 71). And judging from existing evidence, this influence could be said to extend to Lewis's works 'Creation' and 'Kermesse'.

But Isadora Duncan, too, had been known in London since she first danced there in 1909. Her free body movements, centred, as she argued, in the solar plexus, were a protest against the formal and supposed unnatural discipline of ballet, and along with her daringly flimsy costumes, libertarian sympathies and challenge to stock notions of femininity (she danced while pregnant) found a more receptive audience in Europe than in the United States. In Russia she impressed Lunarcharsky who was to become the Bolshevik Cultural Commissar ('she has broken through the limbo of...fossilised ballet', he said) and Mikhail Fokine who saw her in St Petersburg in 1904 and was, in 1909, to become Diaghilev's choreographer and *premier danseur* (Drummond, 1985: 21, 23).

Unlike Duncan, Loïe Fuller was untrained. Duncan's free style and Fuller's swishing veils were a likely influence on Nina Hamnett's readiness to dance naked or near naked (the opening programme of the Cabaret included a 'Veil Dance') while Fuller's inventive use of lighting would have set a standard for Ford's shadow play – and was even perhaps an influence on the spotlight segments of some of Lewis's studies for the Cave.[5]

Both Ford, in *The Marsden Case*, and Sitwell make mention, too, of ragtime at the Cave. The accompanying dance form according to Ford was the tango. The popular shows *Hallo Ragtime!* and *Hallo Tango!* opened in London in 1912 and 1913 and in its second season the Cabaret Club offered 'Tango Teas' in the afternoons and 'Champagne Tangos' at night, as well as weekly lessons (Strauss, 2001: 183). However, 'ragtime' appeared to serve as a generic name for 'jazz' and the Latin American tango was hardly a jazz dance – unlike the 'Vorticist' bunny hug and turkey trot. The latter had begun in the USA as rough 'animal dances' in the south and west and thence migrated to New York and Broadway where they were adapted or censored. 'Drop the Turkey Trot, the Grizzly Bear, the Bunny Hug etc.' instructed the well-known teaching duo Vernon and Irene Castle, 'These dances are ugly, ungraceful, and out of fashion' (Stearns and Stearns, 1968: 97). What the Castles meant was that these dances were Black – like the 'negroid' band Ford describes at the Golden Calf. The Castles replaced them therefore – so successfully that any family resemblance was wiped out – with a slower more 'civilised' dance, which they named the 'Fox Trot'.

Perhaps distinctions such as this did not matter much in the hullabaloo and social mix of an evening on the town. As Tickner suggests, contemporary audiences would have been familiar 'with current developments in the music hall, the Russian ballet, opera, the legitimate theatre and popular music' (1997: 83). It's true too that this heterogeneity of people, dress styles and dances is what Bohemia meant and made possible, and precisely what set it against normative codes of bourgeois society. However, this was also the moment of emerging and closely defended distinctions in the inner world of contemporary avant-garde movements, and it is difficult not to think these distinctions had their equivalents in the realm of a more broadly defined social aesthetic. The figure of the dancer evidently belonged to both worlds, to the canvas as well as to the cabaret dance floor. But if the 'revolution in dance' coincided with developments on both these fronts and was a part of what was 'modern' in the arts and society, it was not necessarily 'modernist' – not even in the way that American jazz and jazz dances could be seen as modernist. The difference could be seen, argues Paul Edwards, in the opposite positions taken in the journal *Rhythm*, launched in 1913 by Middleton Murry and the Scottish-born Fauvist, J.D. Fergusson, on the one hand, and Lewis's 'Kermesse' and associated studies of dance and dancers, on the other. *Rhythm*, says Edwards, was one of those manifestations of an idea of dance as retaining a 'primordial unity' of self and world and identified by Frank Kermode as emblematic of 'the Romantic Image' which Lewis would have found bland and sentimental (Edwards, 2000a: 82). In drawing on popular dance crazes, in the way that Tickner shows, Lewis was instead staging the 'sexual violence...more truly...released in Dionysian revels' (82). His model of cramped and crashing folk and popular dances upended the idea of ethereal unity and derided 'the genteel or merely pastoral visions of dance celebrated by Dalcroze, Diaghilev and Duncan' (82). At the same time, for all he set his face against the languid and balletic, Lewis's works of 1912, says Tickner, 'refer to a variety of contemporary dance forms' from the Apache dance to the Russian Ballet, to veil dances, Spanish flamenco and Breton folk dance (Tickner, 1997: 88–9).

'If I can't dance I don't want to be part of your revolution', famously declared the American anarchist, Emma Goldman. But what or whose revolution do we have in mind? In other words, after the cabaret and the polite dinner, when things got wild in the early hours, did Wyndham Lewis actually get up and dance? And if he did, how and who with? William Roberts remembered the 'provocative swagger' in Lewis's 'bearing...striding along, the broad shoulders slightly tilted, like a boxer advancing to meet an opponent' (Roberts, 1957: 470). This was all part of the act, of course, along with the practised grimace and costume of 'heavy overcoat and grey sombrero and scarf flung flamboyantly over one shoulder', but it was the pose of the intellectual pugilist rather than comrade or consort. You fancy Lewis would have challenged you to put up your dukes rather than join him in a turn round the dance floor. Or, rather, the invitation would have been to strut your stuff in the ring since dancing – for both Lewis and Roberts – was like fighting. Witness Kreisler, whom Lewis sends crashing through a ball in the novel *Tarr*, or his own and Roberts's paintings of aggressive, agonised or mournful dancers, now bunched together, now torn apart in contorted, combative relationships.[6] We might note, too, that while *Blast* blesses half a dozen music-hall stars, the list also includes six boxers (Young Ahearn, Colin Bell, Dick Burge, Petty Officer Curran, Bandsman Rice, Bombardier Wells; see Wees, 1972: 222–7).

Roberts, says his wife, liked to dance and was a good dancer (Cork, 1985: 244). All the same, he kept this between themselves, at home, as if the outside world was a bruising arena where you had to be on your guard. In a sense of course, this was more than explained by the aggressive circumstances of war-time modernity. Thus the dancers Lewis and Roberts and others showed on canvas, in poems, in the pages of novels helped reflect an altered modern subjectivity in which the body itself became the scene of depersonalised social technologies and self-estrangement. Anything else may well have seemed naive and sentimental.

So, then, how did Lewis dance? Like a marionette or flamenco dancer perhaps? In fact, only one dance seemed likely for Lewis – that of the gangland apache with its associated narrative, so like his own sexual adventures, of attraction, jealousy, betrayal, and violence. Still, there are one or two things to add to and subtract from this. Commenting on his own youthful 'cryptic immaturity', Lewis recognised that his social 'gaucherie' and 'wooden responses' (his silent moods with women friends) would 'erupt... with intensity and with the density of what had been diluted by ordinary discourse' (1984: 126). He might just explode, therefore, into aggressive dance action, arms jutting, legs kicking. But at the same time we know that Lewis's artist must disparage the uncontrolled display of passion. And could the artist then hope to dance the steely abstraction of his paintings? Also, trivial though it might seem, we should remember how Lewis dressed. He had his Brook Street tailor cut his clothes 'into the oddest shapes' (1984: 250) and Kate Lechmere says that before he bought a new suit for his role in the Rebel Arts Centre, he looked like the portrait painted by Augustus John. This suggests a dark jacket, moustache, hair divided in bangs and, in the familiar photograph from 1914, a silk cravat and pin (see Figure 6). C.R.W. Nevinson remembers an occasion, before the Cabaret Club had opened, when Mme Strindberg invited London society and its young artists to the opening night of a supper club. 'Many of us appeared... overdressed à l'apache', says Nevinson (Nevinson, 1937: 41). Maybe Lewis joined in this lark in fancy dress – he and Nevinson were friends at this time and in Nevinson's view he was 'essentially histrionic and enjoys playing a role' (56). It's unlikely, though, that Lewis would have earned the nickname 'l'apache qui rit' bestowed upon Nevinson in Montparnasse (65), principally because playing a role for Lewis meant being ahead of the type. Laugh or no laugh, Lewis would no more wear this stage tough-guy outfit, not at least without a heavy coat of irony, than don the floppy tie and velvet jacket of the effeminate aesthete.

If Lewis drew on popular styles and taste, therefore, this did not mean that his paintings were dance diagrams, or his writings melodramas, or that he looked like a cartoonist's idea of the artist. And if he distinguished himself in one direction from the popular, through the intellectual abstraction of his work, he maintained his singularity in another, in a disdain for the haute bourgeoisie whose very patronage he depended upon – turning up at a society dinner 'in ordinary clothes', as Nevinson remembers, was just one sign of this apartness (Nevinson, 1937: 58). All of which is to say that Lewis was not only not likely to dance, since it would risk too much exposure, but didn't actually need to. For one thing because he and his dancers were already everywhere on the walls of the Cave of the Golden Calf, in the stage curtain, in the programme notes, brochure and invitations he designed. The patrons all danced, that's to say, to Lewis's tune.[7] For another thing, Lewis didn't need the dance floor because he was very busy dancing after his fashion in another arena – in the dance of serial affairs he conducted with middle-class and aristocratic women, swirling them round in a repeated tango of passion, cruelty, indifference and separation.

Was there another way? Well, there was Pound's way for one. Stella Bowen reports how Pound evolved a 'highly personal and very violent style' with much 'springing up and down as well as swaying from side to side' (1984: 49). If his off-beat movements converted the turkey trot and bunny hug into a Vorticist dance, it's clear no one could partner or follow him. The Vorticist male dancer was fittingly the performing 'Egoist', the new title to be bestowed upon the previously named *New Freewoman* in January 1914. Then there was the example of Isadora Duncan. Her Romantic notion of a primary unity, released through the free and intuitive movement of the female body, was linked to a defiant nonconformity, critical at once of US materialism and sexual stereotyping. Perhaps she would have brought some other meaning to the 'Cave' than the phallic symbolism of the Golden Calf. And perhaps she offered an example to the new freewoman – though not if they followed the lead of the paper's editor Dora Marsden, none of whose contributions mentioned Duncan, nor mentioned dance, not even in an ethereal discussion 'Concerning the Beautiful'.[8] Others however, Jessica Dismorr among them, had already found a model in Isadora Duncan. (And is there not some echo of Duncan in the strong limbed, confident figure, her arms aloft, which Lewis drew for the Cabaret Theatre Club poster?) (Figure 19). Before her role in *Blast* and the Rebel Arts Centre, Dismorr had studied in France and was associated with the Fauvist painting of

J.D. Fergusson and the circle associated with *Rhythm*; an early number of which had carried a black and white etching by her of 'Isadora'. In 1912, when Dismorr exhibited at the Allied Artists exhibition, Katherine Mansfield became co-editor of the journal with Middleton Murry. The following year, in London, Duncan danced at the Trocadero and Fergusson met and married Margaret Morris, whose troupe performed across Europe and had appeared at the Cave with her Greek Children dancers. Rebecca West, in this nest of connections, recalls seeing Mansfield at the Golden Calf performing not very well as a *commère*, but looking 'very pretty in a Chinese costume' (Meyers, 1978: 77). This rival aesthetic wasn't entirely elbowed off the floor of the Cave by Lewis therefore.

And there was Rebecca West herself, a socialist feminist firebrand, 'a dark young maenad' and 'one of the two or three acutest critics in England', in Lewis's opinion (1984: 131, 217) and who at eighteen had become an associate editor of the *New Freewoman*. It was West who suggested Pound to Dora Marsden as the paper's literary editor. She had met both him and Lewis at South Lodge and became a life-long friend and supporter of Violet Hunt. Lewis took her to dinner and sat brooding silently (as he did with Kate Lechmere; Wees, 1972: 146; Meyers and Lechmere, 1983: 161). She praised his novel *Tarr* and contributed her own feminist Vorticism to *Blast* in the story 'Indissoluble Matrimony', though it's possible Lewis took the story without her knowing (Scott, 2000: 119–20).

In another very early unpublished story, West writes of the heroine, Adela, that she was 'not only a beauty: she was also that seething whirlpool of primitive passions, that destructive centre of intellectual unrest, that shy shameless savage, a girl of seventeen' (1992: 18). All Rebecca West's life, comments Antonia Till, this precocious, fiercely witty, clear-minded and highly politicised intellectual 'was susceptible to the charm and value of such minor arts as couture and jewellery, and alive to female beauty' (West, 1992: 8). Her writing attests to both. In another very early story in *The New Freewoman* in July 1913, the narrator responds to the dance in a café in Seville ('an extremely disreputable place') of 'Nana', 'a woman of about thirty five' who unlike three other dancers gamboling in red chiffon skirts 'wore a white silk shirt and black satin trousers'. She smiles a generous, bountiful smile, sings badly and performs a striptease. 'And there she stood.' Her nakedness is 'inspired' and 'wholesome' and not at all indecent, and the narrator applauds, wanting to rub against her 'as though I was a child'. The watching males smile as if in friendship but misunderstand (1913a, 26–7). In contrast, the heroines of a group of later stories from the 1920s are sophisticated show girls and cabaret dancers whose lives move between London, Paris,

Nights at the Cave of the Golden Calf 89

New York and Monte Carlo. Theodora in 'The Magician of Pell Street' dances at Rigoli's on Broadway. Ruth Waterhouse in 'Sideways' dances 'like running water, like wind in standing wheat: and she was covered with fame and legend and jewels' (West, 1992: 98). She collected evening dresses 'masterpieces of lace and tulle and satin that matched the masterpiece that was herself' (108). These women's lovers are shocked but reconciled to their 'colourful' pasts and careless ways with money. The men themselves, meanwhile, are plain dealing and home loving, like Izzy Breitman in 'Sideways' who was 'five feet in height! He was fat! He was funny. He was fussy ... the most grotesque partner imaginable for lovely, slender still Ruth' (101).

Rebecca West herself 'dressed flamboyantly' says Harold Orel (1986: 8). He has in mind Violet Hunt's description of her first visit to South Lodge: 'She had a pink dress on and a large, wide brimmed country-girlish straw hat' (Hunt, 1926: 203). 'She doesn't look like anyone else', adds Hunt, with 'her slightly academic air *tres chic*, worn with a Paris gown' (204, 205). Soon after her arrival in London she went to the Cave of the Golden Calf with Austin Harrison, journalist and editor of the *English Review*. The entertainment included a lecture by Frank Harris, rough-hewn editor of the *Saturday Review* in the 1890s, close acquaintance of Wilde, Beerbohm and Shaw and a member of the General Committee of the Cabaret Club. His lecture was 'On Style':

> I admit it was plucky of him, for he was very drunk. His manner was foully offensive: a barking arrogance with oily declensions at the points where he moved to speak of the necessity of the artist to feel pity and love – awful passages as though the Sermon on the Mount had kittened, and there were its progeny. But the thing that really horrified me was that his lecture consisted entirely of a criticism of an incident in *Madame Bovary* which that book does not contain. He had invented it. There is nothing in any of Flaubert's books remotely resembling it. I sat there with the intense solemnity of eighteen, horrified by this charlatan: and even more horrified by the way that not a soul in the room – and it was full of writers, Moore and Hueffer and Housman and Cunningham-Graham and s[u]ch – had detected him. So this, I thought, was London. (Scott, 2000: 37)

It seems unlikely that she stayed. But, if she did, on this or another occasion, how, after the cabaret and the supper and the talk were over, did *she* dance her kind of revolution? Would she have tangoed with Hueffer or Housman, flounced with Pound, or struck attitudes with

Lewis, her whirlpool of primitive passions matching the cut and thrust of his Vortex in a dance of sex antagonism?

Rebecca West, says Antonia Till, needed to recreate her own youth in her writing. And part of this life story was romance with a Byronic lover, a Heathcliffe or Mr Rochester (West, 1992: 6). A picture does emerge therefore, in which West's feminist, 'Devilish well informed and yet *tres femme*' (Hunt, 1926: 205) drifts towards Lewis's devilish superior, smoldering Tyro. But it is a picture. The real sexual dance, for West as for Lewis, was less this big-screen production than something untidy and more painful. In September 1913 she met H.G. Wells. He was 'small, plump and middle aged' (Glendinning, 1987: 46), already married and not a bit Byronic, but he became an obsession, as in later years did Max Beaverbrook. Almost immediately, in late 1913, she became pregnant. Though a product of and active contributor to this era of new art and new ideas, as Wells in his own way was too, she spent the last months of the life of the Cabaret Club in early 1914 out of public view in Hunstanton, Norfolk. She was there still when her story was published in *Blast* two weeks before the birth of her child and the declaration of war (Glendinning, 1987: 51–2). As ever, Bohemia was shadowed by the codes of bourgeois respectability and the horrors of 'daily life' the Cave had meant to escape.[9]

All this time too, from the beginning to the end of the life of the Cabaret Club, Frida Strindberg had been pursuing Augustus John. It was probably John who suggested she employ Spencer Gore and Lewis for the decoration of the Cave, and for a time Lewis was 'thick with Strindberg (in his way)' (John, 1952: 103–4). This strand of the story had, first of all, its own legendary outcome. The Club had been a financial risk from the beginning and within months it was clear that Strindberg's lack of business sense meant she could not pay her artists. One evening, so it is said, Lewis pocketed the money he was owed from the takings at the till. When Mme Strindberg confronted him he kicked her down the stairs. Richard Cork received this story in 1981, almost seventy years after the event, from Spencer Gore's son who heard it from his mother (Cork, 1985: 112, 306 n.190).[10] True or false, it's an inevitable legend, with the overstated symbolic truth of other such incidents. Lewis had kept quiet, so he said, about his mounting frustration at the way things were going, and true to character, as he came to describe his younger self, he had erupted, kicking out like one of his dancers. His only dance at the Club then, so far as we know, was a final round with its *maitresse de ceremonies*.

Frida Strindberg's real struggle, however, was with Augustus John. She had arrived in England in 1908 with behind her an experience in journalism, an acquaintance with European cabaret, a short-lived marriage with August Strindberg and a number of subsequent affairs, with, among others, Franz Wedekind. She also had two children – though they did not accompany her to London. In the Romantic bohemian John she saw another Strindberg, whose greatness, despite all hostility and resistance, she could serve. She was obsessed with both men and this trait, if little else, she shared with Rebecca West. In another of West's early stories, 'At Valladolid' (1913b) written for *The New Freewoman* after a first separation from Wells, the heroine, in despair over her lover, twice attempts suicide, by overdosing on veronal and by shooting herself. Frida Strindberg simulated suicide on at least two occasions by taking veronal and once threatened John with a revolver. This high melodrama carried over into both women's letters. Thus West wrote to Wells in March 1913 'During the next few days I shall either put a bullet through my head or commit something more shattering to myself than death ... You've literally ruined me ... You have done for me utterly. You know it' (Scott, 2000: 20–1). For her part Strindberg wrote to her daughter how she 'was under the influence of a great passion ... Twice I took Veronal which harmed no one but me. I don't know how often I wanted to die and died in spirit. It destroyed me completely. I was dead for years' (Strauss, 2001: 172–3).

John referred to Strindberg as the 'mad Austrian', the 'Wild Woman' 'the walking hell bitch of the Western World' (Strauss, 2001: 170–1). To her he was 'A magnificent animal, but wild' (172). In an age of Fauves ('wild beasts') and the cultivated primitivism of which the Cave of the Golden Calf was an example, the language of wildness was nevertheless evidently gendered. 'I was a pretty sadly tracked animal', Strindberg wrote to John after the war, though she was adroit enough to ask 'why madness should always adopt an unpleasant aspect' (John, 1952: 234–5).[11] Augustus John lived the wild life of a gypsy bohemian with two 'wives' with impunity. When Frida Strindberg appeared with her maid, Anushka, he eyed the maid and proposed they flee to the Pyrenees together (John, 1952: 116–17). His grand gestures – 'Alas and a million devils' as he exclaimed to John Quinn when Strindberg seemed to have bought a picture of his – and Quinn's brutal advice that he treat her with 'absolute, contemptuous indifference' (Strauss, 2001: 174) were all of a piece. If Strindberg's later letter to John is to be believed, her thoughts were gushing but desperately positive: 'I have been thinking of you often and never of one unpleasant hour. Every thought was beautiful and joyful' (John, 1952: 235). Strindberg did, however, have the edge, even if she didn't quite appreciate it. John's painting was precociously accomplished but increasingly conventional. By contrast she had a sure instinct for new talent. His attendance was counted on at the Cabaret Club where she had engaged a gypsy band to please him, but he famously passed on at the sight of 'the seething mob outside its doors, on the opening night' never to enter (John, 1952: 233).[12] What dance these two performed of hunter and hunted tumbled to a ragged halt. She re-made herself in the USA where she became a scriptwriter, lecturer, and virtual caretaker of Strindberg's complete works, installed in 58 volumes in the New York Public Library. Her memoir of Strindberg, *Marriage with Genius* (1937) meant, says her biographer, that 'She was no longer the woman behind the scene' but stepped 'out front as Strindberg's representative' (Strauss, 2001: 261). This does not sound much like stepping out front, though. Not compared with what, surely, had been her real independent art work – the lost creation in 1912 and 1913 of the 'palace of art' at Heddon Street.

5
1914: 'Our Little Gang'

Rebels, allies, enemies

Wyndham Lewis said how after 1914 he would never forget seeing the summer house in the centre of Soho Square upside down. He was introduced to this perspective by T.E. Hulme who upended him by the cuffs of his trousers on the railings opposite. This was after Lewis had 'seized Hulme by the throat' (Lewis, 1982: 36). Hulme's writings contain no comment on this legendary incident. And Lewis offers no further details or explanation other than to set this contretemps in a general picture of the 'big bloodless brawl' among artists and men of letters before the declaration of war. Henri Gaudier-Brzeska 'was spoiling for a fight' and had to be kept off the painter David Bomberg, while Bomberg and the sculptor Jacob Epstein settled another feud with a kiss and T.S. Eliot (after the war, but no matter, says Lewis) challenged St John Hutchinson to a duel. In another pre-war incident Ezra Pound had challenged Lascelles Abercrombie to a duel after Abercrombie had called for a return to the example of William Wordsworth. Fearful of Pound's famed skill as a fencer, Abercrombie proposed they throw unsold copies of their books at each other (Wilhelm, 1990: 117–18). Then there was the march on the Doré Gallery on 12 June 1914 when Lewis led a band of Vorticists or friends of Vorticism, or enemies of Futurism, in a counter *putsch* against the one-time ally and inspiration F.T. Marinetti and now determined Futurist, C.R.W. Nevinson, who had dared to hijack the movement. Gaudier-Brzeska who 'was very good at the *parlez-vous*' heckled Marinetti non-stop from a standing position while the Lewis party set up a 'confused uproar' in support (Lewis, 1982: 33). A letter to the *Egoist* denouncing Futurism and the turncoat Nevinson followed.

All this – what Lewis termed 'the next thing to barricades' (1982: 36) continued in the tradition of the inaugural row between avant-garde and bourgeois taste at the first performance of Victor Hugo's *Hernani* in 1830 – in which Théophile Gautier had worn his sensational red waistcoat: only now, in 1914, avant-garde set itself against avant-garde in a nervy prelude to real combat. Shortly after being upended in Soho Square, Lewis was to return to revising the novel *Tarr*. In 1915 he submitted to the discipline of an army uniform and haircut and experienced first-hand the shuddering transition from the staged battle of books of avant-garde factions in London to the crashing bombardments of Flanders fields. When Hulme was killed in 1917, Lewis witnessed the event from the next battery (1982: 99). He had no great 'personal liking' for Hulme's circle, he said, and restricted his opinions of Hulme to 'respectful, but no more than that' (1982: 107). Fate accordingly placed him at the appropriate symbolic distance of a quarter of a mile away; nearby, but as far apart as life and death. Again Lewis does not comment further. *Blasting and Bombardiering* does open though with a frank recognition of the association of art and war. Hulme's death, like Gaudier-Brzeska's earlier in 1915, confirmed the profoundly depressing truth, as it was bound to seem, that the new, savagely mechanical art had been in a way complicit with war. Lewis, like Ezra Pound, watched as their peacetime foes and confreres alike paid the price of this wretched bargain.

As J.J. Wilhelm paints the earlier incident in Soho Square it was an unequal combat between the 'brawny philosopher' Hulme and 'the frothing Bohemian' Lewis, who Hulme took by the scruff of 'his flowing scarf and cape' (1990: 148). But this was not Lewis's style. When he was not shouldering his way down Percy Street in his brooding Russian overcoat he cultivated the exacting look of the dandy who persuaded his tailor to assist in his self-fashioning. Kate Lechmere who sponsored his Rebel Arts Centre tells how he got her to buy him a new suit. This had 'a black and white check lining and a fold on the side of the trouser leg and a stitched band' (Meyers and Lechmere, 1983: 162). When Lewis presented himself in it, flapping open the jacket, she barely noticed – but knew this was a statement against the bohemian cliché of 'velvet jackets and floppy ties' (161). There was only one person Lewis took at all seriously who dressed like this – Ezra Pound.

In January at Kensington Town Hall the three men joined in a three-part presentation to G.R.S. Mead's theosophical 'Quest Society'. Lechmere reports how Hulme and Lewis mumbled their way through their talks and Pound, witty and confident, dressed 'in a velvet coat, red tie and framed by a halo of hair and beard', stepped forward to rescue the evening with his renderings of new verse (Jones, 1960: 123). The event has entered the record – in so far as it has, since it is not one of modernism's set pieces – in pretty sketchy terms.[1] This humdrum occasion, however (imagine the interior of Kensington Town Hall on a January evening in 1914), did deliver some momentous content. Hulme was newly returned from Europe armed with the theories of Wilhelm Worringer's *Abstraction and Empathy*. His lecture announced a new tendency towards abstraction and an accompanying anti-humanist sensibility which found its resources in the paradoxical combination of Egyptian and Sumerian art and culture and the modern machine. The result was a 'geometrical art' whose examples were Epstein and Lewis – who was sitting within touching distance. [2]

There's not much doubt that Hulme's new thinking was more important than Pound's verse renderings with a Yankee twang. If Pound rescued the evening from Lechmere's point of view, he was out of place from Hulme's, who hardly had Pound in mind as the new type of artist. Nor, in fact, was Lewis quite convinced that Pound suited his plans (Lewis, 1984: 138). Epstein records how Pound had tried Hulme's patience from the beginning. When asked how long he could tolerate him Hulme answered in self-mythologising fashion that he knew exactly when he meant to kick him downstairs (Epstein, 1955: 59–60). In this story Pound appears as the self-absorbed, pretentious aesthete to Hulme's no-nonsense philosopher of modern art. A.R. Jones, Hulme's early biographer and editor, makes even more of this antagonism. Pound liked to remember the time he put to Hulme a point on 'the difference between Guido's precise interpretative metaphor, and the Petrarchan fustian and ornament'. Hulme responded, Pound said, with a 'That is very interesting. It is more interesting than anything I ever read in a book' (Pound, 1934: 361). Jones assumes that Hulme treated Pound and his Imagism as little more than a joke, and that the tone-deaf Pound simply failed in this exchange to detect Hulme's 'contemptuous irony' (Jones, 1960: 34). We can never know. Nor could Jones. He takes sides in a battle over the making of reputations and the literary history of Imagism which F.S. Flint was to bring to public notice in the *Egoist* in 1915. Flint's article, which Jones sees no reason not to accept as 'a factual account' (34) claimed that Hulme, not Pound, was the originator of Imagism. The more standard account (Hugh Kenner proving more influential than F.S. Flint and A.R. Jones) has since come to credit Pound more than the others.

It is easy, on this as on other occasions, to sketch a more ravelled history, since everything suggests there were at different times different kinds of contributions to the new poetry and to making it known. And there were times too, surely, at the Eiffel Tower Restaurant or a Kensington or British Museum teashop or at Ford and Violet Hunt's South Lodge when there was a lot of talk and not much actually got said or done. There was, that is to say, an eagerness for change, a 'tendency' as Hulme had spotted, which stirred up animosities and alliances but ran through its ordinary and extraordinary days, or days which didn't yet know which they were – such as the January day which brought these three different figures together at Kensington Town Hall.

Jones decides on a history of fools and heroes and promotes Hulme as the instant leader of the contemporary 'metropolitan intellectual scene' (1960: 150). He based himself at Mrs 'Dolly' Kibblewhite's Georgian house in Frith Street (a former Venetian embassy) and held open house in its 'magnificent spacious lounge' (91). Pound had met both Lewis and Hulme by 1909 and Hulme had introduced him to Orage at the *New Age*. For both men Mondays meant the *New Age* editorial meetings at the ABC Restaurant in Chancery Lane or at Orage's table at the Café Royal, while Tuesdays meant Frith Street, followed by dinner at the Tour Eiffel Restaurant or the Sceptre Tavern and Chop House or on to the Café Royal.

Everyone at one time or another attended Hulme's Tuesday evenings: Sir Edward Marsh, Rupert Brooke and the Georgian poets, Pound, Aldington, Flint, John Cournos and the Imagist poets, Ford Madox Ford, A.R. Orage, Walter Sickert, Lewis, Gaudier-Brzeska, Jacob Epstein, Spencer Gore, C.R.W. Nevinson, Robert Ross – Oscar Wilde's literary executor, D.L. Murray – a fellow member of the Aristotelian society, Richard Curle – Conrad's biographer, Ramiro de Maetzu who later became Spanish Ambassador to the Argentine, the philosopher Henry Slominsky, the poet W.H. Davies, the artist Charles Ginner. Jones mentions all of these and more. We're put in mind of Nick Carraway's list of guests at the magnificent parties held by Scott Fitzgerald's Jay Gatsby, the mid-westerner who went to war and then to 'Ogsford' and became a myth – busy creating the platonic idea of himself, a sober visionary in a world of revelry. Hulme was a teetotaller and a bit of a ruffian but didn't have Gatsby's serious criminal 'connegtions', nor did he sum up a national psyche. The 'myth' Jones sets out to verify, does, all the same, remain mysterious. This is partly due to the sketchy account we have of Hulme's early years, much of it derived, even after Robert Ferguson's new biography (2002), from Michael Roberts's early short account of 1938. Born to a farming family in North Staffordshire, sent down from Cambridge in 1904 for heckling the actors at the Cambridge New

Theatre, lumber-jacking in Canada, studies in the philosophy of art and culture, reading and translating Bergson and George Sorel's *Reflections on Violence*. He tried and for a second time abandoned formal academic study for contemporary intellectual life in Europe and once in England gave a lead to the Poets' Club and set up his salon at Mrs Kibblewhite's. He resembled Henry VIII and had the candour of Samuel Johnson, reports Jones (1960: 92, 94). There 'was something Prussian-looking about him', says Roberts (1982: 26). Anthony Quinton terms him a 'muscular intellectual' (1982: i); he was, said Epstein, bulky in manner and build – 'with legs like a racing cyclist', Lewis noted (Lewis, 1982: 105). He was genial, kindly, charming, aggressive, argumentative, dogmatic, plain, honest, ironic, rude, polite, truculent and talkative; a genius, an astonishingly original mind, a second-hand philosopher. Such are the opinions of visitors to Frith Street and such was the figure who returned again from Berlin in late 1913 to present his thoughts on a paradoxical modern primitivism at the Kensington lecture.

Similar thoughts had been emerging in discussions in the *New Age* at the end of 1913, but it was really Hulme's uncompromising case for an epochal shift towards abstraction that gave it definition. Pound, for one, fell rapidly into step. In one of his most intense essays he reported on Hulme's lecture in the *Egoist*. The lecture had been 'almost wholly unintelligible' but in Hulme's thinking and in the temper of the times, Pound detected the emergence of a new art, especially a 'new wild sculpture', and a new artist, 'who recognised his life in the terms of the Tahiytan savage ... equal to that of the bushman'. Civilisation is defunct and brainless, he concludes, and 'we who are the heirs of the witch-doctor and the voodoo, we artists who have been so long the despised are about to take over control' (Pound, 1914a: 67–8). Earlier, in the first number of the *Egoist*, Lewis's 'The Cubist Room' had promoted the work of Etchells, Hamilton, Wadsworth, Nevinson and himself as a revolutionary group, whose profound, seismic analysis of the 'geometric bases and structure of life' took art beyond Futurism and cubism (Lewis, 1914: 9). And in March Gaudier-Brzeska joined the ranks of those on the side of artistic abstraction and the 'the barbaric peoples of the earth' against cold reason and the Greek legacy (Gaudier-Brzeska, 1914: 118).

At this point Gaudier-Brzeska had already begun work on the hieratic head of Pound which was to stand in the Whitechapel Gallery and then gather moss in Violet Hunt's garden – some distance from its inspiration in the statues of Easter Island. In June, Pound offered the highest praise for Lewis as 'a man at war' with his age to whose emerging 'youth-spirit' he nevertheless gave abstract expression (Pound, 1914b: 233). Hulme arguably gave a significant lead to this thinking. However, he came soon to think Lewis belonged to a dilettante, gratuitous and incoherent abstractionism (Hulme, 1914: 661–2). His favoured examples were Epstein and David Bomberg, both of whom were careful not to sign up to Lewis's foremanship. Nevinson too, though he named the new journal, betrayed the movement for Futurism. A letter sped its way to *The Times*, the *Egoist* and other papers, disassociating the new movement from Marinetti's Futurism and from Nevinson, who was twice damned for having used Rebel Arts Centre notepaper. In November 1913 Lewis had attended a dinner in Marinetti's honour with Etchells, Hamilton, Wadsworth and Nevinson. On 12 June 1914, he and others set out after a hearty meal to disrupt the Futurist gathering at the Doré Gallery. Interestingly, Hulme was named as one of Lewis's party (Lewis, 1982: 33).[3] Rivalries and pacts were intricate, intense and casual all at once, patterned by an unstable mixture of principle, personality, comradeship, spite and insult. Such was the tenor of these restless and inventive times on the eve of war.

What was at stake in a sense was a name: cubism, Futurism or Imagism. Whatever the differences between these movements, including the geometric semi-naturalism favoured by Hulme, the new journal Lewis was launching was not as yet aware of them. As late as April in two advertisements a fortnight apart it was advertised in the *Egoist*, for example, as discussing 'Cubism, Futurism, Imagisme and all Vital Forms of Modern Art'. But then by 13 June *Blast* was announced in the *Spectator* as 'The manifesto of the Vorticists', the 'parallel movement' to cubism Expressionism, and Imagism and the 'Death blow to Impressionism and Futurism'. When Pound hit upon the term 'Vorticism' it suited the arch-individualist Lewis to think of himself as the charismatic Vorticist leader at the still point of the Vorticist whirlpool (Goldring, 1943: 65). There was an emerging Vorticist 'group' all the same, as Pound emphasised in December 1913 to William Carlos Williams, identifying Gaudier-Brzeska and others as 'our little gang' (Paige, 1971: 27). The Vorticist arts, Pound was to theorise, were joined in a common aesthetic through their attention to their 'primary pigment' (1970: 88). The same unifying motive encouraged him towards the end of 1914 to consider launching a College of Arts which would recruit Lewis, Gaudier-Brzeska, Arnold Dolmetsch and Alvin Langdon Coburn, the photographer.[4] The term 'Vortex' which he had used in the letter to Williams was a fitting one for both the artistic practice and the movement: a vibrant compound of alliances and divergencies, 'a radiant node or cluster...from which through which and into which ideas are constantly rushing' (1970: 92).

The 'little gang' of Vorticists included a heterogeneous mixture of arts, nationalities and ethnicities – with William Roberts, Epstein, Wadsworth, Gaudier-Brzeska, Pound himself and Lewis at its core – who put together the premises of a experimental art based in the metropolis. Lewis bridled at what he felt was Hulme's attack on him in the *New Age*. Even up to the assault on the Futurists, however, Hulme might have been thought one of the gang. A month later, though, with the appearance of *Blast*, he was out of it.

There are two other things to comment on here. The many guests attending Hulme's evenings, as reported by Jones at least, were, all but one, men. Similarly, Vorticism's most publicised exponents (even those who stood at its boundaries like Epstein and Bomberg) were male artists. The artistic programme and the men were indeed made for each other (see Tickner, 1992; Beckett and Cherry, 2000). For all that the new art was an intended escape from the humanised body and the fuss of human sentiment, a welter of masculinised forms and emotions were impressed upon the canvas or cut into stone along with the turmoil of the times. Pound's name for the new movement brought those latent emotions to the surface. Whatever its earlier provenance 'Vorticism' came to mean the pulsing engine of the new art – thrusting the new 'into the vortex' (1970: 117) and 'the great passive vulva of London' (Pound, 1958: 204). Such was the phallic logic of Pound's psychogeography. The 'marble phallus' as Lewis frankly described it, of Gaudier-Brzeska's hieratic head of Pound was displayed in May 1914 (Edwards, 2000b: 44); Epstein's 'Rock Drill' combined his obsession with sex and new technology. The masculinised aggression and sexuality of the new art were blatant.

On this score, the estranged Lewis and Hulme had much in common. As Jones concedes, Hulme's attitude towards marriage and women was 'basically Victorian' (1960: 118). Like Lewis he compartmentalised women into wives and mothers, on the one hand, and sex and 'shop girls' on the other. Lewis's compartments of bourgeois and bohemian women were perhaps more refined,[5] but had the same effect: to sanction the use of women for sex and protect the world of art and ideas for men. Lewis suggests Hulme tried to draw him out on his sexual attitude and conquests: 'He would cock an eye, sneer and throw out an inquisitive hint' (1982: 107). Not surprisingly, Lewis was as guarded in his conversation as he was in his actual sexual exploits. So the two sparred with each other, art-school dropout and rusticated undergraduate; rival campaigners for the new art but joint opponents of an effete Bloomsbury who called in outsiders to do the 'rough and masculine' work for them.[6]

Elsewhere, Hulme referred to Fry's 'faked stuff' and wrote how the dissenting *New Age* art critic, Ludovici, 'needed a little personal violence' (Hulme, 1994: 661, 260). They did not need to swap notes on their sexual conquests because they were reading from the same script; both of them 'rough bohemians' who wore their heterosexuality on their sleeve – or elsewhere about their person. While Lewis chose a personally tailored suit and pin in his silk cravat, Hulme sported a knuckleduster – apparently made for him by Gaudier-Brzeska. It was 'a sex symbol', said Kate Lechmere (Hutchins, 1965: 125) as if this clears his name of a reputation for violence, when in fact it compounds sexuality with aggression and the art object. You can almost hear Hulme rhythmically cupping his knuckleduster in his hand, thinking what Bloomsbury needs.

Kate Lechmere, so far a witness, plays a vital role in this story. When Lewis walked out of the Omega Workshop it was to lead the Rebel Arts Centre, funded by Lechmere and opened in Spring 1914 at 38 Great Ormond Street, just off Queens Square in the enemy territory of Bloomsbury (see Cork 1985: 190–204). Lechmere had known Lewis since 1912 and wrote to him from Nice in 1914 with the idea of an atelier of which he would be the professor (Wees, 1972: 68). The result, named probably by Lewis, comprised a large exhibition, lecture and meeting room, a picture store and office and an upstairs apartment for Lechmere. The press were enthralled with its lemon walls, gold curtains, red doors and 'dreamy blue' carpets (Wees, 1972: 68; Beckett and Cherry, 2000: 64). There were plans, at least, for the production of decorative works – Lechmere is said to have made curtains and clothes – and fans, scarves and a table were later exhibited so that, to this extent, the project presented itself as a would-be alternative to Fry's Omega Workshops. It charged a guinea per annum for membership and for this there were open days on Saturdays accompanied by cakes and tea, served (naturally) by Lechmere or some other woman, and lectures – by Marinetti, who came, and by 'Schoenberg or Scabine' who didn't, and by such as Pound and Ford, who felt the symbolic blow of one of Lewis's canvases on his head as he talked of Impressionism or some other heresy. Lewis hid the canvases he was working on in the side room, so that when the Pounds came on Saturdays, only Ezra could see and try to fathom them (Stock, 1970: 99). Vorticism as such was not publicly invented until June 1914 but Lewis was brewing up the idea of a journal and Nevinson who joined the Rebels' cause – and wanted no 'damn women in it' (1937: 76) – found the name for the magazine on his lips. Damn and Blast!

Lechmere herself was out of sympathy with Vorticism and increasingly with Lewis who insisted she dress professionally, in the white blouse and long dark skirt of 'a high class shop girl' (Wees, 1972: 146). She could not paint in such circumstances and there were mounting problems over money. Lewis grew neglectful and insulting and her letter of late July rebuking him for losing 'your self command & using such ugly insulting language' (Beckett and Cherry, 2000: 63) conveyed how cool things had grown between them. She had met Hulme at Kensington in January and later that year when he called at the Rebel Arts Centre they 'clicked' reports Cassidy (9 January 1954 interview). Hulme proposed, apparently, in an ABC Restaurant (Cork, 1976: 160) which it's tempting to think was the same one in Chancery Lane where the *New Age* held its regular meetings, but there's no knowing. When he heard of this Lewis rushed off to Soho Square. Did he want Kate Lechmere or the Rebel Arts Centre? What he feared most of all, it seemed, was Epstein taking over: 'Hulme is Epstein, Epstein is Hulme' he repeated to her (Cassidy, 1954 interview). With this in mind he raced off to strangle Hulme.

The story of Soho Square has been told many times – remarkably, given its source in just two sentences from Lewis. It suits us to think of Lewis and Hulme coming to blows. Did it really happen we wonder.[7] Was it in jest or in earnest? Did Lewis barge into one of Hulme's Tuesday evenings demanding satisfaction? Did Hulme judge this the moment to kick him, if not Pound, downstairs and frog-march him to Soho Square? Did anyone follow them from Frith Street? And who let Lewis down from the railings? Did someone call the police? Did someone call the press? After all, the *Daily Mirror* had followed the course of the Rebel Arts Centre. Here was a jape worth a picture you would have thought. *Blast* was due out, and Lewis stepped forward as the propagandist for the new movement. The press were avid for news of its 'arch-exponent' (Lewis, 1982: 32, 36). Perhaps Lewis thought there was a picture in it too. One of those upside-down modernist pictures.

What of Kate Lechmere? She chased after Lewis, she said, pleading for him not to kill Hulme (Jones, 1960: 123). Did she laugh when she caught up with them? Did she join Hulme back in Frith Street? Not in Dolly Kibblewhite's presence. And what kind of alternative, anyway, was Hulme who, so Jones reports, felt a woman's place was in the nursery not the artist's studio. Surprisingly, given her tart reaction to Lewis's ugly behaviour, Lechmere agreed with Hulme's views, says Jones once more (125).[8] We end with a further mystery therefore. Lechmere (or is it Jones?) asks us to appreciate how an Edwardian woman artist could be both a Victorian and a modern woman. Hulme and Lewis were similarly strung across the conformities and stereotypes of one era and radical inventiveness of another. Their desire to lead the new art movement and possess the woman artist-patron were in a crooked sense one. Out of such tensions sprang the scene in Soho Square.

The after-effects left Lewis without the Rebel Arts Centre and without Kate Lechmere. Hulme got the girl, Lewis the fame. Lechmere was blessed in *Blast* but otherwise not represented.[9] Her memoir of the Rebel Arts Centre remained unpublished until the 1980s and the record of her work as an artist and designer is extremely thin. Hulme too was shut out. He had been marginalised in Pound's Imagism and was entirely absent from the pages of *Blast*[10] and the contemporary accounts of Vorticism's geometrical art. It is difficult not to detect some revenge upon an enemy who, in another turnabout, Lewis was ready in 1937 to see as the theorist of his own practice: 'All the best things Hulme said about the theory of art were said about my art', he asserted, 'We happened...to be made for each other, as critic and "creator"' (1982: 100). Even then we might feel there is some elbowing for position, since for Lewis to enlist Hulme to his cause once more displaces Epstein – the artist Hulme just might have thought he was theorising.

Bohemian girls and new freewomen

She was unmistakably striking – her height emphasised by her diminutive companion, though you looked from one to the other and were meant to take them as a pair. Both had had their hair cut short; their make-up was theatrical and they were dressed to shock their mothers and please themselves, one in pantaloons narrowing at the ankle, the other in a patched skirt affair you could imagine someone had run up in Fry's workshop. And both were smoking. John was immediately interested and was already painting them in his mind. He'd stopped talking and caught Nevinson's eye. 'Nancy!', said George Moore brightening, 'well here you are!'

The entry of Nancy Cunard and Iris Tree into the Café Royal 'in all probability' for the first time in 1914 is one of those legendary moments of London's café society (see David, 1988: 112). The one sure memory, though it is of a first rapturous sighting and not necessarily of the first visit of the two women, is that of the 22-year-old David Garnett, later novelist and publisher:

> I was with Francis Birrell talking I think to 'Saki', or to Geoffrey Fry in the Café Royal when a party came in with one or two of Sir Herbert

Beerbohm Tree's daughters and stopped to greet my companions. With them was a young girl – Nancy – who made a great impression on me. She was very slim with a skin as white as bleached almonds, the bluest eyes one has ever seen and very fair hair. She was marvellous. (Ford, 1968: 26)

In 1914 Nancy Cunard was eighteen. Everybody in those years, as later, noticed her blue eyes ('sapphire', 'arctic', 'untroubled'), her fair hair (like 'pale sunshine'), extreme thinness, gliding, confident walk and high squeaky voice. Nevinson, who was a habitué of the Café Royal, had been aware of her at earlier functions when he and Lewis were being lunched and dined by 'all the rich and great of the land'. She 'was then about fifteen or sixteen, the brightest, prettiest and naughtiest little girl, with a vivid intelligence that often embarrassed her mother' (Nevinson, 1937: 58). What both he and Garnett spotted in Nancy Cunard was the rebel. And what Garnett could see, aside from her appearance, was that there was something remarkable in her simply being there. Unattended women at the Café Royal were either, with some ambiguity, dancers, artists' models, or prostitutes. The legend which remembers Nancy Cunard and Iris Tree making an entrance alone (Garnett suggests they were in a party) emphasises the shock of their newness. But if they weren't the usual type, what were they? Garnett comments:

The world she inhabited was that of the rich and smart and the gulf between us seemed then unbridgeable. But the fact that she should appear in the Café Royal at all, even without her mother's knowledge, might have made me see that it was not. (Ford, 1968: 26)

Garnett forgets Iris Tree in his fascination with Nancy Cunard. And if the cultural memory echoes this occlusion, in making their symbolic entrance into the Café Royal in the hot early summer of 1914, the two teenage friends (were they girls or women?) chose jointly to defy their mothers and step out of their class into another social realm. And not simply into an artistic realm, since this wasn't a reading in Yeats's rooms, for example, but the disreputable domain of artists and artist types – 'bohemians' in short – which Stella Bowen on her first accompanied visit saw as 'a sink of iniquity' (Bowen, 1984: 36). In fact of course the Café Royal wasn't exactly the scene of temptation in 1914 it had been in an earlier era, and its seedy opulence wasn't likely on its own to satisfy adventurous young women. Adrian Allinson's picture of 'The Old Café Royal' shows both women firmly installed here, though Nancy is noticeably in the foreground and Iris Tree barely distinguishable, but in fact they ranged further afield, and Nancy, certainly, was to help make the reputation for the next generation of the Eiffel Tower Restaurant, off Tottenham Court Road. At this earlier date, too, there is a strong sense that it was all a bit of a dare, and, most importantly, a flight from home to some 'fugitive haunt unknown to our parents' (Ford, 1968: 18). As Iris Tree remembered: 'we were bandits escaping environment by tunnelling deceptions to emerge in forbidden artifice, chalk white face powder, scarlet lip rouge, cigarette smoke, among roisterers of our own choosing' (18–19). They made their way across London's bohemian landscape, from the Café Royal to Bloomsbury studios, the 'coterie' organised by their friend Diana Manners, motor bike rides with 'stray Tommies', the Cheshire Cheese, pubs in Limehouse, river barges and cab shelters. 'I wanted to run away and be a vagabond', Nancy Cunard had confessed to George Moore as a young girl (6) and both women prepared themselves for this roaming lifestyle in a studio they secretly rented in Fitzrovia and stocked with theatrical make-up and a wardrobe of fancy dress clothes (Fielding, 1974: 49).

Daphne Fielding, Iris Tree's biographer, comments that she 'was the most truly Bohemian person' she had ever known – 'totally unconcerned about public opinion, material matters and conventional society' (13). Rupert Hart-Davies, among others, remembers Nancy Cunard was 'very "Bohemian" in her habits' (Ford, 1968: 29). Gaudier-Brzeska was a bohemian of the type Henri Mürger would have recognised: poor, dedicated to his art in a way that made his poverty tolerable. If he was the 'archetypal bohemian', in Amy Lowell's eyes (Gregory, 1958: 108), Cunard and Tree could only be bohemian in another sense. Theirs was plainly a well-heeled unconventionality, all too obviously free in fact of any concern about 'material matters'. Their bohemian rebellion was defined, accordingly, precisely by their privileged family background and by the additional fact, not simply that they were women, but young upper-middle-class women born to the new rich in Edwardian society. They were debutantes who 'came out' in a different society to the one their parents had in mind. And once we identify them in this way as financially liberated women who used their freedom to join, indeed in some ways give a lead to, a new rebellious generation, we can see other differences between themselves and their women friends and contemporaries.

Nancy Cunard was the daughter of the English baronet and inheritor of the fortunes of the Cunard shipping line, Sir Bache Cunard, and his younger wife, a Californian heiress, who was to change her name from

Maud to Emerald. Friends advised her that as an American she should not attempt directly to enter London society. Instead she played hostess to that society at Nevill Holt, the couple's country house in Leicestershire. Here Nancy Cunard's life alternated between long periods of solitude when she was in the care of servants and governesses and the sudden activity of the season which her mother returned to orchestrate. Her 'first friend' was George Moore who took a somewhat self-serving interest in her education, and who some speculated was her actual father (Chisholm, 1979: 15). When she was fifteen her mother left Sir Bache and the Leicestershire home for London and there entered into an intimate but scandal-free relationship with the married, rising conductor, Thomas Beecham. This handed Nancy the licence to do as she liked – or so she is reported to have said to friends (31). She had met Iris Tree at an experimental private school in London, completed her education in Munich and Paris, but after the bohemian outings in pre-war London, in 1915 married the gallant but conventional middle-class young officer, Sidney Fairbairn. The relationship lasted 20 months. Was this a distorted parody of her mother's example, or an impulsive escape from her control?[11] Her mother's influence was all-important but ambiguous, for what she also introduced her daughter to were the arts, including the figure of her admirer, George Moore. This ambience changed too. At Nevill Holt, the house-guests had included titled members of old families, leading politicians and, among writers, establishment figures such as Edward Marsh, Alfred Austin and Somerset Maugham (13–14). At her London home in Cavendish Square, fashionably decorated after the style of Bakst's designs for the Russian Ballet, Lady Cunard extended invitations to the Sitwell brothers, Tommy Earp, Ezra Pound, C.R.W. Nevinson and Wyndham Lewis.[12] These young rebel artists presented Nancy with the prospect of a life and contacts of her own. Her first poems appeared in the Sitwells' *Wheels* in 1916 and in 1918 she shared an Oxfordshire house with her 'liberator', Sybil Hart-Davis, and the latter's children. Here she wrote poetry and, as one of the children remembered, life seemed a 'perpetual party' (Ford, 1968: 29).

Iris Tree was also a close friend of Sybil Hart-Davis. She didn't need to make the radical break that Nancy Cunard did, however. Her home life was shaped by the increasingly celebrated actor-manager Beerbohm Tree and his sometime actress wife, and was directly rather than indirectly or 'bogusly' artistic, in Lewis's term. Beerbohm Tree had built Her Majesty's Theatre in the late 1890s and held supper parties there for persons of rank and style in 'High Bohemia', and for writers and artists, including Oscar Wilde (Fielding, 1974: 32). Iris wrote poetry from an early age, as accomplished young women did, and went to the Slade School of Art when she was seventeen. There she met Dora Carrington and was introduced to Bloomsbury. She was one of the first young women to bob her hair and scrupulously monitored her appearance for the ways it fell short of her ideal. Her father indulged her fantastical theatrical imagination while her mother came to indulge his philandering and gave her attention to her children. All this, quite unlike Nancy Cunard's young life in detail and quality, Iris Tree remembered as a formative idyll: a time of 'unalloyed happiness' in Fielding's words, 'provided by beloved and loving parents' (43).

There were other broader distinctions too. For these two young women's lives, touching but divergent as they were, found a place in a regime of artistic patronage which included Lady Diana Cooper, Lady Drogheda, Lady Low and Ottoline Morrell. On a lower social rung, there were the house parties, teas and readings organised, for example, by Violet Hunt ('a poor woman's Lady Ottoline Morrell' in Glendinning's opinion; 1987: 39), Mrs Fowler and Olivia Shakespear in Kensington. These gatherings, orchestrated by middle-class women, were different again from Bloomsbury 'at homes', evenings at Hulme's Frith Street address, or at Yeats's or Pound's rooms, or those held in cafés and studios. Mme Strindberg was a further exception – or another kind of bohemian. She had no aristocratic pretensions, no money to speak of, no country or town house in which to entertain, but could claim an artistic pedigree, and, certainly, an experience of the avant-garde in Europe sufficient to inspire something new in London. Often she seems like an unacknowledged forerunner to this later generation of artistic, strong-minded, but vulnerable younger women.

Nancy Cunard and Iris Tree therefore stepped out as the rebellious products of one internally differentiated section of the English upper middle-class. They carried their wealthy, somewhat hypocritical, sophisticated and artistic backgrounds with them to the Café Royal. Some of its customs and manners they left at the door, some they could not shed so easily. What shadowed them, in particular, in the shape of their mothers, were the conventional irregularities, as we might say, of their class towards sex, home and marriage – including the role of the mother and the idea of motherhood.

Marriage, especially, and the status it conferred had been a vital issue, plainly enough, for an older 'new woman' and suffragette such as Violet Hunt and a moderately liberated woman such as Olivia Shakespear when thinking of her daughter. The more outrageous Mme Strindberg was haunted by her short-lived relationship with the playwright, and continued to use his name after their divorce. And for all their differences, marriage and its associations of financial solvency and social respectability, dogged the lives of younger new women. Estranged from her husband in the early 1920s, Brigit Patmore needed to conduct her relationship with Richard Aldington away from London in Europe (Patmore, 1968: 103). Rebecca West, 'New Woman though she was', thought of escape from home and family in terms of marrying (Glendinning, 1987: 49). Her affair with H.G. Wells and having a child brought shame and disappointment to her mother. 'How I wish', grieved West in later life, 'I could have made her happy by marrying early and never meeting H.G.' (51). Marrying, Glendinning confirms, 'was the only acceptable reason for a young girl to leave home' (49). Women such as H.D., Mary Butts and Iris Barry, like Nancy Cunard, embarked consequently upon short-lived marriages dictated by a confused mixture of convention, pique or impulse. The alternative was an 'unacceptable' bohemian life-style as unmarried mistress and/or mother or lesbian partner. The change of name by Rebecca West (born Cicely Isabel Fairfield) and Iris Barry (born Iris Crump) and the spelling of Helen Saunders name as 'Sanders' in *Blast* 1, was a double mark, in all this, of a bid for independence and the strong influence of the family's respectable 'name'.

Many of these women did of course choose the bohemian option, and this entailed making a break from their own mothers and families, and indeed from the idea of family. Mary Butts, 'at loggerheads with her mother' and class, seemed to Stella Bowen when she met her in East London, to have wrenched herself from her 'formidable background tooth and nail' (Bowen, 1984: 39). Cunard similarly defied her mother and her class attitudes. Others, like Nina Hamnett or Kate Lechmere or Iris Barry, seemed not to belong to families at all. Hamnett dealt with the 'problem of sex' in a business-like way (deciding upon a likely young man who on cue asked her take off her clothes: 'So I did and the deed was done') and was equally determined to look and dress differently. The loss of virginity and cutting her hair short gave her a similar 'sense of freedom' (1984: 44, 46). And to declare this to the world she put together a deliberately provocative outfit of clergyman's hat, check coat, a skirt with red facings, white stockings and men's dancing pumps. As planned, she 'got stared at in the Tottenham Court Road. One has to do something to celebrate one's freedom and escape from home' (47–8). Becoming a bohemian was like undergoing a physical operation and stepping through a wardrobe all at once, generally accompanied by a magical journey from the English provinces and regions (or from

New Zealand and Australia in the case of Katherine Mansfield and Stella Bowen) to the metropolis and the playgrounds of Europe.

Once embarked upon, this life meant, for some at least, the life of the artist. More likely, it meant the role of minor artist or co-worker, editor or sponsor of others' art. The Vorticist painters Helen Saunders, Jessica Dismorr and Dorothy Pound, and again, Nina Hamnett, Iris Barry, Stella Bowen, Kate Lechmere and Nancy Cunard were, in one way or another, examples of this. It also meant, for the more conspicuous examples, a life of masquerade in which their leading art exhibit was their own public image. Hamnett and Nancy Cunard, in particular, helped foster the myth of themselves as crowned queens of bohemia and were mythologised, in turn, in the press and by way of the many drawings, portraits and fictionalised sketches of them by such as Augustus John, Roger Fry, Lewis, Man Ray and Michael Arlen. The latter, as male artists, could meanwhile enjoy the double security of an artistic vocation and public image denied to most women. The Bohemian option for women was to be first an artist-in-life and only secondly an artist in words or paint, and true to Mürger's narrative, this testing role could bring dissipation and a raggedly tragic end.

The shape is plain to see, for example, in the story of Nina Hamnett and comes also to overtake Iris Barry. Nina Hamnett entered bohemian life in London and Paris with energy and enthusiasm. Her autobiography, *Laughing Torso*, is a series of endless encounters and adventures. Parties, affairs, bursts of spontaneous naked dancing and some painting and drawing pass by like entries in a day-by-day diary. Her beguilingly simple prose manages to hold off the deleterious effects of drink and age, but from the late 1920s, when she teamed up with Augustus John and Tommy Earp, the frazzled pub life of Fitzrovia began to take its toll. She was remembered in the 1930s and post-war years as a pathetic figure, obviously drunk and bemoaning the loss of a new beautiful young man or singing lewd ditties for a drink; a tramp on the cadge (Elizabeth Wilson, 2000: 107; David, 1988: 234–5). The price of Bohemia was that her work was neglected and little regarded by herself or others.

The aspiring poet Iris Barry left her Birmingham home in 1916 to join Pound's London circle and the cause against censorship only to find there were limits to freedom of expression for young women. She lived with Lewis on his terms until he became indifferent and in the end hostile. Their two children (if there were two) were placed with her mother and put out for adoption. In the 1920s, she made a life as a novelist, biographer and pioneering film reviewer and was briefly married. Her *Let's Go to the Pictures* (1926) prioritised the role of women in the industry and as film's main audience. Subsequently, as Curator of Film at the Museum of Modern Art in New York she campaigned for the merits of both art and popular film, but in 1950, having left her second husband, she abandoned her career for a life selling antiques in southern France with a young Frenchman, Pierre Kerroux. When this romantic-bohemian episode ended in the early 1960s, she gave way to alcoholic barbs at old acquaintances and tall tales of lost, earlier times.

In December 1956, after a period in hospital, Nina Hamnett fell from her small second-floor flat in Westbourne Terrace, Paddington and impaled herself on railings below (David, 1988: 244–5). Iris Barry died from cancer 'abandoned by all', in a Marseilles hospital in 1969 (18 April 1979; Schiddel). Nancy Cunard looks like an exception. She published three volumes of poetry in the 1920s and her independent Hours Press made a major contribution to modernist writing. She maintained a literary life well into the 1950s when she published respected memoirs of Norman Douglas and George Moore. In the following decade, however, her elected persona of sophisticated vagabond in a life laced with liquor surrendered to failing physical and mental health and she too died alone, her memory gone, under an oxygen tent in a Parisian charity hospital (Chisholm, 1979: 335–6).

Their first meeting was in February 1913. Miss Weaver (she was Harriet only in the family home) had subscribed to the WSPU journal Votes for Women *but was not convinced that the vote alone would solve women's problems. She had seen too much in the East End to believe that. When two years previously she had seen a copy of the* Freewoman *on the news-stands she had bought it. I remember your words, she said, 'that woman is an individual, and that because she is an individual she must be set free ...'*

'And if she is an individual she is free', Dora Marsden helped her.

'When I was younger, you know', Miss Weaver began again, 'my parents forbade me to read the novel Adam Bede. *Ever since I have been moved to defend the right, a woman's right, to freedom of expression, to read and think as we wish.'*

Both were modestly dressed, though there was more colour and originality in the second woman's costume. They smiled briefly. She was beautiful, Miss Weaver thought.

Dora Marsden was thirty-one. She was an arts graduate from Manchester University who had been an active member of the WSPU. Harriet Shaw Weaver was thirty-six. She had been bought up in a strictly evangelical background in Frodsham, Cheshire and then in a large house off

Hampstead Heath. Her adult life had been devoted to social work, chiefly in the East End, where she had overseen the support given to invalid children and later helped young girls and women into apprenticeships and paid work. In 1909 with the death of her mother she had come into a substantial inheritance. In the spring of 1913, around the time she met Dora Marsden, the foundation stone was laid for the South London Hospital for Women and Children for which she had been the fund-raiser. She had joined the 'Freewoman Discussion Circle' in 1912 and reacted as others did to W.H. Smith's decision to boycott the paper in October. She wrote to its editor, Dora Marsden, offering support and financial assistance. Hence their meeting. The result was the re-launched *New Freewoman*, renamed the *Egoist* in January 1914, and later the Egoist Press.

The women associated with the cause of suffrage, with the *Freewoman* and *New Freewoman*, seemed to belong to a distinctly un-bohemian world. Marsden's ideas, moreover, which took the magazine away from the specific question of suffrage, simultaneously took her away from the life of the metropolis to Southport and subsequently to Glencoin, a remote miner's village in Cumbria where she lived with her mother. The changing fortunes of the *Freewoman* become the *New Freewoman* and then shortly afterwards, the *Egoist*, prompt us to ask, too, about the relation between the contemporary women's movement and the artistic avant-garde. Marek (1995) argues that Pound hijacked the *New Freewoman* and the *Egoist* on behalf of a male-dominated modernist agenda. However, Rebecca West, although she came in later life to adopt something like this view had, as editor briefly of both the *New Freewoman* and *Egoist*, differed from both Pound and Marsden over the content and direction of the *New Freewoman* (Scott, 2000: 400–5). She didn't see why Marsden's 'gospel' shouldn't be connected to the 'movement towards freedom of expression in literature' and recruited Pound as literary editor to fill this gap (Glendinning, 1987: 40). The differences between the arts and feminism were not gendered in a simple binary fashion, therefore, and 'freedom of expression', in the broadest sense, for women and for the arts in their battle against censorship was probably the one banner uniting the parts of the paper. 'There was also liberty to uphold, injustice and Mrs. Grundy to combat and right to protect', insisted Iris Barry, thinking of the suppression of Lawrence's *The Rainbow*, the censorship of Joyce and of lines in *Blast* (1931: 163).

These issues remain of interest.[13] I'd like here, however, to consider not so much the relation between the male modernist and contemporary women's movements as between bohemian and other 'non-bohemian' women involved in the arts. In some instances this is a question about the relation between bohemian and feminist or in other ways politicised women. Rebecca West, once more, to some extent crosses these worlds (see Chapter 4). So in different ways did Violet Hunt and May Sinclair and at the other end of London, Virginia Woolf. Mary Butts also, before she published in the 1920s worked for the Children's Care Committee in the East End while she studied at the LSE (Bowen, 1984: 39). During the war she worked for the National Council for Civil Liberties, helping conscientious objectors. Nancy Cunard too, in what Arthur Waley saw as a thorough change of identity (Ford, 1968: 3) became from the late 1920s a publisher and editor, most notably of the volume *Negro* (1934), as well as a committed anti-racist and communist sympathiser. Surprisingly, she comes at this stage to resemble Harriet Shaw Weaver, publisher and editor, life-long socialist who in the 1930s supported the united front against Franco and became an active member of the Communist Party (Hanscombe and Smyers, 1987: 148).

There were 'no plays, no dancing and...no romances' for Harriet Weaver (Hanscombe and Smyers, 1987: 140) but she did, according to her lights, cross the other way in the late 1910s to join Pound's weekly company at Belotti's in Soho. Her carriage and appearance were rigid, 'so very straight with severe hat and nervous air', and her modesty was extreme, never speaking of herself or the *Egoist* 'save under extreme pressure or when business and nothing else made it essential and then only in the lowest tones and unutterable detachment' (Barry, 1931: 167). Helen Saunders recognised a kindred type, 'she was as silent in "company" as I was myself', though she saw too that Harriet Weaver's marked plainness made her 'distinguishable from the rest' (Lidderdale and Nicholson, 1970: 119–20). Her careful attire was an expression of her independence, just as extravagant clothing was for others. And if she desired above all to be 'a person alone', this person was a companionable person. H.D., Violet Hunt, May Sinclair, Dorothy Pound, Mary Butts, Aldington, Lewis, Eliot and others, were part of this company at Belloti's and, on those evenings, Harriet Weaver joined original subscribers to the *New Freewoman* and sometime assistant editors of the *Egoist* of which she had herself become editor after Marsden's departure. Her Egoist Press was to publish Lewis, Pound, Eliot and most significantly and consistently, Joyce. Aldington, H.D. and Eliot, in the sequence of assistant editors, shared the *Egoist* offices at Oakley House, Bloomsbury Street. Once a week, therefore, while Pound spun the Vortex, she sat as its quiet centre, the fulcrum to this working group on its regular evening out. And she was also actively in touch with a wider company. She continued to visit and assist Dora Marsden; she regularly offered Iris Barry a meal and bath, and gave her employment and a paid holiday in Paris seeing to the binding of Joyce's *Ulysses* (Lidderdale and Nicholson, 1970: 182, 203–4); she was close to H.D. and Bryher and Robert McAlmon in Paris; and was in regular contact with Sylvia Beach, co-publisher of Joyce. Friendship, partnerships and loyalties were therefore a significant feature of her life as they were of the lives of other modernist women.[14]

In this wider network bohemian women arguably found the women-centred context which gave their art another expression than their performative selves. They found too a common set of concerns and commitment. The *Freewoman*'s great service to its country, said Rebecca West, was 'its unblushingness'; it 'mentioned sex loudly and clearly and repeatedly' (1982: 5–6). Its themes, aside from the cause of suffrage, were marriage, chastity, male and female sexuality, 'uranians' (homosexuality), divorce and unmarried motherhood: precisely the themes which governed the personal lives of rebellious bohemian women (see Hanscombe and Smyers, 1987: 161–78; Bland, 1996). It was this wide agenda, too, and the cause of freedom of speech which had attracted Harriet Shaw Weaver to the project. Or perhaps we should say 'Josephine Wright', the name Harriet Weaver chose to write under in the *Egoist* at the age of thirty-eight when she moved for the first time into a flat of her own at Gloucester Place, Marylebone. Dancing, dresses, romance and modesty aside, she was not immune to the appeal of an alternate, performative self. And perhaps it's not impossible to see this independent person in the making when she arranged to meet Dora Marsden in early 1913. A year later friends took to calling her 'Josephine' – 'a new name to fit her new life', as Hanscombe and Smyers put it (143). On occasion, therefore, in irregular combinations and different registers, the bohemian freewoman and freewoman bohemian could and did consort together.

6
Café Society

Two for Dieudonné's

As Richard Cork tells us 'cafés were a crucial part of a London artist's life' in the pre-war period (Cork, 1985: 217). This would have met with universal agreement even in the longer period from the nineties to the immediate post-war years, before the social and artistic tone of London life changed significantly. Ford was carried in the 'extraordinary rush' of the months before the war on a tide of engagements: 'There would be a dinner, a theatre, or a party, a dance. Usually a breakfast at four after that' (Ford, 1921: 181; 1932: 410). Cafés were places to parade, be seen and hold court, to plot and plan, to write and edit in, and places to paint. The Café Royal continued to be used after its heyday under Whistler and Wilde but the scene shifted in the 1900s and 1910s to cheaper restaurants in Soho and further north in Fitzrovia. Arthur Ransome's explorations of bohemian London took him especially to the Dieppe, the Roche and Brice's, all in Old Compton Street. Pound used Pagani's in Great Portland Street and later began to gather fellow artists around him in Belotti's in Old Compton Street. Already in 1914 the newly married Dorothy Pound travelled by bus, a copy of *Blast* under her arm, to meet Pound after a *New Age* meeting and go on to Soho. The *New Age* editorial meetings themselves – taking in the culinary extremes across the eras and areas of London – were held downstairs at the ABC restaurant in Chancery Lane and at the editor, A.R. Orage's table at the Café Royal. The ABC chain had 'numerous shops (often crowded)' reported Baedeker (1908: 16). They offered ices, cake and tea, were cheap and a sign of the new mass society. John Cournos used them regularly. And Lewis blessed them in *Blast* 1, partly in spite of their 'vulgarity', for if they were vulgar they were also an inspiration to the new geometrical art. In *Blast* 2 Lewis damns Lyons '(without exception)'. Most of the world wouldn't have detected a radical difference between the two chains. However, Lewis's contemporary and rival David Bomberg liked Lyons (Cork, 1985: 217) and perhaps this was sufficient reason for Lewis to shun them. Another venue was The Florence on Rupert Street and here C.R.W. Nevinson arranged a dinner for thirty guests in honour of the Italian Futurist, Marinetti, in November 1913.

There were celebrated meetings elsewhere: between Pound and Lewis at the Vienna Café, as we have seen; at Miss Ella Abbott's teashop in Holland Street, Kensington where scrambled eggs on one piece of toast cost Pound 1/3d (Hutchins, 1965: 135) and where – so one story goes – Pound edited H.D.'s poems and invented her as an 'Imagiste' (Aldington, 1941: 134; and see H.D., 1979: 57). This location and Pound's preferred Frenchified name for the movement (which he pronounced 'mouve-mong' said Aldington) caught the mixture in these years of a dainty English ordinariness and French *savoir vivre* – as did a life measured out by bus rides between tea and cake at the ABC and dinner at the Café Royal. For the West End restaurants were still rather grand. Even a modest Soho restaurant offered five courses while Frascati's in Oxford Street offered ten. Dinner at the Café Royal cost 4/-. The magistrate at Wilde's committal had not known where to find the fashionable Kettner's, where dinner cost from 5/- to 7/6, and the judge later marvelled that 'chicken and salad for two' at the Savoy should cost Wilde 16/- (David, 1988: 5).

Most of the later generation of artists could not have begun to follow Wilde's example if they had wished to. Pound, Lewis and the Eliots and figures such as John Cournos and Nina Hamnett were dogged by money problems. Gaudier-Brzeska lived a bohemian life on principle and refused to go into relatively modest Soho restaurants because they were too bourgeois. On one such occasion, with Horace Brodzky, he instead bought bread and cheese and salami and they ate it with their backs to the wall at the corner of Old Compton Street and Dean Street (Brodzky, 1933: 78). Pound could not afford De Marias on Church Street Kensington (Hutchins, 1965: 134); hence the choice of Belotti's. It was all the more surprising then that the two dinners, arranged two days apart in mid-July 1914, to celebrate Vorticism and Imagism, were staged at Dieudonné's in Ryder Street. The Baedeker considered this a restaurant of the 'highest class'; evening dress was usual and dinner cost between 7/6 and 10/- (1908: 11–12). A ticket for the Vorticist dinner, Kate Lechmere confirmed, cost 10/- (Meyers and Lechmere, 1983: 165), and the menu was elaborate and extensive (Wilhelm, 1990: 161). Gaudier-Brzeska couldn't afford this and had to pay in kind with a small carving which he delivered to Pound's table (Cork, 1982: 15). One wonders just how he and Pound and Lewis were received in their assorted bohemian garb. Why Dieudonné's then? It's easier to see why in the case of the second dinner. This was arranged by Amy Lowell for 13 guests: the Pounds, Aldington and H.D., Ford and Violet Hunt, Amy Lowell and her companion, Ada Dwyer Russell, Flint, Upward, Cournos, Gaudier-Brzeska and John Gould Fletcher. Amy Lowell was new to London, a millionairess who entertained Pound, Fletcher, H.D. and Aldington in the five-room suite she'd taken in the Berkeley, and a recently published poet, determined to promote Imagism. Her intervention was meant to distinguish her conception of free verse from Pound's 'Imagisme' and her dinner meant as a deliberate riposte to Vorticism, which she had taken against at the Vorticist dinner on the 15th, but of which, says Wilhelm, she didn't have 'the foggiest notion' (Wilhelm, 1990: 160). Promoting Imagism appeared to entail literally taking over the territory occupied by its rival.[1]

The effect was, from one perspective, the opposite. Allen Upward and Pound were ready to satirise her diffuse brand of 'Amygism', in Pound's coinage. At one point in the evening while Gaudier-Brzeska and Aldington carried on a running tussle over Greek art, Pound brought in 'a large tin bathtub' on his head and set it down by the table (Fletcher, 1937: 151). The Imagist school was at an end, he announced, and was superseded by the 'nageiste' school – a movement Lowell had inaugurated with her poem 'In a Garden' which ended 'Night, and the water and you in your whiteness, bathing'. As if on cue, Upward read out an expansive parody of Lowell's poem. One wonders in passing, at the availability of an old tin bath at Dieudonné's (Pound juggled with a waiter's tray, says Damon, 1966: 233[2]) but this is the story with minor differences – Pound put the bath-tub on the table, or at Amy Lowell's feet – as we have it, largely through John Gould Fletcher's account of 1937. Others in this company of thirteen – Dorothy Pound, Violet Hunt, Ada Russell, Flint, H.D. – had a view on this event, we can be sure, but such is the partiality of the historical record, we know nothing of them. Pound probably felt the joke paid off: Amygism was 'blasted' off its feet. As a second perspective emerges, however, so the usurper recovers to earn the sympathy of John Cournos and the warm admiration of Fletcher. For Cournos, who admired Pound and found Amy Lowell 'overbearing and aggressive', the evening was 'an uncomfortable affair'. The 'undercurrent of hostility' and 'condescension towards the hostess' climaxed with Upward's 'rollickingly witty after-dinner speech' which left the table 'shaking with laughter'. Still, Cournos 'could not help feeling for Miss Lowell, who was the butt of the excruciatingly witty if cruel jest' (1935: 271). Fletcher does not mention Upward's performance. Everybody laughed at Pound, he says, though, for his part, Fletcher felt 'Pound had considerably overplayed his own intellectual arrogance'. Amy Lowell rose above his insult and 'everyone felt, as I did' that they should pay homage to her 'gallant spirit'. The evening confirmed the 'understanding, warmth, and sympathy of a complete alliance' between this new pair (Fletcher, 1937: 152).

For Fletcher, therefore, the event marked a decisive shift of allegiance; hence its place in his memoir. As so often, an event such as this, bringing writers and others together, worked upon latent tensions, opened splits and effected new alliances. We're left here with the picture of a divided and slightly discommoded company, with, on one side, Pound, Upward and Gaudier-Brzeska, the quarrelsome Vorticist gatecrasher, and, on the other, Fletcher and Lowell, with Ford, Cournos, Aldington and the others leaning more this way or that, or holding off as silent witnesses. We can imagine that Dorothy Pound's and Violet Hunt's sympathies were more with Pound and Ada Russell's were with Amy Lowell. Of the rest H.D. and Aldington later sided with Amy Lowell and Flint was to produce his case for Hulme against Pound as the originator of Imagism. The split between Vorticism and Imagism was replicated, that is to say, by splits *within* Imagism, on this occasion as much on a matter of social decorum as aesthetics. Out of tune with Pound, Fletcher nevertheless struck the note by which others would soon come to judge him. The picture Pound and Upward conjured up of the 'hippopoetess', Amy Lowell, bathing in the moonlight perturbed and vexed her 'puritanic soul', says Cournos (Cournos, 1935: 271). Pound's manner vexed Fletcher too, just as his involvement in *Blast* would offend its more 'puritan' readers. Rather disarmingly, Fletcher and Lowell shake hands at the end of this evening on the prediction that Pound's 'irresponsibility' would wreck his own career (Fletcher, 1937: 152). They do not consider their own role. For in fact what would derail Pound's career in London was exactly the kind of uncomfortable clash this evening had produced, between his attempted satire – for which, as his contributions to *Blast* indicated, he had little natural gift – and more staid but sensitive egos such as their own.

We don't ourselves have to take sides in any of this to see how the Imagist dinner, arranged to celebrate the publication of *Des Imagistes*, did in a real sense mark the end of Imagism as a *new* movement. Pound was positioning 'Imagisme' within Vorticism, and T.E. Hulme, the other serious contender as co-founder, had himself moved on to discuss the new painting. Flint's account of Hulme's role in 1915 was soon in fact to confirm that Imagism was history. At the dinner no one wanted to define Imagism and only one or two, H.D. and Aldington, said Ford, could be thought to represent it (Fletcher, 1937: 149). Imagism therefore passed, circa July 1914, into a broader poetic stream – whether now 'diluted' as Pound's antics emphasised, or newly launched upon a common poetic quest as Fletcher envisioned (148). The bath-tub is what is remembered from this scene and the watery verse and bathing versifier it conjures up conveys the contrast between the 'hard' and 'definite' poetry called for by Hulme and Pound and the more liquid, 'polyphonic' verse of Lowell and Fletcher. Pound's association of Amy Lowell's programme with her physical person, and indeed her naked body, also underlines how gendered this opposition was (Thacker, 1993). And this is emphasised for us in another way by the lack of any record from the women present, and the way, according to Wilhelm, 'everyone studiously avoided' the close relationship between Amy and Ada Russell, to whom many of Lowell's later sensuous and more synaesthetic poems were addressed (Wilhelm, 1990: 161; Thacker, 1993: 54–6).

It's both too much, because too explicit, and not enough to say this was a battle between the masculinist Pound (and Upward) and the lesbian intruder. For one thing, because other figures were sidelined by both tendencies, including Cournos and Flint, and for another, because as a Lowell from Boston, Massachusetts, Amy Lowell also represented something else: the social and class power of one of America's first families. She was at once haute-bourgeoise and 'bohemian', the wealthy patron the movement needed (but who rejected Pound's leadership) and a woman poet whose personal life and writing belonged to the coded lesbian context shared by a number of other modernist women authors. Pound's spiteful jest and continuing jibes played jointly across the material signs of her untold wealth and body size. Questions of sexuality were present too no doubt, but remained unspoken, as the silent figure of the unacknowledged guest, Ada Russell, bore witness.

Perhaps the loosening of ties with Imagism's beginnings which this dinner enacted makes some sense of holding it at Dieudonné's. For here was an appropriate venue for the inception of Amy Lowell's more broadbased 'Some Imagist Poets', a project launched in earnest on Lowell's own ground at a meeting a fortnight later, at the Berkeley and literally on the eve of war, between herself, Fletcher, H.D., Aldington and D.H. Lawrence (Aldington, 1941: 139). This only confirms, though, that the earlier more strictly delimited 'Imagisme' belonged elsewhere – in the modest setting of the Kensington teashop or British Museum café, for example.

But then if this earlier Imagism(e) didn't belong in Ryder Street, Vorticism seemed to belong there even less. Recalling the crowded months after Henri Gaudier-Brzeska began working on his 'hieratic' head at the beginning of 1914, Pound comments 'My memory of the order of events from then on is rather confused' (1970: 51). Certainly the hazy and somewhat bizarre picture that emerges from the flimsy record of the Vorticist gathering at Dieudonné's confirms the fallibility of human memory. It confirms too just how like fiction the reiterated tales of biography and literary history regularly become, tied here and there to the few documents bearing the authentic stamp of dates and first-hand recollection. Indeed, as we have seen, this kind of assemblage of fact and fiction comes to seem inevitable. We are bound then to work across the tissue of texts by which we know anything of such past events. Something other than the play of textuality is revealed by this scrutiny however. We see the tensions and enmities, loves, friendships and admiration marking the social relations of these groups and get a sense too of how these fluctuated as moods and circumstances changed. In addition, as if to vindicate Pound's confusion, the surviving recollections show how the drama of events over these few critical months in 1914, pitching London Bohemia into new coteries, new liaisons and separations, marriage, war and death, did crowd confusingly in upon each other. The immediate pre-war period was commonly viewed as a time of 'fever', 'ferment', and 'tremendous change' (Wees, 1972: 11). Europe in 1914 'was full of titantic stirrings and snortings', said Lewis, a 'new art' had arrived 'to announce a "new age"'; the feeling was, said Ford '– truly – like an opening world' (Lewis, 1982: 253; Ford, 1921: 137). Oddly enough, therefore, the imperfect reminiscences of this one evening in the exceptional heat of July 1914, took the 'true' impression of these harried times.

Pound had first met Amy Lowell at the Berkeley Hotel in July 1913 and chose her poem 'In a Garden' for his future Imagist anthology. Almost exactly a year later, he wrote to her announcing: 'BLAST dinner on the 15th...Will be glad to come to *your* dinner' (Paige, 1971: 37). Remembering the dinner once more a year later, after Gaudier-Brzeska's death at Neuville St Vaast on 5 June 1915, Pound writes 'The feast was a great success, every one talked a great deal' (1970: 52). Gaudier-Brzeska, he remembers, 'spent a good part of the meal in speculating upon the relation of planes nude of one of our guests though this was kept to his own particular corner' (52). Later still, in the *Pisan Cantos*, now that Dieudonné's and so much else had gone after another war, Pound remembers still 'Gaudier's eye on the telluric mass of Miss Lowell' (1975b: 469). Evidently the persistent image and gaze were as much Pound's as Gaudier's.

Pound's *Memoir* to Gaudier opens with excerpts from Ford Madox Ford's essay on *Blast* from *The Outlook* of July 1915, shortly after the appearance of *Blast* 2 and Gaudier's death. Deeply conscious of the loss, in Pound's words, of a 'great spirit' and 'great artist', Ford writes of Gaudier '*as I last saw him*, at a public dinner' (my italics) with 'his radiant and tolerant smile' answering 'objectors to his aesthetic ideas with such a gentleness, with such humour, with such good humour' (Pound, 1970: 18). This public dinner, says Pound, was the Vorticist dinner at Dieudonné's which comes then to stand for this 'last' time, the moment of youth and enormous promise in the arts before both are cut down. An 'emotional content' in H.D.'s words in her reflections on her own memories of Pound comes through the '*cloud* of memories' (H.D., 1979: 24). But the cloud lingers too, through the versions Ford gives of this incident in the *English Review* in October 1919, in *Thus to Revisit* in 1921 and in *No Enemy* in 1929. In *Thus to Revisit*, for example, Ford remembers less and remembers differently. Here he recalls Gaudier, doubtful '*that I had ever noticed him before* [my italics] ... amongst a crowd of dirty-ish, bearded, slouch-hatted individuals', rising to speak like a 'supernatural' visitation 'inspired by inward visions' and again 'with such humour and such good humour'. The occasion was 'late July 1914' and the place 'a low teashop ... an underground haunt of pre 1914 smartness' ... a 'cave' with a band and 'nasty foreign waiters' a function of which Ford otherwise remembers 'disagreeable sensations, embarrassments' (1921: 173, 176). He adds that the host whom he 'can't remember' (the host at the Vorticist dinner was Wyndham Lewis) 'must have been someone I disliked' and on such occasions 'the food seems to go bad' (176). This last at least was a pity since Ford was a gourmet and the menu on the 17th was an 'elaborate affair', running from 'Norwegian hors d'oeuvres and lobster bisque to filets of sole and lamb ... and ended with various "bombes" and other desserts' (Wilhelm, 1990: 161).

Ford's description of the place is confirmed by the *English Review* essay titled 'Henri Gaudier: the story of a low teashop'. The venue sounds more like the Cave of the Golden Calf than Dieudonné's but then neither could be called a teashop. Goldring recalls an inaugural party to celebrate *Blast* at the Cave of the Golden Calf and does not mention Dieudonné's (Goldring, 1943: 70). And Violet Hunt confirms there was 'a *Blast* evening at the Golden Calf to celebrate the foundation of our review' (1926: 214). Since the Cabaret Club closed its doors in February

1914 this could not have been a publication party, though it may well have followed the announcement of the magazine in the *New Age* in January. Still, it would be odd for Ford not to name the Golden Calf, if this is what he has in mind, since, as we have seen, he names it readily elsewhere and it was enough in his mind to use it for parts of the novel *The Marsden Case* (1923). There is something odd too if this occasion in 'late July' was one when Ford first noticed Gaudier-Brzeska ('I do not know that I had ever noticed him before'; 1921: 176) if the Vorticist dinner, held on the 15 July was also when Ford 'last saw him'. One answer to some of this confusion is that Ford's accounts slip from one party to the other. When he recycled this material in the fictionalised 'tale of reconstruction' of *No Enemy* (1929), the host is clearly Amy Lowell. The 'disagreeable sensations – embarrassments' are now linked directly to her and the dinner 'an "affair" – one of two – financed by a disagreeably obese Neutral whom I much disliked' (1929: 205). She is a 'very fat, very monied, disagreeably intelligent being' (205). In the *English Review* article of 1919, he prefers 'monstrously fat, monstrously monied, disagreeably intelligent coward' (1919: 297). In both 'the Neutral' replaces 'the host' he can't remember in the more modest account in *Thus to Revisit* of 1921. Aldington's response to the essay in the *English Review*, in a letter alerting Amy Lowell to Ford's bad manners and sexism, confirms that he and Flint saw it as referring to the Imagist dinner (Aldington, 1992: 53). Ford therefore confused one dinner with the other – or in a more extraordinary implication, given what has always been assumed, he was in fact only at one. But even so, if this was the Imagist dinner, Ford does not mention Pound and the bath-tub; nor does anyone else mention a band playing. And why describe Amy Lowell as 'the Neutral' and suggest she was keen to flee the city (1919: 297; 1929: 205) when war had not as yet been declared?

Chroniclers of modernism depend a good deal on Ford's prolific recollections. He loved to embellish and stretch a twice or thrice-told tale – even venturing back through his literary connections on one occasion to suggest that he had met Byron (Aldington, 1941: 151). Ford's social persona and writing career, where occasional journalism and fiction exchanged hands, were built out of his instinct for creative reminiscence. The more he wrote the more he left a record of adjacent and divergent versions of events. His stories and the manner of their telling do, however, give us the temper of the time, the 'extraordinary rush' in which two, three or four parties could become one, or a restaurant, a cabaret club and a teashop seem like the same place. In part the memory that comes through is of Ford's reshuffling of times and places, but in part, too, it is a recollection of the singular radiant image of the 'supernatural' Gaudier. As H.D. once again said, confessing 'I didn't always listen and I can't remember everything', what is involved is 'hardly a process of remembering, but almost of "manifesting"' (1979: 46).

It's not that we are entirely without details on the Vorticist dinner. We even know something – possibly – of the seating arrangements. Kate Lechmere, for example, remembered that she was seated between Gaudier-Brzeska, who arrived late, and Arthur Symons.[3] She recalls that Symons said he had not read *Blast* but 'given it to my children in the nursery to teach them their ABC' (Meyers and Lechmere, 1983: 165). Lewis objected, adds Cork, and asked that the speaker apologise to Lechmere since she had financed the magazine and had fifty copies under her chair (Cork, 1976: 237).[4] It's a mere detail of course but one wonders what Symons was doing at this dinner, hosted by the 'anti-aesthetic' Lewis. Symons was now aged fifty; he had never entirely recovered from his mental breakdown of 1908, and had had nothing directly to do with Imagism or Vorticism. His biography and letters suggest he was 'almost exclusively' at Island Cottage in Wittersham, Sussex during the period 1909–19, including the summer of 1914 (Lhombreaud, 1963: 291). And there is no evidence that he had any children. If anything, Symons would seem to have been more at home at Violet Hunt's party for *Blast* at South Lodge, alongside Mr Thesinger, Lady Aberconway and Mrs Leopold Hirsch who bought a copy half-price and returned it the next day because of its bad influence upon her daughters (Hunt, 1926: 215).

We can't be sure, given the above, that Ford and Hunt were themselves at this dinner at Dieudonné's, though in two of his four accounts Ford presents himself as the somewhat reluctant 'Grandfather of the Vorticists' (1919: 297; 1921: 176). He had met Symons, 'that marvellously skilful writer', once, he says, many years earlier at St James's Hall with Verlaine, and is unlikely to have forgotten a second meeting – if there was one.[5] Others said to be at this dinner, along with Kate Lechmere, were Amy Lowell and the American novelist Mary Borden Turner. Ford, with all the provisos above, is commonly said to have disagreed with Lowell over 'literary principles' (Foster Damon, 1966: 232–3; Saunders, 1996: 464); she to have tried to woo him (Wilhelm, 1990: 160). Whatever passed between them, if the dinners are not being muddled, both Ford and Lowell are, like Symons, unlikely guests at a Vorticist event. Aside from Pound and Gaudier-Brzeska and Lewis himself, it's unclear what other potential members of the broad movement – Roberts, Wadsworth, Nevinson, Bomberg, Etchells, Atkinson, Saunders, Dismorr, Epstein – were present. Bomberg was known as fiercely independent and had never appeared at the Rebel Arts Centre. Roberts said he himself had only spent 'about five minutes' there and that though Lewis included him as a signatory to *Blast*, 'I, in fact, personally signed nothing' (Roberts, 1956–58). Of the others, Nevinson, now a confirmed Futurist, disagreed with Lewis. And Hulme for certain wasn't there. It's surprising too that Lechmere and Borden Turner, both in a relationship of sorts with Lewis, should attend or be invited, unless Lewis enjoyed this kind of risk. Mary Borden Turner wrote to Lewis the next evening from the Savoy to say how they got on each other's nerves and bored and offended each other. She proposed they 'abandon this attempted intimacy and take refuge in a more gentle formality or a more formal gentleness' (O'Keefe, 2001: 159). It was on this new understanding, perhaps, that Lewis, along with Ford and others, later joined her at Charterhall, a country house on the Scottish Borders rented by her husband.

Lewis's relationship with Kate Lechmere was also eventually placed on what he called a more 'adult' and friendly footing after the war. Lechmere thought him a genius and remained fond of him but she did not like Vorticism.[6] No more did Dorothy Pound who, though she was to adopt a Vorticist style later, in March predicted that *Blast* would be 'horrible' and thought Lewis's paintings 'filthy' (Pound/Shakespear, 1984: 333). Violet Hunt, too, though she and May Sinclair succumbed to Lewis's influence and wore Vorticist costumes, thought that the murals at Great Ormond Street – much admired by the national press – made the Rebel Arts Centre look like 'a butcher's shop full of prime cuts ... the blood running down in gouts and streaks on the cornices and folding doors' (Hunt, 1926: 217, 213).[7] What is more, Lechmere and Lewis, as we have seen, were at odds over the Rebel Arts Centre. She wrote to him towards the end of July complaining about difficulties over the distribution of *Blast* – involving some tension between herself and Helen Saunders who in this episode appears devoted to Lewis (O'Keefe, 2001: 160).[8] This incident seems immediately to have brought the Rebel Arts Centre to a close. Lewis wrote a threatening note to her on the 25th July and the next day ('after your language and behaviour of this morning') Lechmere effected a spirited withdrawal from the project. She was no longer prepared to pay the rent – and eventually went to court, unsuccessfully, over what Lewis owed her. Within three days, in this last week of July, Lewis had decamped to 4 Percy Street and his studio in nearby Fitzroy Street.[9]

A good time was had by all, says Pound. And Wees (1972: 46), Cork and many others appear to agree. 'The dinner must, above all, have been Lewis's finest hour', Cork concludes (1976: 237). This seems hardly to catch the underlying mood of the evening. The only detail Pound supplies is of Gaudier-Brzeska eyeing Amy Lowell and we have some sense of the animosity underlying this. Did he know of Lewis and Borden Turner and Lechmere, of the likely tensions between both women and between Lechmere and Saunders and over the running of the centre? If so, it didn't dent his impression of a jolly occasion. There were further tensions outside the restaurant of course between Lewis and Hulme, the absent ghost at both feasts. He and Lechmere had met first at Kensington, later at the Groupil Gallery in March when Lewis thought they were giggling over his drawing for *The Enemy of the Stars* (O'Keefe, 2001: 148) and then one lunch time at the Rebel Arts Centre. And Hulme had already or was soon to propose to her. Who knows, perhaps he was waiting outside Dieudonné's to see Kate Lechmere home?

Paint the legend: the Restaurant de la Tour Eiffel

What all this amounts to is that the Imagist and Vorticist dinners should have taken place somewhere else, at the right place and with the right people. Douglas Goldring remembers 'a Blast dinner, held in the room in the Eiffel Tower Restaurant... which Lewis had decorated for its proprietor' (1943: 70). This was not in fact a *Blast* dinner but a later 'Vorticist Evening' held on the 23 February 1916 to celebrate Lewis's painting of a Vorticist Room at the Tour Eiffel. But one begins to see why Goldring and Ford should forget where this dinner was or merge it with others at the more appropriate venues of the Cave of the Golden Calf and the Eiffel Tower Restaurant. In memory both seem in fact to have pushed Dieudonné's off the record. This is especially true of the Eiffel Tower Restaurant, as remembered most famously by William Roberts as the venue for the *Blast* dinner. Roberts' painting is captioned 'The Vorticists at the Restaurant de la Tour Eiffel: Spring 1915'. One diner holds open a copy of the first pink or puce issue of *Blast* and another copy, its title obscured, is on the table. 'Spring 1915' is a year in advance of the Vorticist dinner to celebrate Lewis's Vorticist Room, and too late by several months to make sense of the inclusion of the first issue of *Blast*. But these discrepancies are in a perverse way what matter, of course, as proof of how dates are subservient to the symbolic social meaning of events and places. Roberts paints a dinner that should have happened. Indeed, we might almost feel that the associations swirling through the period and subsequent memoirs have made it happen. In a more daring move than Goldring's unwonted elisions and Ford's 'creative' mis-remembering, Roberts' painting seeks to mythologise

Vorticism and to present his imagined event as the historical document. At the same time, however, his painting has to struggle to affirm the meaning of Vorticism – at this moment that never quite was – against the lesser events that did occur and the meanings the movement otherwise acquired. Also, though the dates are subservient to the making of this preferred symbolic meaning, one date is crucial: the date of its composition in 1961–62.

But first we should appreciate why the Tour Eiffel was the magnet for Roberts' Vorticism. 'The Restaurant and Hotel de la Tour Eiffel' at 1 Percy Street, off Tottenham Court Road, was acquired in 1908 by Rudolph Stulik, and for thirty years he and the restaurant served as honorary players in the artistic life of bohemian London. The first connection between the Tour Eiffel and literary society was via T.E. Hulme, himself returned in 1908 to London from Germany. As honorary secretary of the 'Poets' Club' he determined it should meet once a month at the United Arts Club at 10 St James Street to dine, read 'original compositions in verse' and receive 'a paper on a subject connected with poetry' (Jones, 1960: 29). In January 1909, the club issued a small volume of verse *For Christmas MDCCCCVIII*, including poems by Lady Margaret Sackville, Mrs Marion Cran and Henry Simpson. 'I think of this club,' said F.S. Flint, 'and then of Verlaine at the Hotel de Ville ... in a café hard by with other poets, conning feverishly and excitedly the mysteries of their craft – and I laugh' (1909: 327). Hulme derided Flint's 'belated' romanticism but soon quit the Poets' Club's suave West End venue and polite versifying for the kind of obscure bohemian café the Francophile Flint thought essential. Hulme, Flint and a handful of other proto-imagists began on a more irregular basis to meet to con French verse and to craft their own at the Eiffel Tower Restaurant. Thus began one of the shifts, as ever trailing the French example, from an English amateurism to the professionalism of international modernism. That this was at first a slow evolution we know from Pound's taste for 'poesy' and his operatic performance of the poem 'Sestina Altaforte' at the restaurant when he first joined the group in April of this year. Hulme simply did not take him seriously.

The next phase of the café's bohemian life is associated primarily with Lewis who began to use it regularly when he moved to 4 Percy Street in late 1914 to convalesce from a bout of gonorrhoea and to revise the novel *Tarr*. He became a great favourite with Stulik ('I vould do anyting for Mr. Lewis' William Roberts remembered the Viennese Stulik intoning; 1957: 470) and later, in 1915, assisted by Helen Saunders, Lewis painted an upstairs 'Vorticist Room' for his benefactor.[10] Lewis's interest in interior design and architecture developed considerably in these years and one can see how the production of murals, fabrics and furnishings at the Rebel Arts Centre, short-lived though this work was, had made them a would-be competitor of the despised Omega Workshops, some of whose workers, like William Roberts, had used and continued to use the Tour Eiffel.[11] Others included Mark Gertler, Gaudier-Brzeska and Nina Hamnett, who, with Augustus John, drifted from the Café Royal to John's Crabtree Club in Soho and on to the Tour Eiffel. Michael Holroyd paints a picture of the restaurant bustling with politicians, personalities from high society and bohemian artists whom Stulik subsidised or occasionally, as with Lewis, allowed to eat for free (Holroyd, 1976: 536). As depicted in three panels executed by Roberts in 1919 in the lobby to Lewis's Vorticist Room, the key occupations of the café's clients were dining, dancing and bedding (Cork, 1985: 245). The last took place between courses or after hours in the hotel adjoining the restaurant. Others who came to witness or join this night life, from the Café Royal or studios in Fitzrovia, were Walter Sickert, also a close friend of Nina Hamnett's, and Iris Tree and Nancy Cunard, who was inspired by the Café's mixed pleasures to name it 'our carnal-spiritual home' (Cunard, 1923: 24).

Here was, in a sense, Vortex London, a mixed congregation of 'high society' slumming it on the edge of Soho alongside attitudinising artistic coteries at a restaurant with distinctly Parisian and European associations. The area itself, bordering Fitzrovia, was the site of a territorial battle of the kind Amy Lowell had entered into – even if some of the feuding between Rebel Artists and Bloomsbury was manufactured. At this distance, moreover, the personal and theoretical differences between Roger Fry and Lewis appear less interesting than others – between, for example, young Jewish artists from the East End such as Roberts and Gertler, the French émigré Gaudier-Brzeska, Europeanised Anglo-Americans such as Pound and Lewis, and the English political and upper classes.[12] Hugh David suggests they all tumbled into a 'classless' pot-pourri (1988: 127) and perhaps the Tour Eiffel did offer such an oasis. Even so, this libertarian artistic scene was marked by blatant and subterranean inequalities, especially as experienced by women in relation to men and by women of different social classes. Many of the young women of this set belonged to the generation after the 'new women' of the turn of the century and suffrage campaigners such as Violet Hunt and May Sinclair. This was one kind of difference. They brought a new daring to the social scene with their boyish hairstyles and colourful fashions, by smoking in public, entering restaurants and walking London's streets unchaperoned, and in their freer sexual attitudes. Several also, Nina Hamnett, Helen Saunders, Jessica Dismorr, Iris Tree and Dora Carrington, were among the first women to attend the Slade School of Art, and though they may not all have used the Tour Eiffel to the same extent, collectively brought a new aspect to London's café society. There were, however, differences between them. Helen Saunders and Jessica Dismorr, for example, who were modest in company and came from well-to-do families, did not have the same cachet as Iris Tree, daughter of the celebrated actor–manager, Herbert Beerbohm Tree, nor did they share the liberated, hugely wealthy and aristocratic background of Nancy Cunard. Nina Hamnett, by contrast, though she plunged into the bohemian life of London and Paris, was an average artist who came from Tenby in South Wales and struggled financially thoughout her life.

Hamnett and Nancy Cunard both served as examples in the late 1910s and 1920s of the 'archetypal Bohemian', as David describes Hamnett (132), and both were associated, particularly in novels and through their own drawings and writings, with the Tour Eiffel.[13] In some ways, in a kind of class distinction among bohemians, they were opposites, for as David suggests, when the 'fugitive bohemians', led by Hamnett and Augustus John, found the bolt-hole of a working-class pub in the Fitzroy Tavern, it was at last to 'be themselves, untroubled by the likes of Nancy Cunard' (135). But if Hamnett persuaded herself and others that she was the 'real thing', Nancy Cunard 'was famous for *being* bohemian' (Elizabeth Wilson, 2000: 149). She looked the part, or aided by paintings, photographs, and drawings, she became the look; a type English society was always likely to produce, and then did, significantly, in the new century in the person of a young woman: the rebel aristocrat as bohemian girl. Novels by Evelyn Waugh (*Decline and Fall*, 1928), Aldous Huxley (*Antic Hay*, 1923; *Point Counter Point*, 1928), and Lewis (*The Roaring Queen*, 1936) reinforced this image of the bold young modern woman and connected it especially with café society.

Michael Arlen was one of the first to both see and make this happen in his novels *Piracy* (1922) and *The Green Hat* (1924). The first is anchored in the Eiffel Tower, called here the Mont Agel, and draws on Nancy Cunard for the character of Virginia Tracy, daughter of Lady Carnal. At one point Arlen sets her in the shuttered café alone at night, a 'lady of high fashion in all her finery' writing off notes to artist friends in London over a prolonged half glass of Vichy water. Then, leaving the café 'in the early hours of the morning...Swiftly she would penetrate the black solitudes of Soho in war-time: a rich and fragile figure braving all the dangers of the city by night, an almost fearful figure to arise suddenly in a honest man's homeward path: so tall and golden and proud of carriage, so marvellously indifferent to his astonished stare.' She understands and mocks the coarse desires of men in her 'swift and solitary vagabondage' (Arlen, 1922: 167, 169).

The male protagonist of Arlen's novel is a wealthy, brooding, young man, Ivor Pelham Marlay: a tall 'darkly serious young man ... something of a fop' who was 'of an angry habit' (14, 15). Marlay was expelled from school, failed therefore to go to Oxford, and before he lost an arm in the war, had became a writer ... of romances, titled *'Fair Ladies of London* (1914)' and *'Legend of the Last Coutezan. A Romance* (1918)'. He is neither T.E. Hulme nor Wyndham Lewis, therefore, but Michael Arlen, author of *The Romantic Lady*, and *The London Venture*. Marlay is introduced sitting alone at a table in the Mont Agel on 1 May 1921, after the introduction of the café itself and its owner, M. Stutz in the book's 'Prologue'. The novel then goes on to tell of Marlay's life, his affair in Europe with the twice-married Virginia, of her death after an operation on something dreadful 'inside', before returning him to the café, 'a recurrent fact' in his life 'for now ten years' (1922: 9).

But if this is a novel about a decade in the life of the Tour Eiffel it is not about Imagists or Vorticist Rooms or dinners. Arlen uses the recognisable figure of Nancy Cunard and the icon of Augustus John in the café's background, to mythologise the Tour Eiffel in a particular direction. Its bohemian aura along with the presiding oracle, M. Stutz, are appropriated, that is to say, for high society. Arlen's strategy in this way indirectly sharpens the class differences between its heroine, aka Nancy Cunard and other real-life well-heeled artist bohemians, and figures such as Hamnett and Iris Barry. There is indeed some recognition of this gulf and an attempt to bridge it at the end of the novel. After his solitary visit to the Mont Agel on 1 May 1921, Marlay encounters 'Pamela Starr' in a passage-way off Piccadilly. Marlay recognises her as the subject of a famous painting by Augustus John of 1916. She has now become 'the richest woman in the world' on the death of her older lover and guardian, but was born 'Pam Snagg', a plumber's daughter, and remains a woman 'of the people' (331). The novel closes on the promise of romance and adventure for Pamela and Marlay.

Lewis would have run into Arlen at the Tour Eiffel and was by no means unacquainted with 'those delightful people' in Arlen's words who comprised English high society (Lewis, 1982: 47). He had been introduced to Lady Cunard by Lady Drogheda, whose house in Belgravia he decorated in sensational fashion in 1913–14 (Cork, 1985: 177–90) and he was to have an affair with Nancy Cunard in London and France in the mid-1920s. *Blast* had earlier put him on the guest list of London salons and drawing rooms. But though he was lionised by the press and London aristocracy he found himself treated as an amusing oddity, 'lion-hunted from expensive howdahs' (1982: 47). His attendance in a boiled shirt at these functions would, he hoped, help the cause of rebel art, but he found only the smooth surface of snobbery, 'a long established blank of genteel fatuity' sleepwalking its way towards war (1982: 47). Patronage by way of the British class system fell down, in other words, on the idea of civilisation. In Arlen's novel, M. Stutz who represents the figure of Stulik, is credited with having produced an air of 'sensible civilisation', casting a dignified, pleasantly formal, appropriately familiar, artistic atmosphere upon yeomen, burghers and beaux alike (1922: 6–7). But this is not the idea of civilisation the Vorticists Lewis or Pound had in mind. 'Civilisation is individual' they jointly intoned and for this the spokesperson was to be the artist rather than the restaurateur. The cultural comparison on civilisation both Lewis and Pound drew was – as ever – with France and Paris. To this effect Lewis quotes Disraeli's *Coningsby*: 'Nothing strikes me more in this brilliant city [Paris] than the tone of its society, so much higher than our own...There is, indeed, throughout every circle of Parisian society, from the *chateau* to the *cabaret*, a sincere homage to intellect' (Lewis, 1982: 48).

The war, as everyone said, changed things dramatically. Lewis had assumed that 'artists always formed militant groups...seeing how "bourgeois" all Publics were' but since he 'was so little a communist...it never occurred to me that left to itself a group might express itself *in chorus*. The leadership principle, you observe, was in my bones' (1982: 32). The catastrophe of war 'altered the face of our civilisation', it 'extinguished' the arts which were to herald 'the great social changes necessitated by the altered conditions of life' (1982: 257–8). And such a change could only in the end amplify Lewis's instinctive individualism and dampen the chorus.

Even the tone of life at the Tour Eiffel was affected. When Roberts visited the restaurant on leave from the trenches he met Nina Hamnett but found it otherwise empty of rebel artists. At a later luncheon party, the twenty-three year old private Roberts felt intimidated by a show of rank from 'Colonel Ford-Hueffer of the Welch Regiment'. 'The old sense of camaraderie had vanished', comments Cork (Cork, 1985: 238–9): 'military uniforms and shaven chins had replaced the sombreros and beards', says Roberts, while Joe, the waiter, scrutinised 'over-exuberant bohemians...and their warrior companions' through a peep-hole before granting them admission (Roberts, 1957: 470). Lewis and Roberts, who moved to a flat at 32 Percy Street, continued to use the Tour Eiffel and to enjoy Stulik's patronage, but in the 1920s both restaurateur and restaurant went into an evident decline. Overweight, drinking too much, careless of the restaurant's business, Stulik hung on until the late 1930s when everything was sold off. Lewis's panels and other furnishings of the Vorticist Room were lost. Roberts' lobby panels were auctioned as three anonymous 'futurist panels' and subsequently disappeared (Cork, 1985: 247). Fittingly enough, after the slow death of this experiment of bringing Paris to London, the Tour Eiffel was anglicised as the renamed 'The White Tower'.

Roberts' imaginative reconstruction of the Vorticists in the Tour Eiffel provided in one of its functions some compensation for this loss. The painting's meanings are more particular than this, however, and were prompted by the exhibition at the Tate Gallery of 'Wyndham Lewis and Vorticism' in 1956. Notoriously, Lewis claimed in the catalogue to this exhibition that 'Vorticism was what I, personally, did and said in a certain period' (Lewis, 1956: 3). In addition to over 40 years of Lewis's work, the exhibition itself included a selection of paintings in an adjacent room intended to demonstrate Lewis's 'immediate impact' upon his contemporaries. Roberts responded to this misrepresentation, as he saw it, in a set of privately published *Vortex Pamphlets* (1956–58). Here, in three sardonic, insistent, but ignored essays and unpublished letters, he laid out his case against Lewis and Sir John Rothenstein, friend and supporter of Lewis, biographer of Roberts, and the Tate's artistic director. Roberts objected to the exhibition because it endorsed Lewis's claim to be the sole inspiration of Vorticism, because it suggested that all Lewis's work was Vorticist and because it maligned and marginalised his contemporaries. Of the latter, Jacob Kramer and Frank Dobson were not at any time Vorticists, said Roberts; David Bomberg and C.R.W. Nevinson were strong-minded, independent artists; and the paintings included by Roberts himself, *The Dancers* and *Religion*, were, he said, 'pre-Vorticist'. The exhibition was, in short, a 'fabulation' to 'bolster up the Leader Legend' (Roberts, 1956–58). A fourth article demolishes Rothenstein's biographical essay on Roberts in the 'Modern Painters' series as poorly researched and gratuitously insulting.

Like many other commentators, Jeffrey Meyers sees Roberts' reaction as a 'puerile' display of petty jealousy (Meyers, 1980: 327). Certainly Roberts' complaint is repetitive but it is precise too and in fact more than personal. The exhibition falsely supposed that Lewis's contemporaries could be considered in terms of Lewis's 'impact' upon them when the truth was more a matter of impact against impact, said Roberts. It thus ignored the complex dynamics of this sometime group. As Roberts puts it, 'the scene as it was in reality at that time' was composed not of 'Wyndham Lewis surrounded by a herd of Adherents, Disciples and Professed Followers, influence-drenched and impact-dazed, but on the contrary a criss-cross of opposed interests between rivals eager to establish themselves and their own particular brand of abstract art' (1956–58).

This gives another sense to the living vortex of the 'Vorticist Group' who in a further unpublished letter to *The Times* Roberts lists as 'Gaudier Brzeska, Wadsworth, Etchells, Dismorr, Saunders, Roberts, Lewis'. Roberts prefers to think of these artists as working in the manner of cubism and to see Vorticism as an offshoot of this. As evidence he cites a series of essays by Hulme in the *New Age*, titled 'Contemporary Drawings' from December 1913 to July 1914. A following single page dedicated 'To Hulme and the English Cubists' and listing Epstein, Wadsworth, Nevinson, Bomberg, Roberts and Gaudier-Brzeska underlines his point. It is churlish of him to omit Lewis and unthinking to omit Saunders and Dismorr, but this is remedied in the later painting. What Roberts went on to depict in 'The Vorticists at the Restaurant de la Tour Eiffel' was an expanded version of 'our gang', as Pound had put it. Here Lewis is shown as prominent but not alone. On his right, from the left of the picture, sit Hamilton, Pound and Roberts and on his left, Etchells and Wadsworth. Stulik presents one of Lewis's favourite sweets, a *specialité de la maison* Stulik named, 'Gateau St Honoré' which was a large custard tart ornamented with pastry balls around its edge (Roberts, 1957: 470). More pointedly, Dismorr and Saunders, appropriately enough given the way this group positioned them, are shown arriving late, ignored by all but the waiter, Joe. When Roberts painted this picture Dismorr, Hamilton, Wadsworth and Lewis had died. So too had Epstein and Bomberg. The painting therefore revives the personalities of the core group in its legendary public setting and stands as a celebration of the energies of this moment of collective creative life.

Cork feels Vorticism and the avant-garde's role in public life has been forgotten in the late twentieth century (Farrington, 1980: 29). The response to Roberts, at the time of the pamphlets and since, shows how, in a version of this neglect, his memory of the alliance of independent, individual artists in a common tendency has still to struggle with a historical sense which wants to see leaders and disciples, large egos and also-rans, whales and sprats. His *Vortex Pamphlets* charged the Tate with poor art history. But in the end, his group picture doesn't vie with 'history' so much as with Lewis's self-mythology and the way criticism has endorsed this. Lewis and too many of his commentators prefer the image of the artist as outsider, the paradoxically heroic lone enemy, to the idea of a generation of inventive artists who met in rowdy, companionable and competitive association. Roberts' painting captures this social and artistic bohemia in one of its symbolic metropolitan places. Such a counter-image must struggle with the persistent coupling of art and romantic individualism. It evokes a frankly idealised picture, of course, but that's the idea: a tougher idea, in the end, of the situated sociality of modernist art.

7
The Nerves in Patterns

'An ex-dancer, I believe'

> This was the last dance; a horrid One Step. Sibylla gave Mike a good deal of harsh instruction. 'Now dance, for a change,' she said. 'Don't spring and leap, for God's sake! Glide, don't lurch. Lean over me – don't drag at me. That's better. Now you're dancing, for a change – you never do dance, you know, you simply march about. Come on, let's get a move on – you've got no energy, that's what's the matter with you. Dance, I say.'

The Eliots liked to dance. It was one of the things they did together. At their flat in Crawford Mansions he would roll up the carpet and 'seriously' dance the fox trot to music on the gramophone. He had taken lessons in Boston, and in London on one occasion cancelled a meeting with Wyndham Lewis because he and Vivien were going to a dance studio. At one time too they went on Sundays to a dance hall in Queensway with Brigit Patmore. She was unnerved by Eliot – he could be 'winning and cordial' but lacked 'a grace, a carelessness' – but on this occasion she was impressed by his attitude towards Vivien who practised a step like the ballerina Karsavina in a chemist's shop on their way home. Vivien took ballet lessons, paid for by Bertrand Russell, so it seemed, and was more of an accomplished dancer than Eliot; more accomplished even than her brother Maurice's wife, Ahmé Hoagland, who was a professional cabaret dancer (Spender, 1967: 58; Eliot, 1988: 122; Patmore, 1968: 84–5, 89–90; Seymour-Jones, 2001: 242). Sometimes, dissatisfied with Eliot, she would find other partners, at the Savoy in earlier years and later with 'Freddie' or 'Hawkinson' who she met at Caxton Hall or the Elysée Galleries. There too she was 'Picked up by three

Canadian flying men, all exquisite dancers' and 'Danced as I never have since before the war' (Diary, 1919: Bodleian[1]).

The passage about Sibylla and Mike appears in Vivien's story, 'Thé Dansant', published in the *Criterion* in 1924. It was one of a dozen such items by her, including one other short story, 'Night Club' set in London; three stories set in Paris; an incisive review of Virgina Woolf's 'Mr Bennett and Mrs Brown'; and other reviews, sketches and a poem. These were published through 1924 and 1925 at a time when she was collaborating with Eliot on editing the journal at their flat in Clarence Gate Gardens after his day working at Lloyds bank. She wrote under the pen names, Fanny Marlow, Feiron Morris, Felix Morrison, F.M. and I.P. Fassett. One piece 'On the Eve: a Dialogue', published in early 1925, was assigned to Eliot, but was probably by Vivien and edited by him (Seymour-Jones, 2001: 655–6). In 1926 it was thought the Eliots' marriage was dead in all but name; in March 1928 Eliot took a vow of chastity, and in the autumn of 1932 separated himself definitively from her. He left England to lecture in the USA and returned to live in hiding at addresses known only to a few close acquaintances (Seymour-Jones, 2001: 453, 454, 465). To Pound he wrote that he was 'leaving no addresss until my wife gets used to it'; he had 'no intention of ever returning' (21 September 1933: Beinecke). Staff at Faber and Gwyer which he had joined in 1925 put Vivien off when she called at their offices while Eliot hid in the toilet or made his way out down the back stairs. Ottoline Morrell, Mary Hutchinson and Virginia Woolf were in touch with and visited Eliot but would not put Vivien in contact with him. She was sure he was in need of protection and sent him the keys to the flat so that he could return to his home to work in peace. In September 1935, she drafted an advertisement to appear in *The Times*: 'Will T.S. Eliot please return to his home 68 Clarence Gate Gardens, which he abandoned September 17 1932', and later, in the summer of 1936, in a desperate mimicry of his behaviour, let it be known that 'Daisy Miller' now occupied the flat while Mrs Vivien Eliot (as she insisted – they were not after all divorced) was in Cambridge, Boston (Seymour-Jones, 2001: 542–3, and see Bodleian[2]).

They met three times during these years: once at his solicitors; once, shocking Eliot's nerves into a panic for the rest of the day, by accident in a London street; and once when, after several such attempts, Vivien attended a lecture he gave in November 1935. She was dressed in the uniform of the British Union of Fascists which she had joined a year before and had three of his books and her dog Polly under her arm; 'he seized my hand and said how do you *do*, in quite a loud voice'. She joined him on the platform after the lecture while their dog scampered around his feet: 'I cannot talk to you now', he said, rapidly signing the books before leaving with the young man who had introduced him (Pearson, 1978: 278). He had sent a letter through his lawyers when he was in the USA but he never spoke to her to explain his actions.

Virginia Woolf described Vivien in the early 1930s as a 'torture... biting, wriggling, raving, scratching, unwholesome, powdered, insane, yet sane to the point of insanity' (Woolf, 1980: 331). She smelled often of ether, she took bromide and chloral and other drugs, possibly cocaine, on a regular basis. Her face was blotchy, she was overdressed. Like others, Woolf thought of 'poor Tom' dragged down by this little vampire, 'this bag of ferrets...Tom wears round his neck' (331). Edith Sitwell reported that when she met her on Oxford Street, Vivien denied she was 'that *terrible* woman who is so like me' (Pearson, 1978: 278). In August 1938, Eliot and her brother Maurice had her committed to a private mental asylum in Finsbury Park. Eight and a half years later, she died, in January 1947, most probably from an overdose, possibly self-inflicted (Seymour-Jones, 2001: 568). During this time Eliot never once visited her.

Hers seems the more bohemian tale. From the beginning, she had a vaguely 'artistic' air. She was 'an ex-dancer, I believe', said Aiken (1965: 93); she was 'An artist I think he said', reported Betrand Russell, 'but I should have thought her an actress' (Russell, 1967: 54). She sketched – her father had been a fashionable Royal Academician – and tried most other things. She was an expert dancer and was, like others, Eliot included, entranced by the Ballets Russes. She took part with Eliot in amateur theatricals and at one time had a part in a play in Hampstead, and on another occasion, in a macabre double disguise, dressed up as the mistress disguised as a cabin boy to Eliot's Dr Crippen, the wife murderer. In the mid-1920s she began writing and in the mid-1930s she started singing lessons. Throughout her life, too, she was, again like Eliot, interested in fashion – a photograph shows her in a multicoloured dress and head scarf at Garsington playing croquet. In another, the 'last photograph' from 1934 she is dressed in a suit by Philips et Gaston. Vivienne, or Vivien Eliot, as she chose to call herself from the mid-1910s, was therefore a 'modern' girl; a flapper and dilettante, part flighty gamine, part spirited but frustrated talent. Also, for all Eliot's calculated, surgical separation from her, and the indifference of earlier critics to such matters, his early years in London are permanently associated with her, as partner and muse, just as his later career and reputation were shadowed by her ghost.

They married in June 1915 after he had come at the beginning of the war from Marburg to London and two months after their first meeting at Oxford. He was sexually naive and inhibited but by his own account full of hope. When after a month he returned alone to the USA to face his parents' disappointment, he wrote beforehand to his father to say he was '*convinced* that she has been the one person for me ... I owe her everything' (Eliot, 1988: 110). If he had stayed in America he might have become the Harvard Professor of Philosophy his parents hoped for. That he defied their wishes and returned to London and Vivien showed what he had invested in the alternative life of struggling poet with her. She married him to 'stimulate' him, said Bertrand Russell (1967: 54); she was to be the vivacious feminine to his listless male, the life of 'emotions and feelings' out of which the impersonal poet (Eliot's 'filament of platinum') would form a new compound – the poem which would stand as the 'objective correlative' to the life (Eliot, 1951: 18, 145). To Conrad Aiken, Eliot wrote in early 1916 that he had in the last six months '*lived* through material for a score of long poems'. He did not have enough 'detachment' to write yet but was meanwhile 'having a wonderful life' (1988: 126).

The idea seemed to be working. When the one long poem appeared as *The Waste Land* a half-dozen years later, his friends recognised it as 'Tom's autobiography – a melancholy one' (Woolf, 1978a: 178). The tone had changed but, even so, the poem is not the evident record of a failed and miserable marriage it is often taken to be. The section thought to disparage Vivien ('My nerves are bad tonight ...') she described as 'wonderful' (Eliot, 1971: 11), and later when the poem was published, she thanked Sidney Schiff for his 'real and true appreciation of it ... it has become a part of me', she added, '(or I of it) this last year' (Eliot, 1988: 584). Certainly there were well-known difficulties in the marriage from early on. Eliot's sexual shyness was combined with a studied courtesy that cooled into icy reserve. Vivien was by contrast flirtatious, chatty and impulsive – though sex if not romance was complicated for her by the experience of very heavy periods. Her mother, in the language of the day, termed this 'moral insanity'. Vivien carried a basket with her when she stayed away from home to take away the bloody bed sheets, have them washed and returned clean. Eliot was unaware of this when they married but was advised she should not have children. If Eliot's 'maleness' was in some way wanting, her female body became associated with an embarrassing excess. On his return from the United States, according to Hastings, Eliot spent the nights of their 'second honeymoon' at Eastbourne 'in a deckchair under the pier. With a bottle of gin' (Hastings,

1984: 61).³ Vivien had in the meantime begun a long-term liaison with Russell in which Eliot later possibly colluded.

The couple settled into a small flat in Crawford Mansions in Marylebone but the marriage began to look like a mistake: the 'awful daring of a moment's surrender', in the words of *The Waste Land*, to an idea of the bohemian life in a seedy part of the city with a waif of a girl who was a bit of an artist or dancer or actress. As Eliot's timidity found another level in moods of depression and disgust, this was not a pose he could sustain in the easy terms of the mythology. His reaction was to establish a compensatory regime of order out of the damaged materials of their marriage or in the alternative sphere of work. Indeed, in a life which their letters represent as a series of unrelieved vexations, they together found a modus vivendi based exactly on a rendering of their lack of 'normality' as itself routine. They shared the anxieties, in other words, of sexual incompatibility, money worries, illness, and the as yet unachieved ambition for him to be a great poet. Arguably some of this was exaggerated – since they did receive money, for example, from Russell, from Eliot's brother and father, from Vivien's family and later from Eliot's stocks passed to him on his father's death in 1919 – by which time he was also earning £420 per annum at Lloyds bank (rising to £500 the following year). His total income in 1924 when he complained he was financially *in extremis* was £1000, while Ezra Pound in 1922 made barely £300 (Seymour-Jones, 2001: 369, 317; and see Delany, 2001).⁴

Again, though they were plagued with illness, the Eliots were both given to hypochondria (Read, 1967: 32). Their letters frequently begin and end with a record of aliments. Vivien suffered from acute neuralgia, colitis, migraine, spinal problems and bouts of influenza and pneumonia – he at one point from 'suppressed influenza' he told Ottoline Morrell after serious attacks of the real thing (Seymour-Jones, 2001: 409). She saw a series of 'specialist' doctors who prescribed various drugs, rest cures in the country or sanatoria and over-severe regimens and painful treatments. Some of this was not uncommon. We think of the experience of Virginia Woolf, for example. But others too, including Ottoline Morrell, Roger Fry, Clive Bell, Richard Aldington and F.S. Flint suffered from nervous disorders or 'neurasthenia' which, compounded by a widespread and devastating flu epidemic in 1918, came to characterise the mental and physical condition of this war-time generation.

If, therefore, a combination of factors helped shape the character of the Eliots' lives together – medical ignorance, quack cures, and the trauma of war – they also helped make it themselves, and bore its real and aggravated misery together. All the same it was not all grim nightmare, and

Vivien's one extant diary from the period of their life together, for 1919, presents quite an unexpected contrast to the usual saga. She tells here of regular teas and dinner parties with the Sitwells and Pounds and of boat trips and picnics with Mary Hutchinson, when, on one occasion, Vivien sailed from Bosham, Sussex to Hayling Island and back. Both the more relaxed and the more energetic events took place when Eliot was not present, whether in the country, or in town, when she went dancing with 'Freddie' or 'Hawkinson', or they went with others to see the Ballets Russes or performances at the Phoenix Society. In this same year she cared for Eliot, their maid, and her mother during periods of ill-health. Her diary entries convey a vigour and boldness which are not otherwise associated with her, together with an expectation of a time when things would be settled for him and when she could begin writing (Diary, 1919: Bodleian).

By 1919, too, the Eliots were established within the circle of Bloomsbury associates and were both especially friendly with the Sitwells, the Schiffs, Mary Hutchinson and Lady Ottoline Morrell. This was less the café society of Pound and Lewis than of the teas, dinners, picnics and theatre visits Vivien describes. It included invitations too to the Woolfs at Richmond and Ottoline Morrell's Garsington Manor. While Bloomsbury for the most part found enough amusement and puzzlement in its own complex inner world, Ottoline Morrell entertained Diaghilev in London and at Garsington where Augustus John, Russell, Middleton Murry and Katherine Mansfield as well as the Bloomsbury regulars were guests. This was what Garafola (1998) calls the 'lifestyle modernism' of high bohemia, a world of relative wealth, connected to the establishment but in some respects critical of it – as in Bloomsbury's and Ottoline Morrell's pacifism, unconventional manners, and liberal sexual attitudes. At first sight then the Eliots in their unstable, 'open' marriage and 'triple ménage' with Russell, as Vivien described it (2 August 1915: Thayer), seemed sufficiently irregular to join this non-conformist society within a society.

Not surprisingly they were introduced to Bloomsbury by Russell. In early March 1916, the same month they moved into their own flat in Crawford Mansions, they met Ottoline and Philip Morrell at a dinner in Soho after a lecture Russell had given the previous evening at which Clive Bell, Mark Gertler and others had also been present. The next day the Eliots were invited to tea at Ottoline Morrell's house in Bedford Square. These early meetings didn't go particularly well, however, and the invitation to Garsington came later rather than sooner, and was initially for Eliot alone, since Ottoline had found Vivien odd and hysterical.

Eliot's entrée was the poem 'Prufrock' but his hostess wondered at this too ('where does this neurasthenic poetry come from?') and found him 'dull, dull, dull', like an 'undertaker' (Seymour-Jones, 2001: 137). Later, there was a different response from the retinue at Garsington when Clive Bell presented the 'brochure' *Prufrock and other Observations* and Katherine Mansfield read the poem aloud to 'much discussion and some perplexity' (Bell, 1948: 17). The Woolfs, too, were sufficiently impressed to print Eliot's *Poems* for the Hogarth Press in 1919.

'Prufrock' was *the* poem of this era and somehow caught a nervy and unnerving cultural tone in its debilitated, 'feminised' male persona. Woolf found Eliot a little sinister and was never friendly towards Vivien, and in the event the Eliots turned out to be just too irregular. Vivien said the wrong thing, while Eliot said far too little, and what he said he said in an over-deliberate, unctuous and courteous English. To Bloomsbury's lauded wit and informality, Eliot brought a creepy gravitas whose emotional core was shuttered behind his formality and 'four-piece suit' (Bell, 1948: 16).

Given Eliot's singularity, it made a peculiar sense that he should decide to take a flat of his own in 1923 at Burleigh Mansions in the theatre district in Charing Cross Road. Here, in a version of the artist's garret, he received the Sitwells, the Woolfs and Léonide Massine, dancer and choreographer with the Ballets Russes. Seymour-Jones associates this secret life with Eliot's supposed homosexuality. Among other suggested liaisons, she believes Eliot continued to grieve over 'a love cut short' by the death in war of the young Frenchman, Jean Verdenal, who Eliot had met in Paris in 1910 and to whom 'Prufrock' was dedicated, and that he was 'in love' with and an 'intimate' of Léonide Massine (Seymour-Jones, 2001: 291, 349, 419, caption 426–7). None of this is confirmed by Eliot's immediate contemporaries. Thus if his homosexuality, if such it was, was known to his Bloomsbury associates, or to Pound, Lewis and Joyce, to say nothing of Vivien herself, we have to conclude they did not comment directly on it, or, that this evidence has in some way been censored. If such a comment were to surface, the most remarkable thing still would be that it had been so repressed.

Eliot, it is true, was given to secrets. And so was Vivien. One they shared was the 'Guy Fawkes plot' of the *Criterion*. It was going, possum style, to explode slowly under the establishment (Eliot, 1988: 553, 589). The short episode of editing and writing for the journal was the high point of this best period for Vivien. But if there was a shared *Criterion* conspiracy, there was the scent of another plot against her. Her poem 'Necesse est Perstare?' published in April 1925 exposed the tedium of

Bloomsbury:

> And there was an end (for a session)
> of the eternal Aldous Huxley –
> Elizabeth Bibesco – Clive Bell –
> unceasing clamour of inanities.

Bloomsbury objected. The offending author was discovered and silenced. Did Eliot allow Vivien free rein as his own double, indiscrete, satirical voice, knowing Bloomsbury would require her suppression? She, anyway, published no more. The late 1910s and early 1920s had been years of promise and waiting for them both, and, strange perhaps though their compact was, they had come this far together. At this point, however, the classic destiny of the bohemian, on the road to the academy, the hospital or the morgue, divided. Her talents were blocked and she declined, heading for the mental hospital and mortuary. He meanwhile was destined for fame and a place in the groves of academe.

'Some of the actor in Tom'

> Oh the moon shone bright on Charlie Chaplin
> His boots were cracking
> For want of blacking.

> Eliot was a 'A Wonderful fellow. Marvelous sense of humor. We were both addicts of the comic strips, made the rounds of bars and burlesque shows, talked about everything from free verse to love and human folly.' (Lorenz, 1983: 19)

Conrad Aiken was Eliot's contemporary and close friend at Harvard, the freshman to his sophomore. Both men were poets and both were looking for a new idiom. 'From the moment they met, in the offices of the *Harvard Advocate* in 1908', reports Aiken, 'for the next five years, this was their constant concern... We were feeling our way towards it, something less *poetic*, more inclusive, more quotidian admitting even the vernacular, and lower in pitch: a new poetic voice, one in which one could *think*' (1971: 5). Aiken thought he was on to something with the youthful 'The Clerk's Journal' and 'London Symphony'. The first, written in 1910, 'is already talking of lunch-counters, plates of beans, the moon among telephone wires' (4). Aiken believes this was 'several years before "Prufrock" ' (4), though Gordon tells us 'Prufrock' was completed when the two men met in Paris in the summer 1911 and that Aiken commented on a longer draft version (Gordon, 1998: 63, 66). At which time, of course, Eliot had long discovered Corbière and Laforgue through Symons's *Symbolist Movement in Poetry*. There are certainly echoes of Eliot's verse in Aiken's second volume, *Turns and Movies* (1916): 'At ease on sawdust floors, he lean and drinks', 'She will not turn to him – will not resist / Impassive, she submits to being kissed', 'She paused, fatigued with combing out her hair...She was getting old' (1916: 4, 9, 11). Reuel Denney sees the influence as going the other way (Denney, 1964: 85). But if this was the case, Aiken did, on the other hand, have more caché as a published poet than Eliot, with four volumes to his credit by 1917, and did significantly help 'Prufrock' into print by showing it around London and, most importantly, when pressed, to Pound. The poem 'bordered on "insanity"', Harold Munro had said (Aiken, 1948: 22). Eventually it appeared in *Poetry: A Magazine of Verse* in June 1915 after a nine month's campaign by Pound, and some four years after its first composition. 'Prufrock' and Eliot, we should remember, were frighteningly avant-garde.

Aiken and Eliot's careers developed in quite different directions and Aiken, though a Pulitzer prize winner in 1930, never achieved Eliot's success. Eliot said he regretted this, though Aiken's letters in the 1920s on his possible contributions to the *Criterion* suggest that Eliot did not particularly admire his work, nor actively seek to promote it. By this time, too, Aiken's sense of the writer's purpose could not have been more different from Eliot's proclaimed doctrine of impersonality. 'Give yourself away, come clean', Aiken wrote to Malcolm Cowley in the late 1920s, 'Get down to the real business of the poet [which is] consciously or unconsciously to give the lowdown on himself...what do you think of yourself or feel which is secretly you? shamefully you? intoxicatingly you, drunkenly or soberly or lyrically you?' (Aiken, 1978: 23). Both men were said to be shy, but whereas Aiken would have the poet crash through his inhibitions, Eliot found a more guarded outlet: 'Letters should be indiscretions' he wrote to Aiken in 1914 'otherwise they are simply official bulletins' (1988: 75). Few though such moments are, Eliot's letters to Aiken do sometimes jolt into a confession of something 'secret' and 'shameful'.

Aiken, too, proved a consistently astute observer of the different sides of Eliot; from his early 'composite photograph' of Eliot 'posed as a "decadent"' (Aiken, 1978: 26) to his reading of *The Waste Land* as an 'anatomy of melancholy' (Grant, 1982: 156–61). At Harvard, Eliot, said Aiken, had 'the most beautiful manners' and 'enviable grace'

(1965: 92); he was 'a singularly attractive, tall and rather dapper young man' (1948: 20). 'There was an element of... Laforgue already in him', Howarth confirms, 'it was easy to progress to the pose from the urbane dandyism, the perfection of dress, manners and accomplishments, which was the Harvard style of the time and in which he excelled' (Howarth, 1965: 105). Aiken saw how 'extremely controlled, precise and disciplined' Eliot was (1965: 92), how he schooled himself to attempt 'certain varieties of experience' so as to overcome his shyness. 'The dances and parties' of his social life at Harvard 'were a part of this discipline', adds Aiken, as were the boxing lessons he took in Boston after his year at the Sorbonne. Eliot returned to Harvard 'perceptibly Europeanised', said Aiken, and took self-consciously and conspicuously to 'carrying a cane – was it a malacca?' (1948: 21). 'There was some of the actor in Tom', he reflects 'and some of the clown, too. For all his liturgical appearance... he was capable of real buffonery' (1965: 92).

This composite Eliot shuffled different types – the dandy, clown, buffoon and specifically in relation to Laforgue, the figure of Pierrot. Baudelaire had defined the dandy as possessing an 'aristocratic superiority' of personality and stoical reserve of which an 'interest in personal appearance and material elegance' were the mere symbols (Graña and Graña, 1990: 577), and Holbrook Jackson reinforces this in his reflections on the English 1890s. 'The dandy is the product of boredom', writes Jackson (1976: 114). His 'revolt against the ennui of conventions' appears in a cultivation of artifice and an aesthetic of 'unexpectedness' (111). Dandyism was, on this reckoning, less 'a phase of life' than 'a phase of art. It was really the art of posing' and as such found expression not only in clothing and manners but in a state of mind or a 'dandyism of the temperament' (110). Baudelaire was the latter's true philosopher, says Jackson, and was led by his 'acute consciousness of sin' not to resist evil but to explore the 'purgatory in every sensation' (110). At the source of this temperament was the dandy's attitude towards sex and towards women. As Jessica Feldman underlines, for Baudelaire 'woman' is 'the opposite of the dandy': the 'natural', 'abominable' and 'vulgar' to the dandy's civilised, artificial and artistic (Feldman, 1993: 6). The dandy's misogyny was less than secure, however, for while women were by definition expelled from the realm of culture, the dandy's 'yearning for the female' meant he internalised an idea of the feminine. Contemptuous of women he nevertheless existed, like them through a self-fashioning persona, since for both 'To appear is to be' (Feldman, 1993: 7). For Feldman, therefore, the dandy emerges as a transgressive figure, poised between the customary polarities of gender.

We have met something like this already in Wyndham Lewis. The young Eliot came at it differently however. Holbrook Jackson observes that dandyism in Europe was 'the Pagan's reply to Puritanism' (1976: 111). Turn of the century Harvard was neither Paris nor London, nor was it the most likely place for the puritan to convert the other way to paganism. It did nonetheless present the arena of a bounded, highly coded male society and Eliot chose to observe its 'laws' of personal manner, dress, conduct and intellectual style to a point of conspicuous perfection.[5]

For Eliot, as for Baudelaire's dandy, this role required strict self-discipline and the stoical submission to a regimen, ranging as Baudelaire puts it, from 'the impeccable care of the person to the most dangerous forms of sport' designed as 'a gymnastic exercise ... to fortify the will and discipline the soul' (Graña and Graña, 1990: 577). The result was a super-conformity, 'originality, within the apparent bounds of convention' as Baudelaire has it (ibid.), which allowed, by that same token, for the singular and exceptional. For Eliot, all the same, too much of the ways of Harvard, family society in Boston, and holidays at Cape Ann proved tedious (Gordon, 1998: 46). His 'revolt from this ennui' took him in 1911, not surprisingly, precisely to the home in Paris of those poets who presented a model in both literary and personal style of how to be modern. Through Symons, Eliot found in Laforgue an ironic dandysim he could identify with: 'strictly correct, in a top hat, a sober cravat, an English jacket, a clergyman's overcoat, and in case of necessity, an invariable umbrella under his arm' (Symons, 1958: 56). And once in Paris he 'looked', Gordon confirms, 'for the decadent Paris of *Babu de Montparnasse*' (1977: 39). 'He hunted down decadence, and allowed lust and drunkenness to circle round him, so that he might contemplate with horror a life bereft of morale or dignity' (40).

Somehow the experiment fell flat. Aiken joined Eliot briefly in the summer of 1911 to sip 'sirop de fraises' and learn that his friend had decided to return to Harvard to study philosophy (1948: 20–1). Eliot had set himself to study Parisian decadence; he had inspected its tawdry streets and caught the eye of a prostitute or two, but found Paris or himself, or both, wanting. Not for him the 'sexual marathon' the otherwise respectable court tutor Laforgue had enjoyed in the low dives of Berlin (Gordon, 1998: 58). The 'Europeanised' Eliot therefore returned to Harvard with the symbolic prop of a Malacca cane but with no actual advance on his sexual education. His achievement had been a sheaf of poems, including 'Prufrock', 'Portrait of a Lady', 'Rhapsody on a Windy

Night' and 'Conversation Galante'; all of them suffused with a Laforguian idiom and the temperament of Pierrot.[6]

Characteristically this pose is defined in relation to older women, among them the Boston hostess, Adeline Moffatt; 'Miss X' as Aiken calls her, 'the *precieuse ridicule* to end all preciosity, serving tea so exquisitely among the bric-a-brac' (1948: 21; Gordon, 1998: 37). In 'Portrait of a Lady' this woman is given to a watery, flattering emotionalism which her young male guest parries with non-committal smiles and trivia in a non-exchange that matches Eliot's Laforguian switch between the banal and esoteric. Typically and with an almost palpably stiffening body language, the speaker makes his self-protective retreat, exiting on a tepid note of self-doubt. The man's demeanour thoughout is marked by a barely controlled tension between politeness and weary contempt – for which the only social form is a watchful, resentful silence.

These poems exhibit a fastidious, enervated defensiveness which Gordon interprets as a 'distrust of women' (Gordon, 1998: 38). Eliot enjoyed women's company (his sisters and female cousins were strong, career-minded women) and he liked to flirt, thereby holding off any sexual relationship – as he did during a long off/on relationship with Emily Hale who he first met in 1912. This is not so unlike, but more anaemic than the more blasé Laforgue (Storey, 1978: 158–9). While Eliot's self-possession 'flares' and 'gutters' (Eliot, 1974: 21), Laforgue's Pierrot is more acerbic and unflappable. Thus what emerges is less the haughty but showy dandy than a distant, would-be-suave but nervy Pierrot, permanently on guard against active involvement or invasion. This Prufrockian sensibility was what, in part, Eliot brought to Oxford and war-time London. He was open to the foreignness and noisy variety of the capital but was pulled up, not for the first time, by his own reactions, amounting to 'one of those nervous sexual attacks which I suffer from when alone in a city'. This time, he confided to Aiken, in a proffered 'indiscretion', was 'the worst since Paris':

> One walks about the street with one's desires, and one's refinement rises up like a wall whenever opportunity approaches. I should be better off, I sometimes think, if I had disposed of my virginity and shyness several years ago; and indeed I still think sometimes that it would be well to do so before marriage. (Eliot, 1988: 75)

The 'several years ago' was probably Paris in 1910–11. Eliot's 'refinement', once more, owes less to the dandy's blasé hauteur than to the gauche sexual innocence which condemned him to the role of frustrated spectator upon an urban scene of anonymous, fantasised sexual opportunity: this very scene indeed comprising a major trope, in Baudelaire, Symons, and others, for the fleeting, contingent sensations distinguishing urban modernity. In Eliot, however, the nervous excitement of the city is a source of torture rather than tantalising opportunity or decadent perversity.

The shy virgin poet was not entirely unaccompanied however. Aiken remembers this period for the early poems, but also 'more immediately', he says, for giving 'rise to the series of hilariously naughty *parega* which was devoted spasmodically to the singular and sterling character of King Bolo' (1948: 22). These verses Eliot wrote into but cut out of his early notebook 'Inventions of the March Hare' but regularly enclosed – a further 'indiscretion' – in letters to Aiken. One such, a 'war poem', titled 'Up Boys And At 'Em', ran:

> The captain pac'd the quarterdeck
> Parading in his corset.
> What ho! they cry'd, we'll sink your ship!
> And so they up and sink'd her.
> But the cabin boy was sav'd alive
> And bugger'd, in the sphincter. (Eliot, 1988: 59)

In the notebook, 'The Triumph of Bullshit' began:

> Ladies, on whom my attentions have waited
> If you consider my merits are small
> Etiolated, alembicated,
> Orotund, tasteless, fantastical,
> Monotonous, crotchety, constipated,
> Impotent galamatias
> Affected, possibly imitated
> For Christ's sake stick it up your ass. (Eliot, 1996: 307)

The 'strictly correct' Thomas Stearns Eliot was shadowed therefore by the incorrect ribald balladeer and outright misogynist. Underlying the tedious and puerile incantations, as Gordon sees it, of ' "big hairy balls", a black "knotty penis", "assholes" and quantities of "shit" ' in these verses, there is 'a sick fury...an obsessional hatred of women and sex, punitive in its virulence' (Gordon, 1998: 77). Elsewhere, Gordon warns us, persuasively I think, against assuming Eliot was 'queer', for if the 'repressed' 'King Bolo' poems were pornographic and, in fact, depressingly conventional, Eliot did, as in the letter to Aiken, outwardly express a troubled desire for women. And 'who' writes Gordon, 'can now determine the exact ways people of the past bent their inclinations in order to construct gender according to absurd models of masculinity and femininity?' (53). Absurd and constructed the 'King Bolo' poems certainly were; to the point, one feels, of sheer rhetorical invention. For in the main they served in a homosocial exchange with Aiken, and perhaps with Pound, another recipient, to express an aggressive sexuality Eliot did not possess nor reveal in other than this kind of crude 'hilariously naughty' outburst. Thus they helped confirm a lewd cameraderie which bonded male companions in a shared knowledge of what is 'secretly you, shamefully you' (Aiken, 1978: 23). It was of course women who were kept out of this secret and in Eliot's case the very particular woman, his mother, who – the unspeakable transgression of these verses to one side – he was very concerned in 1920 should not see the published poem 'Ode' which refers to 'blood' upon the bridal bed.[7]

The 'King Bolo' poems belonged therefore to a hidden and 'darker' male discourse, which Aiken, paradoxically, could easily place on the other 'lighter' side of Eliot as the 'cynical counterpoint to the study of Sanskrit and the treatise on epistemology' (1948: 22). Thus, too, in later life, 'the two men at lunch laughed over Eliot's Bolo poems – of which Aiken had been appointed Royal Keeper, and Aiken's limericks' (Aiken, 1971: 7). We might choose to see something else: the bluff and brazen side of a shyness and fear of women which could only be appeased through gross sexual caricature.

But what becomes of Pierrot? Laforgue's figure has moments of 'nice cruelty' (Storey, 1978: 162), and *commedia dell'arte*, says Martin Green, traditionally teams the 'highly aesthetic, wistful, elegant, graceful' with 'madness and murder'. 'Pierrot and Harlequin' he adds, 'can be terrifying' (Green, 1987: 18). Harlequin is a 'wry and agitated joker', a coarser, more lawless figure than Pierrot (28). In the modern age, he takes to the music hall and vaudeville stage, 'legs apart' as the big-bellied 'comedian' of Eliot's 'Suite Clownesque' – only then, like some quick-change artist, to step out from behind the screen as Sweeney – 'broadbottomed', 'apeneck' – to shoulder Pierrot and Prufrock to one side. American readers, Eliot supposed, would find him 'disgusting'. 'Do you think', he asks, anxious again about his mother, 'that "Sweeney Erect" will shock her?' (1988: 363).

Eliot's anxieties, whether as Puritan, Pierrot, Harlequin or the pagan Sweeney, are focused upon the female body (the 'female smells in shuttered rooms'; 1974: 28), but extended to an extreme self-consciousness about his own male body. Apparently, he would not allow anyone to see him shaving and was shocked by Bloomsbury's open discussion of bodily functions, and, in one incident, by Leonard Woolf's pissing when they were out on a country walk (Bergonzi, 1972: 70). The likelihood is that Eliot was sexually shy of both men and women, generally lacking in 'crude insistent passion' as Russell put it (Gordon, 1998: 91). Before this lack of feeling was worked up into moods of complaint and bitterness – and eventually a doctrine of celibacy, there was one brief episode at least, however, in London, communicated again to Aiken, when Eliot sounded amazingly carefree. He was dissatisfied with his verse but asks 'why should one worry about that? I feel such matters take care of themselves, and have no dependence upon our planning.' He had – with Byron – ' "nothing plann'd / Except perhaps to be a moment merry" ' (1988: 69).

This was in late 1914. Eliot had met Pound and was soon to fall in with Lewis and other modern artists in London, the 'radical' Gaudier-Brzeska, the 'interesting' Hulme, and Edward Wadsworth 'whose work I like exceedingly' (1988: 94). London agreed with him and he felt part of the Vorticist or as he termed it 'cubist' crowd. In April 1915 he wrote to Pound apologising for his 'ravings' after a 'debauch' the night before and hoped to meet Pound in town or at Lewis's on Saturday (1988: 96). And he was to be published in the second issue of *Blast*. In February 1915, Eliot confessed to Aiken that he didn't know his own mind: whether to marry, have children or retire at fifty to a table on the boulevard viewing the world through the fumes of an aperitif. Both conventional bourgeois and artistic options seemed 'thin', he said (1988: 88). There is something languid about all of this, even to allowing he would be 'forced to a decision in a few days'. Within a matter of months rather than days things were indeed decided: London was attractive; he had a dozen friends and was married. Two days after the wedding Pound wrote at Eliot's request to his father with 'some sort of apologia for the literary life in general and London literary life in particular' (1988: 99). Eliot wrote to his brother explaining his change of plans: it was 'what I always wanted':

> The only really surprising thing is that I should have had the force to attempt it...I know that you will agree that the responsibility and independent action has been and will be just what I needed. Now my only concern is how I can make her perfectly happy, and I think I can do that by being myself infinitely more fully than I have ever been.

I am much less suppressed, and more confident than I have ever been. (104)

Literary life and Viven were an inseparable expression of independence, a way of 'being myself infinitely more fully'. But what did it mean for Eliot to be himself? Would the real Eliot remove or openly display the mask? And which self, masked or unmasked, decided to send two obscene poems, 'The Triumph of Bullshit' and 'Ballade pour la grosse Lulu' to Lewis for inclusion in *Blast*? Lewis was keen on these 'excellent bits of scholarly ribaldry' but stuck to his policy to have 'no "Words Ending in -Uck, -Unt and -Ugger"' – a decision Eliot put down to Lewis's 'puritanical principles' (1996: 306). Had Eliot abandoned his puritan principles then and gone pagan?

Eliot 'plunged' into marriage, in a way Virginia Woolf thought was beyond him and against both his own and everybody's expectations (see Woolf, 1978a, 104). 'I think that all I wanted of Vivienne', he was to say later, 'was a flirtation or a mild affair: I was too shy and unpractised to achieve either with anybody' (1988: xvii). The casual bohemian way with women was not one Eliot could muster and he was drawn into something he 'did not naturally "take" to' (Aiken, 1948: 20). But really the struggle with himself was a battle he had to win with his parents and the Eliot family. To get free he persuaded himself he loved Vivien, 'because I wanted to burn my boats and commit myself to staying in England' (1988: xvii). To be a poet not a Harvard professor he had jumped, eyes closed, but misjudged and floundered. His moment had gone. He clung to the poetry but almost immediately his daring 'surrender' felt like a long awful drop into purgatory.

On his return from visiting his parents in late July, Eliot and Vivien took their disastrous 'second honeymoon' at Eastbourne. We survey the scene of the virgin groom, self-conscious about his congenital hernia and his nakedness, shocked and appalled by Vivien's heavy and irregular menstrual flows. Henceforth he retreated into a solicitude for Vivien's health and for his own, constructing the routines that characterised the fretful drama of illnesses, doctors, cures and money which comprised so much of their married life.

Pierrot and Sweeney meanwhile twisted about. In late 1923, Virginia Woolf went to a small party he had arranged and discovered him completely drunk (Woolf, 1978a: 278). He apologised profusely but the damage was done; by now he'd shown all that was weird and gruesome in the blurred composite of himself. He had started from Laforgue and the Jacobeans, he said, and the latter had come to claim their own.

When Osbert and Sacheverell Sitwell called on 'Capt. Eliot' at his Charing Cross hideaway, they found Sweeney had ursuped the more delicate Pierrot and was sitting in his place, 'a dusting of green powder' on his cheeks (Pearson, 1978: 239). Then, in the mid-1920s, his relationship with Vivien worsening, a raw, shamefully indiscrete yell burst through the air of nervous debility. Aiken wrote in fulsome praise of Eliot's *Poems 1909–1925*. Eliot replied from France where he'd gone alone, leaving Vivien at a Health Institute in Watford, with a page torn from the *Midwives Gazette*. He had underlined the words 'Model Answers' for students taking nursing exams, and below this, in a column describing forms of vaginal discharge, underlined the words 'blood, mucous' and 'shreds of mucous' and the phrase 'purulent offensive discharge' (Aiken, 1978: 109). In reply Aiken quoted from an advertisement recommending the sanitary towels Kotex – used with success he added by 'Blue eyed Claude the cabin boy' – 'the clever little nipper / who filled his ass with broken glass / and circumcised the skipper' (110). Extraordinarily enough, soon after this 'deepest darkest... most malignant' exchange 'the air was cleared and our friendship resumed' (Aiken, 1978: 110; 1965: 93). They were both very good at covering things up.

Pierrot, un peu banquier, on Margate Sands

I.A. Richards was stunned by Eliot's poetry: 'I remember sunlight on those large, fine pages and a breathless exhilaration as I came away with it', he says of Eliot's 1920 volume *Ara Vos Prec* after discovering it in a Cambridge bookshop; he was – 'unable NOT to read it in the Market Place ... – spreading the resplendent thing open: lost in wonder and strangeness and delight' (Richards, 1967: 2). He followed this up with a visit to Eliot's basement office at Lloyds bank. The office was in Henrietta Street, said Richards, later correcting this to Queen Victoria Street (Lloyds). Both addresses, in a manner typical of such memories, were wrong. From 1917–20 Eliot worked at 17 Cornhill, then at Lombard Street and from 1923–25 at 20 King William Street. Richards remembers Eliot in a 'little room' on his own 'almost entirely filled' with a 'big table', beside which there was 'just room for two perches' (1967: 4). 'Within a foot of our heads when we stood', he recalls 'were the thick, green glass squares of the pavement' (4). It is highly unlikely that a clerk of Eliot's status would have had a room of his own and Richards tends to remember the scene by way of Charles Dickens's London. We do have an idea, though, of what kind of world he stepped into. A rule book at the bank stated that male staff could talk to women only on business matters and that the clothing of female staff must be 'of a dark colour and quiet of character' (Lloyds). Women were employed on a temporary basis during war-time, but the bank and the City remained a predominantly male preserve. As someone who thought there were 'too many women' associated with the *Egoist* (1988: 198) Eliot may well have welcomed their subdued role in the world of work where along with hundreds of others he happily adopted the formal City uniform of black jacket and sponge bag trousers. His friend Pound, he said later, thinking no doubt of Pound's conspicuous bohemian get-up, 'would have looked rather out of place in King William Street' (Southam, 1977: 79). In a sense the City was a transplanted Harvard and the dandy in Eliot distinguished himself here, as there, by his smooth ultra conformity. To the bank clerk's regular dress he brought the discrete transgression, as a colleague reported, of wearing 'large tortoise-shell rimmed glasses which, at the time, were a new thing and not generally worn, even at managerial level' (Lloyds). At the same time, as his fellow clerks knew, he was in the other part of his life, a poet – who 'often seemed to be living in dreamland' and would 'break off suddenly' from dictating a letter 'to grasp a piece of paper and start writing quickly when an idea came to him' (Lloyds). On one occasion Eliot judged a short story competition among staff. And after work, he would join the Sitwells and Vivien for tea, or, as Iris Barry reminds us, Pound's weekly gatherings in Soho, dressed as for the bank. If Pound stayed clear of King William Street, Eliot, in a sense truer to the workings of modernist estrangement, brought the banker to Bohemia, at a stroke converting the clerk's suit into the poet's garb.

Richards remembers Eliot's 'big table covered with all sorts and sizes of foreign correspondence' and Eliot himself as 'a figure stooping, very like a dark bird in a feeder' (3). In commentaries on the modern city, by Benjamin and by Poe, for example, the clerk is the drudge and marionette, or, elsewhere, in English fiction, he is the dogged aspirant to culture. Both types appear in *The Waste Land* drafts and published texts and we might read the poem as the successful attempt to separate this figure from Eliot himself (Brooker, 2002). Pound was one of those who in reality attempted to rescue Eliot the poet from Eliot the banker, notably in his 'Bel Esprit' campaign to provide Eliot with a guaranteed independent income of £300 p.a. The plan failed and embarrassed Eliot who did not leave the bank until an alternative was absolutely secure in 1925 when he joined Faber and Gwyer.

In fact, the two halves of poet and city clerk were more like patches on the same Harlequin costume than a case of schizophrenia. The writer's block Eliot reported in 1916 eased from the following March when he began at the bank. There followed poems in French, the first 'Eeldrop and Appleplex' in May, a job as assistant editor on the *Egoist* in June, and in July the publication by the Egoist Press of *Prufrock and other Observations*. The bank gave Eliot the disciplined regimen and, quite crucially, the degree of financial security he needed in order to enter dreamland. In this respect, though more cautious than Pound, he was the more 'modern' poet whose creative life was regulated and made possible by the routines of time-keeping characterising urban modernity. We might note, too, with Hugh Kenner, that Eliot was the poet of this newly technologised world (1987: 26–7) and remember that this division, if such it was, between poet and banker took place inside Eliot, and was not felt by him as a disabling conflict between incompatible parts. The immaculately black-coated Eliot sorting papers at the bank is, after all, not so far removed from the poet pondering the very miscellaneous foreign materials of *The Waste Land*.

The eventual transition in the 1920s from bank clerk to editor of the *Criterion* and publisher was an enormously significant one. Even so, if we are to believe his friend and colleague, Frank Morley, this too involved less a jump into another sphere than a step across and steady climb up another ladder close by. Morley met Eliot in 1925 at what he calls the 'Criterion bar', when Eliot joined him and others, including Herbert Read and F.S. Flint, for weekly dinners at the Grove pub in South Kensington (Morley, 1948: 60, 64). Joining Faber and Gwyer had provided a magical solution for some of Eliot's immediate difficulties. He could quit the bank but continue in the steadying routines of office work with the security of a five-year contract at four-fifths of his Lloyd's salary. It gave him time to write, a publisher for his own work and a way of orchestrating literary taste through Faber's list and through the *Criterion* which the company took on in October 1925. In Morley's view, Eliot's literary reputation 'had not spread very far', and 'it was as a man of business ... that he was taken on' (1948: 61, 62). In truth, both sides of Eliot were relevant to Faber, and Eliot himself, who as businessman and poet, the defender of a self-correcting tradition and original creative talent, now discovered the ideal accommodation of both in the role of a businessman of letters. The routines of office life, the camaraderie of practical jokes and clubbiness which later developed between Morley, Geoffrey Faber, Eliot and John Hayward (nicknamed 'Whale', 'Coot', 'Elephant' and 'Tarantula') confirmed his settlement with a male bourgeois establishment – which licensed, indeed sponsored, his criticism and poetry.

Part of the bond with Morley turned out to be a shared fondness for Sherlock Holmes. Eliot, says Ackroyd, would quote passages from memory as one of his party pieces (Ackroyd, 1984: 167) and Morley opens his contribution to a Festschrift on Eliot's sixtieth birthday with a quotation from Dr Watson and ends with regret at the loss of 'my Sherlock Holmes' (1948: 60, 70). Eliot was attracted to Holmes as 'in some important respects a sport' who transgressed the 'laws' of the English type of detective fiction (Eliot, 1927: 140) and by a nostalgia for nineteenth-century London ('the hansom cabs, the queer bowlers... Holmes in a frock coat after breakfast'; 1929: 553). But perhaps there was something else too. For Holmes was himself a divided figure who swung between a firm exercise of and loss of will, a devotion to the methods of scientific inquiry and moods of depression, ennui and drug taking. In Holmes, in short, Eliot was presented with a displaced rendering of the Larforguian persona ('strictly correct, in a top hat... an English jacket'), the urban dandy turned detective, in a version, now closer to Eliot himself, of the uneasy contract between decadent aesthete and impersonal arbiter, safely removed from the world of feminised emotions.

Maybe Morley's 'my Sherlock Holmes' credited Eliot – linguist, scholar, practical joker, businessman, poet and publisher – with some of Holmes's all-round genius. But he has Eliot's appearance and manner in mind too. Thus, when in the early 1920s, Eliot went from the Grove pub to discuss the *Criterion* with its then patron, Lady Rothermere, he set out in 'a costume much more sportif', says Morley, than his usual banker's outfit '(he could never resist a touch of the dramatic)' (1948: 64). Of the 'usual outfit', he comments:

> He still looked very much the City man. His strong-set aquiline features and his well set-up figure were observed to advantage in the traditional costume of bowler hat, black coat and striped trousers... Was that a deliberate disguise? It might fool you to know which of his disguises was which. He carried a malacca-handled umbrella which was always neatly rolled, and with which, when he wished for a taxi-cab, he paved in the air. Such a display, however, was unusual; for the most part his behaviour was subject to an iron control. (61)

Some of the controlled theatricality Morley speaks of appears in the photograph of Eliot in 1926 outside the offices of Faber and Gwyer (Figure 8). 'He looks almost too perfect to be entirely serious' Ackroyd comments 'as if he were posing in fancy dress' (1984: 153). It's a portrait of Eliot as

Laforgue become banker become Faber's Sherlock Holmes. But there's another echo too surely: of the sometimes jaunty 'sort of Pierrot' of the silent screen, Charlie Chaplin (Chaplin, 1964: 225) whose 'egregious merit' Eliot had detected in a 'rhythm' of abstract caricature. Chaplin explained his creation this way:

> You know this fellow is many sided, a tramp, a gentleman, a poet, a dreamer, a lonely fellow, always hopeful of romance and adventure. He would have you believe he is a scientist, a musician, a duke, a polo player. However, he is not above picking up cigarette butts or robbing a baby of its candy. And of course, if the occasion warrants it, he will kick a lady in the rear – but only in extreme anger. (154)

Thus Chaplin. And from Eliot:

> Politic, cautious, and meticulous
> Full of high sentence, but a bit obtuse;
> At times, almost ridiculous –
> Almost at times the Fool. (1974: 17)

And:

> En Amerique, professeur;
> En Angleterre, journaliste ...
> En Yorkshire, conférencier;
> A Londres, un peu banquier, ...
> En Allemagne, philosophe. (1974: 49)

Eliot played all the parts, said Kenner: 'the Archdeacon, the Publisher, the Clubman, the Man of Letters in Europe, the Aged Eagle, the Wag, and Public Spirited Citizen' (1960: x). The list could go on: student of vaudeville, boxing, dancing, fan of the funny papers, detective fiction and silent cinema; humourist, would-be actor, drinker, moody hypochrondriac, misogynist. Ask for Mr Eliot, Elephant, the Possum, the Poet, the Publisher, Mr Holmes, Dr Crippen.

In late September 1921 after Eliot had experienced severe headaches, a London doctor diagnosed a nervous disorder and ordered him to take an extended period of rest. His staff card at Lloyds includes in a pencilled note dated 12.10.21 the stark legend, 'Three months sick leave (nervous breakdown)' (Lloyds). So, between 22 October and 17 November, he went to stay at the Albemarle Hotel, 47 Eastern Esplanade, Cliftonville,

Margate. During this time he became convinced that he was suffering not from a nervous disorder but from 'an *aboulie* and emotional derangement' (1988: 486), and determined, on the advice of Ottoline Morrell and Julian Huxley, to apply to Dr Roger Vittoz in Lausanne for treatment. He felt he needed less a 'nerve man' than 'a specialist in psychological troubles' and was assured that Vittoz was 'just the man I want' (1988: 480, 482). Before leaving Margate he wrote the draft of the third section of what was to become *The Waste Land*. He then travelled back to London and on to Lausanne via Paris where he showed the unfinished poem to Pound who had now permanently left England. At Lausanne, while under Vittoz, he drafted the remainder of the poem. By 24 January 1922, after commenting again on the poem, Pound declared it a triumph: 'The thing now runs from April...to shantih without [a] break...and let us say the longest poem in the English langwidge... Complimenti, you bitch' (Eliot, 1988: 497–8).

Vivien had accompanied Eliot to Margate and stayed with him at the Albemarle for four days in October. Among their luggage was a mandolin she had bought him.

Not what I intended, what I desired, was not to surrender just for one minute but always continually sink back down among the dead men.[8]

Sunday faces, bonnets and silk hats and gloves in hand in endless procession, sad and glad and haggard and merry faces, our journey affording a fleeting view of the Thames, the lamps shining on the silent water, flitting from the gloom and into the light and so into the gloom once more and though I am not subject to impressions, the dull, heavy evening with the strange business upon which we were engaged combined to make me nervous and depressed, to lose a little my self-possession. At the Lyceum Theatre the crowds were already thick at the side entrances. In front a continuous stream of hansoms and four-wheelers were rattling up, discharging their cargoes of shirt-fronted men and beshawled, bediamonded women. Not yet nine before after so dreary a day another day and the dense drizzly fog that lay low upon the great city slipped brown and yellow below the pavement and so across the crowded thoroughfare.

Travel by undergound tube railway! From 5.30 a.m. to nearly midnight, at intervals of 3–10 min. and of 20 min. before 7 a.m. and after 9 p.m. The carriages are of first and third class only. The third class is apt to be inconveniently crowded between 8 and 10 a.m. and 5 and 7 p.m. by passengers going to and returning from their daily work. The fares are extremely moderate, seldom exceeding a shilling even for considerable distances. The names of the stations are called out by the porters, and are always painted at different parts of the platform and on the lamps and benches, though frequently difficult to distinguish from the surrounding advertisements. Baker Street, Portland Road, Gower Street, King's Cross, Farringdon Street, Aldersgate Street, Moorgate Street – close to Finsbury Circus, 5 min. from the bank, chief station for the City. (Baedeker, 1908: 30, 31)

Fastidious, punctilious, oblivious he held his open notebook upon his knee. Below stairs. You must ask for Mr Eliot.

It was Sunday we went to Queensway with Brigit and then with the Morrells when Massine was with them in town. Brigit was mentally lazy, I said, when all the world knew she was the most beautiful woman in London, and he was, yes, I said, the most beautiful actor. The most beautiful poem was Hulme's. And then in the cab with Virginia, later, towards Richmond, when the masks dropped. She plunged, she thought.

And shall I wear my face painted, my trousers, hat, jacket, overcoat, hat umbrella, waiscoat? Tell me. Pound used Coton the tailor for swank. Vivien wrote to mother how she would purchase new socks and underwear and a new winter coat for me. Those shoes for Joyce. How would we look stood together? His black patch after the operation standing with his son; his voice was a singing voice and you could tell he was a dancing man, so she said.

Margate, Eastbourne, Torquay, her healthy bloody cheeks then. They went and I went later and later the boat trip but not upon the sea she couldn't. Not like the Isis the real sea where you see yourself below the waves. Twisted things turn up, a child's toy, the claw I saw still twitching. She would rush out in her black silk pyjamas. Pure torture, after which any man would. Did you never visit Dublin, says she, not that I would, not now. Jim looking on. Nor London. Where the stairs climb at Sandymount. Bathing for men only. Cold would excite the membrane. Red hot to stimulate the husband. After a night upon the strand enough to make any man any man think twice. I remember how mounting the stairs at midnight my mind shook. Always shave first thing when she's out of the bathroom and into her bedroom. I was in the hall when she ran out past into the blackness. Well then my girl, if that's your game. Murder in mind. Ask for Capt. Eliot atop. He'll fit you. You can see the dome below, the crowd curling around the Coliseum, the wind twisting the smiles and faces. The way it smooths out the beach, my hair smoothed back, hers on end like stray, twisted bits of words the way she spoke them.

> Like fractured atoms we are spars upon the floors. Something along those lines.
> Bits of verse by means of which the artful French fought off the female stench,
> the bloody murder upon the bloody bed. Imagine mother reading it. Imagine
> marrying such a one if such a one as Ezra should say 'Sodomy!'
>
> One hand smoking, the ash falling, her scent all about me – let's dance, she
> said, a new step, let's try a modern dance. At Crawford Mansions where we
> had the gramophone. And after there was tea and cake and crumpet and would
> you mind please and excuse me's in the ABC. The cups in the garden rattling
> like bones. That afternoon when I wrote about her breasts shaking and did she
> see how hard I needed to concentrate, to collect my thoughts to hold myself
> together because it takes all your energy.
>
> I have done a rough draft of part III, but do not know whether it will do and
> must wait for Vivien's opinion as to whether it is printable. I have done this
> while sitting in a shelter on the front – as I am out all day except while
> taking rest. But I have written only some fifty lines, and have read nothing,
> literally – I sketch the people, after a fashion, and practise scales on the
> mandoline. (Eliot, 1988: 484–5)
>
> Once on the cliff or promenade, the visitor could stroll past ornate cast-iron
> bandstands and shelters, listening to 'nigger minstrels' or the ubiquitous
> German bands. From the early 1890s al-fresco troupes of Pierrots regularly
> performed along the Thanet coast. No more dapper troupe could be found
> than Harry Gold's entertainers whose first all-Pierrot show opened on
> Margate Sands in 1905. Will Catlin's troupe played the Sands in the 1910s
> and H.G. Pelissier's Pierrot Company appeared at the Winter Gardens in
> the early 1920s. (From Williams, 1992: 101–5)

Roger Vittoz's short monograph *The Treatment of Neurasthenia* was published in translation in England in two editions in 1911 and 1913. His thesis was that 'every form of neurasthenia is due to the brain working abnormally' (1913: vii). The problem and the cure therefore lay respectively in an insufficient or proper degree of 'brain control': 'brain control dominates the psychological and even the physiological life of man', Vittoz argued, and again, suggesting how the mind and physical symptoms may be connected, 'psychically speaking, the sufferer looks without seeing, as also he may be said to listen without hearing' (8). We think of lines and half lines in Eliot's 'Gerontion' and *The Waste Land*, and he, in what could only have been a retrospective linkage between the poem and his own condition at the time, marked the following passage in his French edition of 1923. 'There is in fact often an excessive excitability which makes the sufferer aware of the slightest noise [' "What is that noise? ... What is that noise now?" '] and is frequently a case of insomnia' [' "My nerves are bad to-night ... Stay with me" '] (Vittoz, 1913: 27; Eliot: 1974: 67; and see 1988: 480). Above all, Eliot found confirmation in Vittoz of the condition of 'aboulie'. Insufficient or unstable brain control results in fatigue and fits of anger or despair, said Vittoz, but also in indecision and an apparent lack of will due to fear of future consequences. Thus, in a passage Eliot marked and might have cross-referred to 'Prufrock', Vittoz's text runs under the heading, 'Lack of Will (Fr. *Aboulie*)', 'It may be that every neurasthenic lacks will power; in fact there exists every degree of this, from the undecided man who puts off an action indefinitely to the one with no will power whatsoever' (25).

In Lausanne Eliot had presumably been guided through the exercises Vittoz recommended to regain brain control and will power. Patients were, for example, asked to concentrate on an idea, a curve, or the symbol of infinity, to mentally repeat the ticking of a metronome, to retain the impression of a touched object, or to imagine figures in the mind and efface them 'gradually and voluntarily' (Vittoz, 1913: 27). If Eliot followed these exercises, the immediate effect seems quite the opposite of a more determined will, however. To Virginia Woolf he explained that he wrote the final sections of the poem in a trance; 'I wasn't even bothering whether I understood what I was saying', he remembered later (Hall, 1977b: 105). To Ottoline Morrell he wrote from Lausanne that he felt 'more calm than I have for many many years – since childhood' (1988: 490).

Perhaps Eliot's words can be understand as a gloss of a kind on the passage, in this final section of *The Waste Land*, headed 'Damyata (control)', 'The boat responded ... with controlling hands', and much has been made of this in accounts of the poem's emerging stability and order. However, as a whole and not only in its last section, the poem drifts across and between its many fragments in a mimetic and, we might think, transfigured alternative to the pollution of bottles, sandwich papers, silk handkerchiefs and other 'testimony of summer nights' afloat on the river (1974: 70). The poem spills, moreover, beyond its published text into the drafts and other earlier drafts and fragments. What degree of control and editorial decision was brought to the poem was brought, famously, by Pound who 'performed the caesarean operation' that gave it birth (Eliot, 1988: 498). Eliot's indecision on the form and on matters of detail is evident in their correspondence, even once he had returned to London (504). Pound gave *The Waste Land* some shape and precision where it was structurally incoherent. Even so, generations of readers have felt that the poem's formal or mythological order is superficial or unconvincing. Its fragments, as Conrad Aiken argued early on, are just that, fragments, and are, by that same token, suggestive beyond themselves (Grant, 1982: 159). This is interesting in a way that most readers don't often consider and which Colleen Lamos (1998) suggests we take account of. Troubled though the Eliots' marriage was, they were, as suggested above, arguably at their closest during these years and were united by and in the poem, as well as in the joint enterprise of the *Criterion*. 'As to Tom's *mind*, I am his mind', Vivien insisted (Gordon, 1977: 79). Lamos argues that Eliot strives to repress errant, liquid female energies in his work and personality and *The Waste Land* has, with reason, been seen in this connection as a poem of abjection; its women are mad, sexually threatening or unfeeling, or careless working-class gossips who exist in reported rather than active first person speech (Tate, 1988). On the other hand, we may well understand the calmness which came over Eliot at Lausanne as a relaxing not the tightening of self-restraint; a *loss* of the will to control which in turn implied an openness to the 'female' as to the independent life of disseminated meanings. When we prefer its fragments to its putative order we are responding to its errant and transgressive 'feminine' potential. Typically, too, we reach for watery and liquid metaphors in describing this, as does Ackroyd in positing Eliot's 'retreat from worldly cares into that amorphous sea which he had known as a child, to slide out...' (1984: 116). But why must we view this as a 'retreat'? The poem opens itself, we might think, into the realm of the 'semiotic' with the mother–child and womb-like associations this term is given by Julia Kristeva and carries in the remarks by Pound, Ackroyd and Eliot himself above. In this realm male and female co-exist, as in Tiresias, perhaps, but more in the poem's dissonant tones and rhythms, its demotic and scholarly, nostalgic and fretful voices. *The Waste Land* stages these voices upon a screen of passing tableaux, in a manner true to Eliot's taste for impersonation. Far from cured of a lack of will power or 'aboulie', therefore, Eliot arguably surrenders to it (for a second time) in an irregular, misshapen, collaborative work in which his own double-sidedness and he and Vivien, co-exist. This is clearer still when we think of what an actual show of will power was to mean in Eliot's later unyielding determination to shut Vivien out of his life. She belongs at her best, like Laforgue, and like the best of Eliot, to the richly unbalanced, heterogeneous earlier period, full of its melancholy tensions of self and other, male and female.

8
Bloomsbury's Bohemia

Temps perdu, temps retrouvé

'Saturday 6th March 1920... Then on Thursday dine with the MacCarthys, & the first Memoir Club meeting' (Woolf, 1978a: 23). The idea of the club had been Molly MacCarthy's who hoped this would be a way of getting Desmond MacCarthy to write the 'big book' he had always promised but frittered away in talk and journalism. The dozen members were to gather at one of their houses once a month to read a chapter of what was to become their full-length autobiography. In the event this proved too ambitious and members read occasional papers, some of which much later found their way into print. So there they were, on 4 March, twelve friends, according to Virginia Woolf's diaries, or eleven according to Quentin Bell or according to Leonard Woolf thirteen; the same thirteen, he said, who had gathered together shortly after 1904 and now met again, in the same room at 46 Gordon Square. Thus Leonard Woolf names the MacCarthys, Clive and Vanessa Bell, himself and Virginia Woolf, Roger Fry, Duncan Grant, Lytton Strachey, Maynard Keynes, Adrian Stephen, E.M. Forster and Saxon Sydney-Turner (Woolf, 1967: 114; see Bell, 1968: 14–15; Edel, 1981: 258). 'A highly interesting occasion' thought Virginia Woolf of that first meeting of the club on 4 March. 'Seven people read – & Lord knows what I didn't read into their reading' (1978a: 23). Clive Bell was 'purely objective'; Roger Fry, 'Good: but too objective'; Duncan Grant was 'tongue enchanted'; Molly MacCarthy was 'composed at first' but suddenly broke out with 'Oh this is absurd I can't go on' before shuffling her sheets, starting again on the wrong page, and continuing through to the end. And 'Nessa' started out 'matter of fact' before she was 'overcome by the emotional depths to be traversed; & unable to read aloud what she had written'. 'I doubt that anyone will *say* the interesting things', comments Woolf, 'but they can't prevent their coming out' (23).

Not Hoxton, not Brixton – not even Chelsea or Kensington or Soho – but Bloomsbury. 'It is lucky perhaps that Bloomsbury has a pleasant reverberating sound, suggesting old-fashioned gardens and out-of-the-way walks and squares; otherwise how could one bear it' (Bell, 1997: 95). Vanessa Bell felt this way after the event – long after, in 1951, in her 'Notes on Bloomsbury' for the Memoir Club, at a time when, before Bloomsbury became fashionable once more, it was subject, she thought, to hostility, popular misconception and plain error. The formation and very name of the Memoir Club suggested, as Vanessa Bell strongly felt, that Bloomsbury, as such, was over, but evidently not lost to memory. All of her own talks returned to the early years of Bloomsbury's infancy and the halcyon days of the early 1910s. It was for her an unrepeatable, utopian time, full of the thrill of an innovative collective life and artistic creativity. 'How full of life these days seemed', she muses, when 'Everything was brim-full of new life and ideas and it certainly was for many of us "very heaven" to be alive' (111). Her nostalgia is obvious but magnetic, and also, in one of the paradoxes of Bloomsbury, responsive to, indeed the product of change.

At the same time, obviously, Bloomsbury was not at all lost. Just as her own paintings, drawings and photographs had recorded this life, so Bloomsbury continued, or was in some respects first brought to life, in the talks and papers presented to its members over the forty-five years or more of the club's existence. Beyond the club's memoirs, too, of course there stretch the many volumes of letters, diaries and further memoirs, paintings and novels by other members and associates, to say nothing of decades of biography and critical commentary. All of which has only compounded the recurring motif of Bloomsbury's intrinsic ambiguity: who belonged; and where and when did it exist? Did it really exist? Was it important? The participants felt this ambiguity too. Thus Virginia Woolf could be at times detached and ironic about Bloomsbury and at others committed to both people, places and principles. Bloomsbury was superficial, a mere trick of conversation and manners, she felt, but then in another mood was ready to stand by it as the standard bearer of no less than 'civilisation' (Lee, 1997: 267–8). More importantly, Virginia Woolf, especially, was aware of these fluctuations in her own opinions and thus in the thing itself. 'Naturally I see Bloomsbury only from my angle – not from yours', she began her own talk to the Memoir Club, adding how in presenting the past she would like to present herself both then and now – 'to make the two people, I now, I then, come out in contrast', knowing that as she changed so the past changed (Woolf, 1978b: 183, 86–7). In the end this is surely the truth of the matter: there were several differently angled Bloomsburys at one time and over time. There are endless points before the end, however. At one such, in 1951, Vanessa Bell felt she should respond to the vagaries of opinion and misrepresentation by holding firm. This was the time, she felt, for a true history.

'To begin with then', she offers, 'This is how it all arose' (Bell, 1997: 97). In 1904, the Stephen sisters and their brothers, Thoby and Adrian departed the 'melancholy' house in Hyde Park Gate, Kensington, of their father, the eminent Victorian, Sir Leslie Stephen, and together moved into 46 Gordon Square. 'We knew no-one living in Bloomsbury then' says Vanessa (98) – though she likely knew of Yeats who had lived there since the mid-1890s, and would come to know that Dorothy Richardson, the author of 'a woman's sentence' discovered by her sister (Woolf, 1979: 191) had been Yeats's neighbour. She also soon knew something of the area as a student for a short time at the Slade School of Art in Gower Street. It was a dismal experience. She felt crushed by the Slade Professor, Henry Tonks, and made no friends – but the Slade was surely already one of the symbolic cultural markers of the area and of bohemian Fitzrovia where many artists had studios. Augustus John, pre-eminently, and Gwen John had studied there in the 1890s and were followed over the next decade or so by Wyndham Lewis, C.R.W. Nevinson, Mark Gertler, David Bomberg, William Roberts, Iris Tree, Carrington and Nina Hamnett.

Many of these artists also became direct or indirect associates – or enemies – of Bloomsbury. There was a before and an earlier and a later Bloomsbury, that is to say, and a Bloomsbury which was not 'Bloomsbury'. What initiated the latter was Thoby's decision to entertain his friends from Cambridge at Gordon Square, and 'So it happened that one or two of these friends began to drift in on Thursday evenings after dinner' (99–100). Casually but crucially the sisters were included. There was cocoa and biscuits, and some whisky, for guests, but the true nourishment was conversation – the scandalous freedom to talk 'till all hours of the night' about the philosophy of G.E. Moore, books, painting, sex, or simply but always amusingly about the day's comings and goings. Bloomsbury claimed the right to this freedom to be silent or to talk as and when they wished about anything. Vanessa Bell suggests a democratisation of subject matter and equalisation between young men and women, 'all free, all beginning life in new surroundings, without elders to whom we had to account in any way for our doings or behaviour and this was not then common in mixed company of our class' (102). And principally, for herself, this brought a freedom from parental control and the responsibilities which had fallen to her as housekeeper in her father's house.

So Bloomsbury was about freedoms; above all about the 'freedom of speech' exercised in the fittingly spacious, light and freshly distempered rooms of 46 Gordon Square. But, in Virginia Woolf's memory at least, the freedoms didn't come all at once. First there was the novel company of Thoby's friends. Their reputations went before them, but didn't then seem to enter the room at the same time as these heroes themselves. Strachey, or 'the Strache', 'was the essence of culture... He was exotic, extreme in every way... a prodigy of wit' reported Thoby (Woolf, 1978b: 191). Clive Bell 'was a kind of Sun God', mad with the discovery of Shelley and Keats, who, when he wasn't being a superb horseman, 'did nothing but spout poetry and write poetry'; Saxon Sydney-Turner 'was an absolute prodigy of learning' who had the whole of Greek literature by heart and 'was the most brilliant talker... because he always spoke the truth' (191, 192). In the event the first evening at Gordon Square went very slowly with barely a word until Vanessa found one: 'beauty' (193). Then they were off. It was very abstract and stimulating but somehow irrelevant since it didn't matter what they talked about or what opinions they took as long as there was a lot of opinionated talk. And one major freedom was missing, Virginia realised. The sisters had never given a thought to Thoby's sexuality; nor to their own (140). At Hyde Park Gate, sex and the body had been muffled under gossip about marriage. Now, with these shabby intellectuals there was not even this. Then on one legendary half-remembered, half-invented occasion in Spring 1908, Strachey made the breakthrough. Virginia and Clive Bell were arguing, Vanessa was sitting silently with her needle or scissors, when 'Suddenly the door opened and the long and sinister figure of Mr. Lytton Strachey stood on the threshold. He pointed a finger at a stain on Vanessa's white dress. "Semen?" he said' (200).

Strachey's much imitated voice started low and ended in a squeak. For both Stephen sisters, he found the satirical tone and set the agenda. His 'great honesty of mind' and remorseless sniping at sham and hypocrisy revealed what a 'complete freedom of expression and mind' might mean, said Vanessa (Bell, 1997: 106). And talk of sperm and buggers set off all kind of possibilities, variations on the theme of sex which 'revolutionised' the 'old sentimental views' of fidelity and marriage (Woolf, 1978b: 201). Even so, something was still lacking; the revolution had been more a conceptual and linguistic breakthough, for Virginia especially, than a matter of newly released passions. She had thought the trouble had been 'that there was no physical attraction between us'

(199) and this didn't alter. She turned down a proposal of marriage from Hilton Young and tried midnight bathing with Rupert Brooke at Granchester. No one was much impressed and Brooke and his 'neo-pagans' decided against Bloomsbury queers. Then in 1909, Strachey, the very model of Bloomsbury's queer iconoclasm, proposed to her, only to withdraw the proposal the next day when it occurred to him that marriage might mean having to kiss a woman. More extraordinary than his proposal was Virginia Stephen's readiness to accept. Did this unconventional young woman, now aged 27 and with a married sister, think that she too should be married? She flirted with Clive Bell but he wanted more sex than talk about sex, and only on Leonard Woolf's return from Ceylon in 1911, and after two patient proposals from him, did she agree, the next year, to marry. Still, after all the talk she felt no sexual passion and their honeymoon confirmed to both of them that she was 'frigid' (Jean Moorcroft Wilson, 2000: 87). Thus they embarked on a sex-free, childless, lifetime companionship which was in the event, for Virginia, only different from a marriage to Lytton Strachey because he would have been more of a distraction and rival.

The Stephen sisters and brothers lived at Gordon Square from late in 1904 to the autumn of 1906 when, with Vanessa's marriage to Clive Bell, Virginia and Adrian moved to 29 Fitzroy Square. Here Virginia was now the hostess. In 1907 Thoby had died of typhoid fever but others had joined and sustained the atmosphere of 'acute intelligence' that formed some 'unusual bond' between the members of this emerging set, no matter what 'violent quarrels and differences of opinion of all kinds' started up between them (Bell, 1997: 102). And so, after five years as a quarrelsome twosome in the faded elegance and noisy environs of Fitzroy Square, brother and sister carried Bloomsbury style in 1911 to the experiment of Brunswick Square, where Virginia (the only woman) and Adrian shared number 38 with Leonard Woolf, Maynard Keynes and Duncan Grant. At this point Thursdays 'at home' were given up. Instead the Bloomsbury manner evolved into a daily, communal lifestyle across households, pivoted still on the Bells at 46 Gordon Square. This now became the venue for 'all sorts of parties at all hours of the day or night'; a permanent open house for the inhabitants and friends of nearby Brunswick Square (Bell, 1997: 109).

Thereafter, 'Bloomsbury', bearing the quotation marks which lifted it above a mere literal geography, extended across and beyond the city. In August 1912, Virginia married Leonard Woolf and at his instigation, after her second serious nervous breakdown, moved across homes in

London to settle in 1915 in Richmond where two years later they set up the Hogarth Press. Earlier in 1912, Virginia had leased Asheham House on the Sussex downs and in the war years Vanessa had discovered Charleston near Lewes, Sussex. All the while, the personnel remained remarkably constant, owing to some extent to their non-combatant status during the war. There were new associates such as the Eliots and the Hutchinsons and an emerging younger generation, including Carrington and David Garnett, but for Vanessa people were either Bloomsbury or not Bloomsbury (Garnett, an exception among younger figures, 'was completely of Bloomsbury in its latest moments of disintegration and yet also outside it'; 1997: 113). The triangular relations she began with Clive Bell and Roger Fry and then with Duncan Grant at Charleston were characteristic of Bloomsbury's libertarianism and contrast in their constancy and tolerance with the fractious liaisons and partnerships in other modernist groups. But if her life at Charleston was consistent with Bloomsbury it was in her view no longer the thing itself. Even in 1919 when she returned to London she 'realised very clearly how all had changed. Nothing happens twice and Bloomsbury had had its day' (113). The years she looks to were 'from 1909 or 1910 to 1914' 'when life seemed fullest of interest and promise and expansion of all kinds...brim-full of interest and ideas' (111).

Bloomsbury belongs in this account to a pre-war moment, not of Edwardian twilight stillness, obviously, but of new life and energy which is similar to the sense of creative energies experienced by such as Pound, Lewis and Ford in their different Londons. Still, Vanessa Bell's chosen time for Bloomsbury is somewhat problematic. These best days are 'full' to the brim of the one period container 1909–14. The personal relationships which the Cambridge philosophy of G.E. Moore taught Bloomsbury to value found their form in the frankness and familiarity of their talk but also in the meetings and gatherings in which talk took place and in the diaries and letters which continued the conversation to oneself or one other. It was a world of interiors, in other words, of inner and outer circles, measured as much in terms of passing time as in people and places, moving in a rhythm that focused at points upon the single moment and silent internal dialogue before expanding outwards and returning. This encouraged certain genres and subjects: Bell and Grant's many paintings of objects and figures in interiors opening at some point in the frame through doors and windows beyond themselves, for example; or Woolf's method of interiorised characterisation; or Strachey's loosely conversational but polished treatment of public figures. The personal and personalities were everywhere. But the 'fullness' of the moment and experience of Bloomsbury also spilled over into liaisons and friendships extending to other houses and other friends, associates and lovers. The philosophy, as it were, undermined the physical walls of Bloomsbury and led on to passageways and tunnels which surfaced in another place in the country, or someone else's garden party or drawing room. Once there, from Ottoline Morrell's house in Bedford Square, for example, or from Garsington Manor, which the Morrells acquired in 1915, it might have looked as if the Stephen sisters' Bloomsbury was more the annexe than the main building – particularly since one of them lived in Richmond and one in Sussex.

It was Ottoline Morrell, after all, who many thought of as 'the Queen of Bloomsbury'. Friend to Asquith and Diaghilev, lover of Augustus John, Henry Lamb and Bertrand Russell, she made a different kind of public showing and was the more conspicuous bohemian. She 'worships the arts', Virginia reported – no less than the figure of the divine male artist (Woolf, 1975: 395; 1978b: 205). She dressed in inventive and striking outfits, now a Cossack, now an Oriental princess, her mahogany-red hair ablaze. At Bedford Square, she bore 'down upon one from afar in her white shawl with the great scarlet flowers on it and sweeping one away out of the large room and the crowd into a little room with her alone' (Woolf, 1978b: 205). On the street passers-by stopped to gaze, working men whistled and catcalled. All in all, Ottoline Morrell lived 'an odd life', she confessed to Strachey, 'continually acting upon the different stages of London' (Darroch, 1975: 15, 62, 126). Did Bloomsbury include Bedford Square, asked Virginia Woolf of the Memoir Club? 'Before the war, I think we should most of us have said "Yes"' (1978b: 204). They did not go in for her style of clandestine affairs and serious self-display or intense intimacies, or indulge in more than an ironic tinge of her 'lustre and illusion' (Woolf, 1978b: 206) but they did share with her the camp side of Lytton Strachey who enjoyed a regular tête-à-tête with this aristocratic bohemian about silks and petticoats and his young men (Darroch, 1975: 110–11). During the war, too, Bloomsbury joined in the evenings of crazed dancing to Phillip Morrell's pianola at pacifist gatherings at Bedford Square. While Duncan Grant bounded like Nijinsky, the Stracheys stepped out a courtly minuet and Ottoline threw herself into wild gypsy dances with Augustus John (145–6).

Bloomsbury therefore stretched out and changed under different lights: less the still-point of a vortex in the image of its rival modernism than a wandering rhizome. Its starting point was the already connected, already plural family group which then became further rooted through marriage and friendships and new arrangements in new places, and whose end point, in still surviving relatives and memorialists looks back and carries on. The Imagists and Vorticists, it goes without saying, have no such surviving family members. However, Bloomsbury did more than simply survive, since opinions within and outside its core group changed by mood and moment and correspondent. Thus to Ottoline Morrell after their first meeting Virginia Stephen wrote of her 'great joy' at the prospect of their friendship, confessing how 'delightful' it is 'to know you and like you as I do' (Woolf, 1975: 381) only shortly after to describe Ottoline's growing fondness for her as 'like sitting beneath an Arum lily; with a thick golden bar in the middle, dropping pollen, or whatever that is which seduces the male bee' (394). To Madge Vaughan she described her as having 'the head of a Medusa' (395). Later, when she read Ottoline Morrell's memoirs and realised the effect of Bloomsbury's mockery, and reflected on her own misery at that time, she regretted they had not been greater friends (Lee, 1997: 277).

Bloomsbury was therefore fluid and distinctive at once, a modulating 'small world inside the big world' as Virginia described the conspiratorial alliance between herself and Vanessa (1978b: 144). A figure such as Strachey defined it both ways, the small and eccentric against the big and conventional. His languid brilliance at Cambridge – pictured reclining on a sofa in an embroidered dressing gown sipping crème de menthe (Scott-James, 1955: 8) – was a second-hand pose waiting for the newness of Bloomsbury to happen, while the homophobic reactions of Rupert Brooke, Lawrence and Russell to his 'queerness' in turn decided what was outside the inner circle.

Another important later addition – 'perhaps the most important of all', said Vanessa Bell – who also came simultaneously to define, indeed redefine, inner and outer Bloomsbury was Roger Fry. 'So Roger appeared', wrote Virginia Woolf, his pockets stuffed with intriguing objects, canvases under his arm, and his mind full of projects which were to put some blood into the veins and indolent abstractions of 'old Bloomsbury' (1978b: 202). He brought a practical expertise as buyer for the Metropolitan Museum of Modern Art, an acquaintance with European artists, and a patient critical eye which inspired Bloomsbury's artists, especially Vanessa Bell, and widened their horizons. Fry gave Bloomsbury its emphasis on painting and design, and in the Post-Impressionist Exhibitions of 1910 and 1912, a public image and place in the swing of European avant-garde movements. The Bloomsbury talking shop became the Omega Workshops, just as, in the Woolfs' Hogarth Press, Bloomsbury developed one of the most enduring modes in English modernism of independent production for fiction, essays and poetry. Fry deepened but also extended

Bloomsbury – in introducing English painters and audiences to European art, and, initially, by recruiting figures emerging on the London art scene to the Omega Workshops. This gave purpose to Vanessa Bell and Duncan Grant but also offered the support of paid employment to such as William Roberts, Gaudier-Brzeska, Nina Hamnett and many others, including Wyndham Lewis. Fry had been impressed by Lewis's contribution to the decoration of the Cave of the Golden Calf and in 1912 both he and Clive Bell openly praised Lewis's work, especially the painting 'Kermesse'. In early 1913 Lewis and Fry apparently called on Gertrude Stein together in Paris and in July Lewis joined the Omega Workshops as one of its founding members (Edwards, 2000a: 60, 95; Anscombe, 1981: 25). A day in the life of the Omega Workshops when Fry, Lewis, Grant, Bell, Frederick Etchells worked alongside each other has not come down to us, and in the event of course this collaboration was to provoke a rival anti-Bloomsbury faction into existence. After a few months, Lewis and his soon-to-be Vorticist confrères walked out in protest at what he saw as Fry's perfidy over a commission for the 1913 Ideal Home Exhibition intended for himself (Edwards, 2000a: 96–9).

One reason behind this rift, so Lewis argued, was that Fry's double role as entrepreneur and artist meant he was prone to deceive and misrepresent other artists in his own or the Omega's interests. Worse, as he depicts Fry (the character Hobson) in *Tarr*, he had deceived himself in his artist's bohemian garb. Plainly too, Lewis's own vitalist art was moving away from Bell and Fry's concept of a more mimetic formalism. Lewis's 'Round Robin' written on his departure from the Omega conveyed these differences in revealing terms however. The Omega's 'Idol is still Prettiness', he sneered. 'This family of strayed and Dissenting Aesthetes' needed outside talent to do 'the rough and masculine work' for them; a 'vigorous art-instinct' to upset their 'pleasant tea-party' (Edwards, 2000a: 98, 99). Evidently, Lewis could be as personal and bitchy as Bloomsbury, but the implications are clear. The (heterosexual) Fry who Vanessa Bell found especially sympathetic when she was experiencing post-natal depression, who nursed her through a miscarriage and encouraged her work when the experience of Tonks and others had taught her to expect disdain, was lampooned as effeminate. Pound maintained he couldn't tell the difference between the 'Bloomsbuggars' (Carpenter, 1988: 244) and Gaudier-Brzeska and Hulme chorused the same tune. The rough masculinity of the new combative abstract art needed to work over its enemies with a little 'personal violence' in Hulme's phrase (Hulme, 1994: 260). Thus the Omega's association with women artists and decorative work (which Lewis in fact also attempted at the Rebel Arts Centre) condemned it as merely pretty and feminine, and, inevitably, showed Fry up as less than a man as well as the lesser artist. This animosity was compounded by Bloomsbury's pacifism, and reinforced beyond retrieval, on Bloomsbury's side, by Virginia Woolf's violent rejection of Lewis, Pound and, more ambiguously, Joyce. These high emotions were at all points about sexual power, fairly clearly, but also about class and nationality and rival ideas of freedom and civilisation. Bloomsbury's town and country houses – along with Bell's wealth, the Stephens' legacies and the Strachey family's titled background underline how being 'liberated' in English class society was defined by that society's different kinds, styles and degrees of privilege. Virginia Woolf was, she confessed, a snob. Pound was unquestionably elitist but not a class snob. What Bloomsbury meant by freedom was a degree of equality for women as accepted members of a highly educated middle class – though the Stephen sisters were denied a formal university education. Bloomsbury was to a man and woman white and predominantly English (MacCarthy was Irish) though strongly opposed to a nationalistic war. It shared a common prejudice against Jews, and thence had some difficulty with Leonard Woolf, but practised bisexuality and homosexuality when the latter was a criminal offence. Its emphasis on the personal and interior life was consistent with a collective position within a class whose social codes its members both adhered to and subverted.

Irony was therefore Bloomsbury's inevitable mode, both as a matter of conversational nuance and social position. Their town and country houses were a sign too of this double existence, since they both rented and owned property in the manner of their class – in a way which would have been impossible for Pound, Lewis or Gaudier-Brzeska – but inhabited as they decorated these houses in a bold experimental style. Above all, however, they undermined orthodox bourgeois, gendered and sexual constraints, in word as in deed, and it was in this revolt under the shadow of the Victorian patriarch that Bloomsbury declared its bohemianism. For the internationalist modernist of three cities like Pound (taken for a Jew by British Museum mandarins, and 'szum kind ov a furriner' by an English navvy; Pound, 1975b: 503) English society was soon 'dead as mutton' and an abomination. Like others, he campaigned, in the most fundamental difference between these modernisms for 'impersonality' not the personal. His 'freedom of speech' was the voice of the benighted and needy artist-sage, frustrated by a lack of sponsorship and public platform. However much the Woolfs counted the pennies, Bloomsbury did not need the paid work for journals the way Ezra Pound did; nor did anyone have to work in a bank. No more, with the security of the Hogarth Press, did its main author and associates need to wrangle with editors and publishers. Until 1919, meanwhile, Bloomsbury painters and associates could collect 30/- a week from the Omega Workshops. Commenting on the post-war situation in the arts, by this time Herbert Read felt that Bloomsbury, along with Harold Munro's *Poetry and Drama* and the Sitwells had seen off all rivals (1967: 15–16). One of the reasons for this and for Bloomsbury's longevity is that it established a cultural apparatus as well as a personal and aesthetic style. And for this Roger Fry was the inspiration.

About 1910

> The autumn of 1910 is to me a time when everything seemed springing to a new life – a time when all from all was a sizzle of excitement, new relationships, new ideas, different and intense emotions all seemed crowding into one's life.

This was the memory not of Virginia Woolf, whose thoughts on the pivotal moment of 1910 have become so famous, but of Vanessa Bell in 1934 (1997: 126). Others, like Ford and Lewis, felt this excitement and newness at a more likely, but paradoxical date, in 1914, on the eve of war. Why then, as Woolf put it, 'on or about December 1910' (1992: 70)?

In a way we might say 1910 began in 1904 with the Stephens' move from Kensington to Bloomsbury or in 1907 with the marriage of Vanessa Stephen and Clive Bell which installed the Bells at Gordon Square and Virginia and Adrian Stephen until 1911 at Fitzroy Square. Other things were stirring in 1907 too. Duncan Grant, for example, arrived in London from Paris where he had met, among others, Frederick Etchells and Wyndham Lewis (Bell, 1997: 107,193; Anscombe, 1981: 12). The following year, other soon-to-be-modernists – Pound, Lewis, Hulme, Frida Strindberg and Katherine Mansfield – also decided on a move to London. In 1909 Hueffer started the *English Review* and the Poets' Club began at the Restaurant de la Tour Eiffel. By 1910 Pound had published four volumes of poetry and *The Spirit of Romance*; Eliot had written two 'Preludes' and 'Humouresque (after J. Laforgue)'; Joyce had completed *Dubliners* and published *Chamber Music*. Meanwhile Virginia Stephen had begun reviewing for the *Guardian*, and *Times Literary Supplement*, writing articles for the *Cornhill* magazine and working intermittently on what was to be the six years of writing and rewriting of her first novel, *Melymbrosia*. In May 1910 the King, Edward VII, died, in September Pope Pius X issued a mandatory oath against 'the errors of modernism', and in November the first Post-Impressionist Exhibition was staged under Roger Fry's direction at the Grafton Gallery. This last, so it's said, was what Woolf, at least, had in mind.

But, this too initially takes us back a few steps. Vanessa Stephen had first met Fry in 1904 or 1905, and then again with Clive Bell on a train journey from Cambridge to London. She remembers this as 'early in 1908' (1997: 120), though Woolf sets it in the magical later year. Clive burst into Gordon Square with news of this new amazing man, she says. 'It must have been in 1910...He had just had one of the most interesting conversations of his life. It was with Roger Fry' (Woolf, 1978b: 202). The Bells anyway had by this date secured Fry's membership. They met him at his home in Guildford and at Gordon Square, and in the autumn he went with Clive Bell and Ottoline Morrell and possibly Duncan to Paris to choose pictures for his as yet unnamed exhibition. Vanessa Bell was ill and stayed in Studland with her new born child Quentin: 'I was not very much aware of what was going on' she recalled, though she came later to realise how Fry 'was at the centre of it all' (Bell, 1997: 126, 125). In the summer Virginia Stephen too was ill though she was back in London in November. The press view of the exhibition was on Guy Fawkes day and the private view two days later. On that day Fry took his deranged wife, Helen, to an asylum in York where she would remain until her death. The exhibition then opened under the title 'Manet and the Post-Impressionists' on 8 November.

It wasn't of course the only thing that was going on. In the same week the Prime Minister, Herbert Asquith, a longtime admirer of Ottoline Morrell's, dissolved Parliament and the country prepared for a general election. On 12 November Virginia attended a mass rally at the Albert Hall which called for the enactment of the Conciliation Bill giving the vote to a million women. She was bored and could only find amusement in a crying baby (Woolf, 1975: 438). At the same meeting Violet Hunt 'ardent for the cause' sat in a box with friends and wept at the treatment of women 'mauled in the arena below'. She went on then to a party which was interrupted by two suffragettes. They had approached Asquith who was present and when they were escorted out, she approached him too, and 'said something...as in duty bound, when I shook hands: "I say why don't you give it us?" And he smiled as he always did when tackled on this subject' (Hunt, 1926: 52–3).

On 18 and 23 November, the Women's Social and Political Union organised mass demonstrations outside the Houses of Parliament. For several hours there were violent clashes between police and women demonstrators, during which many women were injured and two died.

Asquith barely escaped the wrath of a deputation headed by Emmeline Pankhurst which returned the following day. In early December Ottoline Morrell was in Burnley supporting her husband Philip's campaign for election. Asquith made two speeches in his support, one attracting a record audience of 11,000. Morrell was elected with a majority of 173. Ottoline Morrell then returned to London where during February and March her relations with Fry, an erstwhile colleague on the Board of the Contemporary Art Society, grew more intimate (Darroch, 1975: 83, 99). The Post-Impressionist Exhibition had run from November 1910 to 15 January the following year and had met with a passionate response; mostly hostile. In February when the new Parliament sat, Asquith refused to extend suffrage to women and thereby provoked militancy of another sort (but was it related?), including the smashing of windows in the West End and at Number 10. An extensive campaign of arson attacks on private and public property followed. One such action by Mary Richardson was to attack the 'Rokeby Venus' in the National Gallery with a meat chopper. She attacked an image of mythological female beauty, she said, in protest at the re-arrest of Mrs Pankhurst, 'the most beautiful character in human history'. Thus an idea of beauty which had, we remember, been Bloomsbury's inaugural theme, was linked with an idea of justice. The Vorticist militant Lewis advised the suffragettes, 'Leave Art Alone, Brave Comrades!' (Lewis, 1997: 152). In *Three Guineas*, Woolf noted how 'burning, whipping and picture-slashing only it would seem become heroic when carried out on a large scale by men and machine guns' (1938: 295). But this was almost forty years later. She was thinking of the 1910s clearly, but not thinking as she had thought then; not if she had meant to suggest the Post-Impressionist Exhibition alone stood for fundamental change. Rather 'the two people', as she was to put it, 'I now, I then, come out in contrast' (Woolf, 1978b: 87).

There's one thing, anyway, we can be sure of. It must have been Sophie. Sophie Farrell had been at Hyde Park Gate, Kensington, and opted to go with Virginia and Adrian when they moved to Fitzroy Square to occupy what had once been George Bernard Shaw's house. They lived there till 1911 – the only people in this one-time genteel neighbourhood with a cook, a maid and a front door bell, said Grant (Wilson, 2000: 59–60). He himself lived on the second floor of number 22 where he was soon joined by Maynard Keynes. Roger Fry opened the Omega workshops in 1913 at number 33 and a number of artists including Walter Sickert and Lewis, as well as Nancy Cunard and Iris Tree and later Vanessa Bell took studios in the area. The Stephens' maid was Maud and their cook was Sophie Farrell. Sophie thought Virginia needed her more than the newly married Vanessa: 'Such a harum scarum thing she wouldn't know if they sold her' she said of Virginia. 'She don't know what she has on her plate' (Wilson, 2000: 60). Later she moved on with Virginia to Brunswick Square delivering the meals to a strict timetable for the five residents to take up to their rooms. So it must have been Sophie who emerged from her basement as a sign of epochal change 'in or about December 1910... now to borrow the *Daily Herald*, now to ask advice about a hat' (Woolf, 1992: 70).

Woolf decided on 1910 in 1923 when she wrote and revised the essay first titled 'Character in Fiction' and later 'Mr. Bennett and Mrs. Brown'. 1910 was an eventful year in public affairs and no doubt these found their way into the copy of the *Daily Herald* at Fitzroy Square. Not only was there the death of the king and the campaign for suffrage and Fry's exhibition but the issue of Home Rule in Ireland. All these things were unquestionably swimming about, but Woolf's comment, as we can't fail to notice, is not directly 'about' any of them. Her essay refers to books and authors, to Samuel Butler and George Bernard Shaw, as themselves recording this transition and is indeed above all concerned with how literature renders character and registers change. But this is a change in 'human relations' – 'between masters and servants, husbands and wives, parents and children', and only then, one word a piece, for the linked changes in 'religion, conduct, politics and literature. Let us agree', she says, 'to place one of these changes about the year 1910' (1992: 71).

But what, first of all, is likely to strike a modern reader is what Woolf herself first of all refers to as a sign of this momentous transition – a conspicuous change from the ways of the Victorian cook to the ways of the Georgian cook:

> The Victorian cook lived like a leviathan in the lower depths, formidable, silent, obscure, inscrutable; the Georgian cook is a creature of sunshine and fresh air; in and out of the drawing room, now to borrow the *Daily Herald*, now to ask advice about a hat. (70)

The fact that Woolf relates to her servant in a new way, and vice versa, could only mean something in a world where there were, or more particularly, where you had servants and you had come (with the same servant) from the Victorian Hyde Park Gate, where the cook did indeed inhabit a dark basement, to the bright and airy Edwardian and Georgian Bloomsbury. The Stephens had a cook and maid. The character Rose in Woolf's *The Years* (1937) notices in the chapter for 1910 that her poor relations cook for themselves. And this was more the situation with the poor relations amongst modernists. The Eliots had a maid cum cook, while Pound and Lewis, to say nothing of Gaudier-Brzeska or Cournos, had to 'do' for themselves. When Pound married Dorothy Shakespear, the product of a servanted household, she did not cook, nor even begin to consider it. Pound was himself an able cook but one consequence of small lodgings and no domestic help meant that, unlike Bloomsbury, the Soho and Kensington based modernists used teashops and cafés for their society and talk of art. Hence, for one reason, their heterogeneous, fractious and short-lived coteries.

As Peter Stansky (1996) demonstrates, Woolf's essay also had its own particular animus. She was responding to Arnold Bennett's dislike of her novel *Jacob's Room* which showed, he thought, in an earlier comment in 1923, her inability to create character. Earlier still, in 1917, Woolf had anonymously reviewed Bennett's *Books and Persons* including his review of the Post-Impressionists. Bennett had praised the new art but the logic of this, Woolf implied, was that he would see the limitations of his own 'infantile realisms' (quoted in Stansky, 1996: 240). In 1919, again, in the essay 'Modern Fiction' Woolf had argued, with Bennett, Galsworthy and Wells in mind, that the novel should turn away from their 'materialism' and instead 'look within', in a famous description, so as to capture the way 'an ordinary mind on an ordinary day...receives upon its surface a myriad impressions – trivial, fantastic, evanescent, or engraved with the sharpness of steel'. It was this 'incessant shower of innumerable atoms' which composed what she proposed we understand as 'life itself' (Woolf, 1925: 189, 192).

All this is entirely consistent with the arguments of 'Mr. Bennett and Mrs. Brown' but with a broader perspective too. For just as Virginia Woolf needs to show the internal life of Mrs Brown, so she finds signs of change in the domestic interior of the home, in relations between mistress and cook. Perhaps even more than the rest of Bloomsbury her orientation is personal and inwards. Roger Fry gave this select interior world of new taste and conversation a public profile, and one which in the Post-Impressionist exhibitions and Omega Workshops challenged and dissented from accepted public taste and the mass market. Fry recruited the Bells, Duncan Grant and Desmond MacCarthy but his project did not take Virginia Stephen with it. She claimed in fact not to understand the scandalised reaction from 'all the Duchesses' to the Gauguins, Van Goghs, Matisses and Picassos displayed at the Grafton Gallery; 'a modest sample set of painters', she said, 'innocent even of indecency' (Woolf, 1975: 440). She was hearing 'a great deal about pictures' but didn't 'think them so good as books' (440). It was books and writing, and especially the novel, not painting which was best able to register change or 'life'. So went a running debate with Vanessa Bell (Dunn, 2000: 151–2). Hence in the same letter her excitement that she is pouring out 'fragments of love, morals, ethics, comedy, tragedy, and so on ... into a manuscript book' (440) which probably meant that she had returned to the draft of her first novel *Melymbrosia*, revised and published in 1915 as *The Voyage Out*.

This puts Virginia Woolf's 1910 in a rather different light. While this year saw protest and schism and the provocation of artistic innovation upon the public stage, she was the earnest but yet to be published and publicly acknowledged novelist. In the event too, the first and second novels were barely noticed and she found her way to her own kind of modernist fiction, somewhat after the event, by what proved an unavoidably compelling analogy with painting, in which 'Cézanne and Picasso had shown the way' (Woolf, 1940: 172). The two stories 'The Mark on the Wall' and 'Kew Gardens', published by the Hogarth Press in 1917 and 1919, showed this tendency to abstraction and colourist impressionism in prose. Fry commented on the first story's 'plastic sense' (Woolf, 1976: 285) while Vanessa Bell's illustrations for the Hogarth Press editions found a way of balancing collaboration and independent expression. These stories were the first signs of Virginia Woolf's new conception and treatment of character as consciousness and were followed by her first full-length, non-traditional novel, *Jacob's Room* (1922), which Bennett had found wanting. Her essay on 'Character in Fiction' in 1923 was therefore written in defence of her 'modernist', perhaps we should say 'Post-Impressionist', method of rendering the inner life.

This is not to say 1910 itself or even December 1910 were simply plucked out of the air and meant nothing but a new understanding with your cook. The year began for Virginia Stephen on the stroke of 1 January with a letter to her friend, former classics tutor and latterly suffrage organiser, Janet Case, asking if she could be of some use to the cause. 'How melancholy it is', she notes, 'that conversation isn't enough!' (1975: 421). It sounds like an indictment of Bloomsbury's particular forte. She cannot 'do sums or argue, or speak', she says – though the latter was precisely what she could and later did do – but was ready for 'humbler work' (421). She found herself as a result 'writing names like Cowgill on envelopes' in an office which was 'just like a Wells novel' and not, that is to say, like a novel by Virginia Stephen. When she did write up this episode in the novel *Night and Day* (1919) it was to reiterate its tedium and express her distance from it. The earlier first novel, *Melymbrosia*, was begun in 1907 and she had shown one hundred pages to Clive Bell in the summer of 1908 and continued with it into the following year. She had had an affair of sorts with Bell, what Lee calls 'a game of intimacy and intrigue' (1997: 249), from around May 1908. 'There were kisses between Virginia and Clive, we know', writes Louise DeSalvo, 'and perhaps more' (DeSalvo, 2002: xii). Whatever the degree of physical intimacy, their flirtatious talks and letters found, for Virginia Stephen at least, a more serious and nervous passion in the topic of her writing. This dual intimacy brought a complicated note of suspicion, guilt, knowingness and, oddly, more emphatic, even erotic, affection to her exchanges with Vanessa (Lee, 1997: 250–1). Matters then changed again and the writing of *Melymbrosia* was suspended because of her illness. This was of course one of a series of 'illnesses' or 'breakdowns' and was preceded by episodes in 1895–96 and 1904, during which she attempted suicide. Her illness in 1910 extended from mid-April when she had 'stupidly made my head bad again' and was under Dr Savage's orders to 'keep quiet' to at least November when she felt 'very well again' but 'Savage has still to decide my future' (1975: 424, 436). She spent June at 'the Moat House' near Canterbury and July at 'Burley' a mental nursing home for ladies in Twickenham, placed there by Savage who was guided by the conventions of his profession and Vanessa Bell's opinion of 'Virginia's still depressed condition' (Woolf, 1975: 428). She was then in Cornwall, Dorset and Oxford and only intermittently in London before returning to Fitzroy Square in late autumn. At 'Burley' she was confined to bed and wrote to Vanessa (addressing her as 'Beloved, or rather Dark Devil') that she couldn't stand much more of it and was ready 'to jump out of a window' (431). Under Savage's regimen she was overfed on a milk diet, had to rest and retire early, and was without 'books and culture' (Lee, 1997: 183; Woolf, 1975: 433). She was thought to suffer, as were so many, from a nervous disorder or neurasthenia: a term Savage applied to 'any "hysteric" and sexually deprived young woman given to invalidism, self starvation, paralysis, masturbation, or eccentricity' (Lee, 1997: 189).

We begin then to see what was important, frustrating and frightening about 1910 for Virginia Stephen. What in general she was seeking, we can say, was a way of negotiating, on the right terms, between her inner life in her Bloomsbury and a more public world. Hence the intention to assist the 'Adult Suffragists' in January. And hence, above all, her longer term need, stymied for pretty much of this year, to establish herself as a writer in an artistic set dominated by painting and the visual arts.

Another bout of mental illness, after the serious attack of 1904, threatened this. That she had resumed work on her novel once more at the end of the year, in the same month she declared her 'time had been wasted a good deal upon Suffrage' (1975: 438), said a lot about her priorities and sense of 'life'. The written word when she returned to it was a strange instrument, the vehicle for a transformed expression of consciousness as she was to theorise, but inescapably associated with her own changed mental state during periods of illness. The 'myriad impressions' of 'life itself' were at these times shut down before they came on again all at once. 'Something happens in my mind', she reflected later, 'It refuses to go on registering impressions... Then suddenly something springs... ideas rush in me' (Woolf, 1980: 287). As Hermione Lee unequivocally puts it, 'There is a relation between illness and modernism in Virginia Woolf's writing life' (1997: 195). To write was to openly present herself and her mind and to risk both, since her attempt to receive and follow manifold impressions might be thought a bit mad.

There were, in addition, two other events, either end of this year, which in their own way took this same risk. The first was the infamous 'Dreadnought Hoax' in February when Virginia Stephen was the only woman in a party of six – four of whom, including herself and Duncan Grant, were disguised as Abyssinian royalty – who conned their way on to the Royal Navy flagship HMS Dreadnought at Weymouth. The second event was a fancy-dress ball in the winter to celebrate the Post-Impressionist Exhibition. In both she dressed up; in the first in black face as an oriental prince. At the Post-Impressionist ball, held at Crosby Hall, 'a group of us', Vanessa Bell recalled, 'dressed more or less like figures from Gauguin'. Practically all Bloomsbury, including three from the Dreadnought Hoax – Roger, Clive, Vanessa, Virginia, Adrian, Duncan and James Strachey – draped themselves in material 'from Burnetts' made for natives in Africa... we wore brilliant flowers and beads, we browned our legs and arms and had very little on beneath the draperies' (Bell, 1997: 133–4). Virginia wrote to Ottoline Morrell of a plan for Clive to dress up as a guardsman and Lytton as a ballet girl as a way of getting them to make up a 'really rather exciting' quarrel between them (Woolf, 1975: 449). The artists in the group decided to put their delight on canvas and in March 1911 Virginia wrote of having 'to dress up again as a South Sea Savage, to figure in a picture'. The fancy-dress ball went off much as the exhibition of Post-Impressionist pictures had; the dancers at Crosby Hall 'stopped and applauded us' while 'Mrs Whitehead was horrified at our indecency' (Bell, 1997: 134).

For Virginia Stephen, we might think, both events were a way of trying on another self. The first was the more adventurous and, Vanessa Bell thought, foolhardy public performance: a bohemian prank which as an act of protest was quite unlike a suffrage march or meeting and instead used the bold device of the practical joke to expose the paper thin security of the self-aggrandising British navy. There was a thoughtlessness about the group's racial stereotyping of course on both occasions (they mumbled 'bunga bunga' on the Dreadnought when bits of Swahili, Greek or Latin failed them) which the British navy fell for because it shared it. But in Virginia Stephen's case particularly, this cross-gender, cross-cultural masquerade entailed a degree of radical self-estrangement, which was diced with modernist primitivism and maybe just a little recklessness.

In the same vein, in one of the few reviews she wrote in 1910, she tells of Lady Hester Stanhope, an English aristocrat in the grand manner, who, frustrated by the obstacles to her sex, 'set sail for the East' there to emerge 'in Syria, astride her horse, in the trousers of a Turkish gentleman'. For the rest of her life she would 'shake her fist at England', surrounded by devotees and natives who thought her 'neither man nor woman, but a being apart' (Woolf, 1977: 197). The more developed forms of masquerade and the notion of the androgynous artist genius in the novel *Orlando* and in *A Room of One's Own*, lay in the future, but we can see how the japes of spring and winter 1910 anticipated them. There was a closer stepping-stone too. In 1920 in the story 'A Society' Woolf imagines a group of women who found a 'society for asking questions'. They each invade a male institution: a court of law, an Oxford college, the London literary scene and the Royal Academy. They dress up as a charwoman, a male reviewer and one as an 'Aethiopian Prince' who goes 'aboard one of his Majesty's ships' (Woolf, 1985: 119, 120).[1]

This story was a reply once more to Bennett, as well as to the Bloomsbury male Desmond MacCarthy who had supported Bennett's argument in *Our Women* that women are the intellectual inferior to men (Woolf, 1978a: 69; Lee, 1997: 286). The change in human relations Woolf talks of in the 'Mr. Bennett and Mrs. Brown' essay was a part, therefore, of this sustained riposte, as were the other ways she found to contest a male establishment. The change between masters and servants, husbands and wives, and parents and children she writes of indeed took place in Bloomsbury households: between Sophie and Virginia (the story 'A Society' ends with a reference to Castalia's cook having bought the *Evening News*), and in the sexual musical chairs between Clive Bell, Molly MacCarthy and Mary Hutchinson; Vanessa Bell and Roger Fry and Duncan Grant; and Grant and Maynard Keynes and David Garnett – since Bloomsbury of course also meant different relations between men and men. Vanessa's children ran free and naked in the garden at Charleston.

But there was more to it than this. 'All human relations have shifted', wrote Woolf (1978a: 71). Perhaps we think of her as more witness than participant. While others experimented she found a precariously sensitive role between celibacy and sexual expression in her relations with Leonard Woolf and with the extravagant, passionate Vita Sackville-West who she was meeting regularly in the years of drafting her thoughts on character in fiction. A touch of the hand, she explained to Leonard, could give her exquisite pleasure; while to Vita she confessed she had broken down more ramparts than anyone else (Wilson, 2000: 102). She was physically reticent, but this tells us just how much was at stake and how much she stood to lose when her extraordinary mind 'on an ordinary day' did indeed open itself to a 'myriad impressions'. 'Life itself' moved along a risky and wavering line and could let in another very strange self altogether. There were bold bohemian moments all the same. Dressing up didn't have much directly to do with contemporary suffrage perhaps, but had quite a lot to do with the performative self Bloomsbury helped introduce and Virginia Woolf the writer was to re-think as the basis of a new idea of character. By December 1910, after months of enforced constraint, she found she could start again to dress up in the pages of a book.

Notes

1 Bourgeois-Bohemians

1. Published in *La Corsaire*. Mürger subsequently collaborated with Théodore Barrière in writing the play *La Vie de Bohème*, based on his stories. The play was Puccini's acknowledged inspiration.
2. Benjamin's much cited early volume on Charles Baudelaire opens with chapters on 'The *Boheme*', 'The *Flâneur*' and 'Modernism'. The second and third are invariably linked. The first and third rarely so.
3. Mürger's bohemians were to be found in Ancient Greece, the first in a lineage that includes 'those illustrious Bohemians' Molière and Shakespeare (Graña and Graña, 1990: 45).
4. An almost identical account appears in Ford's 'Mr Wyndham Lewis and "Blast"', *Outlook*, 34, 4 July 1914: 15–16.
5. Reported in letter from Edmund Schiddel to Victor M. Cassidy, 21 April 1974 (Schiddel papers).
6. Meyers cites an interview with Hugh Gordon Porteus in 1978 in evidence for this story. Whether or not such an event actually happened, Paul O'Keefe disputes that Ida's baby was Lewis's child (Edwards: 2000a: 552, n.2).
7. Barry wrote to Lewis of Masie (who 'is very well and can talk – limited vocab at present but still she talks') and mentions 'Going down to see' her, adding 'I suppose you don't want to come – do if you can'. There is talk of money, 15/-, 30/- sent by Lewis, £3 for shoes, thanks for a cheque; of meetings for dinner of 'popping around' and her work on the *Spectator* and idea for the novel *Here is thy Victory*. Frequently too she addresses him as 'Dearest Lewis'. His letter of 11 April 1930 interrupts this abruptly. He writes 'The endearments you think fit to employ disgust me...The lapse of so many years may have effaced from your memory the fact, but it has not effaced it from mine, that my acquaintance with you was of a most unpleasant nature. Why then in heaven's name these epistles?' Her book he returns as not being 'as you may guess, of any interest to me' (letters from the Wyndham Lewis Collection, Cornell University, sent to Schiddel by Victor M. Cassidy).
8. Michael North (1999: 58–64) rescues Cournos's novel from the shadow cast by the modernist canon. Many events of the novel are mirrored in Cournos's *Autobiography* (1935), though this presents a much flatter account, with no equivalent to the protagonist's relation to women, nor to the theme and imagery of 'Babel'.
9. Peppis (2000) shows how nationalist sentiment, empire and avant-gardist polemics turned out to be implicated one in the other, especially in Vorticism.

2 'The Nineties Tried Your Game'

1. Symons said he had 'never in a single instance been accosted by a woman' at the Empire. Perhaps not. However, he was in 1893 'sharing the favours' with

Herbert Horne of Muriel Broadbent, the daughter of a physician, who had begun working as a prostitute at the Alhambra in 1892 where Symons had met her. He wrote two stories about her as Lucy Newcombe. (See Beckson and Munro, 1999: 102.)
2. He was 'not drawn to brit/pubs' he wrote to Patricia Hutchins 'France, italy, trattorie, yes' (letter dated 1 December 1953; Hutchins, 1965).
3. In a 'Foreword' dated 1964 to the reprint of *A Lume Spento* Pound confesses to 'the depth of ignorance' the poems display – 'ignorance that didn't know the meaning of "Wardour Street"' (Pound, 1965).

3 'Our London, My London, Your London'

1. Pound's room was later occupied by Ito, John Cournos and Agnes Bedford and the vicar who married Eliot and Valerie Fletcher and brought them back to the room for a wedding breakfast.
2. Richard Aldington, H.D., Brigit Patmore and Pound went about as a foursome in the early 1910s. H.D. was particularly taken by English teashops and Aldington was scornful of the discussion of poetry in 'some infernal bunshop' in Kensington. Legend has it that Pound edited H.D.'s poems for her first publication as an 'Imagiste' in Miss Abbot's teashop in Holland Street. By 1915 Pound and Aldington, who had married H.D., were estranged. I imagine Pound meeting Brigit and Eliot there again after Flint's 'History of Imagism' in the *Egoist* in 1915 and the correspondence with Pound that followed in which Flint repeated his claims for Hulme, Edward Storer and the 'School of 1909' against the late-comers, Pound included. The Flint papers are held at the Harry Ransom Center, University of Texas, who presented some of the key correspondence in the pamphlet, *The Imagist Revolution* (1993) (see also Middleton, 1965; and see Crunden, 1993: 212–14).
3. H.D. and Aldington were formally divorced in June 1928, by which date he was in a relationship with Brigit Patmore and she was living with Annie Winifred Ellerman ('Bryher'). See Patmore (1968) and Guest (1984).

4 Nights at the Cave of the Golden Calf

1. See Cork's incomparable illustrated discussion of the work of the artists for the Cave (1985: 61–115).
2. In fact shadow plays (or *Theatres d'Ombres*) were common fare in European cabarets from the 1880s onwards. Kokoschka had performed a shadow play on the opening night in 1907 of the Kabarett Fledermaus in Vienna. Frida Strindberg had undoubtedly known the Fledermaus and other European cabaret clubs and sought to rival and outdo them in the Cabaret Club. Lewis, who she employed to assist Spencer Gore in its sensational decorative scheme, planned a shadow play with Cuthbert Hamilton – but they got into a row with Strindberg over it (Cork, 1985: 111).
3. This italicised subsection presents extracts from Chapters VI and VII of Ford's *Marsden Case* (1923) and closes with some imagined actions and conversations at the Cave of the Golden Calf involving Ford's younger contemporaries or 'les jeunes'. The sources for the words of these participants are given

in a corresponding note. I attempt this as one way – I hope a vivid and analytical way – of recapturing the atmosphere and inner detail of the short, adventurous life of the Cabaret Club. There are unsurpassed accounts of the history of the club, and the Cave of the Golden Calf which it housed, elsewhere, by Cork (1985), as above, and Tickner (1997). Tickner, in particular, sets this avant-garde venue, with Lewis as its centre-piece, in a world of contemporary detail, including its wide coverage in the press, its parodic treatment in popular music hall and melodrama, and the social-sexual dynamics of current dance forms. The 18 pages of notes to her 33-page article are a sign of the scholarship from which her marvellous account emerges. Like others I am in its debt. My own primary concern here, as throughout, is with the figure of the bohemian in the world of bourgeois modernity. What I want also to underline is the inveterately palimpsestic and intertextual nature of the historical and cultural record. Tickner's account spectacularly demonstrates just this. What we also discover, as elsewhere, is how unstable the 'authentic' credentials of much of the documentary evidence often are: memories fade, gaps, contradictions and inconsistencies appear in the tissue of lives and events. As Ford, who regularly recast the 'factual' events of his life in autobiographical and fictional form, writes through his persona Jessop in *The Marsden Case* – itself an example of course of such a recreation – 'I will try to continue my time-table, though it is not chronologically that that long night comes back to me. But it would confuse anyone if I put all those visions, as they really return, one on top of the other' (111). Ford's talk of chronology here is itself naturally a fictional device. I risk instead a little confusion in this chapter by putting one thing on top of or alongside another; fact with fiction and fictionalised recreation. As well as the staging of the shadow play, Ford's story in these chapters deals with the character George Heimann, his sister and Miss Jeaffreson and the latter's attempt to verify George's aristocratic birth. I omit the latter so as to bring out the metaphorical interest in Ford's text with shadows and light, between what is known and unknown, authenticated and imagined in motive and meaning in the borderline realm of the Cave.

4. On Hamnett's dancing with a veil, see her *Laughing Torso* (1984 [1932]: 52). She at one time danced naked, she says, to Debussy's 'Golliwog's Cakewalk' played on the piano, and was recommended to Isadora Duncan, but did not want to dance and 'only pranced about for fun and to be admired' (58). On her coloured stockings and flat shoes and her meeting with Lewis in Paris see pp. 52, 55. Lewis, she says, took her arm and spoke to her in French. Lillian Shelley, a favourite of Hamnett's, sang 'Popsy Wopsy' and 'You made me love you' 'every night at the cabaret' (47). On her friendship with Gaudier-Brzeska, whose drawings she first saw in *Rhythm*, and meeting with Sophie Brzeska who passed for his sister, see pp. 38–41. She tells here the story of stealing a piece of marble which he used to create a torso of her, 'now in the Victoria and Albert Museum' (40) and of Gaudier-Brzeska's making the sculpture of Pound 'now in a front garden in Kensington' (41).

On Gaudier-Brzeska's shirt and relative cleanliness, Violet Hunt remembered 'Henri Gaudier Brjeska was quiet, ill-looking, almost toothless, wearing his blue workman's shirt, clean, on all occasions' (1926: 114). Aldington was however adamant, Gaudier-Brzeska, 'was probably the dirtiest human being I have ever known, and gave off a horrid effluvia in hot weather' (1941: 165).

For Cournos on Gaudier-Brzeska's generosity, poverty, circumstances in Putney where he had his studio, and their friendship, see Cournos (1935: 257–9). Cournos writes how 'Returning from the Café Royal with him late in the night he would dance like a young savage down the street' (258). Sheila McGregor tells how Middleton Murry rowed with Gaudier-Brzeska over his drawings in *Rhythm* and how he reacted to his name being misspelled in the magazine, taking this as a deliberate snub on the part of Katherine Mansfield. He wrote to Murry severing all relations (McGregor, 1985: 15). Rebecca West remembered Katherine Mansfield at the Cabaret Club (Meyers, 1978: 77).

On Pound's dancing, H.D. reports that 'he had no ear for music' and that she 'suffered excruciatingly from his clumsy dancing' (1979: 49). Brigit Patmore remembered how, 'Ezra danced according to no rules I understood. New steps one may invent, but surely the music sets time and rhythm. But for Ezra, no; with extremely odd steps he moved to unearthly beats. One couldn't face it. Easier to waltz with a robot' (1968: 110). Edgar Jepson recalled 'those Vorticist dances, the Turkey Trot and the Bunny Hug' being performed at the Cave (Jepson, 1937: 155).
5. See illustrations in Cork (1985: 86, 87) and Edwards (2000a: 61, 63).
6. See illustrations in Cork (1985: 87–93, 243–5).
7. Corroborating this suggestion of Lewis's dominance, when Mme Strindberg contemplated a revival of the Cave she thought of opening a 'Blast Club' (O'Keefe, 2001: 144).
8. In *The New Freewoman*, no. 6, vol. 1, 1 Sept 1913. Marsden was interested in a super freewoman type at the vanguard of sexual emancipation but increasingly argued for a universal individualism which would be 'genderless, solitary and unique' (Beckett and Cherry, 2000: 62).
9. The 'Aims and Programme of the Cabaret Theatre Club' as presented in its brochure of May 1912 declared that 'We want surroundings, which after the reality of daily life, / reveal the reality of the unreal' (Yale; Cork, 1985: 61).
10. Part at least of this story is disputed by O'Keefe who argues that the person named 'Mr Percy Wyndham' mentioned in the Club's minute book who would have had access to the till was not Lewis (O'Keefe, 2001: 144).
11. Others found her far from mad. Pound declared she had 'more brains than Gertie [Gertrude Stein] or Amy [Amy Lowell] put together' (Mullins, 1961: 99); Ashley Gibson, a critic and habitué at the Cave described her as 'amazingly masterful, intelligent and, in a way fascinating' (1930: 105). Lewis found her 'a very adventurous woman' (1984: 134).
12. The Crabtree Club John co-founded in Soho in April 1914 sounds altogether more down-market – and included boxing (David, 1988: 118–19).

5 1914: 'Our Little Gang'

1. See Roberts (1982 [1938]: 22); Meyers and Lechmere (1983: 165); Lewis (1982: 101). Victor M. Cassidy's typed notes of an interview with Kate Lechmere run as follows: 'She saw Hulme at Kensington Town Hall, reading paper on Modern Art. Way above heads of audience, and in bad platform style. Lewis, with Miss L. kept saying "you've got to hold your head up when you speak," then when his turn came he got up and mumbled. Ezra Pound

stole show reciting poetry. Lewis muttered after that Pound only captured audience because of his accent: "It's rather a joke hearing poetry read by an American."' (Interview dated 9 January 1954; copy courtesy of Paul O'Keefe.)
2. The lecture appeared as the essay 'Modern Art and Its Philosophy', in T.E. Hulme, *Speculations* (1960), 73–109. See pp. 106–7 for this reference to Lewis and Epstein. Lewis is said to have 'read a paper supporting Hulme' (Roberts, 1982: 21).
3. See Wees (1972: 103–18) for a full account of these episodes.
4. The prospectus of the College of Arts was printed anonymously, with surrounding introductory and concluding remarks in the *Egoist*, 2 November 1914: 413–14.
5. This is the kind of distinction suggested by Lewis's *Tarr*. But see Chapter 1, above. Cassidy reports that 'Lewis confided to KL that he found it very difficult to have sex with girls of his own class. He preferred shopgirls and charwomen.' Notes from interview with Lechmere, dated 28 July 1973; courtesy of Paul O' Keefe.
6. Lewis's contempt for Roger Fry, in particular, is well known. This comment is from the 'Round Robin' drafted by Lewis on his quitting Fry's Omega Workshop. See Chapter 8 below, and Rose (1963: 47–50).
7. The suggested references in Martin (1967: 188) to the fight between Lewis and Hulme in the *New Age* of 26 March and 16 April 1914 don't in fact produce this corroboration.
8. Cassidy reports, 'Miss L says she ranaway from Hulme for a time because of his overpowering personality – wanted to make everyone he met into a little Hulme. Then gave in, they apparently became lovers...She considered they were engaged, although Hulme insisted on postponing marriage till after war...Also kept their relationship secret; wouldn't let her meet Kibblewhite Gang, evidently even controlled what she said in letters.' Interview with Lechmere, dated 9 Jan 54. Robert Ferguson reports on the erotic letters Hulme wrote to her from the front. He wanted her to think of herself in purely sexual terms and she, with some reluctance, apparently went along with this in her letters to him (2002: 262–4).
9. Cassidy reports, 'Lewis always liked her work and praised it, encouraged her to contribute to BLAST'. Interview with Lechmere, dated 28 July 1973.
10. However, a 'Tommy', unidentified by Wees in his Glossary on those named in *Blast*, was blessed in *Blast* 1 (1914: 28). This may have been meant to evoke no more than the generic foot soldier, 'Tommy Atkins'. All the same, as Patricia Hutchins reports from her conversations with Kate Lechmere, Hulme was called 'Tommy' (1965: 125).
11. An open, explicit and mutual rejection came later over her relationship with the black musician Henry Crowder. Its public expression was her pamphlet *Black Man – White Ladyship* (1931) which attacked her mother's racism.
12. Lewis made a surprising distinction between Lady Cunard and 'the bogus "high-life" of pre-war Mayfair': she was 'not only intelligent, of superlative party-wit, a live wire in the realm of music, a keen politician, but a very good hearted person – a "classless" virtue' (1982: 47, 56).
13. A further question concerns the relation of these little magazines and the techniques of the emerging mass production industries in the press and advertising. This is the subject of Mark Morrisson's study *The Public Face of*

Modernism (Wisconsin: University of Wisconsin Press, 2000). I would view this as a facet of the relation between artistic bohemia and bourgeois commerce.
14. Examples are the partnerships, and sometimes lesbian relationships, between Weaver and Marsden; Margaret Anderson and Jane Heap, founder and co-editor of the *Little Review*; Sylvia Beach, owner of the Shakespeare and Company bookshop and Adrienne Monnier; Harriet Monroe and Alice Corbin Henderson at *Poetry* (Chicago); Bryher (Annie Winifred Ellerman) and H.D., and the overlapping friendships between Nancy Cunard and Iris Tree, Cunard and Brigit Patmore, Rebecca West and Patmore and Violet Hunt, May Sinclair and Violet Hunt (see Hanscombe and Smyers, 1987; and Marek, 1995). We shouldn't assume there were not supportive or long-term friendships between male modernists or between men and women – though the last appear at first sight to be one-sided, as between Harriet Weaver and Joyce, for example. Bloomsbury also of course presented an extensive network of friendships between women and men.

6 Café Society

1. According to Foster Damon, Amy Lowell was given a picnic luncheon by Allen Upward and visited Gaudier-Brzeska's Putney studio (1966: 231). Wilhelm claims she didn't know or approve of other Vorticists, including Lewis, but was intrigued by Gaudier-Brzeska (160). In a particularly wild disagreement among critics, however, Jean Gould reports that Lowell 'could not abide' the 'audacious, atrocious, raffish, if gifted young French sculptor' (Gould, 1975: 126).
2. However, Damon gets other obvious things wrong, about the contents of *Blast*, for example, and seems to confuse this dinner with the Vorticist dinner, borrowing from but not attributing Pound's comments about that occasion. Thus, it 'was a great success, everyone talked a great deal', said Pound (Pound, 1970: 52) and Foster Damon, it 'was very jolly. Everybody talked a great deal' (1966: 233).
3. 'An interesting "*Blast* dinner" was held, I forget where', wrote the 84-year-old Lechmere, 'at the cost of 10/- per head. I sat next to Gaudier-Brzeska and I think Arthur Symons' (Meyers and Lechmere, 1983: 165). If we doubt Symons presence at Dieudonné's, Iris Barry suggests he was one of those occasionally present at Pound's dinners at Belotti's slightly later. 'Arthur Symons, very frail and elegant, just out of a sanitarium, came once or twice', she writes (Barry, 1931: 168).
4. Cork draws on an additional interview with Lechmere, dated 1969.
5. Ford, *Thus to Revisit* (1921: 201). Iris Barry's account suggests both Symons and Ford attended the weekly dinners at Belotti's – though precisely when is not known. We could view the *Blast* dinner as a remarkably catholic gathering of new and older writers and old and new flames, but the first, at least, was not Lewis's style as rebel artist.
6. Lechmere wrote, ' I was interested so much in Lewis's work before Vorticism and it was rather a shock to harbour this very abstract and non-human art and one that I found had great limitations, so I felt frustrated and did practically no painting. After the war he said "Vorticism is out" and his work became much more interesting' (Meyers and Lechmere, 1983: 162).

7. See the startled admiration of reporters from the *Daily News and Leader*, the *Daily Mirror* and *Vanity Fair* in Cork (1976: 147).
8. Lechmere remarked that Saunders and Dismorr 'were like two little puppies – followed WL about, did everything he said'. Victor M. Cassidy 'Interview', dated 28 July 1973: 3.
9. It was here, says Goldring, at a gathering of 'more than twenty people', to whom, under Lewis's instruction, Jessica Dismorr served tea, that the columns of those to be blasted and blessed had been drawn up. The company proceeded after this tea party, Goldring remembers, to 'a Blast Party at the Golden Calf' (1943: 70).
10. Beckett and Cherry suggest 'the possibility of a more direct and equal collaboration' and ask if a third panel, in addition to two known to have been by Lewis, was not the work of Helen Saunders (2000: 64–5).
11. In addition to the Vorticist Room with its wall panels, light fittings and table decorations, Lewis began a corner mural; Hamilton or Atkinson designed curtains which were sewn by Lechmere and a friend; and Lechmere painted a divan red and covered it with a striped red, white and blue covering from Liberty's. The doors of her 'Futurist' apartment were painted black and the walls cream. Also, though Lewis insisted she wear a black skirt and white blouse like 'a shop girl', a picture taken by the *Daily Mirror* in March 1914 shows her in a 'Vorticist' or 'Futurist' outfit perhaps made by herself after the style, suggest Beckett and Cherry, of the designer Paul Poiret and the Ballets Russes (Cork, 1985: 195–8; Beckett and Cherry, 2000: 64, 66). After the war Lechmere designed a dress for Vanessa Bell and began to design and sell hats in a London shop called Rigolo (Meyers and Lechmere, 1983: 160).
12. Gaudier was French and added the surname of his Polish companion, Sophie Brzeska, to his own name. Lewis's father was American. The circumstances of Lewis's birth, famously on board his father's yacht while it was moored off the coast of Nova Scotia are investigated by O'Keefe (2001: 4–7). Lewis was to declare that he arrived 'At around the age of six...in England, a small American' (O'Keefe: 13).
13. Aside from the many mentions of the Tour Eiffel in her autobiography, *Laughing Torso* (1932), Hamnett also illustrated the original edition of W. Seymour Leslie's *The Silent Queen* (1927) with sketches based on the restaurant.

7 The Nerves in Patterns

1. Bodleian: MS. Eng. misc. f. 532, fols 82r–84r and fol. 21r.
2. Several letters in 1936 were addressed to 'Mrs. V. H. Eliot, c/o Miss Daisy Miller, Three Arts Club, 19a Marylebone Road, NW1': Bodleian, MS. Eng. lett. b. 21. 23 July (fol. 11), 4 August (fol. 57), 6 August (fol. 59).
3. These words are given to Vivien in his play *Tom and Viv*. Seymour-Jones (2001: 116) writes that 'Maurice recalled that Tom spent a night in a deckchair on the beach at Eastbourne'. Her notes suggest this piece of information was derived from Hastings' interview with Vivien's brother Maurice Haigh-Wood (596).

4. £1 in 1922 was worth £36.47; in 1924 it was worth £35.04. John J. McCusker, Economic History Services, 2001: http://www.eh.net/hmit/ppowerbp/.
5. Eliot under-performed in his first year as a student but had sufficiently impressed the Harvard authorities to be taken on as a Doctoral student in 1911 and an Assistant in Philosophy in the following year. In 1914 he was awarded a Sheldon Fellowship to study at Merton College, Oxford. Aiken by contrast was expelled for failure to attend (1971: 3).
6. See, as well as these poems in *Prufrock and other Observations* (1917), reprinted as 'Appendix B' in Eliot (1996), the poems 'Nocturne', 'Humouresque (after J. Laforgue)', 'Spleen' in *Poems Written in Early Youth* (1967) and the sequence 'Suite Clownesque' (Eliot, 1996: 32–60). The notes to this latter volume identify the extensive echoes of Laforgue in Eliot's poetry between 1909–17.
7. 'Ode on Independence Day, July 4th 1918', published in the English but not the American edition of *Ara Vos Prec* (1920). See Eliot (1988: 363; 1996: 383).
8. This italicised section is made up of fragments and echoes of Eliot's early poems, letters and other related writings, including passages from Conan Doyle's 'Sign of the Four' and other sources as indicated. As readers will guess, I have in mind Eliot's 'I can connect / Nothing with nothing' in *The Waste Land*.

8 Bloomsbury's Bohemia

1. *Melymbrosia* satirised the pretensions of male experts to a point where Clive Bell thought her 'prejudice against men' made her 'didactic "not to say priggish"' (Woolf, 1975: 383; see DeSalvo, 2002: xx).

Bibliography

The following collections were consulted and are signalled, as here, in the text:

Beinecke: The Ezra Pound papers, Beinecke Rare Book and Manuscript Library, Yale University.

Bodleian: The Vivien(ne) Eliot papers, the Bodleian Library, University of Oxford. Contains diaries for 1914 and1919; notebooks containing drafts of stories; letters and sketches and miscellaneous items.

Hutchins: The Patricia Hutchins Correspondence. The British Library. Add. 57725–6.

Lloyds: Material held at Lloyds Bank, Lombard Street, London relating to T.S. Eliot's period at the bank, 1917–25.

Schiddel: The Edmund Schiddel Papers, Special Collections, Boston University. Contains Schiddel's correspondence with Iris Barry and with Victor M. Cassidy, including a typed 'Profile' of Iris Barry, dated '1942–3', and copies of Wyndham Lewis's correspondence with Iris Barry, 1920–30, 1939–42.

Texas: The F.S. Flint papers, Harry Ransom Humanities Center, University of Texas.

Thayer: Schofield Thayer papers containing correspondence with Vivien Eliot, Beinecke Rare Book and Manuscript Library, Yale University.

Yale: The Yale Centre for British Art, Yale University. Contains preliminary sketches by Spencer Gore and drawings by Eric Gill and Wyndham Lewis for the Cave of the Golden Calf.

Ackroyd, Peter (1984). *T.S. Eliot*. London: Hamish Hamilton.
Aiken, Conrad (1916). *Turns and Movies*. Boston: Houghton-Mifflin.
Aiken, Conrad (1948). 'King Bolo and Others'. In *March and Tambimuttu*, 20–3.
Aiken, Conrad (1965). 'T.S. Eliot', *Life Magazine*, 15 January 1965, 92–3.
Aiken, Conrad (1971). *The Clerk's Journal. Being the Diary of a Queer Man*. New York: Eakins Press.
Aiken, Conrad (1978). *Selected Letters*, ed. Joseph Killorin. New Haven: Yale University Press.
Aldington, Richard (1941). *Life for Life's Sake*. New York: The Viking Press.
Aldington, Richard (1992). *An Autobiography in Letters*, ed. Norman T. Gates. University Park, PA: Penn State University Press.
Anscombe, Isabelle (1981). *Omega and After. Bloomsbury and the Decorative Arts*. London: Thames and Hudson.
Arlen, Michael (1922). *Piracy*. London: Collins.
Baedeker, Karl (1908). *London and its Environs*. London: Dulau and Co.
Baisch, Dorothy (1950). 'London Literary Circles 1910–1920'. PhD thesis, Cornell University, June.
Barry, Iris (1931). 'The Ezra Pound Period', *The Bookman*, October: 159–71.
Baudelaire, Charles (1964). *The Painter of Modern Life and other Essays*, ed. Jonathan Mayne. London: Phaidon Press.

Beasley, Rebecca (2002). 'Ezra Pound's Whistler', *American Literature*, 74: 3, September, 485–516.
Beckett, Jane and Cherry, Deborah (2000). 'Reconceptualizing Vorticism: Women, Modernity, Modernism'. In Edwards (ed.), 59–72.
Beckson, Karl (ed.) (1977). *The Memoirs of Arthur Symons*. University Park, PA and London: Penn State University Press.
Beckson, Karl and Munro, John M. (eds) (1989). *Arthur Symons. Selected Letters 1880–1935*. London: Macmillan.
Bell, Clive (1948). 'How Pleasant to Know Mr Eliot'. In March and Tambimuttu, 15–19.
Bell, Quentin (1968). *Bloomsbury*. London: Weidenfeld and Nicolson.
Bell, Vanessa (1997). *Sketches in Pen and Ink. A Bloomsbury Notebook*, ed. Lia Giachero. London: The Hogarth Press.
Benjamin, Walter (1973). *Charles Baudelaire: a Lyric Poet in the Era of High Capitalism*. London: Verso.
Bergonzi, Bernard (1972). *T.S. Eliot*. London: Macmillan.
Bergonzi, Bernard (1973). *The Turn of a Century*. London: Macmillan.
Bland, Lucy (1996). 'The Shock of the *Freewoman* Journal'. In Weeks, Jeffrey and Holland, Janet (eds), *Sexual Cultures*. London: Macmillan, 75–96.
Bottome, Phyllis (1944). *From the Life*. London: Faber and Faber.
Bowen, Stella (1984). *Drawn from Life*. London: Virago.
Brodzky, Horace (1933). *Henri Gaudier-Brzeska*. London: Faber.
Brooker, Peter (1979). *A Student's Guide to the Selected Poems of Ezra Pound*. London: Faber.
Brooker, Peter (2002). *Modernity and Metropolis. Literature, Film and Urban Formations*. London: Palgrave Macmillan.
Brown, Dennis (1990). *Intertextual Dynamics within the Literary Group: Joyce, Lewis, Pound, Eliot*. London: Macmillan.
Buck, Louisa (2002). At http://www.bbc.co.uk/arts/tate/cruikshank/alcohol/caveofcalf.shtml.
Carpenter, Humphrey (1988). *A Serious Character. The Life of Ezra Pound*. London: Faber.
Chaplin, Charles (1964) *My Autobiography*. London: The Bodley Head.
Chapman, Robert (1973). *Wyndham Lewis: Fiction and Satires*. London: Vision Press.
Chisholm, Anne (1979). *Nancy Cunard*. London: Sidgwick and Jackson.
Cookson, William (ed.) (1973). *Ezra Pound. Selected Prose 1909–1965*. London: Faber.
Cork, Richard (1976). *Vorticism and Abstract Art in the First Machine Age*, Vols. 1 and 2. London: Gordon Fraser Gallery.
Cork, Richard (1982). *Henri Gaudier and Ezra Pound. A Friendship*. London: Anthony D'Offay, Curwen Press.
Cork, Richard (1985). *Art beyond the Gallery*. New Haven and London: Yale University Press.
Cournos, John (1922). *Babel*. New York: Boni and Liveright.
Cournos, John (1935). *Autobiography*. New York: G.P. Putnam's Sons.
Crunden, Robert Morse (1993). *American Salons. Encounters with European Modernism, 1885–1917*. Oxford: Oxford University Press.
Cunard, Nancy (1923). *Sublunary*. London: Hodder and Stoughton.

Damon, S. Foster (1966 [1935]). *Amy Lowell: a Chronicle*. Hamden, CT: Archon.
Darroch, Sandra Jobson (1975). *Ottoline. The Life of Lady Ottoline Morrell*. New York: Coward, McCann & Geoghegan, Inc.
David, Hugh (1988). *The Fitzrovians. A Portrait of Bohemian Society 1900–55*. London: Michael Joseph.
Davie, Donald (1975). *Pound*. London: Fontana.
Davie, Donald (1991). *Studies in Ezra Pound*. Cheadle: Carcarnet.
Deghy, Guy and Waterhouse, Keith (1955). *Café Royal: Ninety Years of Bohemia*. London: Hutchinson.
Delany, Paul (2001). *Literature, Money and the Market from Trollope to Amis*. London: Palgrave Macmillan.
Denney, Reuel (1964). *Conrad Aiken*. Minneapolis: Minnesota University Press.
DeSalvo, Louise (2002). 'Introduction' to Virginia Woolf, *Melymbrosia*. San Francisco, CA: Cleis Press.
Dismorr, Jessica (1915 [1981]). 'Poems and Notes', *Blast* 2: 65–9.
Drummond, John (1985). 'A Creative Crossroads. The Revival of Dance in Fergusson's Paris'. In Scottish Arts Council, 18–23.
Dunn, Jane (2000). *Virginia Woolf and Vanessa Bell. A Very Close Conspiracy*. London: Virago.
Edel, Leon (1977). *The Life of Henry James*, Vol. 2. London: Penguin.
Edel, Leon (1981). *Bloomsbury. A House of Lions*. London: Penguin.
Edwards, Paul (1992). *Wyndham Lewis: Art and War*. London: the Wyndham Lewis Memorial Trust in association with Lund Humphries.
Edwards, Paul (1996). 'Lewis's Myth of the Artist: from Bohemia to the Underground'. In Edwards, Paul (ed.) *Volcanic Heaven. Essays on Wyndham Lewis's Painting and Writing*. Santa Rosa: Black Sparrow Press.
Edwards, Paul (2000a). *Wyndham Lewis. Painter and Writer*. New Haven: Yale University Press.
Edwards, Paul (ed.) (2000b). *Blast. Vorticism 1914–1918*. Aldershot: Ashgate.
Eliot, T.S. (1923). 'Dramatis Personae', *Criterion*, 1: 3, April, 303–6.
Eliot, T.S. (1927). 'Books of the Quarter', *Criterion*, 5: 1, January, 139–43.
Eliot, T.S. (1929). 'Books of the Quarter', *Criterion*, 8: 32, April, 550–6.
Eliot, T.S. (1951). *Selected Essays*. London: Faber.
Eliot, T.S. (1970 [1928]). *For Lancelot Andrewes*. London: Faber.
Eliot, T.S. (1967). *Poems Written in Early Youth*. London: Faber.
Eliot, T.S. (1971). *The Waste Land. A Facsimile & Transcript*, ed. Valerie Eliot. London: Faber.
Eliot, T.S. (1974). *Collected Poems 1909–1962*. London: Faber.
Eliot, T.S. (1988). *The Letters of T.S. Eliot. Vol 1, 1898–1922*. London: Faber.
Eliot, T.S. (1996). *Inventions of the March Hare. Poems 1909–1917*, ed. Christopher Ricks. London: Faber.
Eliot, Vivien(ne) [as Feiron Morris] (1924). 'Thé Dansant', *Criterion*, 3: 9, October, 72–8.
Eliot, Vivien(ne) [as 'F.M'] (1925). 'Necesse est Perstare', *Criterion*, 3: 11, April, 364.
Ellman, Richard (1973). *Golden Codgers. Biographical Speculations*. London: Oxford University Press.
Epstein, Jacob (1955). *Let there be Sculpture*. London: Michael Joseph.
Evans, Sara M. (1989). *Born for Liberty. A History of Women in America*. New York: Free Press.

Farrington, Jane (1980). *Wyndham Lewis*. Exhibition catalogue. London: Lund Humphries in association with Manchester Art Galleries.
Feldman, Jessica R. (1993). *Gender on the Divide*. The Dandy in Modernist Literature. Ithaca: Cornell University Press.
Ferguson, Robert (2002). *The Short Sharp Life of T.E. Hulme*. London: Allen Lane.
Fielding, Daphne (1974). *The Rainbow Picnic. A Portrait of Iris Tree*. London: Eyre Methuen.
Fletcher, John Gould (1937). *Life is My Song*. New York: Farrar and Rinehart.
Flint, F.S. (1909). 'Book of the Week', *The New Age*, 11 Feb, 327–8.
Ford, Ford Madox (1919). 'Henri Gaudier. The Story of a Low Tea-Shop', *The English Review*, 19 October, 297–304.
Ford, Ford Madox (1921). *Thus to Revisit*. London: Chapman and Hall.
Ford, Ford Madox (1923). *The Marsden Case*. London: Duckworth.
Ford, Ford Madox (1929). *No Enemy. A Tale of Reconstruction*. New York: Macaulay Co.
Ford, Ford Madox (1932). *Return to Yesterday*. New York: Liveright.
Ford, Ford Madox (1934). *It Was the Nightingale*. London: Heinemann.
Ford, Ford Madox (1995 [1905]). *The Soul of London*. London: Everyman.
Ford, Hugh (ed.) (1968). *Nancy Cunard: Brave Poet, Indomitable Rebel 1896–1965*. Philadelphia: Chilton Book Company.
Garafola, Lynn (1998). *Diaghilev's Ballets Russes*. New York: Da Capo Press.
Garnett, David (1953). *The Golden Echo*. London: Chatto and Windus.
Gaudier-Brzeska, Henri (1914). 'To the Editor', *The Egoist*, 16 March, 117–18.
Gibson, Ashley (1930). *Postscript to Adventure*. London: Dent.
Glendinning, Victoria (1987). *Rebecca West. A Life*. London: Weidenfeld and Nicolson.
Gluck, Mary (2000). 'Theorizing the Cultural Roots of the Bohemian Artist', *Modernism/Modernity*, 7: 3, 351–78.
Goldring, Douglas (1943). *South Lodge*. London: Constable.
Gordon, Lyndall (1977). *Eliot's Early Years*. Oxford: Oxford University Press.
Gordon, Lyndall (1998). *T.S. Eliot. An Imperfect Life*. London: Vintage.
Gould, Jean (1975). *Amy: the World of Amy Lowell and the Imagist Movement*. New York: Dodd, Mead.
Graña, César and Graña, Marigay (eds) (1990). *On Bohemia. The Code of the Self-Exiled*. New Brunswick: Transaction Publishers.
Grant, Michael (1982). *T.S. Eliot. The Critical Heritage*, Vol. 1. London: Routledge.
Green, Martin (1987). *The Triumph of Pierrot. The Commedia dell'Arte and the Modern Imagination*. London: Macmillan.
Gregory, Horace (1958). *Amy Lowell. Portrait of the Poet in her Time*. New York: Nelson and Sons.
Guest, Barbara (1984). *Herself Defined. The Poet HD and her World*. Garden City: Doubleday.
H.D. (Hilda Doolittle) (1979). *An End to Torment: a Memoir of Ezra Pound*. New York: New Directions.
Hall, Donald (1977a). 'Ezra Pound', *Writers at Work. The Paris Review Interviews*. 2nd series. New York: Penguin, 35–59.
Hall, Donald (1977b). 'T.S. Eliot'. *Writers at Work. The Paris Review Interviews*. 2nd series. New York: Penguin, 91–110.
Hamnett, Nina (1984 [1932]). *Laughing Torso*. London: Virago.

Hanscombe, Gillian and Smyers, Virginia, L. (1987). *Writing for their Lives. The Modernist Women. 1910–1940*. London: The Women's Press.
Hargrove, Nancy D. (1998). 'The Great Parade: Cocteau, Picasso, Satie, Massine, Diaghilev and T.S. Eliot'. *Mosaic*, 31.1, March, 83–106.
Hastings, Michael (1984). *Tom and Viv*. London: Penguin.
Holdsworth, Roger (ed.) (1974). *Arthur Symons. Selected Writings*. Cheadle: Carcanet.
Holroyd, Michael (1976). *Augustus John*. Harmondsworth: Penguin.
Holroyd, Michael (1994). *Lytton Strachey*. London: Chatto and Windus.
Homberger, Eric (ed.) (1972). *Ezra Pound. The Critical Heritage*. London: Routledge.
Homberger, Eric (1978). 'Modernists and Edwardians'. In Philip Grover (ed.) *Ezra Pound. The London Years 1908–1920*. New York: AMS Press, 1–14.
Hone, Joseph (1971). *W.B. Yeats*. London: Pelican Books.
Howarth, Herbert (1965). *Notes on Some Figures behind T.S. Eliot*. London: Chatto and Windus.
Hulme, T.E. (1914). 'Modern Art III. The London Group', *The New Age*, 26 March, 661–2.
Hulme, T.E. (1960 [1924]). *Speculations*, ed. Herbert Read. London: Routledge.
Hulme, T.E. (1994). *Collected Writings*, ed. Karen Csengeri. Oxford: Clarendon Press.
Hunt, Violet (1926). *I Have This to Say. The Story of My Flurried Years*. New York: Boni and Liveright.
Hutchins, Patricia (1965). *Ezra Pound's Kensington*. London: Faber.
Hyde, H. Montgomery (ed.) (1948). *The Trials of Oscar Wilde*. London: Hodge.
Jackson, Holbrook (1976 [1913]). *The Eighteen Nineties*. Brighton: The Harvester Press.
Jepson, Edgar (1937). *Memories of an Edwardian and Neo-Georgian*. London: Richards.
John, Augustus (1952). *Chiaroscuro. Fragments of Autobiography*. London: Jonathan Cape.
Jones, Alun R. (1960). *The Life and Opinions of T.E. Hulme*. London: Victor Gollancz.
Kenner, Hugh (1960). *The Invisible Poet. T.S. Eliot*. London: W.H. Allen.
Kenner, Hugh (1973). 'D.P. Remembered', *Paideuma*, 2: 3, Winter, 485–93.
Kenner, Hugh (1975). *The Pound Era*. London: Faber.
Kenner, Hugh (1987). *The Mechanic Muse*. Oxford: Oxford University Press.
Kenner, Hugh (1988). *A Sinking Island. The Modern English Writers*. London: Barrie and Jenkins.
Kermode, Frank (1957). *Romantic Image*. London: Routledge.
Kolocotroni, Vassiliki, Goldman, Jane and Taxidou, Olga (eds) (1998). *Modernism. An Anthology of Sources and Documents*. Edinburgh: Edinburgh University Press.
Lamos, Colleen (1998). *Deviant Modernism: Sexual and Textual Errancy in T.S. Eliot, James Joyce, and Marcel Proust*. Cambridge: Cambridge University Press.
Lee, Hermione (1997). *Virginia Woolf*. London: Vintage.
Lewis, Wyndham (1914). 'The Cubist Room', *The Egoist*, 1 January, 8–9.
Lewis, Wyndham (1956). 'Introduction' to 'Wyndham Lewis and Vorticism'. London: Tate Gallery.
Lewis, Wyndham (1970 [1921]). *The Tyro, no. 1*. London: F. Cass.
Lewis, Wyndham (ed.) (1981 [1915]). *Blast 2*. Santa Barbara: Black Sparrow Press.

Lewis, Wyndham (1982). *Blasting and Bombardiering. An Autobiography (1914–1926)*. London: John Calder.
Lewis, Wyndham (1984). *Rude Assignment. An Intellectual Autobiography*. Santa Barbara: Black Sparrow Press.
Lewis, Wyndham (1990). *Tarr. The 1918 Version*, ed. Paul O'Keefe. Santa Rosa: Black Sparrow Press.
Lewis, Wyndham (ed.) (1997 [1914]). *Blast* 1. Santa Rosa: Black Sparrow Press.
Lhombreaud, Roger (1963). *Arthur Symons: a Critical Biography*. London: Unicorn Press.
Lidderdale, Jane and Nicholson, Mary (1970). *Dear Miss Weaver*. London: Faber and Faber.
Lorenz, Clarissa M. (1983). *Loreli Two. My Life with Conrad Aiken*. Athens, Georgia: University of Georgia Press.
Mackworth, Cecily (1974). *English Interludes, Mallarmé, Verlaine, Paul Valéry, Valery Larbaud in England, 1860–1912*. London: Routledge.
Mallarmé, Stéphane (1977). *The Poems*, ed. Keith Bosley. London: Penguin.
March, Richard and Tambimuttu (eds) *T.S. Eliot. A Symposium*. London: PL Editions Poetry.
Marek, Jayne E. (1995). *Women Editing Modernism*. Lexington, Kentucky: University Press of Kentucky.
Martin, Wallace (1967). *'The New Age' under Orage*. Manchester: Manchester University Press.
McGregor, Sheila (1985). 'J.D. Fergusson and the Periodical *Rhythm*'. In Scottish Arts Council, 13–17.
Meyers, Jeffrey (1978). *Katherine Mansfield*. London: Hamish Hamilton.
Meyers, Jeffrey (1980). *The Enemy. A Biography of Wyndham Lewis*. London: Routledge.
Meyers, Jeffrey (1984). 'New Light on Iris Barry', *Paideuma*, 13, 285–9.
Meyers, Jeffrey and Lechmere, Kate (1983). 'Kate Lechmere's "Wyndham Lewis from 1912"', *Journal of Modern Literature*, 10: 1, 158–66.
Middleton, Christopher (1965). 'Documents on Imagism from the papers of F.S. Flint', *The Review*, 15, 35–51.
Morley, F.V. (1948). 'T.S. Eliot as a Publisher'. In March and Tambimuttu, 60–70.
Mullins, Eustace (1961). *This Difficult Individual, Ezra Pound*. New York: Fleet Publishing Corporation.
Nevinson, C.R.W. (1937). *Paint and Prejudice*. London: Methuen.
Norman, Charles (1969). *Ezra Pound. A Biography*. London: MacDonald.
North, Michael (1999). *Reading 1922. A Return to the Scene of the Modern*. Oxford: Oxford University Press.
O'Keefe, Paul (2001). *Some Sort of Genius. A Life of Wyndham Lewis*. London: Pimlico.
Orel, Harold (1986). *The Literary Achievement of Rebecca West*. Basingstoke: Macmillan.
Paige, D.D. (ed.) (1971). *Selected Letters of Ezra Pound*. New York: New Directions.
Patmore, Brigit (1968). *My Friends When Young*. London: Heinemann.
Pearson, John (1978). *Façades: Edith, Osbert and Sacheverell Sitwell*. London: Macmillan.
Peppis, Paul (2000). *Literature, Politics, and the English Avant-Garde*. Cambridge: Cambridge University Press.

Pound, Ezra (1913) 'Status Rerum', *Poetry*, January, 123–7.
Pound, Ezra (1914a). 'The New Sculpture', *The Egoist*, February 16, 67–8.
Pound, Ezra (1914b).'Wyndham Lewis', *The Egoist*, June 15, 233–4.
Pound, Ezra (1920). 'The Island of Paris. A Letter'. *The Dial*, LXIX, 406–8.
Pound, Ezra (1934). *Make it New*. London: Faber.
Pound, Ezra (1958). *Pavannes and Divagations*. New York: New Directions.
Pound, Ezra (1960). *Literary Essays*. London: Faber.
Pound, Ezra (1965). *A Lume Spento*. New York: New Directions.
Pound, Ezra (1968). *Collected Shorter Poems*. London: Faber.
Pound, Ezra (1970). *Gaudier-Brzeska. A Memoir*. New York: New Directions.
Pound, Ezra (1975a) *Certain Radio Speeches*, ed. William Levy. Rotterdam: Cold Turkey Press.
Pound, Ezra (1975b). *The Cantos*. London: Faber.
Pound, Ezra (1977). *Collected Early Poems*. London: Faber.
Pound/Shakespear (1984). *Ezra Pound and Dorothy Shakespear. Their Letters 1909–1914*, eds. Omar Pound and A. Walton Litz. London: Faber.
Puccini, Giacomo (1983). *La Bohème*. Italian and English translation. Story adaptation by V.S Pritchett. London: Michael Joseph.
Quinton, Anthony (1982). 'Introduction'. In Roberts, Michael.
Radford, Jean (1991). *Dorothy Richardson*. London: Harvester.
Ransome, Arthur (1907). *Bohemia in London*. London: Chapman and Hall.
Read, Herbert (1967). 'T.S.E. – A Memoir'. In Tate (ed.), 11–37.
Richards, I.A. (1967). 'On TSE'. In Tate (ed.), 1–10.
Richardson, Dorothy (1939). 'Yeats of Bloomsbury', *Life and Letters Today*, 21, April, 60–6.
Roberts, Michael (1982 [1938]). *T.E. Hulme*. Manchester: Carcanet.
Roberts, William (1956–8). *The Vortex Pamphlets*. London: Canale Publication.
Roberts, William (1957). 'Wyndham Lewis, the Vorticist'. *The Listener*, 21 March, 470.
Rose, W.K. (ed.) (1963). *The Letters of Wyndham Lewis*. London: Methuen.
Russell, Bertrand (1967). *The Autobiography of Bertrand Russell*. London: George Allen & Unwin.
Saunders, Max (1996). *Ford Madox Ford. A Dual Life*, Vol. 1. Oxford: Oxford University Press.
Scott, Bonnie, Kime (ed.) (2000). *Selected Letters of Rebecca West*. New Haven and London: Yale University Press.
Scott-James, R.A. (1955). *Lytton Strachey*. London: The British Council.
Scottish Arts Council (1985). *Colour, Rhythm and Dance. Paintings and Drawings by J.D. Fergusson and his Circle in Paris*. Edinburgh: Scottish Arts Council.
Seymour-Jones, Carole (2001). *Pained Shadow. A Life of Vivienne Eliot*. London: Constable.
Sheppard, Richard W. (1989). 'Wyndham Lewis's *Tarr*: An (Anti-) Vorticist Novel?', *Journal of English and Germanic Philology*, 88: 4, October, 510–30.
Showalter, Elaine (1990). *Sexual Anarchy, Gender and Culture at the Fin de Siècle*. New York: Viking.
Sitwell, Osbert (1948). *Left Hand, Right Hand! An Autobiography*, Vol. 3. London: Macmillan.
Southam, Brian (1977). *A Student's Guide to the Selected Poems of T.S. Eliot*. London: Faber.

Spender, Stephen (1967). 'Remembering Eliot'. In Tate (ed.), 38–64.
Stanksky, Peter (1996). *On or about December 1910. Early Bloomsbury and its Intimate World.* Cambridge, MA: Harvard University Press.
Stearns, Marshall and Stearns, Jean (1968). *Jazz Dance. The Story of American Vernacular Dance.* London: Macmillan.
Stock, Noel (1970). *The Life of Ezra Pound.* London: Penguin.
Storey, Robert F. (1978). *Pierrot. A Critical History of a Mask.* Princeton, New Jersey: Princeton University Press.
Strauss, Monica (2001). *Cruel Banquet. The Life and Loves of Frida Strindberg.* New York: Harcourt.
Symons, Arthur (1905). *The Poems of Ernest Dowson.* London: John Lane, The Bodley Head.
Symons, Arthur (1908). 'Introduction' to *The Latin Quarter ('Scènes de la vie de Bohème').* Trans. Ellen Marriage and John Selwyn. London: Lotus Library Series.
Symons, Arthur (1918). *Cities and Sea-Coasts and Islands.* London: W. Collins Sons & Co. Ltd.
Symons, Arthur (1923). *The Café Royal and other Essays.* London: Beaumont Press.
Symons, Arthur (1958 [1899, rev. edition 1908]). *The Symbolist Movement in Literature.* New York: Dutton.
Symons, Julian (ed.) (1989). *The Essential Wyndham Lewis.* London: Andre Deutsch.
Tate, Alison (1988). 'The Master-Narrative of Modernism. Discourses on Gender and Class in the *Waste Land*', *Literature and History*, 14: 2, Autumn, 160–71.
Tate, Allen (ed.) (1967). *T.S. Eliot. The Man and His Work.* London: Chatto and Windus.
Thacker, Andrew (1993). 'Amy Lowell and H.D.: the Other Imagists', *Woman: a Cultural Review*, 4: 1, 49–59.
Tickner, Lisa (1992). 'Men's Work? Masculinity and Modernism', *differences: a Journal of Feminist Cultural Studies*, 4: 3, 1–37.
Tickner, Lisa (1997). 'The Popular Culture of *Kermesse*: Lewis, Painting, and Performance, 1912–13', *Modernism/Modernity*, 4: 2, 67–120.
Vittoz, Roger (1913). *The Treatment of Neurasthenia by Means of Brain Control.* Translated by H.B. Brooke. London: Longmans & Co.
Wees, William C. (1972). *Vorticism and the English Avant-Garde.* Toronto and Buffalo: University of Toronto Press.
Weightman, Gavin (1992). *Bright Lights, Big City. London Entertained 1830–1950.* London: Collins and Brown.
Weintraub, Stanley (1979). *The London Yankees. Portraits of American Writers and Artists in England, 1898–1914.* New York and London: Harcourt Brace Jovanovich.
West, Rebecca (1913a). 'Nana', *The New Freewoman*, 1 July, 26–7.
West, Rebecca (1913b). 'At Valladolid', *The New Freewoman*, 1 August, 66–7.
West, Rebecca (1982). *The Young Rebecca. Writings of Rebecca West 1911–17*, selected and introduced by Jane Marcus. Bloomington: Indiana University Press.
West, Rebecca (1992). *The Only Poet and other Stories*, ed. Antonia Till. London: Virago.
Wilhelm, J.J. (1990). *Ezra Pound in London and Paris.* University Park, PA and London: Penn State University Press.

Williams, John T. (1992). 'Pierrots', *Bygone Kent*, 13: 2, 100–5.
Williams, William Carlos (1967). *The Autobiography of William Carlos Williams*. New York: New Directions.
Williams, William Carlos (1969). *Selected Essays*. New York: New Directions.
Wilson, Elizabeth (2000). *Bohemians. The Glamorous Outcasts*. London: I. B. Tauris.
Wilson, Jean Moorcroft (2000). *Virginia Woolf's London*. London: Tauris Park Paperbacks.
Woolf, Leonard (1967). *Downhill all the Way. An Autobiography of the Years, 1939–1969*. London: The Hogarth Press.
Woolf, Virginia (1925). *The Common Reader. First Series*. London: The Hogarth Press.
Woolf, Virginia (1937). *The Years*. London: The Hogarth Press.
Woolf, Virginia (1938). *Three Guineas*. London: The Hogarth Press.
Woolf, Virginia (1940). *Roger Fry. A Biography*. London: The Hogarth Press.
Woolf, Virginia (1975). *The Flight of the Mind. The Letters of Virginia Woolf*. Vol.1: *1888–1912*. London: The Hogarth Press.
Woolf, Virginia (1976). *The Question of Things Happening. The Letters of Virginia Woolf. Vol. 2: 1912–1922*. London: The Hogarth Press.
Woolf, Virginia (1977). *Books and Portraits*. London: The Hogarth Press.
Woolf, Virginia (1978a). *The Diary of Virginia Woolf. Vol. 2: 1920–1924*, ed. Anne Olivier Bell. London: The Hogarth Press.
Woolf, Virginia (1978b). *Moments of Being*. St Albans: Triad/Panther Books.
Woolf, Virginia (1979). *Women and Writing*, ed. Michèle Barrett. London: The Women's Press.
Woolf, Virginia (1980). *The Diary of Virginia Woolf. Vol. 3: 1925–1930*, ed. Anne Olivier Bell. London: The Hogarth Press.
Woolf, Virginia (1985). *The Complete Shorter Fiction*, ed. Susan Dick. London: The Hogarth Press.
Woolf, Virginia (1992). *A Woman's Essays*, ed. Rachel Bowlby. London: Penguin.
Woolf, Virginia (2002). *Melymbrosia*. ed. and introduced by Louise DeSalvo. San Francisco, CA: Cleis Press.
Yeats, W.B. (1955). *Autobiographies*. London: Macmillan.
Yeats, W.B. (1964). *Selected Criticism*, ed. A.N. Jeffares. London: Macmillan.

Index

Abercrombie, Lascelles 93
aesthetes, and bohemianism 7
Aiken, Conrad 134, 135, 139, 140–1, 142, 143, 144, 145, 146, 148, 157
  'Clerk's Journal, The' 139
  'London Symphony' 139
  Turns and Moves 140
Aldington, Richard 57, 65, 68, 107, 111, 115, 117, 120, 136
  Death of a Hero 55
Allied Artists Group 14
Allinson, Adrian, 'The Old Café Royal' 103
Arlen, Michael 108
  Green Hat, The 126
  London Venture, The 127
  Piracy 126–7, 128
  Romantic Lady, The 127
art
  exhibitions: Allied Artists 88; Group X 22; Post-Impressionist 14, 165, 169, 170, 172; Tyros and Portraits 22; Wyndham Lewis and Vorticism 129–30
  galleries: Doré 93, 98; Grafton 169, 172; Groupil 123; Mansard 22; Tate 129
  geometrical 95
  romantic individualism 131
  sociality of 130–1
  war 94
Asquith, Herbert 169, 170
avant-garde 94, 130
  and dance 84–5
  and women's movement 110–11

Ballets Russes 50, 80–1, 82–3
Barry, Iris (Iris Crump) 18, 19, 46, 67, 68, 107, 108–9, 110, 112, 149
  Let's Go to the Pictures 108–9
Baudelaire, Charles 3, 4–5, 141, 142
Beach, Sylvia 112

Beardsley, Aubrey 34, 35, 36
Beckford, William, *Vathek* 28
Bell, Clive 136, 138, 158, 161, 162, 163, 169, 174, 176
Bell, Quentin 158, 169
Bell, Vanessa (née Stephen) 158, 159, 160, 163, 165, 166, 168, 169, 170, 173, 174, 175–6
Benjamin, Walter 3, 7
Bennett, Arnold 2, 47, 172, 176
  Books and Persons 172
  Our Women 176
Bergonzi, Bernard 40, 41
Binyon, Laurence 28, 53
  London Visions 46
Blast 14, 69, 85, 98, 99, 101, 102, 110, 122, 123, 128, 146
  Blast 1 16, 19, 21, 113
  Blast 2 21, 25, 67, 113–14
Bloomsbury 106, 125, 137, and class 167
  composition 163
  freedom of speech 161
  Fry's influence 165–6, 168
  hostility towards 166–7
  'lifestyle modernism' 137
  nature of 163–5
  origins 160–1
  pacifism of 167
  security of 167–8
  sex 161–2, 167
  Vanessa Bell on 159
  Virginia Woolf on 159–60
  Vivien Eliot on 138–9
bohemianism
  artist and commodity culture 4–5, 7
  artist and society 3, 5
  Bloomsbury 167
  dress 4, 45–6, 55, 82, 94, 107
  English version 40
  impact of First World War 8–9
  'lifestyle modernism' 137

195

bohemianism – *continued*
  modernist artist 7–8
  origins of idea of 2–3
  received values 35
  ridicule of 5–6
  stereotype figures 39
  types of Bohemian 3
  women 107–9, 110–11, 125–6
Bomberg, David 93, 98, 114, 121–2, 129, 160
Borden Turner, Mary 121, 122
Bottome, Phyllis 57, 65
Bowen, Stella 87, 103, 107, 108
British Museum Reading Room 28, 44
Brooke, Rupert 96, 162, 165
Brown, Ford Madox 39, 55
Butts, Mary 68, 107, 111

Cabaret Club 74, 90, 119–20
  Cabaret Theatre Club 74
  Cave of the Golden Calf 26, 73, 74–9, 82–3, 88
café society 8, 113–31
cafés, important role of 113–14
cafés, restaurants and pubs
  ABC 113–14
  Belotti's 111, 113, 114
  Brice's 113
  Café Momus 3
  Café Royal 28–9, 31, 32, 34, 40, 102, 103, 113
  Cheshire Cheese, The 28, 32, 40
  Crown tavern 34
  De Marias 114
  Dieppe 113
  Dieudonné's 114, 115, 117, 119:
    Imagist dinner at 115–17;
    Vorticist dinner at 119–23
  Fitzroy Tavern 126
  Florence 114
  Frascati's 114
  Grove pub 150
  Kettner's 114
  Lyons 113–14
  Miss Ella Abbott's teashop 114
  Pagani's 41, 43, 113
  Restaurant de la Tour Eiffel 14, 44, 96, 104, 123–9, 168: *Blast* dinner
    at 123; fictional portrayal 126–7, 128; impact of war 128–9; Vorticist evening at 123; 'Vorticist Room' 26, 123, 124–5, 129
  Ristorante Italiano 67
  Roche 113
  Sceptre Tavern and Chop House 96
  Vienna Café 28, 53, 114
  Yorkshire Grey pub 42
Camden Town Group 14
Cannan, Gilbert 47, 57
Carrington, Dora 106, 126, 160, 163
Cave of the Golden Calf *see* Cabaret Club, Cave of the Golden Calf
censorship 68, 110
  music hall 36–8
Chambers, Jessie 57, 62
Chaplin, Charlie 50, 152
cinemas *see* theatres and cinemas
civilisation 128
  Ezra Pound on 69, 70, 71, 97
Coburn, Alvin Langdon 98
Contemporary Art Society 170
Cork, Richard 12, 14, 90, 113, 121, 122, 130
Cournos, John 57, 58, 59–60, 65, 96, 113, 114, 115–16, 117
  Babel 23–5, 49
Cowley, Malcolm 140
Crabtree Club 125
cubism 98, 130
Cunard, Bache 104, 105
Cunard, Emerald (Maud) 104–5
Cunard, Nancy 19, 82, 107, 108, 109, 125, 126, 170
  as bohemian 104
  background 104–5
  Café Royal 102–4
  dress 102
  early marriage 105
  Negro 111
  as rebel 103, 104
Curle, Richard 96

dance, and
  Ezra Pound 87
  modernism 84–5

Index   197

dance, and – *continued*
  music hall ballet   35, 36–8, 80
  new styles of   83–4
  popular   81–2, 84, 85–7
  sexuality   82
  T. S. Eliot   132
  Wyndham Lewis   85–7
  see also Ballets Russes
dandyism   4, 31, 45–6, 94, 141, 142
David, Hugh   3, 6–7, 29, 40, 125, 126
Davidson, John   35, 49
Davie, Donald   62, 65, 66
De Gourmont, Rémy   69, 70
de la Mare, Walter   57
de Nerval, Gérard   3
Denney, Reuel   140
Dismorr, Jessica   25–6, 87–8, 108, 126, 130
  'June Night'   25–6
  'London Notes'   26
  'Monologue'   26
Disraeli, Benjamin, *Coningsby*   128
Dobson, Frank   129
Dolmetsch, Arnold   98
Doolittle, Hilda (H. D.)   57, 60, 64, 65, 107, 111, 112, 115, 117
Dowson, Ernest   34, 35, 36, 38–9, 41
  'Cynara'   41
Du Maurier, George   6
  Trilby   1, 2, 4, 6
Dulac, Edmund   57
Duncan, Isadora   83, 87

Earp, Tommy   105, 108
Edwards, Paul   13, 85
Egoist   15, 21, 24, 67, 68, 93, 97, 98, 110, 149, 150
Egoist Press   111, 150
Eliot, T. S.   2, 41, 80, 93, 111, and Burleigh Mansions   138
  Crawford Mansions   132, 136
  dancing   81, 132
  dress   141, 149, 151
  Ezra Pound   47
  Faber and Gwyer   149, 150
  French symbolists   48, 49
  Harvard   141–2
  hypochondria   136
  image   50–1

  impact of Symons   48
  influences on   48–9
  Lloyds bank   148–50
  London   49, 146–7
  Margate   152–3
  marriage   133–7, 147, 157
  Oxford   50
  Paris   49–50, 142
  player of parts   151–2
  self-consciousness   145–6
  sex   138, 143–5
  Sherlock Holmes   151
  treatment in Lausanne   155–6
  women   143, 144–5
  Yeats   47
Eliot, T. S., literary works
  Ara Vos Prec   148
  'Ballade pour la grosse Lulu'   147
  'Conversation Galante'   143
  'Eeldrop and Appleplex'   81, 150
  'Gerontion'   155
  'Humouresque (after J. Laforgue)'   168
  'Interlude in a Bar'   49, 50
  'Interlude in London'   49
  'Inventions of the March Hare'   144
  'King Bolo' poems   144–5
  'Love Song of J. Alfred Prufrock, The'   48–9, 138, 139–40, 142
  'Ode'   145
  'Paysage Triste'   50
  Poems   138, 148
  'Portrait of a Lady'   142, 143
  'Preludes'   168
  Prufrock and other Observations   138, 150
  'Rhapsody on a Windy Night'   49, 142–3
  'Sweeney Erect'   145
  'Triumph of Bullshit, The'   144, 147
  'Up Boys And At 'Em'   144
  Waste Land, The   49, 81, 135, 149, 153, 155–7
Eliot, Vivien(ne) (née Haigh-Wood)   50, 81, 132–3, 153, 157, and Bertrand Russell   136
  committed to an asylum   134
  dancing   132–3

Eliot, Vivien(ne) (née Haigh-Wood) – *continued*
  death 134
  hypochondria 136
  marriage 133–4, 136–7
  'modern' girl 134
Eliot, Vivien, literary works
  'Necesse est Perstare?' 138–9
  'Night Club' 133
  'On the Eve: a Dialogue' 133
  'Thé Dansant' 133
English Review 10, 11, 44, 53, 54, 55, 80, 119, 120, 168
Epstein, Jacob 57, 73, 74, 93, 98, 99, 101
  head of Pound 97, 99
  'Rock Drill' 99
Etchells, Frederick 166, 168

Faber, Geoffrey 150
Fairfield, Cicely Isabel *see* West, Rebecca
Farrell, Sophie 170–1
Feldman, Jessica 141
Fergusson, J. D. 85, 87
fin de siècle 36
  character of 39–40
First World War
  and art 94
  impact of 8–9, 128
flâneur 3
Fletcher, John Gould 80, 115, 116, 117
Flint, F. S. 44, 45, 55, 61–2, 69, 95, 96, 115, 117, 120, 124, 136, 150
  In the Net of Stars 62
Fokine, Mikhail 83
Ford, Ford Madox 1–2, 4, 8, 46, 47, 53, 70, 74, 96, 113, 115, 118, 121, 168, and
  Cave of the Golden Calf 76
  creative reminiscences 120–1
  Ezra Pound 44–5, 54, 57–8
  family background 55–6
  Gaudier-Brzeska 119–20
  Kensington 63
  London 12
  parties of 56–7
  shifting identities 56
  South Lodge 56–7
  Wyndham Lewis 10–11

Ford, Ford Madox, works
  'Henri Gaudier: the story of a low teashop' 119
  Marsden Case, The 11, 76–9, 84
  'Monstrous Regiment of Women, The' 57
  No Enemy 119, 120
  'On a Marsh Road' 54
  'On Heaven' 54
  Return to Yesterday 10–11
  Soul of London, The 43
  Thus to Revisit 119, 120
Forster, E. M. 158
  Howards End 62
Fowler, Eva 63, 106
Frost, Robert 55
Fry, Helen 169
Fry, Roger 14, 15, 100, 108, 125, 136, 158, 163, 169, 170, 172, 173, 176
  and Bloomsbury 165–6, 168
Fuller, Loïe 83, 84
Futurism 93, 98

Garnett, David 56, 163, 176
  on Nancy Cunard 102–3
Gaudier-Brzeska, Henri 25, 57, 83, 93, 94, 97, 98, 99, 104, 114–15, 118, 120, 121, 125, 146, 166
Gautier, Théophile 3, 4, 94
Gertler, Mark 125, 160
Gill, Eric 74, 75
Ginner, Charles 74, 75, 96
Gluck, Mary 4, 7
Goldring, Douglas 10, 11, 45, 55, 57, 59, 79–80, 119, 123
Gore, Spencer 74, 75
Grant, Duncan 158, 162, 163, 164, 166, 168, 169, 170, 172, 175, 176
Group X 22, 25

H. D. *see* Doolittle, Hilda
Haigh-Wood, Vivien(ne) *see* Eliot, Vivien(ne)
Hamnett, Nina 84, 107, 108, 109, 114, 125, 126, 127, 128, 160, 166
  Laughing Torso 108
Harris, Frank 74, 76
  'On Style' 89

Hart-Davis, Rupert   104
Hastings, Beatrice   18–19
Hayward, John   150
Henley, W. E.   28, 36
Hogarth Press   138, 163, 165
Hueffer, Ford Madox *see* Ford, Ford
   Madox
Hugo, Victor, *Hernani*   4, 94
Hulme, T. E.   7, 14, 44, 93, 94, 95, 96,
   97–8, 100, 102, 116–17, 122, 123,
   124, 146, 166, 168, and
   background   96–7
   character   97
   'Contemporary Drawings'   130
   fictional portrayal of   24
   Kate Lechmere   101
   Kensington lecture   95, 97
   Lewis   101
   marginalisation of   102
   Pound   95
   women   99
Hunt, Violet   47, 54, 56, 57, 64, 70,
   74, 82, 89, 106, 111, 115, 119,
   122, 125, 169
   South Lodge   11
Hutchins, Patricia   45, 63, 71
Hutchinson, Mary   81, 133, 137,
   176
Huxley, Aldous
   Antic Hay   126
   Point Counter Point   126

Image, Selwyn   34, 40, 46
Imagism   7, 24, 54, 95, 98, 114,
   117–18, 165
   dinner at Dieudonné's   115–17
Impressionism   2, 7, 9
industrialisation, and emergence of
   bohemianism   2–3

Jackson, Holbrook   30, 31, 141, 142
James, Henry   2, 56, 69–70
   Roderick Hudson   42
Jazz   25, 84
Jepson, Edgar   47, 81
John, Augustus   4, 13, 90, 91–2, 108,
   125, 126, 137, 160, 164
Johnson, Lionel   35, 36, 63
Jones, A. R.   95, 96, 97

journals and magazines
   Atheneum   69, 70
   Cornhill   168
   Criterion   81, 133, 138, 150
   Dial, The   70
   Enemy, The   22
   Freewoman   21, 109, 112
   Harpers New Monthly Magazine
      37
   Little Review   67, 68, 69
   New Age   62, 67, 69, 96, 97, 99,
      113, 130
   New Freewoman, The   21, 87, 88, 91,
      110
   Outlook, The   69, 119
   Poetry   44, 46, 65, 67, 68, 69, 140
   Poetry and Drama   62
   Quarterly Review   47, 63, 69
   Rhythm   85, 88
   Savoy   29–30, 34, 40
   Spectator   98
   Times Literary Supplement   168
   Tyro, The   22
   Wheels   105
   Yellow Book, The   36
   *see also Blast; Egoist; English Review,
      The*
Joyce, James   2, 15, 110, 111
   Chamber Music   46, 168
   Dubliners   168
   Ulysses   112

Kenner, Hugh   43, 50, 63, 64, 95,
   150, 152
Keynes, Maynard   158, 162,
   170, 176
Konody, P. G.   74
Kramer, Jacob   129

Laforgue, Jules   48, 142, 143, 145
Lamos, Colleen   157
Lane, John   46, 68
Lasson, Bokken   74–5
Lawrence, D. H.   31, 46, 55, 57, 62,
   65, 110, 117, 165
Lechmere, Kate   18, 19, 57, 82, 86,
   94, 100, 101–2, 107, 108, 121,
   122, 123
Lee, Hermione   175

Lewis, Wyndham 2, 13, 22, 44, 57, 80, 102, 105, 108, 111, 114, 118, 121, 125, 146, 160, 166, 168, and
  affairs 18–19, 87, 122, 128
  appearance 10–11, 85, 86, 94
  art exhibitions 14, 22, 129
  Bloomsbury 15
  bohemian artist 13
  Cave of the Golden Calf 73–4, 75
  children 19
  Ezra Pound 53
  Ford Madox Ford 10–11
  First World War 94, 128
  Frida Strindberg 90
  Group X 22
  Hulme 93, 101
  later career 22–3
  Lechmere 101
  multiple personae 11–12, 20–1
  Nancy Cunard 127–8
  Paris 15
  popular dance 85–7
  Rebecca West 88
  Rebel Arts Centre 100, 122
  Restaurant de la Tour Eiffel 124–5
  self-created image 11, 13–14
  Vorticism 14, 16, 19, 98, 129
  women 18–19, 99
  'Wyndham Lewis and Vorticism' exhibition 129
Lewis, Wyndham, works
  Apes of God, The 22
  Art of Being Ruled, The 22
  Blasting and Bombardiering 21, 94
  'Cantleman's Spring Mate' 18
  Childermass, The 22
  'Code of a Herdsman, The' 20
  Complete Wild Body, The 12, 22
  'Creation' 74, 83
  'Crowd Master, The' 21
  'Cubist Room, The' 97
  Enemy of the Stars, The 14, 123
  'Kermesse' 74, 83, 85, 166
  Lovers 83
  ' "Pole", The' 10, 12
  Roaring Queen, The 126
  Rude Assignment 15

Tarr 12–18, 19–21, 22
Time and Western Man 22
Tyro, The 22
'Vorticist Room' at Restaurant de la Tour Eiffel 123, 124–5
London
  Arthur Symons on 31–2, 35, 38
  end of modernist experiment 9
  fictional portrayal of 24, 25–6
  in war-time 68
  Kensington 63
  as 'modern' city 29
  myths of pre-war 12
  Soho 27, 28, 33, 34, 35
Lowell, Amy 57, 68, 104, 115–16, 117, 120, 121, 125
  'In a Garden' 115, 118

MacCarthy, Desmond 158, 172, 176
MacCarthy, Molly 158, 176
Mallarmé, Stéphane 27–8, 35
  'Les Fenêtres' 27
  'The Raven' 28
Manning, Fredric 46, 63, 64
Mansfield, Katherine 88, 108, 137, 138, 168
Marinetti, F. T. 11, 14, 93, 98, 100
marriage, and
  attitudes towards 8, 57
  'modern' 65
  Pound on 64
  women 64, 106–7
Marsden, Dora 15–16, 21, 87, 88, 109–10, 112
Marsh, Sir Edward 96, 105
Massine, Léonide 50–1, 80, 138
Matthews, Elkin 40, 42, 43, 68
  bookshop 46
Memoir Club 158–60
Meyers, Jeffrey 11, 129
modernism 2
  censorship 68
  emergence of 40–1
  modernist artist 7–8
  modernist Bohemia 8
Moffatt, Adeline 143
Monroe, Harriet 44, 65
Moore, George 28, 102, 105
Moore, Mary 42, 43, 65

Moore, Sturge 12, 28
Morley, Frank 150, 151
Morrell, Ottoline 80, 106, 133, 136, 137, 153, 156, 164, 165, 169, 170, 175
Morrell, Philip 137, 164, 170
Morris, Margaret 75, 76, 88
Munro, Harold 140
  Poetry and Drama 168
Mürger, Henri 6–7, 104
  Latin Quarter, The 38
  Scènes de la Vie Bohème 2, 38, 44
Murry, Middleton 85, 88, 137
music hall 29, 33, 34, 36–7, 40, 80

National Council for Civil Liberties 111
National Vigilance Association 36–7
Nevinson, C. R. W. 57, 86, 87, 93, 96, 98, 100, 103, 105, 114, 122, 129, 160
Nichols, Daniel (Daniel Nicolas Thévenon) 28, 29

O'Shaughnessy, Arthur 27–8
Omega Workshops 14, 82, 100, 125, 165, 166–7, 168, 170
Orage, A. R. 80, 96, 113

Pankhurst, Christabel 57
Pankhurst, Emmeline 170
Pater, Walter 35
  Studies in the History of the Renaissance 31
Patmore, Brigit 45, 55, 57, 65, 68, 80, 81, 82, 107, 132
Payne, John 27, 28
Phillippe, Charles Louis, *Babu of Montparnasse* 49
Plarr, Victor 40, 45, 46
Poe, Edgar Allan 3, 27, 28
poetry
  Arthur Symons 30–1
  the professional poet 58
Poets' Club 7, 14, 44, 97, 124, 168
  For Christmas MDCCCCVIII 124
Pound, Dorothy (née Shakespear) 42, 43, 44, 46–7, 62, 63, 64–7, 108, 111, 113, 122, 172
  'Notebook' 64–5

Pound, Ezra 2, 8, 22, 41, 93, 94–5, 96, 105, 110, 117, 123, 130, 146, 168, and
  10 Church Walk 54–5
  affairs 67–8
  ambition of 42–3
  'American Europeanist' 62–3
  Amy Lowell 115–16, 118
  animosity towards 68–9
  approach to poetry 58
  Arnold Bennett 47
  arrives in London 41–2
  Bloomsbury 166, 167
  British Museum Reading Room 44
  career 1913–17 67
  civilisation 69–70, 71, 97
  domination of social events 59–60
  Dorothy Shakespear 64
  dress 45–6, 55
  Elkin Matthews' bookshop 46
  Frank Flint 61, 62
  Ford Madox Ford 53–4, 56–8
  Gaudier-Brzeska 119
  George Prothero 65–6
  Hilda Doolittle 65
  Imagism 54, 95, 114
  Iris Barry 67–8
  literary establishment 65–6, 68–9
  London 43–4, 54, 62–3
  marriage 64, 65
  moves to Paris 9, 70
  T. E. Hulme 95
  T. S. Eliot 48–9, 156
  Vorticism 98, 118
  Whistler 45–6, 55
  women 64–5
  Wyndham Lewis 11, 53
  Yeats 43, 59, 53–4
Pound, Ezra, works
  A Lume Spento 42, 43, 45
  A Quinzaine for this Yule 42
  'Ballad of the Goodly Fere' 44, 55
  Cantos 53, 67
  Canzoni 54, 66
  Cathay 67
  Exultations 43
  'Fratres Minores' 68
  'Histrion' 45

Pound, Ezra, works – *continued*
  Homage to Sextus Propertius 68
  Hugh Selwyn Mauberley 9, 42–3, 47
  'In Tempore Senectutis' 43
  Lustra 66, 68
  Pavannes and Divisions 58
  Personae 43
  Pisan Cantos 63, 118–19
  'Provincialism the Enemy' 71
  Quia Pauper Amavi 68
  Ripostes 67
  'Salutation the Second' 66
  'Satus Rerum' 53–4
  'Sestina Altaforte' 44, 124
  Spirit of Romance, The 44, 168
  'Three Lectures on Medieval Poetry' 63
  'To Whistler – American' 45–6
Prothero, George 47, 63–4, 65, 70
pubs *see* cafés, restaurants and pubs
Puccini, Giacomo, *La Bohème* 1, 2, 4, 6

Quinn, John 67, 91

Ransome, Arthur 31, 32, 113
  Bohemia in London 6, 7
Read, Herbert 150, 168
Rebel Arts Centre 14, 25, 82, 86, 94, 100, 101, 102, 122, 123, 125, 146, 167
restaurants *see* cafés, restaurants and pubs
Rhymers' Club 32, 33, 40
Rhys, Ernest 40, 46, 62
Richards, I. A. 148, 149
Richardson, Dorothy 59, 160
Roberts, William 85, 86, 99, 122, 123, 125, 128, 129, 160, 166
  Dancers, The 129
  Religion 129
  Vortex Pamphlets 129, 130
  Vorticists at the Restaurant de la Tour Eiffel: Spring 1915, The 123–4, 129, 130–1
  and 'Wyndham Lewis and Vorticism' exhibition 129–30
Romanticism 3, 7

Rosetti, Dante Gabriel 56
Rosetti, William Michael 55–6
Rothenstein, John 12, 129
Russell, Ada Dwyer 115, 117
Russell, Bertrand 132, 165
  and Vivien Eliot 134, 135, 136, 137

Sackville, Lady Margaret 124
Saunders, Helen 26, 107, 108, 111, 122, 124, 126, 130
Schiddel, Edmund 67–8
Schiddel, Masie 19
Schiff, Sidney 135
Scratton, Bride 65, 68
sex, and
  Bloomsbury 161–2, 167
  changing attitudes towards 8
  women 107
  Vorticism 99
Shakespear, Dorothy *see* Pound, Dorothy
Shakespear, Henry Hope 63
Shakespear, Olivia 33, 46–7, 59, 63, 106
Shaw, George Bernard 31, 36
Sheppard, Richard 16
Sickert, Walter 125, 170
Sinclair, May 46, 47, 54, 57, 111, 122, 125
Sitwell, Edith 134
Sitwell, Osbert 82–3, 84
Slade School of Art 126, 160
Smithers, Leonard 34
Stansky, Peter 172
Stephen, Adrian 158, 160, 162
Stephen, Julian 160
Stephen, Thoby 160, 162
Stephen, Vanessa *see* Bell, Vanessa
Stephen, Virginia *see* Woolf, Virginia
Strachey, Lytton 14, 158, 161, 162, 164, 165
Streatfeild, R. A. 28
Strindberg, Frida 57, 73, 75, 86, 106–7, 168
  Augustus John 90–2
  Marriage with Genius 92
Stulik, Rudolph 124, 125, 129, 130

Swinburne, Algernon Charles 28
  Atlanta in Calydon 5
  Poems and Ballads 5
Swinley, Ion 50
Sydney-Turner, Saxon 158, 161
symbolism, Arthur Symons on 30
Symons, Arthur 29–30, 46, 121, and
  affairs 33–4
  bohemian London 34
  bohemianism 35
  Café Royal 32
  decadence 30
  Ernest Dowson 38–9
  London 31–2, 35, 38
  mental breakdown 48
  poetry 30–1
  Savoy 34
  women 36
  Yeats 33, 35
Symons, Arthur, works
  A Symbolist Movement in Literature 48
  'Bohemian Years in London' 38, 39
  'Clair de Lune' 31
  'Confessions' 38
  'Décor de Théâtre' 31
  Book of Aspects, A 31
  Memoirs 38
  'Stella Maris' 36
  Studies in Prose and Verse 31
  Symbolist Movement in Literature 30, 31
  Symbolist Movement in Poetry 140
  'The Decadent Movement in Literature' 30, 33
Symons, Rhoda 35
Synge, J. M.
  Playboy of the Western World 43
  Riders to the Sea 46

theatres and cinemas
  Alhambra Theatre 33
  Coliseum 81
  Covent Garden 1, 80
  Drury Lane 80
  Empire 29, 33, 34, 36–8, 83
  Her Majesty's 105
  Leicester Square Empire 80

Shepherd's Bush Empire 80
  see also Cabaret Club
Thevénon, Daniel Nicolas *see* Nichols, Daniel
Tree, Beerbohm 105
Tree, Iris 105, 125, 126, 160, 170
  appearance 102
  background 105–6
  Café Royal 103–4
  rebel 104
Turner, Mary Borden 19

United Arts Club 124
Upward, Allen 115

Valéry, Paul 28
Vaughan, Madge 165
Verdenal, Jean 138
Verlaine, Paul 28, 31, 35, 38, 39–40
Vittoz, Dr Roger 153, 155–6
  The Treatment of Neurasthenia 155
Vorticism 12, 68, 98–9, 100, 118, 122, 165
  Cournos's fictional portrayal 23
  dinner at Dieudonné's 119–23
  masculinity of 99
  'Vorticist Room' at Tour Eiffel Restaurant 26, 123–4
  Wyndham Lewis 14
  'Wyndham Lewis and Vorticism' exhibition 129–30

Wadsworth, Edward 99, 130, 146
Waley, Arthur 111
Weaver, Harriet Shaw 68, 109–10, 111–12
Wedekind, Franz 91
Welden, Harry 80
Wells, H. G. 2, 90, 91, 107
West, Rebecca (Cicely Isabel Fairfield) 21, 57, 88–90, 91, 110, 111, 112
  affairs 90
  dress 89
  marriage 107
West, Rebecca, works
  'At Valladolid' 91
  'Indissoluble Matrimony' 88
  'Magician of Pell Street, The' 89
  'Sideways' 89

Whistler, James McNeill 29, 45–6, 55
  Nocturnes 5
Wilde, Oscar 29, 105
  Salome 36
  trial of 1, 2, 5
Wilhelm, J. J. 94, 115
Williams, William Carlos 43, 45, 54, 60, 70, 98
women, and
  attitudes towards 99
  Bloomsbury 167
  bohemianism 107–9, 125–6
  bohemianism and feminism 110–11
  changing role of 8
  fictional portrayal of 17, 19–20, 21, 23, 24, 126–7
  lesbianism 117
  marriage 64, 106–7
  rebellion 104
  sex 107
  suffrage movement 57, 109, 110, 169–70
  Vorticism 26
Women's Social and Political Union (WSPU) 109, 169–70
Woolf, Leonard 146, 158, 162, 167, 177
Woolf, Virginia (née Stephen) 111, 133, 138, 147, 156, 158–9, 162–3, 164, 165, 167, 168, 172–3, and
  Bloomsbury 159–60, 161
  Dreadnought Hoax 175
  Fitzroy Square 162, 170–1
  Gordon Square 160–2
  Hogarth Press 163
  mental illness 174, 175
  Roger Fry 165, 169
  social change 171–2
  Vivien Eliot 134
  writing 174–5
Woolf, Virginia, works
  A Room of One's Own 176
  'A Society' 176
  'Character in Fiction' 171, 173
  Jacob's Room 172, 173
  'Kew Gardens' 173
  'Mark on the Wall, The' 173
  Melymbrosia 168, 173, 174
  'Modern Fiction' 172
  'Mr. Bennett and Mrs. Brown' 171, 172, 176
  Night and Day 173
  Orlando 176
  Three Guineas 170
  Voyage Out, The 173
  Years, The 171
Worringer, Wilhelm, *Abstraction and Empathy* 95
Wright, Josephine *see* Weaver, Harriet 112

Yeats, W. B. 30, 34, 36
  distances himself from his past 40
  Oxford Book of English Verse 40
  Poems 43
  Pound 59
  Rhymers' Club 40
  Symons 33, 35
  Wind among the Reeds, The 43
  Woburn Buildings 59–60
Young, Hilton 162